THE NIGHTSHADE

AVEENAN NIGHTS : PART ONE

SHAY RODRICKS

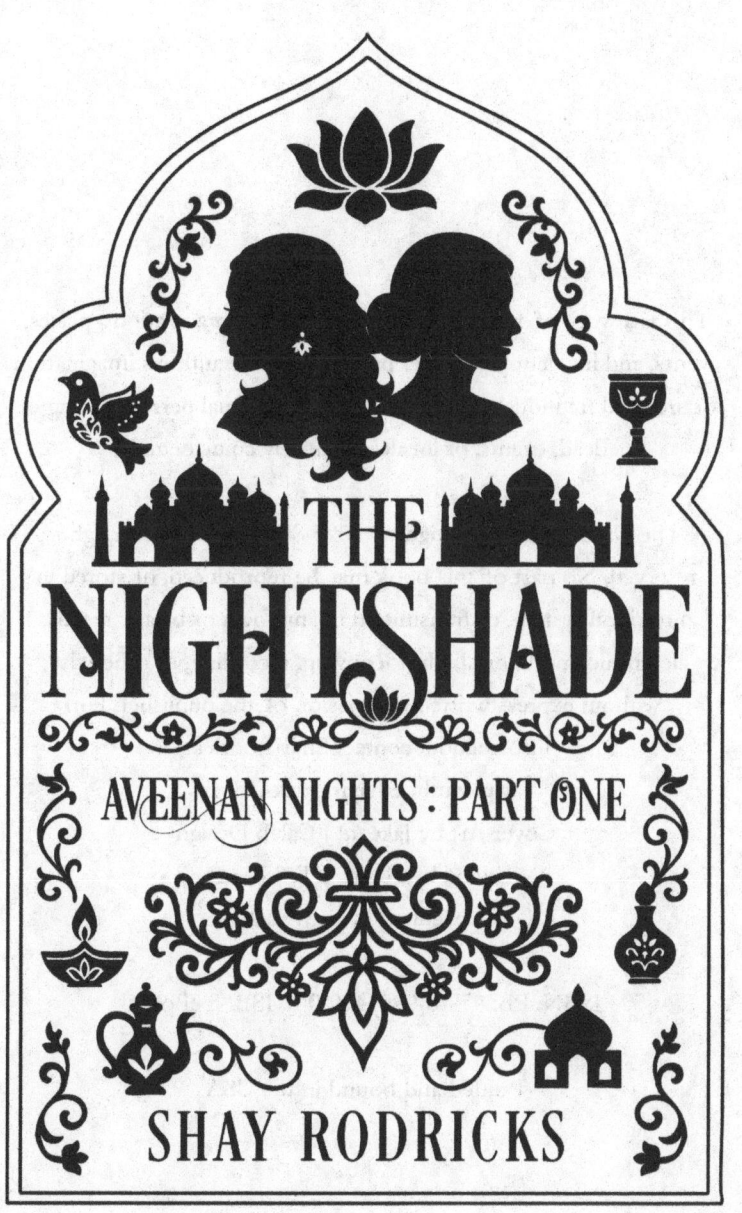

THE NIGHTSHADE

AVEENAN NIGHTS : PART ONE

SHAY RODRICKS

www.authorshayrodricks.com
Cover Art by Jake @ J Caleb Design
Edited by Hannah Teachout
Copyedited by Sam Sachs

ISBN: PB: 979-8-9993410-0-6; ISBN: eBook:

Printed and bound in the USA

In memory of Dada
From one of your mango girls.
We miss you.

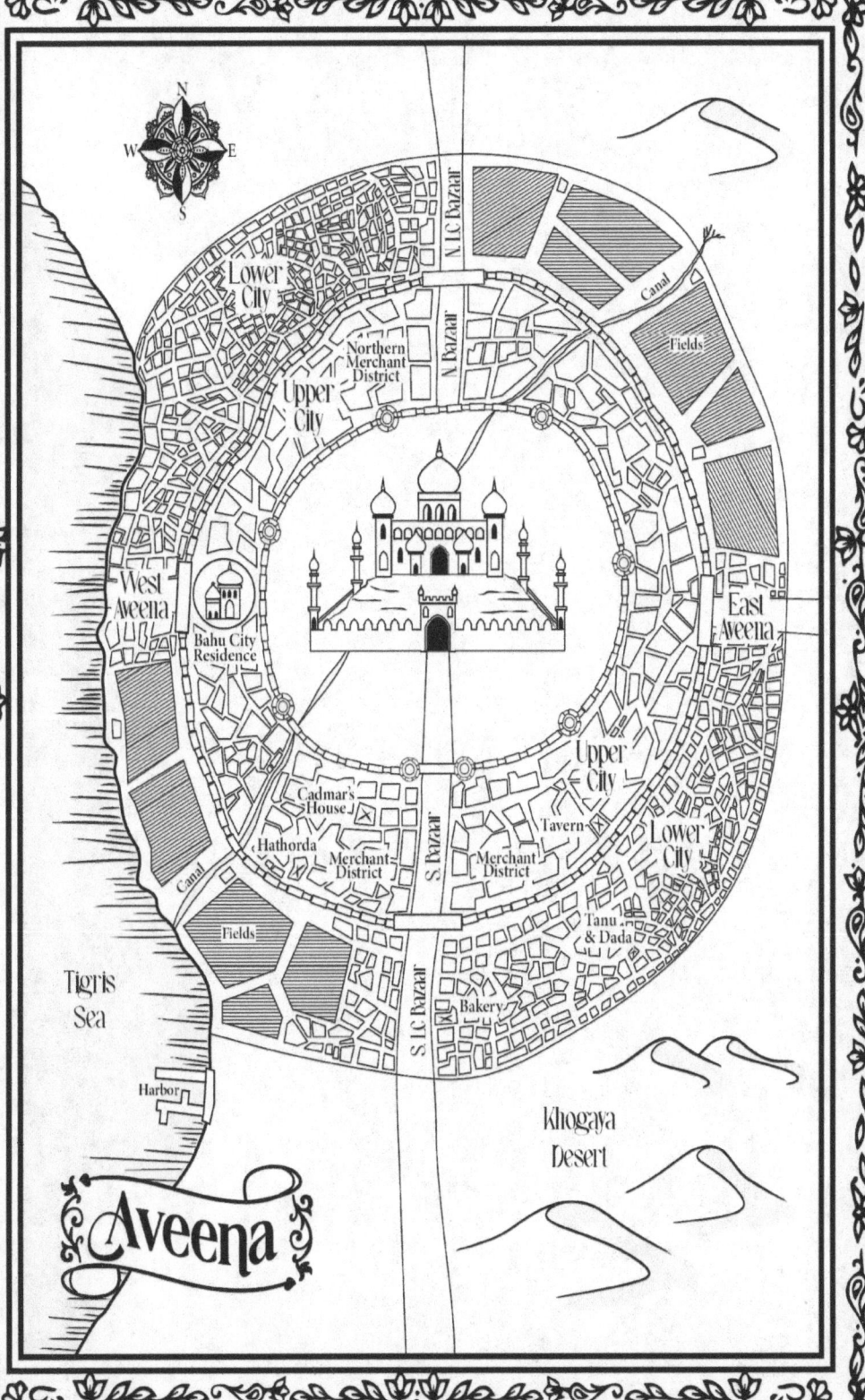

For a list of content warnings, please refer to my website, authorshayrodricks.com. Take care of yourself, take care of your mental health.

1

I crumple the parchment and drop it into the ditch on the side of the dusty street. It disappears into the accumulated muck.

One hundred thousand gold rupees.

The desperation of the Suraksha reeks like the refuse pile beside me. This is the third increase in reward money since the notices were posted a year ago. And yet the guards that swarm the city like flies still need information on the thief calling *himself* the Nightshade. I glance down at the subtle lines of my curves and grin.

Good luck finding *him*.

I walk towards the eastern gate, the wanted poster already forgotten, and secure the hood of my cloak over my head, hiding my choppy, midnight hair. When I took the knife to my hair last night, like I do every moon, I made sure to leave it just long enough to pull it back.

Aveena is quieter than usual, the strict mourning curfew forcing the Lower City into their dilapidated homes by sundown each night.

In the faint starlight, the wall is a massive shadow looming above me, separating the Upper and Lower City, allowing the merchants and Aristocracy to hide from the Lower City folk like we don't exist. The eleventh chime of the temple bell reverberates in the night, leaving a deafening silence in its wake.

Perfect timing.

I hurry past the abandoned stalls in the Lower City bazaar and reach the guard post nearest the eastern gate. Velo promised me three minutes—I guess the Suraksha respected rupees more than they respected the sanctity of the mourning period.

Slipping into the shadows of the wall, I inhale the cool night air, feeling the tingles rippling through my body, and release my controlled breath. The sandstone wall prickles against my back as I listen. The echo of the last temple bell's chime lingers; the sounds of rats' feet patter nearby; the rest of Aveena is silent.

I allow myself a flicker of a satisfied smile before I get to work picking the lock. The Suraksha on night watch enjoys Velo's bribes.

The pin in my hand subtly vibrates as the tumblers of the lock fall into place. I enter the guard post and lock the door behind me. Reports are scattered across the enormous table, taking up most of the space in the cramped room: business permits, housing transfer requests, gate logs. I resist the temptation to read through the papers and cross through the post to the door to the Upper City. My three minutes are almost up. The door closes with a click, and I scurry off. A thrill dances in my stomach as I vanish into the winding darkness of the Upper City.

After darting through several alleyways, I slow to a stop near a tavern, catching my breath. Energy pulses through me as my breathing calms the manic rush of adrenaline. That's the key to working in the Upper City; a few deep breaths are the difference between a successful night and imprisonment in Niraash. Wind ruffles my hood, pushing its fold into my face.

Right. A few deep breaths and the help of Wind Mother.

I kiss my fingertips, acknowledging Her presence. Immediately my hood stills, the breeze calming. I peer around the corner, scanning my surroundings. Rough grumblings come from the tavern entrance punctuated by random shouts. Typically, this area is still bustling late into the night; however, only a handful of merchants walk unsteadily along the street. They do not fear the Suraksha's wrath for breaking the mourning curfew like those in the Lower City. They mingle close to my hiding spot, enjoying the unusual chill in the night air. Normally, Aveena radiates heat long after the sun withdraws for the night.

Tonight is different.

A group of young men stumble out of the tavern, singing a bawdy song about one-eyed Shiv. I lean into the shadows and let the group pass. Adjusting my hood, I stumble behind the group, allowing myself to trip on a small hole in the dusty road. A small gurgle escapes my mouth, and I lean against a nearby building as if I need to stop a dizzy spell.

"Aye, you a'right there?" An enormous shadow looms over me. The man pats my back, knocking me into the wall again. "A little rum ne'er did no harm."

I hiccup and rest my head on the man's shoulder.

"Aye now, don't be snugglin' all up on me like I was part of the Harem. Get going."

With a firm shove, the giant extricates himself and stomps back to the tavern. I laugh. Too easy.

Once out of sight of the tavern, I discard my drunken walk and prowl confidently into the Upper City. The breeze twirls playfully through my stride, enjoying the mischief as much as I do.

The road steadily inclines, the buildings grow taller. The Ari can't help showing off their status. They've got to prove that what they have is bigger than everyone else's around. Ornate stonework decorates the doorframes of several of the houses. Rooftop porches. Even a few doors gilded in gold, glimmering in the starlight. Ornate indeed.

My first target of the night, the Asfour family, is in the middle of the Ari section closest to the eastern gate. My excitement mounts as I near my destination.

"Halt!"

I freeze, straining to pinpoint where the shout came from.

"Get off me!" a second voice whines.

"What are you doing out, street rat?" the Suraksha growls. "You know the order."

I dart between the buildings and crouch, becoming one with the shadows. Closing my eyes, I listen to the scuffle, thankful that my racing heart can't give me away. My hand reaches for the stones woven into my anklet, the uneven edges a soothing touchstone to my panic. I inhale, ignoring the grunts and scuffling, and the familiar chill works its way up from my left ankle, grounding me, connecting me to the earth. A breeze swirls around my feet, following the cold sensation up my body, before settling.

A thunk and a moan.

"That's what ye get for sneaking into the Upper City." I keep still as the sound of flesh striking flesh echoes in the night, pressing my back against the rough sandstone and willing the darkness to swallow me whole. "And that's for giving me trouble, scum."

A groan is the only response. My nails dig into my palms as I wait, the whacks and groans continuing. The stomp of more boots finally disturbs the pattern. The new Suraksha's voice holds a note of authority as it barks, "Is it him?"

"Couldn't be, Captain. Look at the shape of him."

Shit, a captain.

I exhale slowly then cautiously peek around the corner from my hiding space. The scene unfolds several meters away: the captain and the other Suraksha standing over their captured prize. The first Suraksha's hands are behind his back as he reports to his superior; both are ignoring the panting, disheveled man laying below them.

"And are you an expert on the Nightshade?" the captain rumbles.

"Well, I—well, sir, this man—"

The captain smacks the lower ranking Suraksha on the back of the head. He flinches but remains at attention. Shaking his head, the captain nudges the man on the ground with his boot. "You. Where are you headed?"

"Home, sir."

The captain squats down next to him and whispers, "*Liar*. You reek of the Lower City."

"But I—" The man starts, but the captain slaps him. Hard.

"There's no excuse to break the mourning period. Damn disrespectful to our dead sultan." My heart sinks. The trapped man stutters, unable to respond. "You the Nightshade?"

"No–no, sir."

I hold my breath, waiting.

"Got any information on the Nightshade?"

"How could I, sir?"

The captain viciously kicks the captured man in the ribs, causing him to cry out. I turn away from the scene, my stomach churning with the mixture of guilt and relief as I listen to the two Suraksha continue to interrogate the poor sod. The temple bell chimes again, urging me to keep working, but I squash the feeling.

"He's useless like the rest of the Lower City scum," the captain snaps. "Make an example of him in the southern bazaar as a warning to the Nightshade."

"Yes, Captain."

"No! Please!"

The stomp of captain's boots recedes into the night followed by the shuffle of the Suraksha dragging the man away. I wait a few more heartbeats before slipping out of my hiding spot, shaking the guilt off me like sand off a rug.

He should know better than to enter the Upper City.

I let the silence of the night wrap around me, pushing the encounter out of my mind.

I have a job to do.

I encounter no one in the last few streets to the Asfour house. Panting slightly, I slip into the gap between houses to assess my entry point. Without a doubt my destination—the bedroom of Mr. and Mrs. Asfour—is on the top floor of the house. Ari are predictable.

My arm brushes against something soft. I spin and grin in spite of myself. The Asfours decided to demonstrate their wealth by planting a vined trellis up the side of the building—an impressive feat since Aveena is scorching hot and lacks consistent rainfall to keep plant life alive. The extra water required to keep the foliage green is more expensive than the rest of the house decorations on the street combined.

And, as usual, the Ari's stupidity is my gain.

I remove my cloak and hide it behind the base of the trellis. Making sure my lockpicks are secured on the band around my wrist, I remove one of my dusty slippers, grab hold of the vine, slip off my other shoe, and begin climbing.

Flowing water always returns to its source.
-Aveenan Proverb-

2

The vines are thick in my hand as I test out each branch before trusting my weight to it. My toes dig into the edges of the house as I climb. Heat builds in my arms, and I glance up to check the distance. Still several more meters before the top floor.

Up and up I climb, pausing with any noise in the night. My fingers finally brush the windowsill, and I can't help the triumphant smile. I hang, suspended above the Upper City, listening for movement. Silence invites me in.

I pull myself over the ledge and crouch, assessing. Once my eyes adjust, the bed across the room looms into view, the silhouettes of two people asleep on top. I creep towards the right wall where the outline of a large dresser takes up much of the space. A good place as any to start my search for Lady Asfour's necklace.

Jewelry lays scattered on the dresser, haphazardly strewn about. Disgust at the blatant disregard for their wealth roots in my chest. Despite the many glittering options, the necklace Velo described isn't among the pieces. I check each of the drawers and the gap behind the dresser to make sure but no such luck. If the necklace isn't here, then it must be–

One of the Asfours grumbles, and I slink down, but they just roll over and continue sleeping.

Shit, of course.

I crawl towards the smaller of the two sleeping figures, willing myself to stop breathing altogether so as not to wake her. Lady Asfour sleeps peacefully. A delicate golden chain dangles around her neck, the pendant hidden beneath her nightgown.

This has to be the necklace Velo described but I can't know for certain. I center myself, running my fingers along my anklet to send the cooling sensation through my body anew, and shake off the flickering shame. I *need* the gold from this job.

I scan the chain carefully in the darkness, and hope fills me when I spot the clasp. Tentatively, I pinch the clasp and unhook it. Lady Asfour shifts slightly in her sleep, and I freeze, my heart thundering. The open necklace starts to slide away, and I nimbly catch it and slip it off the sleeping Ari.

As I scurry away, I shove the lotus necklace into my pocket, disappearing over the windowsill. The adrenaline coursing through me makes the descent quick. Once I reach the bottom, I carefully slide into my shoes and disappear through the alleyways.

The clouds shift, and moonlight both illuminates my path and creates deeper shadows to hide in. The deserted streets are like an old friend as I easily navigate my way towards the southern gate. Wind Mother must be watching over my shoulder tonight—I encounter no one. She alone knows why I risk this, why I am the Nightshade.

I scurry onto the last street and pause in the deep shadows, hurriedly counting the houses. My second target's house is two thirds down the street, squished in the row between other nondescript houses. I raise my brows in surprise. Jelani Cadmar is popular for the Aristocracy, known to even the lowest in the Lower City, but this unremarkable house does nothing to announce the Ari, to make his status known to his merchant neighbors. For a moment, I hesitate, but I'd only done half the job.

Briefly, I touch my anklet once more before slinking into the shadows towards Cadmar's house. I step into the gap between houses, listening for signs of pursuit, but only the normal nighttime sounds reach my ears.

I lean back, counting the windows above me. The Ari who had contacted Velo had given clear directions to Cadmar's office, saving me time. I run my fingers over the sandstone wall, feeling for the rough grooves and edges that sandstone naturally gives.

I feel higher, letting my instincts take over, finding the next. Slowly, carefully, I begin to climb the wall, my fingertips precariously digging into each ledge, my feet following suite. Sweat beads down my back, but I ignore it, focusing on the burning of my muscles and the handhold.

The shutters are blessedly open, and when I peak inside, the office is unoccupied. I silently slip into the room, searching for the perfect spot.

There.

I place Lady Asfour's lotus necklace in the gap between the cushion and arm of the extra chair. Satisfied with the placement, I tiptoe to the window and disappear into the night.

The moon is descending by the time I finish with Velo's assignment.

Victory dances for joy in my chest. I'm one job closer to saving enough money. After two years of working for Velo, I'm finally close to being able to bribe the Tribes on their next annual visit. Confidence swells in me—the Ari will be at each other's throats with the death of the sultan, plenty of opportunity for the Nightshade to take advantage.

The gentle rush of the canal reaches my ears, and tension worms its way into my gut. I falter but then push forward. I avoided the canal until recently. Too many memories tainted by bitterness. All gifts of my past life in the Upper City.

I swallow the lump in my throat as the moonlit canal comes into view. The canal's old wooden fence—probably the last wooden structure in Aveena—was built to help stumbling drunks avoid an icy wake up call. I run my hand along its smooth surface, forcing my thoughts out of the darkness of my past.

One day I won't need to be the Nightshade. I won't be desperate for the only gold that I can earn to survive. One day I'll be free of my past, and I'll be able to help Tanu.

One day…

The glint of a golden lotus pendant hangs innocently on the wooden post, shocking me out of my dreamy state. I freeze, staring. My breath hitches in my chest.

How is it here?

I stare at the golden necklace. It takes everything I have to not scurry away like the street rat I am.

Or to scream.

C'mon, Laila. Get your head together.

I stroll past the necklace, snatching it off its post and pocketing it. Plans jump through my mind, flashes of ideas fluttering out of reach, each as useless as the last. I turn abruptly away from the canal and let the shadows welcome me again.

This scandal should have given the Ari fuel for their gossip for weeks. The employer on this job wanted Cadmar disgraced. And Tei Asfour was Cadmar's biggest supporter. Two vultures, one price. At least that's what the employer banked on. I never bothered with the reasoning behind the money; gold is gold no matter which way you turn it. And Wind Mother knew how much I needed those rupees.

Through my mess of thoughts, one thing is clear: Someone knows what I've been up to tonight.

Thieves must be marked for all to see the evidence of their treachery to their fellow Aveenans.
-from the Ordinances of Aveena-

3

Sunlight pushes its way through the cracks in the ceiling above me, intruding into the tiny place I call home. Groaning, I roll over, trying to block out the harsh rays. The red haze pokes through my closed eyelids, chasing hope of sleep away.

The sounds of the street outside fill my ears in a rush— shouts of vendors offering their wares mixed with the voices of those bold enough to haggle prices. The smell of hot, fresh naan tantalizes me.

I stretch, but my hand knocks the roof above me, ending the moment. Sighing, I crawl across the dusty floor to my water pitcher, careful to make as little noise as possible. The bakery owners below are among the few who can afford a storefront in the Lower City; they would not appreciate my use of the meager attic space.

A shimmer in the corner catches my eye—the necklace.

I grab onto one of the roof beams to steady myself, needing something solid. That was real. The necklace looks insignificant. Its delicate chain is tangled together on one of the attic beams.

I snatch the chain and stare at it. Velo was extremely clear about thieves who got caught.

Two years ago, I was on the crowded streets of the Lower City, scrambling for food and trying to get hired for *any* job that would pay me. No one would hire me—they didn't trust the fact that I didn't have a male relative to speak for me. Fear was my shadow, never leaving me alone, always following my steps. My cheeks sunk into my face, making my features sickly and sharp—that scared off more potential employers. And the worry: that I would starve to death or that the Suraksha would arrest me. Worry for Tanu, my niece, the only person left that I cared about.

And it was in that state that Velo found me. He appeared out of the shadows as I lay slumped against a wall. After nudging me to make sure I was still alive, Velo offered two bronze rupees for a job. I accepted without even hearing the terms.

That was the first time that I ever stole from someone.

Velo tested out my abilities with each job. A few missing coins here. A reclaimed bracelet there. I impressed his underhanded self. The guilt I might have felt was wiped away by my need to keep Tanu alive. For three months, I worked my way up in Velo's network of thieves and spies until one day he offered the largest sum of money yet *if* I could sneak into the Upper City without being detected. Velo knew there was a market among the Ari, but he'd been incapable of branching into this line of business. His network couldn't blend in with the Upper City.

"I'll give ye the chance if ye can do it without getting caught. Them Ari are getting crazy. If ye get caught, ye never hear from me again. Not having ye failure tainting my reputation."

Since then, I have been the Nightshade. Velo passes along jobs, I get them done, and we both get paid.

When Velo challenged me to break into the Upper City, he had no idea that I had grown up in the northern merchant district and no idea how successful I would be. Now he couldn't keep up with the demand for the Nightshade's skills.

I crush the tiny necklace in my fist, the edges of the pendant cutting into my palm. Velo cannot find out.

I pull on my lehenga, ducking under the roofbeams as I slip my threadbare kurti over my head. I ignore my slippers—they're the only pair I have, and I need them to blend in with the Upper City.

I glance at the necklace again, hesitating. If I don't bring it with me, I risk someone else finding it. If I do bring it with me, I risk Velo finding it. I unclasp the chain and fix it around my neck, hiding the chain beneath my clothes. A sliver of fabric tied around my head becomes a veil, perfect for blending with those in the bazaar outside. And for hiding the chain.

I creep down the small staircase to the storage room below, skipping the squeaky third and seventh steps. Sweat trickles down my neck as a wave of heat washes over me. The sounds of customers are louder in the storage room as I tiptoe through the crates of grain.

The owner's back is to me as I sneak past her, straightening the moment that I join the other customers and duck out of the store before she can notice me.

24

The sun is nearly overhead, and I squint against the harsh light. The bazaar is in full swing, but I turn away from the chaos and follow the street the opposite way. Soon I reach the edges of Aveena. Workers are hunched over in the fields between the city and the Tigris Sea. Those nearest till the earth in preparation for planting, while others a field away harvest fruit from the trees. I rush past the women bending over the canal filling their earthen pots with water. My bare feet slip on the muddy bank as I step over the pale pink flower buds peeking out through the mud and sidestep the scraggly shrubs threatening to snag my lehenga. The builder never finished lining the canal with stones in the Lower City—just one of the many examples of how the Lower City was forgotten.

I follow the line of the crumbling outer wall until a break in the stones allows me to slip back into the city and out of sight of the workers. Three more steps, and I'm in the hidden alcove.

Soft laughter.

I turn quickly, my breath catching in my throat before I can remind myself to act normal. He knows nothing.

Velo's smirk twists the lower half of his face, stretching the scars across his cheeks. The innumerable scars display the history of Velo's wrongdoing. He embraced them, even shaving his hair to make them prominently stand out.

"Laila."

"Velo."

We stare at each other, neither willing to break the silence first. My stomach clenches, but I keep my face impassive. It's best to reveal nothing to Velo—unless you want the information to be sold to the highest bidder.

Velo's smirk grows.

"So ye've done it then," he says, the rasp more pronounced as it softly echoes off the stone wall. His dark brown eyes narrow in greed as he steps closer.

I swallow, my throat dry. "No," I manage to get out.

A flicker of surprise then his trademark smirk returns. "No?"

"No," I repeat, finally finding my voice again. "Too many Suraksha patrolling for the mourning period."

Velo tilts his head to the side as he watches me. I remind myself to breathe, that he cannot suspect anything other than what lies I feed him.

"Too many for the Nightshade, eh?"

"Yes."

He watches me for several heartbeats. Then he sighs. The action takes me by surprise—Velo is not a man who sighs when frustrated. He'd stab something maybe, but he never sighs. I can see that Velo is debating how much to tell me. As someone who buys and sells information for a living, he knows the value of choosing words carefully.

"The sultan's death is making the Ari fuckin' crazy."

"So?" I cross my arms, the movement causing the necklace to slither across the skin of my collarbone. The hairs on the nape of my neck stand up.

Velo leans against the wall, watching me closely. In two years, I've never questioned the jobs. "They're offering ten times more money than before."

"And?" I ask, mimicking his casual posture. Velo narrows his eyes at me, but I just raise my eyebrows and wait. In the silence, the breeze whistles through the gap in the wall, bringing a mix of the earthy mud and a hint of the salty sea air with it.

"So," he grounds out through clenched teeth, "none of the other sneaks can do it."

Ah, there it is. Velo relies on me too much.

I look away, adjusting the veil, thinking. The exhaustion and worry make everything foggy, and I struggle to find the words to convince him.

"Velo, I can't," I say weakly.

He tilts his head, and I shift uncomfortably. He hasn't been in the underworld of Aveena this long without the ability to read people. His voice is cold as he asks, "Can't or won't?"

"Can't," I say quickly. I gesture wildly, desperation filling me. He has to understand. "You'll have to cancel this one. Tell them the mourning period—"

"And ruin the Nightshade's reputation?"

I balk as a chill runs down my spine. My chest tightens, and my voice sounds breathless even to my own ears. "It won't—"

"It will. All that work destroyed by one job," Velo says, matter-of-fact. He finally looks away from me, staring off in the direction of the workers, letting his words sink in.

It won't be. *It can't.* I need that money.

"Impossible," I counter.

"Reputations have been destroyed for less. But—" he pauses, and the anxiety unfurling in my chest while I wait for him to continue. The necklace chaffs on my collarbone, making my skin prickle. Velo holds my gaze again. "If you succeed, they'll see you as invincible. Unrivaled."

I hesitate.

Velo leans closer to me and adds, "It would be enough to bribe passage with the Tribes."

"What?" I can barely breathe, not sure that I'm hearing him right. How does he even know about...

"Your niece. I've seen her foot, how it twists unnaturally." His voice is calm, soothing, and I hate myself for hanging on to his every word. "Complete this job, and you'll be able to take her to Bhavin. It's what you're saving for, eh? Just one more job, and we can train someone else. You can get her healed."

My heart falters, hopefulness and distrust, excitement and caution. To be free of this, I'd never allowed myself to imagine that possibility. And to be able to take Tanu to Bhavin, to get her healed... I inhale, steadying myself, then ask, "What about the Nightshade?"

"Help train them, and you can get a cut of every job they complete as the Nightshade."

It sounded too good to be true. I could live my life, become an honorable Aveenan again. Just one more job. Finally get Tanu the help she needs.

"Okay," I whisper.

Velo's eyes alight with greed once again, the smirk twisting the lines of his scars. "It needs to be done before nightfall."

"Nightfall!"

"The Ari was pretty fuckin' clear," Velo says, shrugging. I start to protest, but he adds, "Before tonight or else no gold. And mourning is over today, so best get going."

"But I don't—"

Velo pushes me towards the gap in the wall, ignoring my resistance. My arm scrapes against a protruding piece of sandstone as I try to twist back towards him, but his hands are firm on my back. I stumble forward as he says, "We got a deal, girlie. One more job."

When I turn around again, he's already gone.

**Servants are a sign of your status of
Aristocracy and are a gift to those who
serve us. You are not only judged on your
own merits but on those of your servants.
When welcoming other Aristocracy into
your home, ensure that all of the servants
are visible to subtly reveal your wealth.**
-Advice from Lady Shah to her daughter-

4

Under normal circumstances I would never attempt to enter the Upper City during the daytime. The Suraksha are too alert and irritable for my taste. But Velo's promises fill my ears as I join the press of bodies surging into the Lower City bazaar.

His promises and his very short deadline.

The mourning period ended today and the increased number of Aveenans gathered in the bazaar were a reflection of how starved people were for interaction. I heard details about the funeral and the soon-to-be sultan from almost every stand as I pass, but the only words I have room for are *last job*. I can almost imagine coming to the bazaar tomorrow, a free woman.

As I move along edge of the crowded street, my gaze flits back and forth, taking in those passing by. To my left, a young couple in tattered clothes whispers heatedly about something unimportant. On the street, an old horse led by an even older man meanders towards the Upper City. A short boy in need of a good bath stands by one of the buildings in a shadow and one stall over, three barefoot young girls skip through the bazaar, tittering loudly about the goods they will buy when they are all married to rich husbands. The dust swirls and moves through the bazaar patrons, carrying the spicy smells from the food wallas down the street. Gales of laughter bubble from a group of kids playing dice. The vibrant colors of the crowd are dotted with the tan uniforms of Suraksha. I walk past them all, a part of the crowd, and yet still an outsider.

My reflection catches in the sliver of mirror resting against the nearest fabric stall. The plain beige veil is loosely tied over my choppy, uneven hair. My warm brown skin remains smooth. However, after three years of living in the Lower City, my protruding cheekbones make the angles of my face harsh and unwelcoming.

I always keep my eyes hidden in shadow. Amongst the sea of brown eyes of Aveena, my blue eyes are too identifiable. Too other. *Djinn*-eyes. The Lower City has demanded my vanity, but it has not stolen the ferocity burning behind my eyes.

"Nothing is free down here, maid. If you ain't going to buy anything, then ye don't get free looks either." The ruddy-faced mistress of the fabric cart glances at my hands to make sure I haven't stolen anything before she shoos me away.

I bob my head politely and mutter a hurried apology in the woman's direction, but she's already berating the three young sisters.

I join the steady flow of people heading towards the south gate. Aveena stands alone with a sea of dunes encompassing three of her four sides and the Tigris Sea against her back. The dry heat rolls off the dunes and clashes for dominance with the humidity from the sea, making Aveena hot at best, hot and muggy at worst. To protect themselves from the nomadic tribes roaming the dunes, our ancestors built the first wall to surround the border of Aveena. Their descendants enjoyed the wall so much that they built the second wall between the Upper and Lower City. No one knows much about the third wall surrounding the palace—it has been there since the beginning of Aveena, keeping the sultans and select Ari secluded from the riffraff of the city.

The south gate is the largest of the four gates leading into the Upper City, which also makes it the easiest to slip through.

I adjust my beige maid's veil to ensure that the butchered ends of my hair are covered. My palms are clammy. Not a good sign. I wipe my palms against my loose-fitting dhoti and then slip on the borrowed lace gloves. The Ari are more particular about the appearance of their servants than they are about their own appearance, which makes my maid disguise tricky. No self-respecting Ari would hire a maid who had a "Lower City look" about her. An ungloved hand was worse than spitting in the tamarind sauce before serving it, and a short-haired servant was unheard of—unheard of and unemployed.

As a group of gabbing servants pass me, I join their ranks, feeding off of their energy and blending in. I smile brightly and nod along as the women discuss their lazy husbands, the unending cleaning, and their struggles finding suitable matches for their daughters. A slight pang squeezes my chest, and my grin falters. I catch myself before the discomfort reaches my eyes.

I focus on what the middle-aged woman to my left is saying.

"As I was telling her, Riyad is as good of a man as she can expect with her, um, qualities. But does the girl listen to me?"

"Of course not. These girls never know what's good for them," the oldest woman in the group scornfully replies. Her maid's veil is incapable of hiding the wild mass of white hair on her head.

The first woman catches my gaze. I nod understandably.

Fifty paces away from the south gate.

"I love my girl, but she's got to realize that Riyad's offer might be her last chance. She's not getting any younger."

"Or prettier," the opinionated grandmother spits out.

The other women in the group burst into raucous laughter. I cannot tell if they are laughing at the jibe or at the mother's reaction as she turns red beneath her weather-worn skin.

None of the Suraksha pay attention to our group as we pass through the south gate, and none of the laughing women notice as I slip from their group and off into the Upper City. The shouts of vendors and jangle of carts die away as I head further away from the Lower City, and none of the wallas in the Upper City bazaar pay me any mind as I keep my head down, the perfect picture of submissive servant. The Bahu family emblem—the sultan's emblem—adorns a few shops in the southern bazaar. Watchful eyes stare distrustfully from the doorsteps of these royally approved wallas, the crossed swords behind a sun glittering from the window. I walk closer to the buildings, my tan kurti blending with the stone and sand, and expertly weave between the other servants hastening down the narrow streets. Occasionally, I am forced to stop and bow as an Ari walks by. I feel exposed, but thankfully Jelani Cadmar's house is not far.

Before rounding the final corner, I pause. I focus on the sensation of air filling my lungs until my chest tightens and then release the breath slow and controlled. Control. I am in control.

I slip into the alley, resisting the urge to glance over my shoulder. Running my hand along the sandstone, I drag my feet to slow down my pace, a lazy servant killing time in between tasks. Cadmar's back door waits to my right. Clean linens are pinned on the clothesline outside. I take down the sheets and fold them. Then, with the linens balanced on my arm, I turn the knob and enter Cadmar's house for the second time in twenty-four hours.

The inside of Cadmar's house is dimly lit. It takes my eyes a second to adjust to the abrupt change in lighting and to assess my surroundings. The window is cracked open to let a whisper of a breeze enter the modest space. Unlike the other Ari kitchens that I've entered, this kitchen is sparse in comparison: two overripe bananas sit in a bowl in the corner, a few bronze pans hang from the ceiling, and a table with two chairs is shoved against the far wall as an afterthought. A large, worn book rests on the table, open as if someone was perusing its pages.

No other servants.

I stride towards the hallway, searching for the stairs. The hallway is as bare as the kitchen, minus a ceramic vase on an end table with two drooping flowers. Their pollen covers the table in a fine dust. Odd. One of Cadmar's servants should have cleared the pollen by now.

My palms sweat underneath the lace gloves, and the tiny hairs on the nape of my neck stand on end. My instincts are screaming, forget the necklace and go. Now.

I clench my hand, the lace sticking to my palm. Maybe all the servants are out on errands...

The stairs emerge, and they are odd even by Ari standards, spiraling up to the next floor and out of sight. The constant twists and turns make it impossible to see the top. Here and there, books are stacked on random steps, sometimes near the inside of the spiral and sometimes on the edge.

I set the laundry on a pile of books and roll my shoulders, trying to relieve tension. I force myself to ascend without dwelling further on what awaits. My charade of casual servant is ruined as I inch up the spiral like a disjointed, drunken spider, avoiding books as I go.

Halfway up the staircase, I slip on one of the books. I try to grab the railing and snatch the book at the same time, but it is too late. The volume tumbles down the stairs, clanging against each step like an alarm bell.

I sprint up the remaining stairs and hide behind a claw-footed table. The silence that follows in the wake of my mistake haunts the hallway, making my hands tremble.

Five minutes pass without a sign of life.

An ugly oil painting greets me across from my hiding spot, vying for my attention, but I ignore it. Cadmar's office door is propped open by books, but I can't see inside. I stifle my sigh of frustration and nudge the door open.

Inside, a low-burning candle flickers with its last minutes of light. A regal wooden desk sits across from the door, a monstrous painting of the night sky fills the wall on the left, while two cushy armchairs and a floor-to-ceiling bookshelf fight for the rest of the space.

I exhale. I have no other choice. I enter the room.

Information is worth more than all the treasure that one can be offered. Guard your treasure with your life.
-excerpt from *The Thief's Guide* Banned by the Council of the Sultan in the year 151-

5

"You don't want to leave that there."

The voice comes out of nowhere like a slap to the face. My body tenses. I turn, searching for the source.

"I have to say, I didn't think you'd return. When you saw that necklace, you looked as if you'd seen the first sultan reincarnated."

The man's gravelly baritone voice taunts me. There. The oil painting was obscured by darkness last night, but now the dying candle illuminates it. The frame juts out from the wall, too far to be a normal painting.

"Why don't you come out from behind your painting?" I say with more bravado than I feel. "It's rude."

"It's also rude to break into people's houses, but I'm guessing you already knew that," the man says. The painting emits a clicking noise as he steps out from behind the artwork into the office. I square my shoulders and lift my chin—no need to let him know that my heart is fluttering a hundred times a minute. He is surprisingly short, even shorter than my five feet five inches, with a stocky build. His jet-black hair and beard are trimmed close, too short to be fashionable according to Ari standards. The harsh lines of his long charcoal sherwani look like steel, not elegant clothing. His dark eyes glitter with intelligence as they take in my appearance.

Jelani Cadmar.

Although I ignore the frivolous squabbles of the Ari, Cadmar's name is well-known throughout the Lower City. Anyone with the balls to go against the Royal Vizier is someone worth paying attention to.

Cadmar is the first one to break the silence. "You look disappointed."

"You're not what I expected," I say to skirt around the truth.

"Ah, let me guess. You expected someone taller. Or maybe someone more in tune with the, as you Lower City people say, Ari? I promise you, I've got much more to offer than what my height might indicate."

A blush creeps onto my cheeks at his innuendo.

"What do you want?" I ask with as much venom as I can muster.

Cadmar raises an eyebrow at my open hostility. "Seeing as you are the one in my house, I believe *I* should be asking you that question. Let me guess, greetings from the Fawzi family?"

I refuse to take my eyes off Cadmar as he picks up the necklace and then sits casually as if he dealt with criminals on a daily basis. Dunes, he actually might deal with criminals on a daily basis.

"Your placement last night was better than today. Too hasty today." Cadmar clucks his tongue in disappointment and shifts the necklace from hand to hand, his eyes never leaving my face. My mouth is dryer than the dunes outside

Aveena. "I'll be returning this to my good friend, Lady Asfour, shall I? She'll be missing it dearly. She's rather fond of it."

My stomach tightens but I keep my emotions masked, a skill I learned at my mother's knee. Emotions are for the weak, she would say, her gilded bracelets a cheap mimicry of the real bangles.

Cadmar continues in spite of my internal struggle. The sunlight seeps through the window casting shadows behind him. "Or maybe the Moeen family? Or could it be the royal vizier himself? Nassor likes to pretend he's above such scruples, but he could be feeling the pressure of the sultan's untimely death…"

"I never ask."

"Never? That's a dangerous game. Please," he gestures at the other chair, "have a seat. You and I need to have a chat."

I perch on the edge of the seat. His dark eyes take in my rigid posture, assessing me.

"Not knowing who you work for. That leads to nasty complications."

"I do my work and then leave it behind me. And that's where the jobs stay—behind me." I keep my voice and expression neutral. The less I reveal to Cadmar, the better.

"You don't really believe that?"

I hesitate, not sure of how to respond. Cadmar sighs and leans back into his chair. He gives off the appearance of a man who is having a conversation with an acquaintance, not a street rat. If only I felt as calm as he looked.

"You're what? Fifteen? Sixteen?"

"Twenty," I answer truthfully.

"Well, at twenty-years-old you should have experienced enough of life to realize that nothing truly stays in the past."

I bristle at his tone. He's lecturing me like one of my old tutors. I ball my fists at my sides.

"Just name your price and have done with it," I say, feeling my mask of calm peeling like old paint in the sun. Cadmar remains impassive. "You Ari are all the same. So what is it? Name it."

Cadmar does not raise his voice. He doesn't even shift in his seat. He continues to assess me as I squirm under his gaze. I've had enough. I stand and run. If I'm fast enough, I'll blend into the crowd and disappear.

An object whizzes by my head, landing with a thunk in the wall. I freeze. My eyes flick to the left. A knife sticks out of the wooden door frame inches from my face.

"Our conversation was not over, Ms. Nightshade."

Color drains from my face as blood and adrenaline course through my body. But I ignore my flight instincts. I don't dare look at Cadmar. My voice comes out as a breathy whisper, sounding foreign to my own ears.

"I don't know—"

"Don't horseshit me."

"You must have me confused with someone else."

"How so?"

"The Nightshade is a man. Haven't you seen the—?"

"That's the brilliance of your little scheme, isn't it?"

I stop talking. My hopes of escaping dwindle to dust.

Cadmar fills the silence first. "There have been rumors among my fellows for quite some time now. A shadow who creates destruction in his wake. For the right price of course. The opportunities for someone with your skill set are endless when it comes to the Aristocracy. Especially now that the prince is of age. Even the most minor Ari families are scrambling for a leg up against the competition."

Cadmar steps close to me, but I still don't move—out of fear or stupidity, I'm not sure. A hand appears in my peripheral and grabs the hilt of the knife. The knife is buried all the way to the guard. Cadmar works the blade back and forth, easing it out of the door frame. He takes his time.

"Greedy bastards, all of them. And the infamous Nightshade was the solution to many men's problems. I knew it was only a matter of time before I was visited by you." His voice sounds bitter—the first true emotion he's shown. "Your servant's masquerade is quite good. The only problem is, I don't have any servants."

Cadmar frees the knife and walks away. The tinkle of glass starts me out of my frozen state, and I turn to see that Cadmar is pulling the stopper out of a beautiful crystal decanter with an amber liquid sloshing inside. He pours the alcohol into two crystal glasses then reclines in his seat.

"Sit."

I obey, a cold sweat trickling down my spine. My brain is blank. Numb. Useless.

"Have a drink." Cadmar thrusts the crystal glass into my hand. "I will say that I am pleasantly surprised to discover that you are a woman. No wonder you've been able to remain in business for as long as you have."

His grim smile doesn't reach his eyes.

"The damage that you managed to inflict on the Agrawal family was neatly done. You cast enough doubt in their direction that Girish is no longer trusted with the sultan's treasury."

"I didn't—"

Cadmar cuts off my denial as if I hadn't even spoken. "And then Deepak Moeen. Well, he was always a stupid bastard anyway. How did you manage to smuggle those falsified documents into his house? I thought he had hired private guards to watch his property."

My grip tightens on my glass, but I keep my mouth shut. I won't fall into his games.

"And of course there is the matter of getting into the Upper City in the first place. I saw what they did to that petty thief in the bazaar today for violating the Lower City curfew." Cadmar's dark eyes hold my gaze as he continues. "The gates are supposedly impenetrable. The wall is too high to climb. I suppose you could swim the canal, but you were dry when you broke into my home last night."

Cadmar swirls his liquor in his glass, looking thoughtful. "But it doesn't really matter, does it, miss——?"

I refuse to speak, to answer the question. Cadmar grins, bearing a feral smile. "Come, come, my dear. Tell me your name, and I won't involve the Suraksha."

"Laila," I choke out, anger battling the fear inside my chest.

"Miss Laila." He draws out my name as if testing it out before he says, "To the Nightshade."

And with that Jelani Cadmar raises his glass to me and drinks deeply.

Time is short and fast like a sword strike.
-Aveenan Proverb-

6

Snake charmers are powerful. I've watched them in the bazaar—with simple motion and music they entrance the deadliest desert snakes.

As Jelani Cadmar toasts me, I realize that I am at the mercy of his whims—just like a snake to the snake charmer's. I sit, both horrified and mesmerized by what he says.

"Well, down to business. You have an intriguing set of skills. Your ability to disguise yourself, to get into places you are not supposed to be—" he gestures at his office for emphasis "—*and* your intimate knowledge of the Aristocracy from masquerading as the Nightshade. I would like your assistance."

"My assistance?"

Cadmar's polite tone lures me in, eases my fear, despite the fact that I know it's a trap. A snake charmer indeed.

"Yes, your assistance," Cadmar says. He swirls the liquid around his glass, watching me. After a pause, he shrugs his shoulders and adds, "If you refuse, I will call the Suraksha and have this whole messy affair behind me. You can rot in Niraash, and I will find someone else. After all, you did break into my home with Lady Asfour's necklace."

I can't control the shiver that runs through me at the mention of Niraash, the mysterious prison hidden in the bowels of Aveena. No one knows the location; no one comes back from Niraash.

I need to buy myself time.

"Or you can comply, and the Suraksha will have to do their own dirty work to fill Niraash."

"What is it you want, exactly?"

"I have a few people who complete jobs similar to what you currently do. With a set purpose, of course."

I wait. His response doesn't clarify anything. Cadmar takes another sip from his crystal glass and continues.

"If you choose to accept my offer, you will need to meet certain expectations." Cadmar pauses and looks into my eyes. I stare back at him, pushing away my fear.

"First, you will only work for me. I expect your loyalty to me will not waiver. I will provide food, housing, and a small sum of money for extra necessities. You will move out of the Lower City."

I continue to hold his gaze—staring down the snake charmer—and try not to show my surprise when he mentions the money. Of course he would pay his people in order to keep them from seeking other work, but he's blackmailing me. I wonder if the money is enough…

"Second, you will not tell anyone what you are doing."

Well, *duh*.

"And third, you cannot have contact with any family or lovers. From this point forward, your only focus will be on the job at hand. I will not have family ties distracting

42

you from your work. Or the empty promises of some man of the week."

I don't blink or flinch at his words. Relief floods my body—Cadmar figured out that I'm the Nightshade, but he knows nothing else. Good. And as for empty promises, well, I've never known another kind.

Cadmar breaks eye contact first and busies himself pouring another drink. I look down at my crystal glass and trace the engraved patterns with my finger, the liquor sloshing around inside. Cadmar listed his terms as if they were inconsequential. Maybe for him they are, but I pause to consider. I'll be restarting. Again. I'll have to learn the new rules of Cadmar's game like I had to learn the rules of the Lower City when I fled there. And in all of his talk of expectations, Cadmar never said what I'll be doing. Or why. Some questions answered, some avoided. That seems to be how he works.

My finger lingers on the circles etched into the crystal. They loop through, trapping each ring in the link of the next. No end, no escape. There might be a choice, but I know there is only one path. I look up from my glass.

"You know my choice," I say. "When do I start?"

His smile almost reaches his eyes. "You have tomorrow to get your affairs in order. Meet at the Hathorda by sunset tomorrow night."

I nod and stand, hiding my flash of surprise. Twenty-four hours to get my affairs in order? Plenty of time to escape into the bowels of the Lower City and away from this Ari and his schemes.

Cadmar gets to his feet as well and accepts my untouched glass.

"I trust you'll let yourself out. But since it is daytime, be sure to use the stairs. I cannot promise that a neighbor won't see you climbing out of a window."

"For someone who doesn't want visitors, your house is too easy to break into," I snap back.

He lets out a bark of surprised laughter. "Oh, this shall be interesting, Ms. Nightshade."

He extends a hand, and I grasp it, expecting the smooth, unworked skin of the Ari and instead finding calluses on his hands. He grips mine tightly, the smile vanishing from his face, as he says, "Our deal only lasts as long as you follow the rules. Break one, and I will make sure you end up in the darkest cell in Niraash."

He crushes my hand then lets go. I leave without responding, trying not to scurry away too fast. A few books tumble off of his curling staircase as I escape. As I leave Jelani Cadmar's house—for once through the front door—his threat weighs on my mind.

His threat and Tanu.

**You won't like what happens if yer ever
caught, girlie.**
-Advice from Velo to Laila after her first job as
the Nightshade-

7

The flight back to my attic is a blur as I scurry back to my hiding spot. My head swivels left and right, each shadow transforms into the Suraksha coming to imprison me in Niraash. As I hurry back through the southern gate, I swear the Suraksha watch me more closely, causing my heart to flutter frantically.

The smell of hot, unwashed bodies press against me as I shove through the throngs of people, unable to avoid the smudges of dirt that the street urchins leave on my clothes as they push past her in a tiny herd of bare feet. My beige veil catches on the breeze and pulls from my head. I turn and snatch at it, trying to salvage one of the few belongings I have.

My body smashes against a large figure, and a loud crash fills the air as bronze pots are knocked out of a man's hands. I fall to the dusty ground amid the chaos of rolling pots and the anguished shouts of the walla.

"I'm so sorry," I stutter.

The walla's cheeks redden as he gesticulates wildly around us, shouting, "My pots! Stupid girl. Look at my pots!"

The crowd converges on us, entranced by the drama unfolding.

"Let me—" I start to reach for a pot, but he slaps my hand away.

"Don't touch them!" He shoves my fumbling hands away and snarls, "Get away from me, street rat."

His spit lands on my cheek, and I stand and glare at him, wiping the spittle off my face with the veil. He catches my eyes and turns dark under his bronzed skin.

"Djinn-eyes," he mutters, fear flashing across his features. I stumble back at the hatred in his expression. "Get away from me!"

I scamper away, pushing through the gawkers who neither help the walla or offer comfort to me, my heart thrumming in my ears. Three more streets and I'm finally at the bakery, one of the last buildings on the street made of sandstone. I glance furtively at the entrance then slip into the gap between the two buildings.

I grab onto a window ledge and pull myself up. The handholds are nearly invisible in the sandstone, but I work my way up the side of the two-story building using the uneven stone to pull myself up. At the top, I lift one of the roof slats and disappear into the attic through the near-invisible gap.

The dimmed light in the attic and the sweet smell wafting up from the bakery below help to ground me. My fingers run across the beads of my anklet unconsciously, seeking comfort in the one item I've had my entire life. I slump to the floor after that spectacle I made of myself in the bazaar. My hands are still trembling, but I clench them into fists, forcing them to stop. I knock my head back on the wall behind me, squeezing my eyes shut. Maybe I'll wake up, and none of this will have happened.

I scoff.

Unlikely.

When I open my eyes again, I gasp and stare. A dead rat is nailed to the wall above my head. It must be fresh, I think calmly, detached. There isn't a smell. A crimson drip slides from the nail and plops onto my cheek.

I flinch and scramble out from underneath the rat, wiping the blood off on my face.

Velo.

Somehow, he knows.

I've been cut off.

My heart sinks, and I scurry to the loose board and check for the bag of gold. Decaying wood cuts under my nails, but I ignore it. Finally, it pops open, then falls forward desperately searching.

"No, no, no," I mutter over and over, searching for the rupees I've painstakingly saved, one job at a time. But there's nothing but barren wood and sandstone.

My trembling restarts, and I tear through the attic, uprooting everything, tossing my threadbare kurtis to the side. I glance at the dead rat and before disgust can overtake me, I rip its body from the nail. Grabbing my knife, I slice through the rodent, desperate for my gold, frantically hoping that Velo hid it inside the rat as some cruel joke. Blood seeps into the wooden slats and stains my head a dark red.

Nothing.

It's gone.

I collapse, sobbing, the life I've tried to build for myself vanished in a snuff of a candle from an Ari and a greedy thief. My chest constricts as I try to keep my cries quiet so that the bakers don't discover me.

If only Velo had left the rupees, I could have hidden until the Tribes visited and bribed passage with them. I wouldn't have to fall into Cadmar's blackmail of working with him. I was so close to freeing us from this dunes-damned city. To getting Tanu the healing from the magical waters of the Bhavin that she desperately needs but that the Ari gatekeep from the rest of Aveena.

Pressure builds behind my eyes, a headache growing as my sobs slow, replaced by dread and emptiness.

Everything I've done, running away from the Upper City, becoming the Nightshade, saving those rupees, all of it to save Tanu. Now it's gone.

Get your affairs in order.

Scrubbing the tear marks from my face, I take a shaky breath, resigning myself to playing Cadmar's game after all.

I grab the few items in the attic—a pair of scissors, a worn copy of *Wind in the Dunes*, and most of the clothes—and lay them in the center of my blanket. I quickly tie the corners and sling the makeshift bag over my shoulder.

I peek my head out of the window, scanning the street for any observers. A few lingering customers mill about the bazaar, leisurely finding their way home. No one close enough to notice me. A shift in the shadows between two buildings catches my attention. I squint, trying to determine if it was the dying sun or something else. The shadow remains still, but goosebumps still erupt across my arms.

I pull back from the window and tiptoe to the other side of the attic. Plan B it is. I slip through the gap in the slats and roll onto the flat ledge. I'm on my feet and jumping to the next rooftop without hesitation. I fly across the rooftops. The freedom is exhilarating, better than any disguise that I could create out of fabric or facade.

Soon I drop down to the ground and cross the narrow alleyway to my destination.

The flash of red on my fingertips catches my attention, and I cringe. I bury my fingers in the blanket, hiding them from sight.

The one-room house is the same. The disheveled roof clings to the supports of the house in a desperate attempt to not slip off. The plaster walls are a myriad of browns— newer patches of plaster and clay contrast the duller original walls of the house. The wooden door frame sags under the expectation of holding the weight placed upon its shoulders.

It is the most beautiful house that I've ever seen.

A flit of nerves swirls in my stomach, but I push them away. I knock softly on the door to avoid the attention of nosy neighbors. It swings open, and Dada pulls me into a hug, crushing me against his round belly, before ushering me inside.

"Can I wash first?" I ask, still hiding my hands in the blanket.

Dada's forehead crinkles but he gestures to the bucket outside the house "Of course, of course. Let me."

I hesitate then pass Dada my bundle. If he notices the blood on my fingertips, he doesn't say anything, just carrying my bundle into the house.

Hastily, I scrub the blood off then dump the water, washing away the evidence, then follow the old man into the house. Dada's back is to me when I enter, and I notice how his bald patch has expanded since the last time I saw him.

One candle flickers on the table against the wall, throwing the rest of the room into harsh relief. Dada gestures to the table, but I hold up a finger. I walk to the makeshift bed in the corner, hidden from the flickering light of the candle. Tanu curls up in her scrap of a blanket. She takes up so much space for such a small person. I bend down to fix the blanket and kiss her forehead.

As I smooth her wild dark hair, longing piercing my soul as I stare at her tiny features, Tanu shifts then rubs her eyes. She rolls over and peers up at me through bleary eyes, her brow furrowed in concentration. Tanu reaches a hand up and cups my cheek, running her fingers over my face.

"Lala?" she asks, her voice heavy with sleep.

I place my hand over her tiny one, holding her to my cheek. I murmur, "It's me. Go back to sleep, Tanu."

I place the doll I bought her a few weeks ago in her hands so she doesn't have to search for it, and she smiles, closing her eyes again. Finally, I walk back over to Dada, my footsteps softened by the dirt floor, and sit down at the table with him.

"How is she doing?" I ask in a whisper. I don't tear my eyes away from Tanu's sleeping form as I talk. Dada's used to this.

"Your niece is a'right."

"Only alright?" I ask, pulling my gaze away from the sleeping form across the room to scrutinize Dada's features. He smiles, pushing his weathered wrinkles up.

"Our girl is going to eat me out of house 'n' home. Growing like a little weed, that one."

I grin as some of the tension evaporates from the room. "Good. She needs to be strong like her mother."

"She's definitely strong headed like her ma if that's what ya mean," he says with a chuckle. He hesitates then says, "It's getting worse."

My stomach twists, and nausea rises in my throat. I'm running out of time. "Has anyone noticed yet?"

"Not yet," he says with a sigh. I tear my gaze away from Tanu and take in his weathered face. He looks tired. And frail. "Stop worrying over me."

"I'm not."

"Liar," he says, smiling.

I grin back briefly then glance over at Tanu again as she shifts in her sleep. Dada waits patiently as I sit in silence. His serene presence urges me to tell him what's happened in the past few hours. I want to tell him if for no other reason than I just want to tell *someone*, but I know I can't. I set the blanket on the table and untie it, my few possessions presented unceremoniously between us.

"Here. To help with the little weed," I say. "I know it's not much, but you could sell it or…"

My voice trails off as Dada grabs my hand, staring at my face instead of the contents of my life. I look at his shoulder, avoiding his knowing brown eyes.

"I might be gone for a while."

"Okay," he says in that same calm tone.

"I—I hope this helps," I stutter.

"It will."

I want to say more, to tell him about Velo and Cadmar and the dead rat and the necklace, but instead I only say, "Okay."

Silence.

I watch the rise and fall of Tanu's chest, joy and longing swirling together inside me. She looks so serene in sleep—the antithesis of my anxiety.

The temple bell chimes, urging me to leave.

I head for the door. Dada follows, and when I turn to say something else, he hugs me tight. I let him, feeling awkward and emotional, his towering frame making me feel child-like.

"Be careful," he says.

My eyes fill with threatening tears, and my throat feels dry. I swallow the emotions and whisper, "I'll try."

"See you soon."

Over his shoulder, Tanu rolls in her sleep, pulling the ragged blanket tighter around her small body. I turn away and step back into the night, unable to respond to the old man.

I'm not sure if I will see the two of them again.

**And once the body has left this earthly
plane enshrouded in fire, the soul will be
free to join Wind Mother and Sky Father
and all their children amongst the stars.
To force the soul to remain bound to the
land of sand and suffering is to deny them
eternal joy.**
-from the Sacred Scrolls of Wind Mother
translated from Aramak, the Olden Tongue-

8

The Sultana

The acrid smell of incense would forever burn in Chhavi's memory, reminding her of her husband's illness.

And death.

She feels empty. Emotionless. Like Wind roaming across the unending sands.

Gautam built this balcony for her when they were first married, ensuring that she would always be able to see the sky and dunes; ensuring that she would be able to escape the palace in the privacy of their own rooms. He insisted that she was touched by Mother Wind, desirous of whisking away to far off places.

He repeated that he wanted to hold onto her long enough that she would know how much he loved her.

She runs her frigid fingers along the marble banister, her eyes unseeing as she stares across the moonlit dunes. Gautam would grab her hands and tuck them into his own, laugh lines framing his mouth as he joked with her about their perpetual cold.

The silence of Aveena is disconcerting. Normally the sounds of the city would drift along the breeze to her balcony, reminding her of the world outside of her walls.

Reminding her of those entrusted to her care.

Chhavi shivers, pulling her silk shawl tighter around her shoulders, trying to banish the emptiness that had settled into her heart since Gautam's death.

How could her ravi be gone?

The shuffle of slippers across the balcony announces Amara, her maidservant. Chhavi feels her presence at her elbow, Amara's hesitation palpable. All the servants were handling her delicately since Gautam's death, as if they were afraid of shattering the sultana into a thousand shards.

"Yes, Amara?" Chhavi asks.

"Chhaviji," she bows tentatively before saying, "the vizier is here."

Surprise colors her voice. "Nassor is here?"

"Yes, Chhaviji. He wishes for a private audience."

The sultana nods, not taking her eyes off of the sliver of the moon just visible above. Gautam was right—she was one with Mother Wind. The desire to move freely intensified with Gautam's death, as though the death of her ravi removed the center of her universe.

"Condolences, Chhaviji," Nassor says, pulling the sultana out of her thoughts and back to the balcony.

She stares out across the dunes for a moment more, one more moment away from her duties as sultana.

"Thank you, Nassorji."

"Sultan Gautam was a good man."

54

The sultana turns to the vizier, allowing him to kiss the tips of her fingers in greeting. The black of the vizier's sherwani melds with the darkness of the night.

"He was a good man," Chhavi agrees. "Although you two did not always see eye to eye."

The vizier chuckles. "That's true. Still, he was a good man and a good sultan."

Chhavi inclines her head graciously. The cloud behind her shifts, allowing the crescent moon to cast its light on the vizier's face. Chhavi notes the strain evident there, the tightness in his stance. He grazes his fingers across the obsidian bracelet he wears, his one nervous tick. She waits for Nassor to continue. She does not have the energy for the niceties expected in the palace anymore.

"How is Ajani fairing?" Nassor asks.

"As well as to be expected of a young man who just lost his father." It takes more patience than Chhavi currently possesses to not snap at the vizier. It is not his fault how grief weighed on her, smothering her. It is not his fault that she'd answered this same question a hundred times today, already.

"May his soul join the stars above," Nassor says, dipping his head. His golden bangles clink against the black one as he moves. He pauses then asks, "And where might he be tonight?"

Chhavi sighs. "In his room, I suppose. How should I know?"

"He didn't answer when I called upon him to wish him condolences." Lucky him, Chhavi thought to herself. Nassor continues on, oblivious to her disinterest. "He should be among the rest of the Aristocracy, soothing their worries at the shift in sultanship and—"

"He can have one night to mourn in peace," the sultana snaps. Annoyance simmers beneath the surface, fighting with her grief for dominance. That the vizier would insinuate that her son is not attending to his duties is reprehensible.

"I meant no disrespect, Chhaviji," Nassor says placatingly. "I only meant to serve the Bahu family."

"Of course," Chhavi says with a nod. Nassor hesitates, the reluctance on his face evident. She wishes he would just get on with it so that she could go back to her thoughts.

"I've been perusing the Ordinances, Chhaviji."

"Oh?" she asks, turning back to the endless sky. Why would Nassor disturb her grief for this? He was always so focused on protocol—one of the reasons that he and Gautam argued fiercely.

The sultana feels him move to the balcony beside her.

"They provide the guidance that we need in our time of grief," Nassor adds carefully. Chhavi bristles at the condescension but hides her distaste behind her palace mask.

"And what wisdom do they provide, Nassorji?" The vizier shifts his weight, carefully choosing his words before speaking to her. As though he thinks she is incapable of remaining stoic in her grief. Chhavi sighs, saying, "Out with it, Nassor. Nothing you say will be worse than the news of Gautam's death."

"The Ordinances dictate that the sultana should be given time to grieve."

"Oh?"

"Privately."

Chhavi deigns to look at Nassor, attempting to glean any motives, but his face is hidden in shadows again. Gautam was always better at reading people than her.

She grits her teeth. "Speak plainly, Nassor."

"You are being granted three months reprieve from your palace duties, Chhaviji. I have already arranged for your Upper City residence to be prepared for your arrival." Nassor faces her, his dark eyes earnest. "I know you loved Gautam passionately, and he you. The Ordinances have given you the opportunity to rest outside of watching eyes. To be free."

Chhavi's heart flutters at the promise of freedom, but she squashes it. Despite the concern in his voice, her hackles were raised. Narrowing her eyes, she asks, "What of my son? What about his chance to grieve?"

The vizier's grimace answers her. Ajani would not be granted the same opportunity. Chhavi lifts her chin, her voice ringing clear in the silent night air.

"Then I shall remain here with him despite the *opportunity* the Ordinances give."

"Chhaviji, be reasonable—"

Nassor touches her arm, goosebumps rising from the chill, but she shrugs him off, pulling her shawl tighter around herself. The night temperatures could drop rapidly once the sun sets.

"I am being reasonable, Nassor. We are both grieving. I *will* support my son."

"That is not an option," the vizier snaps, his own mask slipping.

Chhavi straightens to her fullest height, her voice cold. "You forget who you speak to, Nassor."

The vizier inhales slowly then bows. "My apologies, Chhaviji."

She notices the half bow he offers—unbefitting of her status. Frustration charges the air between them. The sultana watches as Vizier Nassor collects himself, renewing his calm demeanor.

"Chhaviji, please listen—"

"No," she says, putting her hand out to stop whatever rules he is about to mention. "My son *needs* me. That is all that matters."

"If you remain, you will hurt your son."

"Impossible," she scoffs.

"Please listen to me." Nassor reaches out and grasps her hand between his. "Gautam trusted me to be his vizier, to advise him in difficult times. Please let me do the same for you and Ajani."

The sultana's indignation deflates. She closes her eyes, silencing her aching heart, and pulls her shawl tighter around her.

"Okay, Nassorji. I'm listening."

To his credit, the vizier does not show any relief at her change in tone. He lets go of her hands and gestures to the palace behind them.

"Ajani needs to establish himself as the next sultan. He needs to show that although he is young, he is also wise and capable of leading the Council. Ajani cannot accomplish this if he is hiding in the folds of your saree, mourning the loss of his father."

Chhavi looks out to the dunes again, away from the truths that Nassor lays in front of her. "So, he has to pretend as if his father's death is inconsequential?"

"Of course not."

"Then what are you saying, Nassor?" Unlike the vizier, she can't keep the emotion out of her voice.

"Ajani has to prove that *despite* his personal tragedy, he has the mind of a sultan. He needs to show the Council that he is a man among them."

"And my presence would stop that?"

"It would be detrimental to his success." The vizier steps closer to Chhavi, resting a hand on top of hers. She doesn't shake him off this time. "I know you speak with the heart of a mother looking out for her child, Chhaviji, but Ajani is not a child."

"I know." The sultana's whisper is almost inaudible.

"Trust me, Chhaviji. Following the Ordinances is the best way you can support your son." Chhavi's shoulders sag. The vizier pats her hand condescendingly. "It's for the best."

Nassor excuses himself, leaving her alone once more with the moonlit dunes.

**Deference shall be shown to Aristocracy
at all times. They carry the burden of
protecting Aveena from enemies both
outside and inside its borders.**
-from The Ordinances of Aveena-

9

The night passes in fitful spurts of sleep interspersed with sweaty moments of panic flooding my body. The smell of decaying rat permeates the attic over the bakery even though I disposed of the furry body hours ago. I can't tell if the smell is really there or if my anxiety is imagining it.

I should stay here, rotting away like the rat, like I deserve.

Despair threatens to drown me, thoughts of failure weaving into my soul. If I stay here, by the time the Suraksha found me, I'd be gone. Nothing left to throw into Niraash. Dada would care for Tanu, and they'd...

I sit up and press the heels of my hands in my eyes.

No.

Tanu needs me, she needs passage to Bhavin. It doesn't matter if the rupees are from the Nightshade or from some Ari. So what if I have to start over? Save the gold and save Tanu from certain death. If the Suraksha knew about her failing eyesight, she'd already be sentenced to the dunes. The healing waters of Bhavin—the last evidence of magic that Aveena tolerates—are her only chance to survive.

"Get up, Laila," I mutter, forcing myself to stand. "One step at a time."

I stretch upwards, urging the kinks out of my shoulders. *Rip.*

Air hits my bare shoulder, and I swivel my head. *Fuck.* The seam of my kurti lay open, exposing my back and left shoulder, threatening to slide further down to expose my chest.

I squeeze my eyes closed.

"Can't just one thing go right?" I ask.

Silence answers.

Gingerly, I remove the kurti and artfully tie the fabric around my torso.

Instead of exiting through the bakery, I peek out from the roof. When the coast is clear, I climb onto the roof and leap to the next one, heading toward the southern gate. The rooftops are familiar, and I navigate them with ease. When I'm close to the Lower City bazaar, I drop to the dusty street then scan my surroundings.

A few wallas arrange their wares on the warped wooden stands in the early morning light. Guilt sits heavy in my chest—I don't take from those who are barely surviving like me. But I can't meet Cadmar in scraps of fabric, and I refuse to take the gifts I gave Dada back. He and Tanu need it more.

Reaching down, I rub my fingers across the uneven stones of my anklet, breathing deeply. When the chill shivers down my spine, I know the magic is working.

Silently, I emerge from my hiding place, remaining close to the shadows of the building as I stealthily approach the fabric cart.

"Hurry up, you lazy cow," a stout man snaps. He leans against the wall behind him, the honey from the ladoos he snacks on dripping onto his chin as he glares at the woman who is unloading the clothes.

The ruddy-faced mistress straightens, panting under the weight of the fabrics. "Yes, Amirji, of course."

When she drops the clothes onto the table, one tumbles into the sand. Frantically, the woman scrambles to pick up the lehenga and dust it off, but the stout man is already in her face, yelling.

I dip behind them and snag one of the kurtis out of the cart. Neither of them notice.

As I slip into the alleyway, the sound of a slap echoes behind me. I cringe, but hurry away. Once out of sight, I tuck the kurti into my waistband and climb. I roll onto the rooftop and lay staring up at the one wisp of cloud above me. Guilt gnaws at me—the woman will be blamed for the missing kurti once they notice. As much as I need the clothes, I don't want her to be punished for my thievery.

I blow out a frustrated breath. I shouldn't care and yet...

The slap replays in my mind, and a cold sweat breaks out. My cheek stings, and my father's shadow stands over me, his hand raised again. His anger palpable at my perceived transgression. I try to explain, beg him to understand, but he is oblivious to my words. Ahmed stands smugly behind him, a malicious delight burning in his eyes as he watches.

Bile rises in my throat, and abruptly I sit up, sucking in air. *I'm not there. I am free of them.*

I repeat the mantra over and over as I breathe in and out, shoving the memories to the dark recesses of my mind. I rub my fingers across the rough sandstone, grounding myself. A breeze ruffles my hair.

"Thank you, Wind Mother," I whisper.

Once calm, I pull on the borrowed kurti and stand on shaky legs.

I can't let the woman suffer for my theft. She doesn't deserve that punishment.

Resolved, I sprint and leap across to the next roof and then the next, distancing myself from the bazaar. The wall appears ahead, a few birds perched along the ledge. I lean over the edge, scanning the building underneath me for ledges.

"Good enough," I mutter, lowering myself down.

I brush my hands off, then head towards the southern gate. The Suraksha are busy fixing the wheel of a cart with an irate merchant in the Upper City as I walk by. The hairs on my neck prickle, and I glance over my shoulder but none of the Suraksha pay attention to me. But I can't shake the feeling of being watched.

The Upper City bazaar is already a flurry of activity. The scent of spices tickles my nose as I pass a stand with a rainbow of spices for sale. Next to it, the sizzle of dosas hitting the pan over an open fire underlies the shouts from wallas on either side. As I pass, a jewelry walla glares at me, throwing an arm over her wares distrustfully. I hurry past and duck down the next street before she can call the Suraksha over.

A moan.

The beauty and bustle of the bazaar is marred by the example tethered in the middle. This time it's a younger man, probably no older than thirty, his head and hands trapped inside the rusting metal pillory. Chains wrap around his feet and cuff his neck, his skin rubbed raw. His body trembles from the exertion of holding himself upright in the pillory to avoid getting cut further by the metal. A signpost over his head reads:

Guilty of disrespect to the Aristocracy and failure to show deference as is due to those who care for Aveena

As I pass, a merchant spits on the imprisoned man. The latter doesn't flinch as the spittle slides down his cheek. I grimace and avert my eyes. If I stare too long, the Suraksha might find my gawking *disrespectful* as well.

I stroll purposefully towards the center of the city, closer to the palace. Soon store fronts replace the bazaar stalls. I surreptitiously scan the doorways, looking for the sultan's emblem. The closer towards the palace, the emblem appears— two curved swords crossed behind a sun with a crown wrapped around.

If anyone can afford to lose one kurti, it's a sultan-endorsed walla.

I dip into an alleyway and run my fingers over my anklet, breathing in measured breaths to calm my racing heart. A tingle begins to work its way from my ankle through my legs. I've never used my mysterious skill to blatantly steal during the daytime, and yet, here I am preparing for the second time today to do so.

The tingle stops as the thought distracts me. Fuck. I need to concentrate.

Inhaling deeply, I try again, and this time the chill works its way throughout my entire body. A breeze brushes past, but instead of fluttering my stolen kurti, it passes through me. I hurry towards the sultan-endorsed store, keeping towards the wall to not bump into the crowd.

"Come along, Esha," a pompous Ari woman commands to the younger woman next to her. "Only the best for our family after all."

"Yes, mamaji," the younger woman says. Several servants flank them, a half-step behind. I join the shadows of their group, and as the servants hold the doors open for the Ari women, I'm able to squeeze in behind them.

I sigh softly in relief, and one of the servants glances around for the source. I hold still, waiting until she shuffles further into the shop before heading towards the opposite side.

The soft strumming of a tambura filters through the shop as a veiled woman plays in a corner. Sparkles glitter along the walls, reflections of the sunlight hitting various gem-adorned fabrics near the front windows. The owner bows over the Ari woman's hand while snapping at two assistants behind her to do the same.

I scan the kurtis in the back of the shop, searching for the plainest one I could find.

It's impossible.

Even the less elaborate sarees have tiny mirrors stitched into the bust, mimicking the gem-lined ones. Sweat beads on my neck, my nerves amping up the longer I linger. Finally, I snatch an orange kurti and hurry to the back room. As I whip around the corner, one of the Ari servants stares after, her gaze focused on the orange fabric in my hand.

Heart racing, I change quickly. As I shove my arms through the new kurti, my elbow knocks into a box, and I accidentally knock it onto the ground. The conversation around the corner falters.

Shit.

"Go check the back, Aditi," the owner's voice snaps then turns sweet again. "Lady Shah, if you would care to…"

I can't hear the rest over the roaring in my ears. I snatch a nearby handbag and dump its contents, then hurriedly stuff my clothes into it. Just as soft footsteps round the corner, I duck behind a box. The cooling sensation from my anklet evaporates, and despite my frantic attempts, I cannot get the magic to return. It never works when I'm distraught.

The assistant passes my hiding spot, and before overthinking it, I escape into the store. I wrap my chuni around my head loosely to hide my hair and saunter purposefully towards the exit, pushing out the aura that I belong there.

Ten more steps.

"Have you seen this one, Lady Shah? It would look divine on your daughter."

Five more steps.

"No, no, no, much too bland. She needs to stand out or else the prince won't notice her."

Two more steps.

"You're always so astute, Lady Sha—hey wait!"

I abandon any pretense and rush forward and into the crowd. A quick glance over my shoulder reveals the store owner speaking to Suraksha, gesturing in my direction. Time to go.

Without breaking into a sprint, I quicken my pace, expertly maneuvering through the crowd.

"Stop! Thief!"

One of the wallas gasps at the Suraksha's shout, hovering protectively over her wares, keen eyes scanning the crowd. I meet her eyes briefly, and hers narrow.

"Over here, sir!" she shouts, waving the Suraksha over.

I sprint around the corner, hoping to lose the guards in the bazaar. I wind through several side streets and then to where the food wallas are all lined together, their stalls pressed closely together. The crowd is thicker here as the scents of hot dosas frying on the pan mingle with the earthy smoke smell of the roasting shish kabobs on the other side. I slow my sprint but continue to hurry towards the Lower City where I know I can disappear.

I reach the far side of the bazaar and risk another glance over my shoulder. The Suraksha are scanning the area but further away. I can get away if–

"Oof."

I collide with a muscled body and nearly fall to the dusty street, but warm hands steady me.

"I'm so sorry, miss," he says, letting go quickly once he realizes I'm stable. "I wasn't paying attention and then–"

"It's fine," I say, then glance over my shoulder again. "But I've really got to–"

"Are you okay?" he asks.

The concern deep in his voice halts my frantic searching for the Suraksha momentarily. I look back at him, quickly saying, "Of course. If you'll excuse me."

His brow furrows, but I can't linger to admire how handsome it makes him.

I try to duck around him but a rough hand grabs my arm and pulls me around, and I come face to face with a large, bearded Suraksha.

10

"There you are," the guard growls in my face, his hot breath sour in my nose. "Don't cause more trouble now, and I'll make sure they go easy on you in the stocks."

He chuckles darkly, dragging me back the way I came. My stomach sinks, my thoughts freezing, unsure how I managed to escape the Suraksha for two years for it all to come crashing down on my head over a guilt kurti.

Before we make it two steps, another hand grabs my arm. "And where do you think you're taking my wife?" the handsome stranger asks. The authority in his voice startles the Suraksha into dropping my arm.

"Your wife?" he asks. "She was just seen stealing from—"

"Impossible." The stranger scoffs in the Suraksha's face. He had to be a merchant—that haughtiness is tough to fake. "She's been with me the whole time."

"She's been—" the Suraksha splutters then straightens. "Witnesses saw the thief come to this part of the bazaar. In an orange kurti like what your wife is wearing."

The stranger gestures around the bazaar. "Look around. See any other orange?"

The vibrant attire of the Upper City undulates around us, dots of orange of every shade visible from our vantage point. The Suraksha's face reddens, either from frustration or embarrassment, I cannot tell. I keep my head bowed, as expected of an Upper City wife, not daring to hope that this will work.

Several meters away another Suraksha shouts and starts hustling down the alleyway.

The guard in front of us lets out a frustrated breath, then dips his head. "My apologies for the mix up, sir."

The man next to me scoffs again then says, "I trust it won't happen again."

"Yes, sir," the Suraksha says, then turns on his boot and jogs down another alleyway.

I sigh in relief then look up at the stranger. "Thank you. You really didn't have to–"

"I know," he says with a grin. Dark hair swoops into his eyes as he looks down at me–he's at least a head taller than me. Gold rings glimmer from his ears matching a few on his fingers. Between the gold and the fine fabric of his dark green sherwani, he has to be at least a merchant if not one of the lesser Ari. "Please tell me you didn't actually steal that kurti."

"Of course not," I say quickly, hoping he doesn't notice the heat creeping into my cheeks. "But even still, the Suraksha mistake people all the time."

His grin slips a little. "Do they?"

I bob my head side to side in a non-answer. It's not surprising that this rich boy doesn't know much about Suraksha justice. All in the name of the sultan and all.

The heaviness of eyes watching me prickles along the back of my neck. I glance back towards where the guards disappeared too, anxious to keep moving. They're still gone, but I can't shake the feeling of being watched.

"Well thank you again, but I must—" I step around him, but the stranger touches my arm again, causing me to shiver involuntarily despite the heat of the noon sun.

"Please," he says, his brown eyes earnest, "let me at least buy you lunch for your troubles."

I pause. "Why would you be concerned about my troubles?"

An unknown emotion flashes across his face, but it's gone before I can analyze it further. He shrugs. "Just feels like the right thing to do."

"I should get back," I say. "My mistress, she'll be angry if I'm late."

He pauses, scanning my kurti and veil. "You're a servant?"

"Something like that," I mutter. I step from his gentle hold. "Thank you though. For the offer and for your help."

"Next time then?" he asks, a smile tugging at the corner of his lips.

I shrug a shoulder. "Sure."

He grabs my hand again, surprising me. The interactions between men and women are highly formal in the Upper City. His casual demeanor contrasts my expectations of him based on his attire.

"At least tell me your name."

His gaze is so earnest, so genuine. Despite knowing that I'll never see him again, I whisper, "Laila" before pulling my hand out of his grasp and disappearing into the bazaar. The feel of his eyes follow me until I'm around the corner and out of sight.

The journey back to the Lower City bazaar passes in a haze of hot bodies and jumbled thoughts. Slipping the borrowed kurti from my bag onto the walla's cart when he and his wife aren't looking is simple now that I wear the expensive attire from the Upper City. None of the vendors glare at me with the same distrust as they typically do. In fact, several try to catch my attention to sell their wares, assuming that I have the rupees to buy them.

Although Cadmar said I had until sunset today, I head towards the Hathorda early. I've nowhere else to go, and I've already pushed my luck today.

Plus, I can't shake the feeling of being watched that's followed me throughout the day, causing the hairs on my nape to rise. At least I think I was being watched—I'm second guessing all of my instincts. I repeat my plan over and over, ingraining it into my mind. Reveal nothing, stay silent, observe and wait. It's the best I can do as I figure out how to get out of this mess. New game, new rules.

Dark, smoke-stained fabrics hang across the Hathorda ceiling in an attempt to hide the mosquito nets above our heads. The swaths of blues and blacks are punctuated by a crimson curtain that cuts through the darkness, the blood-red fabric dancing ominously above my head.

The Hathorda is a tavern and inn. Common complaints include bed bugs, substandard food, and unsavory customers. Those who brave the dunes to Aveena do not frequent the

Hathorda, and few people in Aveena know it exists. The shadow world of Aveena sees the Hathorda as a homebase, a neutral zone. *Hathorda* translates to "hammer"—which fits since its clientele visit to get hammered.

My beer sits untouched, I only ordered it to get the barmaid to stop scowling at me. My eyes sweep to the familiar exits once more before I allow my mind to wander. Barmaids flit between tables, giving out the ale as freely as they give out their promises. Men call out to one another over the rumble of conversations. The haze of hookah smoke floats in the still air, hiding the corners of the bar.

My mind goes back to the kind stranger from the bazaar. The warmth in his gaze. The way that he insisted on next time, even though there's no hope of that. Why did I give him my real name?

Reckless.

A part of me wants him to know—wants *someone* to know the innocent version of me that's been long dead. He defended me against that Suraksha so confidently. If only he knew that he'd defended the infamous Nightshade.

Bitterness curls in my stomach.

He was exactly the type of boy that would've caught my attention when I lived with my merchant father: tall, dark, and handsome. Predictable. Oh, and don't forget wealthy. The bitterness sours further. I take a sip of my beer, but it only makes it worse.

My father's biggest concern: was he wealthy?

Thank the dunes I escaped that life.

A shout draws my attention to a nearby group. Two men growl at each other as they try to show off their arm-wrestling prowess. Their arms shake as they battle—although it is unclear if the shaking is due to the alcohol or the wrestling. The other men around them yell encouragement or insults.

With a whoop, the heavier-set arm wrestler slams the other man's arm down on the table. He raises his meaty hands in celebration, waving over a barmaid to get more drinks for the victory. As she saunters off, he slaps her ass like she is part of his victory prize.

Disgusting.

My gaze catches the arm wrestler's attention. A leer spreads across his pockmarked face as he looks at me, revealing a few missing teeth in the process. The haze of a win and the ale seem to bolster his confidence. As if I don't have enough problems today already.

"How ye doing, sweetums?" His breath reeks of alcohol and last night's dinner. I nearly gag as it wafts into my face.

"Go away."

"Aw, but ye look in need of me accompanying services," he replies, leaning closer. Under the table, I uncross my legs, ready to run.

"No. Go away."

He drops his gallant facade, the crooked smile turning into a sneer. He looks me over slowly, his eyes focusing on my curves for an indecent amount of time. He meets my eyes, and I know I won't agree with what he's decided. I've seen that look before.

"Look here, don't go being a bitch about it. I saw ye looking at me. In my book that's a bitch who needs servicing."

Toothless reaches out to grab my arm, using his body to corner me and shield what's happening from onlookers. A swift movement blurs in my peripherals and the dumb brute is on the ground with a woman's foot pushing against his throat. He tries to snatch her foot, but she pushes down and he freezes. It takes a moment before the rest of the bar realizes what happened. The other arm wrestlers burst out in catcalls, laughing at their friend pinned to the ground by the petite woman in front of me.

She leans down so that her face is centimeters from Toothless's face. "You're lucky that you won't be receiving *my* services today. Piss off."

I watch as the newcomer slowly eases the pressure off of Toothless's neck, watching for retaliation. Toothless coughs and stumbles into a standing position. He shoots one final glare at the pair of us, as if that would have an impact.

With the excitement over, the noise in the room returns to its normal level of boisterousness. The incident is already forgotten.

"Attracting trouble?" my savior asks.

"Failing to avoid it."

The petite woman slides into the vacant seat next to me without invitation and points to my full beer. "You going to drink that?"

I shrug in response. The woman downs the beer in three gulps then slams the glass on the table. I resist the urge to check the floor for the contents of the now-empty glass.

"I'm Sala," she says, extending her hand.

"Laila." I offer, returning her firm grip.

"You're the one Cadmar is wetting himself over."

It isn't a question.

"I don't know what—" Sala cuts my denial off with a wave.

"Save it. I've been the one tailing you since you left Cadmar's house yesterday. Good job, by the way. Most new recruits don't even sense a tail. Or shake one off for that matter. Where did you go last night by the way?" I sit stunned as Sala calls over the barmaid. "Another beer for me, and water for my new friend here."

Sala is older than me, but thirty at the most. She exudes confidence as she interacts with the barmaid. Her black hair is braided around her head giving her elegance and practicality. She wears her green kurti more loosely than fashionable. The barmaid returns with our drinks. As Sala reaches for her glass, the fabric of her kurti hugs a long shape against her ribs.

"If you keep staring at my side, everyone in the place will know that I'm hiding more than a sexy physique under this kurti," Sala says.

"Is that a knife?"

"Well, it's definitely not a third boob."

My mouth drops open, and Sala bursts out laughing. I close my mouth, a blush threatening my cheeks. I'm out of my element. Sala sips her beer, her eyes alight with mischief as she surveys me over her glass.

"You have to get used to me. It's why Cadmar won't let me get too close to the Ari—I would send shockwaves through their dignified dispositions."

I smile. "Sorry. I'm not really used to having conversations outside of business."

"All work and no play? You sound like an Ari yourself."

My laugh catches me off guard, and I choke on my water. Sala slaps my back, and I manage to catch my breath, my eyes watering.

"Care for some assistance?" a male voice asks.

"Damn it," I sputter. "No servicing, no assistance!"

I turn angrily to the male voice, thinking it's Toothless, and instead I'm confronted with curls. Curls top the newcomer's head, and a wild beard conceals most of his face. He's also styled the ends of his mustache into two identical twists. He grins, causing the ends of his ridiculous mustache to turn in on themselves.

"Message received loud and clear, my fine lady." He leans in so that his face is inches from mine and lowers his voice. "However, when you change your mind about that servicing, I'll be happy to do the honors."

He winks. My cheeks redden again at his offer. I grab my water and throw it into the newcomer's face, causing his curly mustache to droop.

"*You* clearly need *my* assistance to cool the dunes off."

I face Sala. Her hand covers her mouth, holding in her laughter.

"What?"

"Um, Laila, meet Zahir."

Zahir grabs my hand and bows low over it. Water drips onto my extended hand. "Dearest Laila, it is a pleasure to meet you and to allow you to assist me. I look forward to your assistance in the future."

He kisses my hand.

Choose who you are or it will be chosen for you.

-Aveenan Proverb-

11

"Ah, hm."

Zahir looks up from my hand, and his mischievous grin transforms into a solemn line. As he steps aside, I see Cadmar standing behind him. Cadmar's expression is unreadable, making me wonder how long he's been observing us.

"If you are done playing around," Cadmar says, "follow me upstairs."

His dark eyes stare pointedly at Zahir who straightens and strides to the staircase behind the bar—the perfect example of obedience—and disappears from sight. Cadmar gestures to Sala and me to follow as Cadmar brings up the rear. The stairs are narrow and steep, forcing us into a single file line. Not ideal for an easy escape. I count each step, locking the number into my memory. I'll need every detail just in case. The nerves that I felt before Sala and Zahir distracted me flood back in, causing my stomach to become a jumble of knots.

Reveal nothing. Stay silent. Observe and wait.

I've frequented the Hathorda for two years, but I've never ventured out of the main tavern. I expect to see a hallway and some rooms. Instead, the four of us struggle to squeeze onto the landing at the top of the stairs. A formidable door confronts our procession: the wood is thick, reaching from floor to ceiling. The most intimidating part of the door, however, is its lack of a handle. I want to ask how we open the door, but Sala, Zahir, and Cadmar are unphased by its strange appearance, so I hold my tongue. Zahir bangs his fist on the door three times and then slaps his hand flat against the wood. The door swings open, revealing a dark-skinned woman in a deep maroon kurta and lehenga. Her dark eyes flit over us, and I squirm under her gaze—it feels as if she can see everything about me.

"Thank you, Nimra," Cadmar says, clearly a dismissal.

She bows to Cadmar, fist over heart, and ducks out of the room. Sala nudges me, drawing my attention away from the retreating woman, and she grins. "Nothing like a grand entrance, don't you think?"

The room distracts me from responding. This is *not* what I expected. The room is the same size as the bar downstairs but without the crowd. The floor is open and spotless, with smooth wood paneling—I can't tell if it's smooth from a sanding stone or constant use. There are no windows.

No windows means no escape. Except through the one-way door.

Brackets protrude from the room's four corners, each holding a large oil lamp. I move to the left side of the room where three enormous bookshelves are built into the wall, spanning floor to ceiling like the door. And I thought Cadmar's house was stuffed full of books. I run my hand along the numerous leather-bound books, taking in their worn spines and raised print titles: *Poisons & Their Antidotes, The Thief's Guide, A Brief Political History of Aveena, Human Error: A Study of Human Thinking.* A map of Aveena spans the wall opposite the door. The only furniture, a table and a group of chairs, is shoved underneath the massive rendition of our city. Two wooden crates are pushed against the last wall. I scoff at the locks on the crates—locks in a room styled for thieves. Like *they* could stop me. The locks pique my curiosity, but I squash the feeling. *Observe and wait.*

"I don't think I've ever seen this much open space in Aveena," I whisper to Sala who had followed me around the room.

"Doesn't surprise me. Another problem with the Ari—always feeling the need to fill space with crap."

I laugh. "And then in the Lower City people barely have any space to themselves. Too crammed together to breathe."

Sala gives me a long look. I clench and unclench my hands behind my back, uncomfortable with her scrutiny.

"What?"

"It's interesting that you speak as if you aren't part of the Lower City."

I force myself to breathe normally and maintain eye contact with Sala. "You know how it is being on the darker side of the City Guard. We aren't really Upper or Lower City."

Sala puts her arm around my shoulders and steers us over to the small table. I wonder if she can feel the knots of anxiety forming under her touch. "Whatever you say, Laila."

I slide into the seat between Sala and the wall, trying to isolate myself from this group of strangers, and sling my tattered bag underneath me. I fold my hands in my lap and turn my attention to Cadmar. He doesn't deign to sit with us, choosing instead to hover over our heads—a power play that isn't lost on me.

"Alright," Cadmar says, "you know why you're here."

Actually, we don't, I think, but Zahir is nodding along, and Sala is cleaning her nails with a knife. I squirm in my seat, but keep my mouth shut.

"You have skill sets that are valuable to me." Cadmar emphasizes each word and looks us in the eye as he talks. "I have deemed you trustworthy to join Logonkelie, but first, introductions. Ms. Khatri, start us off."

Logonkelie? I wonder, but Sala is already speaking so I tuck the question away for when I'm alone. If I ever get one…

"Okay. I'm Sala," she says, her attention on her knife.

Cadmar sighs. "Sala specializes in tracking targets, avoiding detection—"

"Pretty much the sneaky shit," Sala interjects, shrugging her shoulders. She twirls the knife between her fingers then slams the point into the table. My eyes widen as I stare at the trembling knife. "Oh, and I'm training you with Cadmarji."

My head snaps up, and I assess Sala more closely than before. Her small build would be useful when blending with surroundings, and she already admitted to tailing me. I needed to be more careful around Sala than I thought. Observant and loyal to Cadmar won't help me escape.

Cadmar glares at Sala, while Zahir's laughter fills the room.

"I'll butt in before Sala pisses off Cadmar more," Zahir says, laughter in his eyes. "I'm Zahir. My ma told me that I'm twenty-six, but she could never remember what day it was so I'm not sure how accurate that is. Probably thirty for all I know. I enjoy long walks by the canal, it's been twenty minutes since my last drink downstairs, and I have been complimented on my kissing technique from time to time."

Zahir smooths his curly beard and winks at me again.

"If you keep doing that, your eyes will get stuck that way," I say.

"It would be worth it for you, sweet—" Cadmar coughs, and Zahir changes the subject mid-sentence. "—and I can kill you with my bare hands."

Zahir reaches his hands into Sala's face as if to demonstrate their brutality, but she doesn't even flinch, cooly watching him from her seat. Cadmar flicks Zahir on the head.

"Ow! What was that for? You said intro—"

"I said introduce, not annoy everyone before we even begin."

Sala snorts. "Nice try, Zahir."

"Well, I—" Zahir begins, massaging the spot Cadmar had flicked.

"No, I think you're done for now." Cadmar cuts him off. I think Zahir purses his lips together, but the wild curls of his beard obscure my vision. "Zahir was annoying the Suraksha with his ramblings when I found him. Accused of stealing."

"They didn't have any proof," Zahir mutters darkly.

"You were caught in the healer's house but successfully pretended to be genuinely confused," Cadmar continues. I glance at Zahir who is glaring at the table, no hint of the lighthearted young man evident his stare. A lump lodges in my throat—I wish Cadmar would stop telling Zahir's story. He's clearly uncomfortable. "He continued to ramble in the stocks for so long that the Suraksha ended up knocking him over the head with his baton to get some peace."

"Wish I could get some peace," Sala mutters. I snort but quickly turn it into a cough when Cadmar looks at me. Zahir shakes his head and looks up from the table. His lopsided grin is forced as he leans back in his chair.

Cadmar continues, ignoring Sala's interruption. "Zahir is useful when it comes to providing a distraction or getting information out of a person."

"They must answer him to get him to shut up," I say.

"Actually, the Ari can't get enough of me," Zahir responds. He leans across Sala to get closer to me, lowering his voice in an attempt to be seductive. "I can be very appealing when given a proper chance. If you'll let me—"

Sala smacks Zahir's throat, causing him to splutter and cough. I freeze.

"Obviously, Laila doesn't need your *appeal*, Zahir, so give it a rest."

Although she keeps her tone light, there is a menace in Sala's voice that wasn't there earlier. I'm grateful if not a little in awe of Sala.

"If you two are done bickering?" Cadmar says, irritation edging into his tone.

Sala crosses her arms over her chest but remains silent. Zahir is too busy rubbing his Adam's apple to respond. Cadmar waits another second, making sure everyone is behaving.

"So that leaves you," Sala says, turning her curious eyes to me. "How did you get Cadmarji's attention, Miss Laila?"

"Well, I, um—"

I fumble over my words, unsure what to say. I make the mistake of glancing at Cadmar. He crosses his arms and says, with an edge to his voice, "Laila stole Lady Asfour's necklace, broke into my house, and tried to plant it in my study. If she had been successful, the Aristocracy would think I was having an affair with my good friend Lady Asfour."

The response is instantaneous.

"You did what?!" Zahir shouts.

"Holy dunes," Sala mutters.

I lower my eyes and sink into my chair. Damn him.

"Yes," Cadmar says. The corners of his mouth twitch up a bit—clearly, he's amused. "Go on, *Laila*, tell them who you are."

I look at Cadmar through my lowered lashes. His gaze is tense, knowing that if I reveal my alias to two more people I will not be able to go back to the way things were. He's covering all his bases. Another sliver of control stolen by Cadmar.

I sit up, square my shoulders back, and take a deep breath. I might not have control, but I will not show fear.

"I am—was—the Nightshade."

**Those of the Lower City are forbidden
from wielding weapons of their own.
Their sacred role is to care for the fields
that feed us all; it is the sacred role of the
Upper City to serve as protectors for their
brethren. To wield a weapon wounds the
harmony between the Upper and Lower
City.**
-from The Ordinances of Aveena-

12

My statement hangs in the air like the haze of the sultan's fireworks after Rangtiu. A blush dusts my cheeks as I glare at everyone in the room.

"But I thought the Nightshade was a man?" Zahir asks, running his hand through his curls absentmindedly.

"You thought wrong, didn't you?" Sala says with a grin. She claps me on the shoulder as she adds, "Thanks for joining us."

Out of the corner of my eye, Cadmar shifts. His face is frozen in his usual mask, but I see the glimmer of discomfort in his eyes. So he *doesn't* want to reveal the full details. Interesting.

"Cadmar did make the prospect... irresistible." I can't help needling him. Zahir babbles but no one acknowledges the constant stream of "couldn't be" and "the Patel job".

"And what exactly is Logonkelie?" Zahir asks, tearing his gaze from me to glare at Cadmar again. "You've had your fun revealing our secrets, Cadmar. I've trained with you for weeks. I deserve some clarity."

Sala's chair grinds against the floor as she pushes away from the table. "Not so fast, Zahir. It's my turn."

She struts over to the large crates and kicks one. "This is your first test."

"Test?" I ask.

"Isn't that what the past three weeks were for?" Zahir asks. Gone is the light-hearted joker as annoyance washes off Zahir in waves. I can't help but wonder what Cadmar has been having Zahir do in order to test him.

"You might have made it out there, but fail my tests and you leave," Sala says, challenge shining in her eyes. "Cadmar selected you, but I'm in charge of your training."

"Later," Cadmar says, meeting Zahir's frustration with a calm only years of being Ari could hone. Zahir's agitation is palpable, but a tense moment later, he nods, turning his attention to Sala.

The swirl of anxiety in my stomach knots further. I have no doubt that I can pass Sala's tests, but with each twist of the conversation my attempts at making a plan shatter. Pass the test and reveal my skill? Or fail and hope I can make it down the stairs before Sala does?

Reality sinks in as Sala curls a finger at me in summons. There's nowhere I can go and still earn enough money to help heal Tanu. I need to play their game long enough to formulate a better plan to escape.

"You first, Little Miss Nightshade. Time to prove yourself."

Cadmar sits in Sala's vacated chair. I hesitate a second longer then shrug nonchalantly and join Sala by the chests. Zahir rests his arms on his knees and leans forward; Cadmar's eyes follow each movement. Their heightened interest raises goosebumps on my arms.

"Okay. Let me guess—get into the crates?" I say with bravado as I glance down at the lock on the box, unimpressed. Most Ari purchase their locks from the same locksmith, Nali Burjandi, who advertises protection and physical appeal in one. They're a joke.

"Of course," Sala says.

"Done."

Before Sala protests, I reach up and grab two pins out of her braid. Sala slaps my hands away but doesn't take the pins back. I bend one pin at a ninety-degree angle and straighten the second, leaving the end turned up in a small hook. Ignoring the watching eyes, I kneel before the crate and insert the bent pin to hold part of the lock in place. Then I push the other pick inside the lock to tumble it. Vibrations tingle my fingers, and a satisfying click echoes in the open space.

Dropping the pins to the floor, I move to push open the crate lid, but Sala sits on top, crossing her legs. "Now, relock it."

"Why?"

Sala raises an eyebrow but doesn't move from the crate. "Cause the Ari will know you've been there if their shit is unlocked."

"So?" I ask, sounding like a petulant child.

Sala's laughter fills the room. "How were you not caught before now?"

"I got in and out before anyone knew I was there," I say, pissed. "I was fast and efficient."

"Fast and efficient are useful. Invisible is better. Relock the lock."

I growl in frustration and pick up my discarded pins, staring at the open lock. I've never locked anything back. I did what I needed to and then got out. The Ari always knew I was there anyway— the effects of my jobs were my calling card. Stealth but not invisibility.

I roll my shoulders back and sigh. Here goes nothing. I'd already removed my two makeshift picks from the keyhole, killing the tension that I used to pop it. I reinsert the bent pick. Wrong angle. I remove the pick and try again. And again. On my fourth go, I finally get the first pick into place and begin work on the second pick. I struggle to keep the tension on the locking mechanism with the awkward angle. My hand slips and loses the grasp I have on the pin.

Sala slaps the top of the crate, startling me. "Time's up."

"There was a time limit?" I ask through gritted teeth.

Sala jumps up laughing and offers me a hand. I ignore her and stand. As I brush off my faded kurti, I slyly adjust my position closer to the one-way door. Twenty steps, and I'm out.

"There's always a time limit," she says.

"So, I failed your test," I state bluntly, watching Sala's body language for clues. I slide one foot behind me, preparing to run.

"Nope."

I stop. "I didn't fail?"

"No. Now go sit and stop inching towards the door."

I offer Sala's bent hairpins back to her, but she pushes them away. "Keep them as a reminder. Next."

Zahir is abysmal at picking locks. He cannot keep the pins in place and jerks his hand whenever the mechanism vibrates, losing the tension. Sala calls time on him before he's able to unlock the crate. I'm not sure what qualifies as a pass after Zahir's miserable attempt.

Sala reaches behind the crate, grabs a key, and unlocks both crates. "Not bad attempts on picking locks, my loves," She dangles the key in front of our faces, smirking. My jaw drops slightly. "But if you'd bothered to check the area, you would've found the key, and we would've ended playtime early."

Cadmar cuts in. "Two lessons: leave everything as it was before and check your resources. No need to make the work more difficult than it already is."

"*And* there's always a time limit," Sala adds.

I resist the urge to roll my shoulders to alleviate some stress. This is going to be more work than I thought.

Sala gestures to the inside of the crates. "Pick your poison, loves."

Inside the crate is a wide array of knives from small kitchen knives to wide blades resembling short swords. I hesitate, nervous. The small dagger I own is only useful for cutting fabric. No way to pass Sala's evaluation this time.

Zahir bumps my shoulder as he walks up to the crate and picks up two curved short swords, weighing them in his hands. "These'll do. Similar to a sickle."

Zahir takes a few practice swings with the wicked curved blades, assessing. I watch as the wide arcs of Zahir's swords become another barrier between me and escape.

"You're next, Nightshade," Sala says. She waves her hand in front of the crate like she has a pile of gold on display instead of a pile of weapons.

I put my hands behind my back to hide the slight tremble.

"I—uh—" I grab the smallest knife I can find out of the crate. It feels unnatural in my hand. "Um, this one. I think."

Zahir stops mid-swing and perks up at my obvious hesitation. His mustache curls in as he attempts at a smoldering smile. "I promised my services whenever you might need them. It's okay to ask for help, Laila. Even strong women like yourself—"

Sala doesn't give Zahir time to react. She slides between his curved blades, close to his body, making it impossible for him to get the right angle to wield them. Zahir brings the swords towards Sala, but she whips around, her back to his chest, and snatches Zahir's incoming wrists. Sala applies pressure to the soft spots, forcing Zahir to drop the swords. The curved blades fall to the floor with a metallic clatter, drowning out Zahir's cursing. Sala kicks both blades toward the crate and out of reach. Zahir tries to extricate himself from Sala's grip by using his weight to throw her off balance. He fails. Sala uses Zahir's momentum and her small stature to trip Zahir over her back and onto the floor, all while maintaining a grip on his wrists. Sala kicks Zahir low on his stomach, causing him to curl around himself in protection.

"Next time I'll kick you in the balls."

Sala is unlike anyone I've ever met.

Zahir lays on the ground, gasping to catch his breath, the wind knocked out of him. My eyes follow Zahir's labored breathing, the knife unforgotten in my hand.

Sala moves towards me, and I raise both arms quickly, backing away. Shit, I forgot who I should be focusing on.

Sala leaps at me. I lift the knife, attempting to fend her off, but she's too fast. Before I move, Sala grips my forearm in both her hands, stopping my momentum. I try to attack, but Sala slams her right hand into my shoulder while keeping her left hand clamped to my wrist. Pain shoots through my shoulder, and I cry out, at her mercy.

Sala knees me in the stomach and twists my arm behind my back. My shoulder burns from the awkward angle, causing my eyes to water. I forgot about the knife in my pain, and Sala snatches it easily from my slack grip. She steps back, pushing the loose hair of her braid back. She isn't even breathing hard.

"Not bad." Sala smiles and gives Cadmar a nod. He chuckles from his perch.

I hunch over, hands on my knees, slowing down my breathing to ease the pain from Sala's blow to my stomach. "That was… good?"

Sala walks up to me and pulls me to a standing position, placing my hands on my head. "Standing is going to be better. And I didn't say good. I said, 'not bad.'"

Zahir rolls over on his side and props his head on his hand like he wanted to be on the floor the whole time. "Sala, you kicked my ass. Not sure how that qualifies as 'not bad.'"

"You each had a fatal weakness."

Zahir groans then asks, "Okay, what was mine?"

Sala reaches down and offers a hand to Zahir. He stands up with her help, grimacing.

"You were distracted. Your obsession with women will get you killed if you don't keep it in your pants."

I laugh but it turns into a groan from the sharp pain. Sala turns to me, brown eyes assessing. "You have no fighting experience, do you?"

I shake my head.

"It's better to fight weaponless than with something you don't know how to use." She gestures to my knife on the floor. "It's easy for a skilled fighter to disarm you and take it. Then you're really in the dunes."

I nod but doubt creeps into my mind.

Sala claps her hand on my shoulder and adds, "Don't worry. That's what I'm here for, Little Miss Nightshade. I'll be here every step of the way."

I force a smile in response until Sala walks away.

That's what I was worried about.

Trust in the Ordinances and let them be your guide. Consistency in leadership is key to managing Aveena—and managing the council.

—Advice from Sultan Gautam to his son Ajani—

13

The evening flies by in a continuation of Sala's tests: strength, flexibility, literacy, and even how long we could hold our breath. I hope to never have to test that skill. With the lack of windows in the room, there is no way to know how long we've been at it when the coded knock on the door finally interrupts the exhausting work.

A tiny, older woman brings in a tray, bowing to Cadmar before exiting again.

Sala is still cheery as ever as she tells us to eat up. The dahl makhani is simple but warm, a combination I haven't had in ages. As I go to take my second bite, Cadmar asks, "Alright. What do you know about the Aristocracy?"

Zahir groans and slams his head against the table. It takes all my self-control not to join him.

"You mean other than the fact that they are selfish, self-righteous bastards?" Zahir asks, voice thick with sarcasm. I stare at Zahir. When he looks at me, I jut my chin towards Cadmar, silently asking Zahir if he remembers who we're talking to. He grins.

"Yes, other than that," Cadmar says calmly, unfazed by Zahir's accusation.

"The Ari are selfish bastards—"

"Already said that, Zahir," Sala interjects, waving her spoon at him.

"Just thought we needed to make it crystal clear." Zahir shoots me another conspiratorial grin and winks. I snort but turn it into a cough when Cadmar looks at me.

"Wrong pipe," I mutter.

Cadmar purses his lips. "Indeed."

Zahir ticks off each answer on a finger as he says, "So, selfish bastards. Don't care about anyone except the other Ari. And avoid the Lower City like Sala avoids baths."

Sala smiles sweetly at Zahir. "Forgot who kicked your ass today? We can fix that tomorrow."

Zahir widens his eyes at Sala and puts his hand over his heart, the picture of innocence. "Sala, I would never—"

"Save it, Zahir, you're screwed," I say.

"Speaking of screwed, I—"

"Enough." Cadmar's finality ends the conversation. "Back to the question. What do you know about the Aristocracy *other* than the fact that *we* are selfish bastards?"

Zahir and I tuck into our food—Cadmar's point is clear: remember who we are talking to. When neither of us answer, Cadmar stares pointedly at me. I choke my food down and say, "I didn't interact with them."

Cadmar scoffs, unimpressed. "Try again, Nightshade."

I take another bite of my dahl to give myself a moment to think. Cadmar pours himself a glass of bourbon and takes a sip all the while watching me.

"I–well, the Ari love the Ordinances."

"Love them?"

"They use them. All the time."

"Use them?" Cadmar asks.

"Like a rule book."

"She's right," Zahir says, running his fingers over his curls. "Fall in line with the Ordinances or get thrown in Niraash."

"And the Ordinances put men on top," I add almost absentmindedly.

"Well, that is a position that we prefer to be in," Zahir says. This time I smack Zahir before Sala can get to him. Sala gives me an approving nod as Zahir rubs his chest.

"Give me some examples of these rules," Cadmar says, ignoring Zahir.

"Women are only allowed in certain parts of Aveena," I say. "When I was the Nightshade, I had to get into those districts without drawing attention by pretending to be a man so I could blend in."

"Yes." Cadmar takes a sip of his drink. "And what is the exact wording for this in the Ordinances."

"Exact wording?" I furrow my eyebrows in confusion.

"Yes, what is the terminology that is used for the law that you've described?"

I hesitate and think. Have I seen a written copy of the Ordinances? My memory comes to a blank; I don't think I know anyone who has seen the Ordinances. It's not surprising since most of the Lower City is illiterate, but when I lived in the Upper City I should have seen them at some point. But I can't even picture what the document looks like...

"I don't know," I say.

"Hm, interesting," Cadmar replies, sipping his drink and giving no hint of his thoughts. "Zahir?"

"Cadmar, you know I've never seen the Ordinances. Get to your point."

Cadmar chuckles. "That is my point, Mr. Juma. The protocol in Aveena consists of customs passed down from previous generations. They are not written in the Ordinances, which are fairly simple when you read them."

"So you're telling me," I say, disbelief etched into my face, "that there is nothing that says that women can't go into the merchant districts without a male escort?"

"There is nothing *written* that says this."

I press my lips together, unsure whether to believe him. Zahir frowns in confusion. "Okay, what about the rule that to get an apprenticeship you need a family member to speak for you?"

"When you are younger, yes, you would fall under the head of the household's responsibility."

"And now?" Zahir asks. It seems like a casual question, but Zahir's eyes darkened, masking his thoughts.

"Nothing written in the Ordinances."

Zahir scoffs and mutters, "That's horseshit."

Cadmar bobs his head side to side but says nothing. He anticipated our reactions; he might even be enjoying himself. I narrow my eyes. "What about the rule that no one can pass through the wall once night has fallen?"

"Nothing."

"That non-Ari have to show respect to the Ari?" I say.

"Nothing." Cadmar watches me closely, but I don't let it go.

"If you are passing an Ari that you must stop and bow your head until they pass?"

"Nothing."

Zahir jumps in. "Marriage cannot happen between Lower City folk and Upper City folk?"

"Nothing."

Zahir and I alternate throwing rules out there, and Cadmar denies each one. Our collective frustration is palpable. My voice gets softer as my anger grows, but Zahir is shouting.

"Parents arrange marriages?"

"Nothing."

"Women cannot show both of their shoulders?"

"Nothing."

"Damn it!" Zahir shouts, standing and prowling away from the table.

Sala tilts her head to the side, watching him pace. "Calm yourself, Zahir."

Zahir looks incredulous. "Calm myself? You just told me that women could be showing more skin all these years!"

"Out of everything that he just said *that's* what you're focusing on?" Sala asks incredulously.

Zahir tries to look seductive as he meets my eyes. "Shoulders are the gateway to other womanly pleasures."

"They're just shoulders, you pig," I say, rolling my eyes.

Cadmar interrupts before Zahir can reply. "The point is—"

"The Ari have been lying to us for years," I whisper.

Silence. Cadmar takes another sip of his drink, letting my words hang between us, before breaking the silence.

"Most of the Ari do not know that the protocols within Aveena are customs, not actual dictates in the Ordinances. Although that does not excuse the abuse they cause others, many are simply ignorant."

"So how did we get stuck with this shit?" Zahir asks.

"A history of abusing power. My ancestors needed a way to control the population, so they manipulated the Ordinances. Now Aveenans don't know the difference either way."

"Is this why you've brought us here?" I ask.

Cadmar's dark eyes meet mine as he nods once.

"It's time for me to give you all the explanation you demanded earlier today."

The Council of the Sultan shall comprise
of men of higher caliber and status. Their
knowledge and discretion will lead Aveena
through the natural internal conflict that
arises in a city such as this and against the
darkness of the Tribes from which we have
separated. They are the only ones capable
of filling such a demand.
—excerpt from *A Brief Political History of
Aveena*—

14

Cadmar walks to the map of Aveena and jabs his finger into the central structure designated on the map: the palace.

"This is why we are here."

Zahir and I stare at the drawing of the palace and wait.

"The Council of the Sultan is in disarray. There is a divide among the men of the Council between those who focus on our traditions and those who focus on our future. The ripples from this divide reach into the Lower City."

I scoff. "The Ari don't give a shit about the Lower City."

"*Some* don't. They believe the best way to deal with the Lower City is to ignore its needs and its existence. To keep the Ordinances strong." Cadmar pauses, staring at the map for a beat before turning back to meet our eyes. "But there are others in the Council of the Sultan who do not agree with the Ordinances. They think that they are outdated."

"Ari like yourself?" Zahir asks.

"Yes," he says simply. As if that was enough.

"So why don't you do something about it?" The accusation is clear in my voice, my frustration mounting.

"How can I speak to those who won't listen?"

I scowl. After all that I've been through because of the Ordinances, I refuse to feel sympathetic for an Ari with actual power. If he was more persuasive, I would have been *safe*. I wouldn't have run away. I wouldn't have worked for Velo. I wouldn't have…

I push the thoughts of Tanu away and focus on what Cadmar is saying.

"The Aristocracy are wrapped up in their own ways of thinking. They will not entertain new ideas, especially from their opposition. I myself am guilty of this. I oppose the royal vizier often, simply because of who he is."

"Ari problems," Zahir states. Both Zahir and I have our arms crossed over our chests, unified as we watch Cadmar.

"Don't you get it, Zahir?" Sala says. "The Ari's problems *are* our problems."

"Exactly. All of the protocols that you listed do one thing—keep the Lower City too downtrodden to protest their treatment. The Aristocracy will not change what benefits them."

"We know this," I snap, the stress of the day making my voice sharper than I intended. "What's your point?"

"Five years ago," Cadmar continues, ignoring my rudeness, "there was an opening for one of the Consulate seats. The Consulate consists of three men who oversee the Council of the Sultan with the royal vizier and the sultan. Several men nominated me—men who supported a newer way of thinking. Tei Asfour was one of them." Cadmar gestures to me, his face grim.

"My election would have ensured that a wider representation of perspectives was working directly with the sultan. Twice the council went to a vote and twice I was denied the position. The royal vizier was the biggest opponent to my appointment. Eventually, Reyanash Al-Sid was elected to the post. I went home disgraced."

I resist rolling my eyes, watching Cadmar stare at the map of the palace, lost in his memories. This was an Ari sob story of being denied what he wanted, not a valid explanation of why I am being blackmailed into subservience.

"I spent a week researching the history of politics in Aveena. I reread the volumes of our six-hundred-year history since our establishment by the first sultan. In every book I read, I saw the same pattern occurring in the Council of the Sultan—two sides but only a few men with real power to make changes in Aveena. Each account of big rivalries within the council ended the same. One Ari would end on top, the other would be disgraced, and no one paid attention to the people of Aveena who were under our care.

In that week I came to a conclusion: nothing will change if we keep repeating the same pattern. I returned to the Council of the Sultan and began my work anew. I continued to make noise and rattle against the royal vizier and those who supported the Ordinances. I looked as if I was continuing business as usual. But I changed my tactics. Under the guise of normal conversation with the other members of the Council, I determined who was an ally and who was loyal to Vizier Nassor. I created Logonkelie."

Putting his hands on the table, Cadmar leans forward and meets each set of eyes.

"*This* is why you are here. Logonkelie works in secrecy to enact small changes within the council in order to have a greater impact in all of Aveena. One lentil can tip the scale. My fellow Ari lack subtlety, but I can use it to help Aveena. Logonkelie works to make those changes. And now you three will work to make those changes."

Zahir lets out the breath that he's held during Cadmar's speech. "And how do we know that you'll have *our* best interests in mind as you make your changes?"

Zahir's distrust takes me by surprise—I thought that he wanted to be here. I wonder what led him to Cadmar if not belief in the Ari.

Before Cadmar can respond, Sala speaks. "Have you been living in a dune, Zahir? Don't you know what Cadmar does?"

"You're asking if I believe the rumors in the bazaar?"

Sala's eyes are wide, disbelieving, as she stares at Zahir. "Cadmarji doesn't act like the other Ari. He is the only one fighting for someone other than himself. For an Ari that's saying a lot."

"Thank you, Sala. I think there was a compliment hidden somewhere in there." Cadmar gives her a rare smile before turning to Zahir. "Why were you in that healer's house?"

"What?" Cadmar's abrupt change throws Zahir off balance.

"Why were you rummaging around in the healer's house instead of hiring her outright?"

"I couldn't hire her."

Zahir remains defiant, distrust etched on his face. I don't blame him, I'm just as unsure about Cadmar. Years of dealing with Ari doesn't wash away that fast.

"And why couldn't you hire her?" he responds calmly.

"I needed her—for my ma. But—" Zahir swallows, the vulnerability in his face a stark contrast to the flirt from earlier. "--but she wouldn't come. I couldn't pay her fee."

"Why?"

Zahir deflates, the fight leaving him. "I slaved away in those fields, day after day, but it wasn't enough. She only had a fever. It should have been quick work."

My stomach drops.

Momentarily, I want to reach out and comfort Zahir. I understood his pain—the pain of being incapable of helping a loved one. It's the same pain I live with each time I think of Tanu and her limping walk.

I tuck my hand underneath my leg though, protecting myself even through my empathy for his struggle.

"She hadn't been able to get work for a while cause of—well, she couldn't get work. I couldn't get an apprenticeship, which left working in the fields." Zahir pauses then looks up at Cadmar. "I did what I had to do."

"You were stuck. You didn't have the chance to take care of your mother."

Cadmar pauses to let his words sink in. Zahir slumps in his chair, the fight deflating from him. I stare at his clenched fists as they open slowly, and I release the breath I'd been holding. Pity and sympathy rush through me, the fear still raw after these past years.

But I don't want to sympathize, to care about their old wounds.

I don't want to stay.

"You've proven your trustworthiness and expertise in skills that Logonkelie can use. But that's not the only reason why you're here." Cadmar gestures to the map of Aveena again. To the walls dividing the Upper and Lower City. "Both of you have been affected by the Aristocracy's indifference. You have motive. Chance led you here. Now let fate move us forward."

I don't look at Cadmar as he speaks. He doesn't know about my life or else I wouldn't be here. He might assume that the Ordinances were the reason I became the Nightshade, but he couldn't understand the depth of that decision.

He might be passionate, but I can't trust him. I'm only here to buy time, to stay free of Niraash.

"Aveena is running out of resources," Cadmar says in a matter-of-fact tone, his jaw clenched tight as he speaks. "Our population has grown exponentially during Sultan Gautam's reign. We can no longer remain in isolation."

"What does that mean?" I ask, speaking for the first time during Cadmar's impassioned speech.

"It means we need trade. We need the Tribes."

My eyes widen, my shock mirrored on Zahir's face. Cadmar dutifully ignores us. "If we open up continuous trade with the Tribes, not this once-a-year nonsense, then Aveena has a chance."

"But people don't trust the Tribes," Zahir says.

Cadmar grimaces. "No, but they need food. Soon they will trust their hunger over their years of prejudice against the Tribes and trade with them. Even if it is begrudgingly at first."

"It's never been done," I add.

"It's never been necessary." Cadmar pauses, letting his words sink in, before he clears his throat. "We move into the palace in three days, which means…"

"The palace!" Zahir shouts, knocking his chair over as he jumps up. My stomach lurches, and wind roars in my ears. "You said nothing about the palace."

"Where else could we—"

But I can't register anything else Cadmar is saying. A cold sweat breaks out between my shoulder blades, and I have to remind myself to breathe. The palace is impenetrable. It's suicide. Cadmar can't be serious.

A hand taps my shoulder, and I jolt, whipping my head around. Sala tilts her head at me, watching me with those intelligent brown eyes. "You've gone pale," she says.

"I–I–," My voice cracks, and I clear my throat and get out, "I'm fine."

Sala raises a brow but doesn't comment. I force myself to breathe slowly, to calm the roaring in my ears. After a moment, Cadmar and Zahir's voices register again.

"...a week's reprieve after the sultan's funeral. Then the Aristocracy are to resume business as usual," Cadmar says calmly. Zahir opens his mouth to interrupt, but Cadmar holds up a hand to stop him. "To enter at another time will be too noticeable. Entering when the rest of the council is bringing their families to make an impression on the prince, well, we need every advantage we can get."

"I still don't understand why—" Zahir begins but Sala cuts him off this time.

"Enough!" Zahir glares at her, but she just raises a brow, waiting to see if he'll defy her order. After a tense pause, Sala adds, "There will be many new faces in the palace. We haven't had an opportunity like this in years."

"So, we're taking advantage of the sultan's death?" Zahir accuses the anger barely beneath the surface.

Sala tilts her head to the side, watching Zahir cooly. "Yes."

"That's despi—"

"That's no more than every other Ari in the council will be doing," Sala says. "We either join in and stand a chance to loosen certain councilmen's strongholds, or we let them take the advantage. Which do you prefer?"

Zahir huffs but doesn't answer. Cadmar casually sips his drink then sets it back on the table.

"I think it is time to retire for the night," Cadmar says. "Sala please show them to their rooms. I'll wait for Nimra to return."

Sala nods, then gestures for us to follow her out of the room.

Once you notice the trap, it's too late to escape.
-excerpt from *The Thief's Guide* Banned by the
Council of the Sultan in the year 151-

15

The roar of the Hathorda's usual clientele filters up the narrow staircase, weaving with the aromatic scent of cumin and sweet hookah smoke from downstairs.

I rub my eyes, frustrated and confused. I guess that's normal when your world is flipped upside-down, but I don't remember being this confused when I ran to the Lower City. Then again, that was about survival. I didn't have to question the way things are. I shake my head to block the memories from resurfacing.

"Here's where you will be staying," Sala says.

She gestures to a door at the end of the hallway. We are on the third floor of the Hathorda. I guess not all of the rumors about the Hathorda were false.

"Cadmarji said that you'd prefer a room with a window."

I'm too tired to respond. I open the door to my room and enter. A pristine bed, an end table, and a dresser furnish the room—my room. A ceramic basin with water sits on the dresser and a chamberpot is hidden in a corner. And, as promised, a decent-sized window cuts into the right wall, the shutters opened to the night sky.

"If you need anything, I'm down the hall," Sala continues. "Food is downstairs, the bathhouse is in the basement, and if you can't sleep, there's always Zahir to entertain you."

I scoff and try to shove Sala, but my arms refuse to respond. Sala laughs as I groan. "You'll get used to it, Nightshade."

"I doubt it," I mutter.

"Your bag is in the dresser. Plus, your Logonkelie supplies."

"Okay. Thanks, Sala."

Sala rests a hand on my shoulder, and I meet her gaze. I didn't notice the lighter browns in her eyes while she was kicking my ass earlier. "You're going to make a difference, you know." I look down. "That's what we do, I promise."

Sala pats my shoulder and then leaves. I close the door and lean my head against the wood. It's comfortingly solid beneath my forehead. I breathe, focusing on the feeling of the wood. Breathe in, breathe out. One. Why did I take that job? Breathe in. How am I going to see Tanu? Breathe out. What if they find out the real reason why I became the Nightshade? Two. This isn't good. I can't stay here.

Breathe—

I push off the door, pure panic rising inside me, raging and swirling like I hadn't felt in moons. My breath is coming in short, rasping pants, and I'm unable to control it.

I stumble, falling back.

Why am I here? How is this going to buy more time? If I enter the palace, I might never make it back out...

I shake my head, trying to clear the panic, but it's impossible. I need to get out of here. Now. Screw Cadmar and his deal.

Screw Velo for cutting me off. I'll figure it out. Anywhere is better than here.

I stagger to the dresser and open the drawer with trembling hands. I grab my bag and shove the drawer closed, causing the washbasin on top to clink. I sprint to the door and pull it open. A quick glance down the hall assures me that it's deserted. I creep towards the stairs, ignoring the cautious voice in the back of my head wondering if I should think through a better plan. How much of this plan was reason and how much was panic?

The tavern was crowded, the press of sweaty bodies filling from wall to wall. I hesitate on the last step, eyeing the intoxicated men nearest the staircase warily, before forcing my shoulders back and walking confidently forward, a hand protecting my bag from pickpockets in the crowd.

"Watch it," a server says as I nearly knock the glasses from her hand.

I sidestep quickly but end up bumping into someone else's back. "Sorry," I say quickly, "I didn't mean—"

My apology dies on my lips as Sala turns around, her eyebrows raised as she appraises me, taking in my bag clutched in my hand. I open and close my mouth, failing to produce an explanation. Sala takes a sip of her beer then sets it down, all while watching me. The panic that had moved me to action dies in my chest, replaced by dread. If Cadmar finds out...

"Damn," Sala finally says. "You were right, Nim."

I'm confused, but then Sala reaches into her pocket and pulls out several silver rupees and passes them to the dark-skinned woman from the Logonkelie room. I hadn't even noticed her standing silently next to Sala. Nim pockets the coins with a shrug, then turns back to the carrom game she was watching.

Sala puts an arm around my shoulders. "Come on then, Nightshade. Back upstairs."

"But I–" I stutter, my tired and overwhelmed brain unable to keep up.

"Yes, yes, you tried to run. Happens to the best of us."

"But Cadmar–"

Sala tuts and leads me to the stairs. "Cadmarji doesn't understand good ol' fashioned fear. You're not the first, you won't be the last."

"But–I–"

"I'm just irritated that Nim was right. *Again.*" Sala sighs as we pass the Logonkelie door and up to the third floor. "She's won too many of my rupees."

"You bet on us?"

"You finally manage to get a word out and that's what you ask?" Sala laughs. Her arm is hot around my shoulders. "What else would we do?"

We arrive at my door, and Sala opens it for me then gently nudges me into the room. I turn and meet her brown eyes, opening my mouth not sure whether to beg, to explain, or to lie. Sala puts a hand on my shoulder.

"Save it," she says. I'm about to interrupt her, but she smiles softly and squeezes my shoulder briefly. "I won't tell Cadmar this time. Just do me a favor and don't try again. I'd hate to have to tell him about your roof entrance to the bakery."

My eyes must've widened because Sala laughs then turns back towards the stairs.

"See you at sunrise, Nightshade," she calls over her shoulder.

I close the door and stumble to the bed, collapsing on it. I curl into a fetal position and stare out of the open window into the pitch-black night, wondering what has become of my life.

I don't know if I sleep for a few minutes or a few hours before Sala's voice jolts me back to reality. Getting dressed is a blur. As I struggle into the loose-fitting dhoti and kurti I find in the dresser, Sala's voice rings out through the third floor of the Hathorda. I glance out the window to see the sun is barely up. I groan and splash water onto my face, struggling to find some semblance of wakefulness, before joining Sala and Zahir in the hallway.

"To the meeting room, my loves!" Sala says in an annoyingly cheerful voice. We drag our feet as Sala ushers us forward. "Pick up the pace, Nightshade."

I groan and stumble ungracefully. Sala laughs as we head down. I hate morning people.

Sala bangs out the coded knock on the door, and it swings inward. The same dark woman from the day before nods to the three of us before leaving. I don't have time to wonder if Nim will tell Cadmar about my failed escape before Sala is spreading us out in the Logonkelie room.

"Is the great Cadmar too good to wake up early with the rest of us?" Zahir mutters as he passes me. I roll my eyes with him, but Sala's instructions cut off the chance for discussion.

My limbs creak as I attempt to follow her stretching sequence. Every time I think I'm in the right position, Sala shouts a new order or reminds me to breathe. Whoever said yoga was soothing had never met Sala the Dictator.

"Laila! Straighten out your legs. And breathe through your nose and out your mouth." Sala slaps the tops of my knees, forcing me into the stretch. "Stretch it out or else you'll be useless to me."

"I'm trying, Sala," I say, panting. "This shit hurts."

Sala reaches the floor next to me and goes into a perfect downward dog—heels flat on the ground, legs straight. My shoulders ache as I push back, mimicking her movements.

"Breathe out and release," Sala instructs. She moves to a plank position before lowering her body to the floor. She controls each pose with ease as she lowers herself to the ground and pushes herself into upward dog. Zahir and I aren't as successful: my arms wobble as I move to plank and Zahir seems like he's stuck in downward dog.

"Mind over matter, my loves," Sala says. "Tell your body what you want it to do. It's your greatest tool. Learn to control it."

Grimacing, I open my mouth to respond, but Sala cuts me off. "Enough. We'll finish with our shavasanah and close our practice." Sala lays down on the ground and extends her arms palm up on either side of her. "Close your eyes, clear your mind, and focus on your breathing."

Zahir's face lights up. "Shavasanah. Nap time."

I follow Sala's lead and focus on my breathing. This is something I'm good at. Breathe in. Breathe out. One. Breathe in. Breathe out. Two. Zahir's snores rumble next to me. How did he fall asleep that fast? I open my eyes a sliver to see that Sala hasn't moved since she began her shavasanah. Zahir is sprawled out like a spider's web, his left leg twitches.

"Close your eyes and clear your mind, Nightshade," Sala says without opening her eyes.

How did she—

I sigh and refocus. After a minute, my mind is clear again.

Bang, bang, bang, slap.

The knock on the door startles all of us out of our meditation. Sala walks over and opens the door. A gray-haired woman bows her head to Sala then shuffles into the room and sets the tray on the table. Cadmar follows her through the doorway. The woman bobs her head to Cadmar before shuffling out the door. The smell of warm parathas wafts over to me. I sit up from my shavasanah, my stomach rumbling.

"Not yet," Sala says. "Cross your legs and open your palms. Finish our practice, my loves."

"I would prefer to finish breakfast," Zahir says conspiratorially, eying the parathas hungrily. I grin, and our eyes meet. Zahir winks playfully as my stomach growls.

"Bring your hands to heart center" —Zahir snickers, Sala glares at him, I groan— "and namaste."

"Namaste," we reply.

"Alright have at it, heathens."

Zahir reaches the table before the words are out of Sala's mouth.

On the tray are parathas—warm, round flatbread—covered in honey and topped with fruit. We grab plates and chow down on the warm breakfast. Honey drips down my chin, but I don't care. I might as well fill up on food until I can manage to escape.

Sala and Cadmar talk in low whispers. Cadmar says something, and Sala nods before the two of them move to the table. Before she grabs a plate of parathas, Sala slaps the back of Zahir's neck.

"What the—"

"Disrespectful ass."

"Okay, okay, I'm sorry." Zahir rubs the back of his neck, but the sting doesn't stop him from his parathas for long. Warmth fills my belly and extends out into my limbs. Cadmar places a slice of lemon in his cup before filling it with hot water. It's odd seeing him with something as tame as hot water to drink—I was starting to think that he ran off of straight liquor.

As everyone eats, I covertly watch them over my plate. Cadmar looks relaxed as he sips his hot water. He's ditched the formal sherwani for a kurta. The deep purple of the fabric is nearly black. Although he looks casual, Cadmar's kurta is worth more than the rest of the clothes on our backs put together. The hint of agitation that radiated from Cadmar the night before while he was telling his story has disappeared. This morning, he's back to his cool and collected self.

Zahir jibbers away between bites of parathas, trying to engage Sala in conversation.

"—well and as I see it, you just can't avoid getting honey on yourself, so why even bother trying to avoid it. I once knew this fellow who lived near the northern gate. His wife would make him bathe after every meal because he couldn't stop getting food on himself. But she was an *amazing* cook, so you can't really blame him. Now that I think of it, I can't remember if it was the husband or the toddler who had to bathe after every meal, but it doesn't—"

"Zahir," Sala growls, rubbing her temples, "if you don't shut up, I will throw you to the dunes and see if you can make it out alive."

Zahir shrugs and says, "I'm just trying to bond here. I mean you do want us to get along and work together, so what better way to serve the Logonkelie—"

Sala's hand snakes out and grabs Zahir's parathas, holding them out of reach. "If you want these back, you will let us eat in peace."

Zahir's eyes widen at the threat to his food. He reaches out helplessly for the parathas, but Sala continues to glare at Zahir until he says, "Fine."

With his plate returned, Zahir begins scarfing down the remaining food as if the threat lingered. Sala pinches her lips together but doesn't say anything else as Zahir eats like a street urchin finding his first meal.

Silence descends as we eat, and the moment everyone is finished, Cadmar nods to Sala and says, "Fittings."

Sala pushes her plate away then gestures to me. "Come on, Nightshade."

I follow her, leaving Cadmar and Zahir in the Logonkelie room talking quietly.

My feet drag as Sala wordlessly leads the way upstairs and down a narrow hallway and opens one of the doors. Inside, I barely register the pristine room before a small form hurtles out of the corner.

"Salaji!" a young boy shouts as he tackles Sala in a big hug.

She ruffles his hair and tries to detach the boy from herself but fails. "Bhaiyya, let go! You need to meet my friend."

My jaw drops slightly, but I close my mouth before they turn my way. Bhaiyya? How can Sala have a brother? The boy lets go of Sala and steps back, and I get a clearer view of him. He's young and gangly, all legs and arms. Although he's barefoot like many of the children in the Lower City, his kurta is clean, and his face has the reddish tint of being recently scrubbed.

"Laila, this is Hrithik, but we all call him bhaiyya." Sala ruffles the boy's long hair affectionately then adds, "Bhaiyya, this is my friend Lailaji."

Hrithik puts his hands together in prayer and then gives a slight bow to me. "Namaste, Lailaji. Nice to meet you."

I return the gesture to this polite little boy then glance at Sala for clarification. She grins and pulls Hrithik into a side hug.

"All of us call Hrithik bhaiyya 'cause he's the little brother we can't get rid of."

Hrithik shouts and tries to pull away from Sala, but she just hugs him closer and ruffles his hair again. "Just kidding, bhaiyya."

Hrithik flashes me a wicked grin before ducking out from under Sala's arm. I smile back, genuinely drawn in by his infectious smile. Someone grunts and trips over the doorway behind Hrithik, spilling swaths of colorful silk onto the floor.

"Careful!" Hrithik yells as he hurries to pick up the fabric from the floor. "Those are delicate!"

Sala smacks Zahir on the back of the head as he stumbles the rest of the way into the room and ungracefully drops bundles onto my bed. Rubbing his head he mutters, "Sure, worry about the clothes."

Hrithik puffs up his chest with pride, glaring at Zahir. "Ma and I did all this for Baba Cadmar ourselves."

I hide my smile behind my hand at Hrithik's name for Cadmar—he's the furthest thing from a sweet little old baba that I can imagine.

"Yes, you did, bhaiyya," Sala says as she helps him fold the sarees that had fallen out of the bundle.

"I know, I know," Zahir says. "You told me the whole way here."

"Then you should take better care of them," Hrithik says as he starts to undo each of the bundles. Zahir opens his mouth to argue, but Sala shoos him out of the room.

"Out!" She commands and closes the door on Zahir's retort. Hrithik's chuckle echoes in the tiny room. "Let's figure out what works best for you."

"For me?" I say, not fully focusing on Sala. The anxiety of entering the palace is still filling me with dread.

"We need you to blend in."

I open my mouth to ask more questions, but at that moment, Hrithik steps away from the bed, the dazzle of colors stopping all thought. He had unpacked fabrics of every color, laying them out delicately next to one another—from glittering gold and pale yellow to a vibrant green inlaid with mirror-like jewels. I gape and step closer to admire the detailed designs in each piece. Embroidered flowers. Gold coins that tinkle when you move. Even a few interwoven with precious stones.

I run my hand over one to my right. Hrithik's Ma certainly knows how to ensconce a girl in glamor. One of the red cropped blouses catches my eye, and I pull it out from its fellows. The red is a deep crimson, almost the color of fresh blood, but with none of the violence. A red that oozes strength and sophistication. The thin straps are inlaid with an ornate pattern that begins on the left shoulder and works its way down to the right. The swirling design makes me question where the pattern begins and if it ever ends. It looks like jeweled waves flowing across the deep red sunset.

"That one is Ma's favorite," Hrithik says from behind me. He grabs the pallu to show me. "She was inspired by an Ari lady who was passing by the bazaar."

"Your Ma made this?" I ask.

Hrithik puts his hands on his hips and fixes me with a serious stare—quite a feat for a seven-year-old. "Ma made everything you see here. She's the most talentedest lady in Aveena."

"She definitely is," I say.

Sala pushes me towards the privacy screen with a pale pink saree, while Hrithik smiles and continues to talk about each of the outfits he brought. Most are inspired by Ari women that his Ma had seen heading towards the palace. Hrithik knew the story of each piece: which ones were his Ma's favorites, which ones he helped her with, which ones gave his Ma the most trouble when putting them together. The more he talked, the more I could feel the tension leaking out of my body.

"You still haven't shown her the best part, Salaji!" Hrithik says after I emerge from behind the screen.

"Why don't you show her?"

Hrithik grabs a midnight kurti with silver beading like stars. He pulls the tunic inside out, hiding the glittering, swirling pattern.

"This is why Baba Cadmar likes us the most," Hrithik says proudly.

On the inside, extra pieces of fabric are sewn on. When I touch one of them, I realize that the fabric is actually a pocket. There are three sewn in different places.

"What—"

Hrithik interrupts me. "These two" —he points to the two lower pockets— "are for small things you need to hide and carry with you. Easy access. This one," he points to the largest pocket, "is for a knife."

I glance at Sala, remembering when she turned yesterday how I could see the outline of a knife pressed against her side. Sala, following my line of thought, nods. "Yeah, you've seen one in action."

"Why don't you get cut by the blade?"

Hrithik points to the pocket. "Look, Lailaji."

The pocket seems to be made of dark fabric like the other two, but upon closer inspection, I notice that it is lined with something sturdier.

"Ma uses really, really thin leather to protect you from getting cut. She stretches out the leather herself in our back room."

"What about the sarees?" I ask, thinking about the cropped blouses and meters of fabric.

A mischievous grin crosses Hrithik's face, and he points to the pale pink saree that I'm still wearing. "Those are extra special. As long as you put it on the right way, you'll be able to get into Ma's special pockets."

I look near the hips of the petticoat. Sure enough, the pockets are hidden in the folds of fabric. I rock back on my heels, whistling softly under my breath. Hrithik's mother was a goddess of disguises.

Sala nudges me and adds, "Hrithik's ma makes sure that we are ready for any situation."

"Look like a lady, but cut like a bitch," Hrithik says in a matter-of-fact voice.

"Bhaiyya!" Sala screeches. She bops him on the back of the head like she would Zahir.

"Ow! But Salaji I heard *you* say it!" he whines, rubbing his head.

Sala and Hrithik glare at each other and I can't help but laugh. Soon my eyes water with my laughter, and I have to put my hands on my knees to hold myself up.

**You cannot relax for a moment.
To relax and forget is to disgrace your
father's name, our family's name, and
your own reputation. Your value is in your
reputation.**
-Advice from Lady Shah to her daughter-

16

After hours of trying on sarees and kurtis, only interrupted by a quick lunch, Hrithik leaves with instructions for his Ma. I'm sad to see the young boy go—he was a welcome reprieve.

Grumbling, I follow Sala down to the training room in a rose-colored saree, exhausted, my feet aching. Zahir opens the door for us, and Sala slides by him. He scans my saree, causing color to rise to my cheeks but before I can think, Zahir grabs my hand and bows over it dramatically, his curls brushing against my captured hand.

"My dear noble lady. How exquisite you look tonight. I cannot—"

I swat him. "Ugh, stop."

"Dearest lady, you wound me—" I try to slip past Zahir, but he's switching between bowing and curtsying, a constant stream of stupidity flowing from his mouth. He meets each of my steps with one of his own, that roguish twinkle dancing in his golden eyes. "Please let me bask in your glory, my lady. My heart yearns for so fine a flower. You are like the mysterious stars above, twinkling in and out of existence before a man can catch you in his grasp. You—"

"*Zahir*," I growl, finally shoving him out of the way. My pallu falls off my shoulder, and I scramble to fix it before Sala berates me for messing it up.

"Actually, that is *exactly* what we are going to practice tonight," Cadmar says from the table.

"What?!" Zahir and I say together, all playfulness forgotten.

A glimmer of laughter breaks through Cadmar's somber Ari mask as he takes in our incredulous expressions. Speaking slowly, as if to two children, he says, "You two need a crash course in Aristocracy manners if you're going to blend in."

I glare at Sala, who's leaning against the wall and failing to hide her smile. "You didn't warn me!"

"If I had told you, you wouldn't have come downstairs," she says.

Zahir appears as put out as I do. He starts backing towards the door.

"I thought we were going in as servants," Zahir says.

With all his nonsense, I hadn't noticed the fine sherwani he wore. The cerulean blue fabric stretches across his shoulders, emphasizing their strength. If it wasn't for the wildness in his beard, he would pass as an Ari right now.

Cadmar crosses his arms and says evenly, "We need you *talking* to the Ari, not just cleaning up after them."

"I did plenty as the Nightshade," I respond, the anxiety from earlier rushing back in. Zahir catches my eyes, and I see my own nervousness reflected in his own gaze. "*Without* talking to them."

"That's no longer enough. Not for Logonkelie." Cadmar's tone leaves no room for argument.

I open my mouth anyway, but Cadmar cuts me off. "Have you ever worked a job in the palace, Laila?"

I grumble at his avoidance. Cadmar and his damn questions. "No, I haven't."

Cadmar nods and sips his drink again. "And why is that?"

"Everyone knows that it is impossible to get into the palace."

"Not impossible," Sala says.

I cross my arms, waiting for *someone* to explain. Cadmar drains the last of his drink then finally turns his full attention to me. "It is not impossible to get in, but you have to learn to play a part."

"So, we'll be servants, right?" Zahir asks, looking back and forth between Sala and Cadmar, waiting for them to agree.

"The only people who make it through the palace wall are members of the Aristocracy and those who serve them," Cadmar says, evading the question again.

I glare at Cadmar. "But once we're in, we'll disappear right?"

"It's not that simple," Cadmar says. "Everyone in the palace is watched at all times. Accounted for. We need you to speak with the Aristocracy, interact with them."

My eyes widen. Play a part? I can't even hide my frustration from those in this room, let alone pretend to be someone I'm not. Sala puts her hand on my shoulder and forces me to look at her. Concern shines in her face, contrasting with Sala the Dictator that we've been dealing with all day. Her concern makes me feel worse.

"Laila, we will train you to blend in. We will teach you to become one of them."

"Can't I be a servant or cook or something?"

"No," Cadmar says. "You and Zahir will have to learn to become Aristocracy. Sala can't do it. Very few can."

Zahir and I exchange incredulous looks, both at a loss for words.

"I'll be with you every step of the way. We'll give you aliases and train you. In a few days, you'll have the Ari eating out of the palm of your hands," Sala adds.

Zahir meets my eyes, reflecting my own fear, then he takes a shaky breath and nods once. He walks towards the table to join Cadmar. Recognizing defeat, I trail after him, afraid that if I argue further that Sala will reveal my attempted escape to Cadmar. I need more time.

"Stop," Cadmar commands from his seat. "Adjust your walk. Both of you."

"Our walks?" Zahir asks.

Cadmar stands and glides towards us. His steps are light, his head held high. He transforms from the Logonkelie leader to an Ari in a matter of seconds. Zahir and I exchange resigned looks before lifting our heads and mimicking his movements.

"You need to straighten here," Cadmar says to Zahir and smacks him between the shoulder blades. Zahir stands taller. I laugh at his expression—he looks like he has an iron rod stuck up his—

"Laila, put more hip into it!"

I stumble over my petticoat and stare at Sala, pissed, as she casually leans against the wall. She's enjoying this too much.

"More *hip*?"

"You need to swish your hips back and forth. Like a cat."

"And why in the dunes would I do that?" I ask, crossing my arms. I've put up with their shit all day, but this crosses a line. When I escaped my father's aspirations of grandeur,

I buried the demeaning customs deep, trusting that I'd never deal with them again.

"Because," Sala says as if I am being deliberately slow, "it is what all the Ari women do."

"Not this one."

"Do you want to get caught within the first day?" Sala challenges, getting in my face. I groan under my breath. I will not make a fool of myself for their enjoyment. I will—

My shoulders sag under the pressure to remain hidden, to fit in. Sensing the fight leave me, Sala pushes. "Swish your goddamned hips, Nightshade."

"Yeah, c'mon, Laila, swish those hips," Zahir teases as he continues to practice gliding. I trip him as he moves past me. Cadmar smacks the back of Zahir's head.

"Ow, what was that for?" Zahir asks.

If Cadmar ever deigned to roll his eyes, he might have in that moment. Instead, he waves a hand in front of Zahir and tells him to pay attention. As Zahir glides away, I take a deep breath, and abandon my pride, forcing my hips to sway in my saree.

"Better," Sala says.

"Yes, Laila, better for—"

Zahir's grunt echoes in the room as Cadmar smacks him again. I sigh and ignore them. If I'm really going into the palace, then I'll have to get used to being ogled by the Ari.

Think of this as survival, Laila, I say to myself as my lower back starts to protest the new movement. *Like learning to climb to the roof. Or picking locks. Survival.*

After gliding around the room, Cadmar instructs us through other Ari protocol. I sweep out my petticoat four times before he's satisfied with the way that I seat myself at the table. By the end of *that* lesson, my back aches from the ridiculous pose Cadmar has me sitting in—ankles crossed, knees together and to one side, hips jutting to the other side, chest pointing in the same direction as my knees. No wonder the Ari women are so rude. If I had to sit with my body in an s-shape all the time...

"Better," Cadmar says tiredly from his seat. A dull ache has started building behind my eyes. Someone knocks on the door, and Sala answers it. I'm tempted to slump in my chair, but I know that Cadmar will only snap at me if I do.

The gray-haired woman divvies food onto our plates—the roasted goat that's been wafting up from downstairs—and bows to Cadmar before seeing herself out. Without waiting for Cadmar's approval, I dig in, savoring the garlic naan. Sala clicks her tongue at me and tosses a napkin my way.

"You'll need to be more delicate than that, Nightshade," she says. "The Ari don't want a gaping fish at their table."

I choke the food down as a blush threatens to emerge on my cheeks. The two of them continue to instruct us throughout the meal, forcing Zahir and I to practice countless Ari faux pas until both of us are bleary-eyed.

Finally, Cadmar says, "Get some sleep. Tomorrow, we go to the palace."

I look at Cadmar before we leave the room. Taking another sip from his glass, he stares unseeing at the map of Aveena.

**The wounds of the mind take longer to
heal than those of the body.**
-Aveenan Proverb-

17

It's past midnight, but I toss and turn, unable to sleep. The bed is too soft, unlike the roof boards I'm used to. The blanket tangles in my legs as I roll over, causing my heart to race irrationally.

I sit up and throw the blanket to the side, grabbing my head in frustration.

This room is a trap. I reach down and touch my anklet, willing it to surge with cooling energy, but nothing happens.

I stand up and begin to pace. Nothing makes sense anymore. I catch sight of myself in the mirror above the dresser—I look wild, out of control.

I need to get out.

Now.

Running my finger through my tangle of hair, I force myself to think. I can't leave–Sala will find me too easily, and I can't trust her to keep a second attempt secret from Cadmar. The tavern is too crowded, and the windowless Logonkelie room is out of the question.

Then it hits me: the window.

126

I thrust the shutters open. They clatter against the side of the building. It doesn't matter—no one can hear it over the noise ascending from the tavern. I close my eyes to the view of Aveena and focus on the humid night, filling my lungs with stuffy air.

No good. I'm still trapped in this damned room.

My eyes shoot open, and I look at the building across the street. Too far. There's no way that I would make that jump.

Think, Laila.

My mind swirls, overfull with the day. Trapped by the Ordinances. Trapped by Logonkelie. Trapped by my choices.

The roof.

I look above my window and see that the sandstone wall extends another ten feet before the roof cuts off its height. The flickering light from the torches on the street below casts odd shadows against the building, making it impossible to tell if there are enough handholds for me to make it to the top.

I rush back into my room and grab the lamp from the wall. I hold it outside the window, protecting the flame with one hand. There. Above me is a stone that juts out more than the others. I can reach that from the window. And above that there seems to be a hole in the wall. And there. I can't wait a second longer, I have to get out of here.

Refusing to look down at the street below, I start to climb. My nervous energy strengthens my sore limbs.

Climbing is easy.

Climbing promises freedom.

The thick ledge of the roof is within my reach. Using my legs, I push off of the wall one last time and manage to pull myself over. I grin and roll onto my back. The light of torches from the street doesn't reach this high. Darkness spans above me. Peace. I count the bright stars, each one a new, calming breath. One star. In. Two stars. Out. Like I used to do when I first ran to the Lower City.

With each star I count, the swirling thoughts in my mind dissipate. The trapped feeling flows out of me. I can handle this. I have handled more than one Ari and his crazy schemes. I'm stronger than this.

At least I used to be.

"I see I'm not the only one with shit on my mind."

I sit up, eyes roving the darkness for the voice. In my haste to get on the roof, I didn't check to see if anyone else was up here.

"Over here, Laila."

Zahir is reclining against the wall. Shadows mask his face, helping him to blend into the darkness.

"Oh, Zahir." I push my hair out of my face as I scramble for the right words to explain. "I, um, couldn't sleep, so I thought I would, you know, get some air."

Zahir chuckles and walks to my side of the roof. He doesn't make any sudden movements, as if I'm a small animal that he might scare off. Dunes, I am a small animal in this game. "Yeah, I thought I would get some air, too. But I used the stairs."

He rests against the ledge, leaving a gap between us. Smart man.

"Ah, the stairs," I mutter, glad that the darkness hides my blush. I stand, uncomfortable with Zahir looming over me. He doesn't seem to notice as he leans over the edge and examines the wall leading from my window.

"I don't know how you did that. My body feels dead."

"I—"

"What in the dunes did you even hold on to? It looks smooth to me."

I sigh, resigned to explaining another secret. Pointing, I say, "See over there? And there? You have to look for the handholds."

"Those aren't handholds, those are miniscule wrinkles in the sandstone."

I shrug. "If that's what you see."

"That's what they are!" Zahir rubs his hand over the nearest crease as if to demonstrate. I grin and stare out over the rooftops—with the aid of the moonlight, I can see the glistening of the Tigris Sea from our perch. Maybe if I could make it past the outer walls of Aveena and to the sea I could find a lone fisherman to usher me away from here. We could find another city and start over, Tanu and I. And when I had enough money, we could travel back and pay the Tribes to take us to Bhavin and–

"Laila?" Zahir asks, nudging me out of my thoughts.

"Hm?"

"I asked if this is how you got over the wall to the Upper City as the Nightshade."

I bob my head in a non-answer, smiling, and then notice planks of wood. "A girl can't give away all of her secrets, Zahir."

"Great. More secrets."

The wood is large but not rotting. Good. I lift the wood and maneuver it over the edge of the roof. A dull thunk echoes in the night air as the wooden slab meets the adjacent rooftop. Slowly, I lower the other end onto the Hathorda rooftop. I wait, listening for an indication that someone heard the thunk.

"I was wondering when you were going to take advantage of my wood."

I feel a blush rise to my cheeks, but I ignore Zahir. "*Your* wood? Last I checked, the only thing you own is a disgusting mouth and a shit ton of curls."

Zahir laughs and nudges the plank. "Last I checked, Laila, Ari women do not say 'shit ton.'"

"Last I checked, Ari women also do not walk on rooftops."

I grab a second board, and before Zahir can protest, I cross the plank to the adjacent roof. I quickly lay the board down, then hurry back to the Hathorda roof.

"What are you doing?" Zahir asks.

"Securing exits."

I bend to pick up the plank. Zahir moves to help, but I notice a heartbeat too late.

"Here, let me—oof!"

As soon as I turn with the plank, I smash the board into Zahir's stomach. The wood crashes to the floor as I grab Zahir's shoulders to steady him, so he doesn't fall off the roof—he's completely winded.

"Zahir! I'm so sorry."

I settle him against the wall and help him slide down. I pull Zahir's arms over his head, forcing him to stretch out. Zahir's breaths come out in rasps as we sit.

"Do you want me to get you anything?" I say, worried by Zahir's uncharacteristic silence. I start standing up, but Zahir grabs my arm to stop me.

"No, I'm okay. Really."

"But you—"

"Really, Laila. Don't go."

I try to stand again. "I'm going to get you some water at least. I just hit you with a plank for dunes' sakes."

Zahir grins and winks at me. "But then I'd have to give up being near you."

I ignore his feeble attempt at flirting. I lay down on my back and stare at the sky. If he's okay to flirt, he really must be okay.

Zahir lays down too. I keep an eye on him just in case.

"You can stop staring me down, Laila, I'm not going to do anything."

"Sorry. Habits."

Zahir laughs. The night breeze carries it off over the rooftop. "You have some interesting habits. More gifts from being the Nightshade?"

"Yeah." My stomach sours. "Something like that. Why are you here?"

"Needed some air. You?"

"Same."

We're both silent for a moment. A distant shout drifts up from the entrance of the Hathorda. The mouth-watering smell of roasting goat wafts up from the open kitchen behind the tavern. The breeze moves the thick, stagnant air, fighting a losing battle to keep Aveena cool. I glance at Zahir. His eyes are closed, the wind ruffling his curls as it drifts by. His broad shoulders are relaxed as he lays on the roof; his face looks more youthful when it's relaxed. I could see how some women might find him attractive, but beards are not for me. They remind me too much of my father and—

A shiver runs up my spine. I can't bring myself to even think of his name.

"If you keep staring, it'll go to my head." Zahir rolls on his side and props his head on his hand. His serious expression takes me by surprise. "Do you buy it?"

"Buy what?" I stare at the stars, not wanting to make eye contact with Zahir. Despite the gap between us, it feels too intimate.

"This whole 'doing things for the good of Aveena'. You buy it?"

I pause before I speak. "I don't know."

He waits. When I don't elaborate, he rolls onto his back again. "I don't know either."

We lay on the roof, and for once, Zahir's comments don't fill the silence. We're both plagued by our own thoughts of what tomorrow holds.

**Wind Mother's magic is most often passed
to Her daughters. They remain open to
Her call.**
-from the Sacred Scrolls of Wind Mother
translated from Aramak, the Olden Tongue-

18

The Sultana

"Then they will announce you: His Imperial Majesty, Sultan Ajani Bahu the IV. And you will enter the ballroom and—"

"I'm not sultan yet," Ajani says, interrupting her.

"Take it in a little more," Chhavi directs the seamstress fitting her son's sherwani. "You will be as soon as the Aristocracy return to the palace. You need to get used to the title. It's your birthright."

Ajani sighs, muttering, "It doesn't feel right."

Chhavi clucks her tongue impatiently. "That will be all, Noor, thank you."

The seamstress straightens and bows first to Ajani then to Chhavi before backing out of the sultan's quarters—now her son's rooms. Although Chhavi puts on a brave face for Ajani, the swiftness in which the servants moved Ajani into Gautam's rooms made her heart ache for her ravi.

Once the door clicks shut, Chhavi asks, "What doesn't feel right?"

"This," Ajani says, running his fingers through his already disheveled hair. "Preparing to be introduced as sultan, no to *be* the sultan. I feel like I'm playing pretend."

"You're not."

"I know I'm not," Ajani snaps. Chhavi remains calm, allowing her son's anger to wash over her and away with Wind Mother. She's the only one he can show his true self with—pain, grief, anger, all of it. He paces back and forth past the glittering gold sconces in the marble walls. "I'm not ready for this. I was supposed to have years to prepare. *Years*, mother."

"I know, Ajani."

"I thought I would have more time to-to—"

"To what, Ajani?"

"To be myself. To be Ajani without being the sultan. I have to face them tomorrow, and yet—" Ajani pauses, and swallows. "I know I'm going to disappoint them."

Chhavi stands from her chaise and carefully approaches her son. She wishes she could take all the fear and doubt from him, take this burden from him, but she cannot.

"You are ready, Ajani," she says slowly, placing a hand on his back and rubbing soothingly. He tenses briefly but then relaxes. "You have been preparing with Gautam for years. Yes, you should have had years more, but it was the will of the stars that your father joined them sooner. You will be great."

"You're my mother. That's what you're *supposed* to say," he says bitterly.

"I am, but that doesn't make it any less true," she replies. "Your fear that you aren't worthy is exactly what will make you a great sultan. You care, not just because it's your birthright

134

but because you want to do what's best for Aveena. *That's why* you'll be great."

"I just wish I–" he hesitates. "I just wish I wasn't so queasy."

"Nothing a little ginger can't solve, Ajani," Chhavi says, tucking her smile away for later.

Ajani turns towards her, his brown eyes pleading, making her chest tight. "Are you sure you cannot stay?"

"The Ordinances…"

"I *need* you, mamaji."

Tears prickle behind her eyes, but Chhavi tucks them away for later as well. She can break down when she arrives at their Upper City home, not a moment sooner.

Cupping his cheek, she smiles softly at him. "You don't need me. I wouldn't leave you if I didn't think you could handle it, no matter what the Ordinances say. You are right where you're meant to be."

"It would be nice to have a friendly face is all," Ajani says, stepping away from her. Chhavi lets her hand fall to her side as Ajani walks towards the balcony overlooking the twinkling lights of the city. "I doubt I'll find one in the council. They're all waiting for me to fail."

Chhavi grimaces, but Ajani still faces away towards Aveena, so he doesn't notice.

"That's not true. They want you to succeed. Your success is best for all." Chhavi hesitates, then adds, "Plus you have Vizier Nassor. He'll be your friendly face."

Ajani scoffs. "He's not the same, mamaji."

The sultana joins her son, leaning against the balcony. The marble is smooth and warm under her arms, the residual heat from the sun. A cool breeze brushes against her cheeks, tugging playfully with her hair. Chhavi smiles at Wind Mother's encouragement.

She continues to gaze at silhouettes of the buildings below them, stepping down from one another haphazardly, as she says, "You know, I remember this boy—"

"Mamaji," Ajani groans, but she can sense his smile.

"When he was younger, the boy would roam the palace halls, following his father, imitating whatever he did or said." Her heart lightens, thinking of Ajani and Gautam together, as she tells the story. "The boy would announce his own presence to the family as he entered the dining room, saying, 'The most wonderful and magnificent Sultan Ajani the IV.'"

"And father would ask what I've done that makes me so wonderful and magnificent." Ajani chuckles, and the sultana grins.

"If I remember right, you told him that you were born to be magnificent, so therefore you didn't have to do anything at all."

They both laugh again. The memory of young Ajani, precocious child that he was, surfaces—dark hair falling into his big, brown eyes, dressing up and imitating his father throughout the palace. His laughter used to ring through the hallways as he played jokes on the palace guards.

As Chhavi's smile fades, tears threaten to fall again, the heaviness of loss settling into her bones. She fights to keep her shoulders back, not slumping forward like she desires.

Strong, she'll be strong for Ajani.

Only for a few more hours.

Relief washes through her immediately followed by guilt. She shouldn't feel relieved to leave the palace and abandon her son, but she can't help but look forward to the simplicity and privacy of the Upper City.

"Thank you," Ajani says so softly Chhavi almost misses it in her mixed-up emotions.

"Hm?"

Her son, no longer a little boy imitating his father, but a handsome young man on the precipice of major change.

Ajani faces her. "Thank you for helping me remember that I have trained for this. That I'm meant to be sultan."

"Of course, Ajani," she says.

"I—I think I'll turn in for the night," Ajani adds. "Rest up for the big day."

Chhavi grasps him gently by the shoulders, holding his gaze. "You're going to be magnificent."

"I'll try my best." Ajani reaches down and kisses her cheek. "Safe travels to the Upper City, mamaji."

Chhavi closes her eyes briefly, holding onto this moment, then steps back. "I'll see you before you know it. I love you."

"I love you too."

Chhavi turns and exits the sultan's quarters, her sight blurring from the tears spilling down her cheeks. Thankfully the hallway is empty—no one is there to witness her weakness—as she trudges back to her room.

Her retinue leaves early in the morning before most of the Aristocracy converges on the palace. Chhavi wants to avoid their gawking and gossiping. Better to slip unseen into the city than to subject herself to more of their blithering. If she had to accept more false words of sympathy, she might combust. The funeral was already horrid enough—sympathies intermingled with requests of her and her son. She loved her people, but the Aristocracy could be relentless.

The candles are already lit when she enters her suite. Amari, her maidservant, bows, and wordlessly helps her to change. Chhavi is grateful that she doesn't comment on her tears, just hands her a handkerchief then braids her hair.

Yes, their Upper City home will be a welcome reprieve. She hopes Ajani will forgive her absence as he navigates the demands of the council on his own.

The original council broke away from the Tribes, fearful of their djinn worship. They built Aveena as a safe haven from the dark power found in the desert, isolating themselves as much as possible.
-excerpt from *A Brief Political History of Aveena*-

19

We leave early, before Aveena wakes up. According to Cadmar, the Ari believe that "only poor people wake up before the sun", which means that we can meet Erol—well, Uncle Erol now—before the rest of the Ari descend on the palace.

My chestnut mare is an easy-going horse, specially selected for my use. Cadmar was right to assume that I didn't know how to ride. The mare's easy pace gives the illusion that I know what I'm doing as I sit on her back, attempting to look comfortable with the new height. My stomach lurches each time I glance at the road. I feel unsteady and out of control on the large beast.

Zahir and I cut our horses to the main road and begin the ascent to the palace. Our ancestors chose to place the palace on top of a hill and build the rest of the city in a sprawling mass around it. The beacon of the palace serves as a constant reminder that the Ari are above us.

I usually love the quiet of early morning, but today, everything is ominous. The last buildings of the Upper City loom higher and higher over Zahir and me. They seem to look down on us and say, "You don't belong here." The wind tugs at the veil concealing my hair, threatening to whisk it away, and I snatch at the fabric. Although it's only wrapped around my hair, the silky fabric cuts into my periphery, obscuring the surroundings like the blinders on my mare.

"If you keep twitching like that, they'll think you like antalesi powder," Zahir says the third time I turn wildly to look down an alley.

"If you sit any stiffer on that horse, they'll think you're riding him for another reason," I shoot back.

"Oh, c'mon, Lai-Lailani. You've got as much experience with horses as Cadmar has with living in the Lower City."

I shift in my seat and try to appear dignified. "I don't know what you mean."

Zahir brings his gelding closer and whispers, "Good impression of an Ari. You almost had the right amount of contempt."

I laugh and some tension dissipates. Zahir smiles and then refocuses on the road ahead of us.

"So have you met Erol?" I ask.

"No. You ever been to the palace?"

"No."

"We will be too familiar with it soon enough," Zahir says.

The gentle ascent transforms into a steep incline as we pass the last Ari house. The clatter of our horses' hooves on the stone pathway announces the end of the Upper City. No buildings exist in the two-hundred-meter circumference around the palace wall; instead, barren earth fills the space. The area lays bare the people who have the audacity to approach the palace. I gulp as the world tilts, and I'm confronted by the palace wall.

The wall that divides the Upper and Lower Cities has four gates. Someone who is determined—like me—can find a way over the wall. The wall that encompasses the outside of the Lower City is a joke: maybe three meters high, crumbling in most places, nonexistent in others.

The palace wall, on the other hand, towers over us at thirty meters high. Guard posts garnish the top of the wall every ten meters, providing a resting place—or hiding place depending on your perspective—for the Palace Suraksha. Even at this distance, the wall's incredible smoothness is apparent, no handholds or rocks out of place. Rumor says two hundred laborers were tasked with smoothing down the stone on both sides to prevent anyone from climbing over.

There is only one gate through the palace wall.

I've never gotten close to it. Even when I was living in the Upper City, I avoided the barren area between the city and the wall. As we approach, my hands sweat, and I adjust my grip on the reins. Zahir shifts in his seat and glances over at me. I nod and we push forward.

Neither of us speak.

As we get closer, I gasp. Sandstone pieces form intricate whorls of design through the center of the palace wall. Stone flowers fan out from the swirled stone vines; the movement of the design makes it seem as if the flowers are real and flowing in the Aveenan breeze. Glimmers of bronze catch the morning sun, illuminating the delicate bronze butterflies. The architect must have taken hours hand-selecting each piece for the wall and placing it in the exact spot to create the image. The enormity of the architect's vision humbles me.

"Did you know?" I ask.

"No," Zahir whispers, silenced by the beauty of the design.

I'm grateful for my steady mare as she keeps pushing forward toward the sole gate in the palace wall. When we are a few meters off, a burly Palace Suraksha steps out of the gatehouse. Behind him, two other Suraksha wait inside. Although they don't move to join the first, their eyes analyze Zahir and me for sudden movements.

"Name and purpose?" the Suraksha asks.

I lower my head, hiding behind my veil, and let Zahir speak for the two of us, like Cadmar instructed. I stare at the guard's black boots and black uniform wondering how they survive the heat of the day. At least the city Suraksha wear lighter colors so the sun doesn't get to them.

Zahir sits tall on his horse and looks down over his nose at the guard. "My name is Zaharian Shaikh, and this is my cousin, Lailani Acharya. My father, Councilman Erol Shaikh, notified you of our early arrival."

The Palace Suraksha stares at us. The pause makes me nervous, and I resist fidgeting with my veil or looking up. I feel the man's eyes roving over me, evaluating me, and I steady my breathing. Lailani does not have anything to worry about. Lailani and her cousin are part of the Aristocracy. They belong here.

After a beat, the guard nods and allows us to pass through the palace gate.

The stone tunnel through the palace wall extends ahead with no end in sight. The only sound is the click of our horses' hooves echoing off the road and walls. I twist my reins tighter, making my chestnut mare prance nervously, and Zahir reaches out a hand to calm her. He and I exchange a look in the murky light—everyone in Aveena sees the magisterial height of the palace wall but who knew about the depth of the damn thing?

I focus on smoothing out my features, hiding my fear, as the end of the tunnel lurks ahead, brilliant sunshine blinding the exit. I glance over my shoulder—the Suraksha watch us from their post, hands on swords. As I feared, our early arrival made us look suspicious.

"Here goes nothing," Zahir mutters grimly as our horses step into the sunlit palace.

Servants in black kurtas rush forward and grab the reins. My eyes adjust to the brightness of the light, and my jaw drops. The palace towers above our heads, higher than any other building in Aveena. The smooth walls are made of marble, not sandstone, seamlessly constructed with no beginning or end. At either end of the building, massive spherical turrets sit atop each corner like glittering emeralds. Crystal blue water separates Zahir and I from the palace, and a long bridge with a golden railing arches over the water. Across the bridge, the wall facing us contains windows carved into the marble, revealing the scurrying palace servants inside. The door is too large to be considered a door; it's a large cutout in the wall bedecked with silver and gold strands that hang from ceiling to floor. A palace maid holds the exquisite curtain to the side.

"Lady Acharya, please, allow this humble one to assist you from your horse."

Two of the black-clad servants stand by my knee, waiting to help me down. Both bow their heads, averting their eyes respectfully. A light blush flushes my cheeks—they had been trying to silently get my attention, but the palace had distracted me.

"Of course. Thank you," I say.

The younger of the two servants looks up, shocked, but the one who spoke smacks him, reminding him not to meet my eyes. *Shit, I'm here two minutes, and I've already forgotten to be an arrogant asshole.* The younger servant kneels down on the ground on his hands and knees, while the other servant offers his hand to me, still avoiding eye contact. I place my hand in the servant's and step on the other one's back. I try to avoid putting too much weight on the young man's back, but my back foot gets caught in the fabric of my skirt and I trip forward. I snatch my veil before it flutters away, and the older servant catches me. The younger servant grunts but does not complain. Both bow their heads and scurry off.

The lack of eye contact unnerves me.

Zahir strolls over and offers his arm. I lace my arm through his, but keep my head down, embarrassed by my ungraceful entrance. Zahir leans over and whispers to me, his beard concealing his moving mouth. "Head up. You are Ari."

I lift my chin and square my shoulders back and summon the best disdainful aura that I can muster. I lower my lashes and glare at any servant who comes close by.

"Better," Zahir says.

A maid steps forward. Unlike the maids of the Upper City, this maid's face is completely concealed by the black fabric of her veil. Her eyes shine through the slit in the fabric, but like the other servants around us, she doesn't make eye contact. Instead, she places her gloved fist over her heart and bows to Zahir. "Shaikhji, please allow this humble one to escort you to Councilman Shaikh."

"If you must," Zahir says in a bored voice.

The maid rises from her bow and turns towards the palace, while Zahir and I follow behind. Arrogant. Ari. Uncaring. Unimpressed. I repeat the mantra in my head as we cross the bridge to the palace. The words wash through me, helping me to maintain my mask of disdain. Water spouts up from the pools below, dancing along the surface, while the sun glitters on the water, causing sparkles to appear sporadically in my peripherals. I ignore the beauty of the fountains. *Disdainful, uncaring, unimpressed, arrogant Ari.*

On the other side of the bridge, we reach the silver and gold curtain. Except it's not a curtain. The silver and gold strands are strands of the precious metals dangling down from the ceiling, creating a curtain worth more than the entire Lower City. I lower my eyes to hide the anger searing through my soul. People are *starving*.

Inside the marble entryway, a long hallway extends before us. Strutting along the hallway are the oddest birds that I've ever seen. Each bird is pure white with a long neck stretching out from its fat body. The tails drag behind the birds for a meter. I pause, unable to help myself. As I stare at the bird nearest us, it turns its beady eyes on me and lifts its long tail. The feathers fan out in a perfect arch that nearly touches both sides of the corridor. The tailfeathers are tipped with bright blue tufts at each end.

"Those are the sultan's peacocks, Lady Acharya," the maid says.

"Of course," I say as if I knew that already. "Lead us to my uncle."

The maid bobs her head and moves further into the palace. We pass marble hallway after marble hallway, turning left, then right, then left again, until I give up on keeping track of the turns. My experience as the Nightshade is useless in this new territory. Soon I'm just focusing on the maid walking in front of me, blocking out the rest of my surroundings. There will be time to understand the layout of the palace once my head stops spinning.

Finally, the maid pauses in front of a teal door. "Councilman Shaikh's residence," she says.

The door swings open revealing an elderly man. His white beard reaches the middle of the man's chest, all of the ends groomed to come together into one point. Zahir's beard is a wild mess compared to the elegance of this Ari.

"Thank you, Niya, that will be all," he says to the maid. She places her fist in front of her heart and bows to the elderly man first and then to Zahir. She nods her head to me and leaves, her feet whispering across the marble floor. "Please, come in."

Zahir and I follow Cadmar's contact into the room, and immediately I notice that he keeps the rest of his hair tied in a small horsetail. I scan the room, assessing the new arrangement. Three large windows—exit points if needed— the door we just entered, and four more doors leading off the main room.

The entry room is vast like the Logonkelie room in the Hathorda, but instead of tools to train us, magenta, green and cerulean chairs and pillows litter the floor. A breeze pushes through the curtained windows. I wander to one of the curtains and pull it to the side, and my heart stops. The sultan had placed bars to prevent intruders from entering the suite—or people leaving unnoticed. My stomach drops. The urge to flee overwhelms me.

"Welcome to the palace," the man says, his gray-green eyes twinkling mischievously. "Where all the fun happens."

The man gestures to the divans that are the furthest from the open windows, and the three of us sit down.

"So we've heard," Zahir mutters.

The elderly man laughs causing the lines of his face to become more defined. "Don't be so jaded, young man. You've got a lot more life to live before you can dole out judgments like an old baba. I'm Erol."

Erol offers his arm to Zahir in the customary greeting. Zahir scowls under his curly beard but grasps Erol's feeble looking forearm as expected. I'm surprised when Erol offers his arm to me as well. Normally, men do not offer their arms to women—that would acknowledge them as their equals. I'm going to like this mischievous old man.

"I'm Laila, and this is Zahir," I say.

"No, that's who you *were*. Don't use those names again. Even the walls have ears," Erol says seriously. I glance at the open windows, but Erol shakes his head. "The windows aren't your concern here."

He doesn't elaborate, and I don't ask.

I put on my façade from earlier and say, "Hello again, Uncle Erolji. We have missed you greatly."

Erol nods approvingly and leans back on his cushion. "Both of you have rooms within my suite. Lailani, your handmaid will arrive promptly at noon to begin preparing you for the afternoon."

"Prepare?" I say, blanching a bit. Zahir snorts but turns it into a cough. I glare at him then turn my attention back on Erol. "What do you mean *prepare*?"

Erol strokes the ends of his beard and doesn't move from his relaxed position on the cushion. "You should know by now that being a lady in the palace requires you to look presentable at all times."

"Yes, Lailani, you have to look *presentable*," Zahir says, sticking his tongue out at me. I try to kick him from my cushion but end up rolling off instead. Zahir loses it and laughs in a most un-Ari-like way. Erol watches the entire exchange from his cushion, gray-green eyes taking in the ease of our undignified joking. I sit back on the cushion and cross my arms, which makes Zahir laugh harder.

"Enough," Erol says, laying a knobbly hand on Zahir's arm. "You two cannot behave that way."

"In what way?" I ask.

"In a way that shows that you two are comfortable with each other. That you interact like equals and not like Ari. You are cousins of the Shaikh family. You were raised Ari. You need to prove it." Erol lowers his voice, and I lean forward to hear his next words. "You can't be too casual at any point with anyone but especially not with each other. They will know that you are not truly Ari."

Erol meets my eyes, and I hold his gaze. "Erol, you called them 'Ari' not 'Aristocracy'," I point out.

Erol smiles, which brings the twinkle back to his eyes. "Who said that you two are the only ones who get to have fun around here?"

He winks at me, and I can't help but giggle.

"Okay, so while I go through beauty torture, what will you and Zaharian be doing, Uncle?" I say at a normal volume. We can't whisper the whole time. It would be suspicious.

"Many of the other Ari will be arriving soon. Zaharian and I will be with the other men, grumbling and socializing and sizing each other up."

"We will?" Zahir asks. He goes pale under his tanned skin.

"Yes, Zaharian, we will." Erol continues on, ignoring Zahir's obvious discomfort. "This afternoon there will be the first meeting of the Council of the Sultan since Sultan Gautam was taken ill. Lailani, you will be attending with us, but you will sit in the Veiled Room with the other Ari women."

I frown. Sala had told me that women are granted permission to attend the Council of the Sultan but only as observers. A screen separates the women from the men, allowing women to see but not be seen. The Ari believe that if women are present in the Council Room, they would distract the Councilmen from their important work.

Absolute horseshit.

Erol notices my frown and smiles kindly. "Lailani, it is necessary for you to be in the Veiled Room not because it is mandated but because it gives you a better perception of the council. You'll see things that Zaharian and I will miss while we are in the thick of it."

I nod, resigning myself to my fate. As the Nightshade, Velo rewarded me for my performance, not my gender. Even Cadmar, as much as I distrusted him, respected my skills as much as he respected Zahir's. I needed to accept my status in order to blend in with the Ari, no matter how much it grated against everything I had built for myself.

"Tonight is the prince's feast, a celebration of Prince Ajani. All eyes and ears will be out during the feast. It is imperative that you perform your roles well."

"Yes, Erolji," Zahir and I say together.

"You have one chance to make an impression. Ensure that you do not get yourselves caught."

I gulp and glance at Zahir. His golden eyes meet mine. There was no turning back.

**Every person shall have his role and serve
it unquestioningly.
Only then will Aveena prosper.**
-from The Ordinances of Aveena-

20

It takes three maids to fill my marble tub with scalding
hot water. After the maids prepare the bath, scattering
oils and flower petals into the water, Erol dismisses them
and leaves the room. The women are confused but do not
question his orders, following him out the door.

I rest my head against the marble rim, savoring the lavender-
scented steam rising from the water and stare around me.
The decorations that litter the room far surpass the opulence
of the Ari dwellings in the Upper City. Even the ceiling is
patterned with a delicate design in the molding—a square
with leafed corners skips around the edges of the room.
Who would have thought to match the cushion patterns
to the ceiling?

A flicker of movement catches my attention. A small lizard
crawls cautiously across the ceiling. His tail has fallen off at
some point, making him appear stumpy for a lizard. I grin
and close my eyes, blocking out the room and my companion.

Not so perfect after all.

The steam from the water clears my face of the last remnants of the Lower City. I scratch my hair lazily.

Crash.

Water splashes out of the tub as I scramble up. The lizard skitters out of sight.

"Hello, Lailani, I'm here to assist you!" Sala says in a sing-song voice. She strikes a pose in the open doorway.

I groan. "For the love of the dunes, Sala, could you tone it down?"

"Tone it down? Me?"

Sala sweeps into the room, and I hear the gentle click of the door as she shuts it. The black of Sala's maid's outfit accentuates her thin waist—and the sharpness of her tongue. Sala spins around, waving her lace gloves, so I can have a good look. "You like, Lailani? Don't I look like the ideal humble servant?" She winks.

"If humble servants talked as much as you do…" I say under my breath.

Sala raises an eyebrow at me. I try to splash water at her, but she dances away.

"So why are you here?" I ask, settling back down into the bath.

"I'm here to get you ready," Sala says. Her cheerfulness makes me wonder if she's forgotten where we are. "And to do your hair."

I sit up and stare at her. It's the first time that someone has mentioned my hair.

"What's wrong with my hair?" I run my hands through my choppy locks to emphasize my point. Sala shakes her head and then opens one of the bags in the room. From its depths Sala pulls—

"A wig?" I screech. More water sloshes onto the floor.

"Shhh! The walls have ears," Sala says. "And no. Extensions. Cadmar's orders. Out of the tub, now. We need to get started."

Sala taps her foot, waiting. I reluctantly get out of the hot water, allowing Sala to wrap me in the silk robe that the other maids left. Sala leads me to the far end of the bathroom, puts her hands on my shoulders, and forces me to sit in front of the mirror. My wet hair sticks up at odd angles.

Sala pulls out three different pieces and holds each up to my wet hair, like a housewife comparing mangos and trying to determine the ripest ones. Finally, Sala settles on the second knot of hair.

"This'll do."

"You still haven't told me—" I begin.

"Lailani, you're supposed to be Ari, right? Have you ever seen Ari with short hair?"

"But I could—"

"No, you couldn't. You have to fit in. That means long hair, expensive outfits, kohl on your eyes, all that shit. You have to be perfection."

Three hours, two arguments, and one headache later, Sala declares that I'm ready. Once she began working, Sala turned me away from the mirror. The worst part was the hair—it felt like Sala was pulling out more hair than she was adding in. The new weight makes me off balance, like my head is being pulled backwards by an invisible string.

I reach back, trying to touch my hair, but Sala swats my hand.

"Don't touch it unless you want me to start over."

I snatch my hand away. There's no way in the dunes that I want to do that again. Sala laughs at my expression. "You'd better get used to it, Lady Acharya."

"Am I allowed to look at myself now?"

"Go ahead. But on pain of death, don't you *dare* touch your hair."

I stick my tongue out at Sala then turn around. The woman staring back at me from the mirror couldn't be me, could she? Pieces of gold ribbon twist through her hair, while long, dark brown waves cascade down her back. Large teardrop gold earrings hang from her earlobes matching the gold teardrop that rests in the center of her forehead. Black kohl lines her blue eyes, sweeping out in wide lines to a point, and hints of pink tinge her cheeks and lips—just enough to add color but not so much that it looks unnatural. And the saree. Sala had selected a pure white blouse with cap sleeves from the trunks of clothes Hrithik's mom sent with us. The fabric of the translucent skirt is layered enough to be opaque, but the pallu is completely sheer, revealing the half blouse underneath. The gold teardrop design gives the semblance of conservativeness.

I stare in awe at the beautiful stranger in the mirror. She doesn't look worn or tired. She doesn't look like a dolled-up street rat. She is beautiful and strong and confident. The skirt hangs low on her hips, revealing bronze skin between the blouse and skirt. She looks like a woman with curves to offer, not one whose wide hips got the better of her.

Sala steps up behind the woman and puts her hand on her shoulder—my shoulder. I blink hard, reminding myself that this woman is me—the Ari version of me at least. The reality hits me hard: I'm not here to be pretty, I'm here to get information for Cadmar.

"I can't wait to see their faces," Sala says with a smile.

"Who?" I ask.

Sala winks and squeezes my shoulder. "All of those snobby Ari."

I smile in return, then glance back into the mirror. The blue of my eyes stands out with all the kohl. Too noticeable.

"What is it?" Sala asks, noting how my smile evaporates.

"Don't you—" I swallow, my mouth dry, hesitating. My father always harped on how no one would want a wife with djinn-eyes, how they would fear me. "Shouldn't we do something about my eyes?"

Sala cocks her head to the side, waiting for me to elaborate.

"The blue it's too—too noticeable," I say. "Won't the Ari distrust me for it?"

Sala scoffs and starts packing up the makeup. "They'll distrust you no matter your eye color."

"But I have djinn-eyes."

Shame surges forward, my father's words repeating in my head. I hated the drops that turned my eyes brown, the way they stank of sulfur and burned for minutes after the tincture was applied. My vision blurred for days after, making me appear clumsier than I was. The stench lived in my earliest memories, haunting me as a child.

"An old wives' tale," Sala says, rolling her eyes. "For superstitious old bitties who have nothing better to worry about."

My mouth gapes open, but I close it. Everyone believed in the bad luck of the djinn-eyes. My father constantly reminded me that his merchant troubles were my fault, punishment for our family because of my eyes.

"But—"

"Do you want the tincture?" she asks.

"Absolutely not." I shudder.

"We need your eyesight clear." Sala's tone brokers no opportunity for argument. "Besides, the blue might be… unique, but the Ari covet what others cannot have."

"Sala—"

"Nope, that's that. Own it. I wouldn't be surprised if you captured some young Ari's affections with those." She bumps her hip against mine, grinning wickedly.

"I *definitely* don't want that," I splutter, anxiety rising swiftly at the thought. "Sala maybe we should—"

The banging of the outer doors interrupts us. Zahir and Erol's voices carry through the door to my suite. Zahir sounds agitated. Erol's voice is low and fast as he speaks.

"I wonder—"

Sala jerks her head towards the door. "No time like the present to find out."

Sala marches over to the door and moves into the main room. I hesitate, looking at myself in the mirror one more time. Glitter and gold and elegance reflect back at me. I square my shoulders back and mutter to myself, "I am Lady Lailani Acharya. I am Aristocracy."

I walk to the main room of the suite and stop in the doorway. Zahir sits on the same cushion as earlier. He's slumped over, head in his hands, while Erol and Sala talk to him.

"—first time that you've been around them," Sala says to Zahir.

"That's right," Erol added, placing a hand on Zahir's shoulder. "You have to let everything roll off you like water rolls off a waterfowl. They are born and bred Ari, and you must be, too."

"How can I be?" Zahir asks desperately. "I want to punch the arrogance out of each one of them. The things they say to each other…"

I move further into the room. "What happened?"

Zahir doesn't look up from his hands as he says, "The Ari happened. That's what."

I snort. "Tell me something I don't know."

"I'll have you know—" Zahir turns quickly, his face contorted with anger, but his retort dies on his lips. He stares at me, and I shift uncomfortably under his gaze. My hand twitches, wanting to pull at the hem of the blouse, but I force my hand to behave. I meet Zahir's golden eyes and tilt my head to the side.

"What?" The waver in my voice ruins my attempt to sound casual.

"You look… like an Ari," he says.

My stomach drops. I cross my arms and glare at him. "No shit, *cousin.*"

Erol stands swiftly and strides towards me. He grabs my hand and kisses it. "I think what your dunderhead of a cousin is trying to say is that you look absolutely radiant, my niece."

I blush and lower my eyes, a small smile playing on my lips. Erol chuckles and squeezes my hand. "Perfect response. You'll have to get used to flattery, my dear. That's the only way these Ari men know how to communicate with those of the female persuasion. But a blush and a playful smile will take you a long way."

I grin at Erol then look back at Zahir. He seems to be struggling with something, but I can't tell what he's thinking. "So, what happened earlier?"

That snaps him out of his silence. "It was fine at first. A lot of formal greetings."

"And then?" I ask. I walk over to the magenta cushion next to Zahir and sit down carefully on the edge. Sala moves forward and adjusts my pallu, ensuring the fabric hangs in the right way to catch the light.

"And then it all went to shit."

"Oh c'mon, Zahir- *Zaharian*. It couldn't have been that bad. This was just the first meeting."

Zahir shakes his head. "You didn't hear them, Lailani. 'The Lower City dogs just need to be stamped out. The whole lot of them.' 'The fewer charity cases in the Lower City, the better for us.' 'The lazy should be left to starve.'"

"They said that?"

"And more. Erol had to keep his hand on my shoulder to remind me to stay calm." Zahir looks up at me again and asks, "How am I supposed to pretend to be one of them?"

The uncertainty in Zahir's eyes makes my heart lurch. I reach out and take his hand between both of my own. I can feel his rough calluses. "You'll have to remember why we are doing it."

"Plus, you have me," Erol says, clapping Zahir on the back. "You're good at distracting, son, but I'll be your distraction."

"We are all in this together," Sala adds.

Zahir smiles at Sala, but it doesn't reach his eyes. He looks down at our hands and then back up at me. The intensity of Zahir's gaze heats me from the inside out, and suddenly, I feel like we're too close. I release Zahir's hand and turn to

Sala. I can feel Zahir's eyes following my every movement; the heat of his hand between mine remains.

"How much time do we have before the council meeting?" I ask.

"At least half an hour," Sala says, glancing at Erol who nods.

"Zaharian and I need to change and then we will leave," Erol says. "Lailani, you'll leave after us. Sala will escort you."

"I can't walk with you?" I ask, a sinking feeling in my stomach. I wanted to rely on Erol's expertise and Zahir's humor to distract me.

"No, you can't. Not to the council."

"I'll make sure you get to the Veiled Room," Sala says.

My shoulders slump forward, but I nod, remaining silent. Zahir has voiced enough doubts for the two of us. I don't need to add to everyone's worries. Erol sees through my silence and says reassuringly, "Don't worry, Lailani. The council meeting will be the easy part of the evening for you. The prince's feast is where the real challenge lies. We will go through that together."

I'm not sure if that's comforting or not.

**Our traditions provide the structure for
our success. The Aristocracy desire to
witness you honor the traditions, honoring
our history and ancestors. The pomp and
circumstance may seem cumbersome now
when you are young, but I promise, son, if
you honor our traditions, you will win over
the hearts of the Aristocracy with ease.**
-Advice from Sultan Gautam to Prince Ajani
on his eighth birthday-

21

Sala secures her black veil in place before leading the way to the Council of the Sultan. We walk at a languid pace so I can memorize the turns we take from Erol's suite to the Council Room. My head is bowed, the picture of subservient Ari woman, as I watch the marbled floor. Sala's slippers pad softly ahead of me, reassuring me of her presence.

The deserted hallways send a chill down my spine. We pass two black-clad servants—they stop and bow their heads as I pass. The wide hallways are a drastic change to the crowded streets I'm used to. The open space feels lonely instead of relieving; the beautiful simplicity of the clean white marble is enough to contrast the dustiness of the city. It offers no places to hide.

After five minutes, Sala announces, "Lady Acharya, we are almost to the Veiled Room."

I nod in response. Ari do not degrade themselves by responding to their servants.

My gold bangles clink together as I square my shoulders back and lift my chin, trying to exude arrogance from every pore in my body. Sala rounds the corner, and we reach the entryway to the Veiled Room. Concealed feminine faces peek out from the minimalist gold decor surrounding the Veiled Room entrance, reminding us of our place. Despite the simplicity of the design, the gold is thick-plated and solid, not just the gilded designs Ari flaunt in their Upper City homes.

Another procession approaches at the same time we do: two Ari women wearing matching sky-blue sarees with white gold bracelets and rings weighing down their fingers. The older woman's nose reminds me of a peacock's beak; her silver hair matches her jewelry. The younger woman is around Sala's age and has the same beaked nose as the older woman. Both women glare down their peacock noses at me. I stare defiantly into the older woman's eyes in return.

Two palace maids open the doors in unison. Sala joins the other handmaids waiting against the wall—the servants must wait for all of the Ari to enter before following suit.

I step forward to enter the Veiled Room when the older of the two women throws a hand out into my path. I glare down at the gaudy rings lining her wrinkled fingers before meeting the woman's eyes.

"And who are you?" the crone asks contemptuously.

I resist glancing at Sala, and instead, match the woman's tone and say, "I'm Lady Lailani Acharya. And who are *you*?"

She doesn't answer my question. Instead, she turns to the younger woman and says, "Acharya? Have you heard of the Acharyas?" The younger woman shakes her head. "Girl, who speaks for you?"

Girl? Who does this old woman think she is? I maintain my haughty mask despite the woman's needling. "Councilman Erol Shaikh is my uncle."

"Councilman Shaikh?" She scoffs. "Esha, stay away from this one."

The younger woman nods. The silver-haired she-devil walks past me without another word, Esha following behind. I take a deep breath and follow the two women. As I pass through the door, Sala catches my eye and winks.

The Veiled Room overlooks the Council of the Sultan from a modest balcony. Deep violet curtains hang from the ceiling to the floor, encircling the front of the balcony, with garlands of purple and white flowers cascading down the delicate fabric. Candles line the walls of the room, providing enough light to see but not be seen. Various shades of lavender and violet combat the harshness of the main curtain, while accents of gold shimmer in the candlelight. I choose a seat in the corner opposite the door where the balcony and wall meet, giving me the opportunity to watch both the Council Room and the Veiled Room. Although Sala warned me that women were not allowed to speak while in the Veiled Room—supposedly our feminine voices could distract from the happenings in the council—several women huddle together, whispering feverishly. As I scan the room, I count twelve Ari women in total: three elders, seven middle-aged women, and two that look closer to my age. Erol said that most of the Ari women would wait in their own suites until the prince's feast tonight, preferring to rest and primp.

The lavender cushion tempts me to sink in and hide from the room, but my saree demands otherwise. As I adjust my sheer pallu, I scan the tops of the men's heads, trying to locate Zahir and Erol in the crowd of beards and black hair. There, on the far left side of the Council Room. I'd recognize those curls anywhere. Zahir's uncertainty from earlier seems to have faded as I watch him engage one of the elderly men near him in conversation. Erol nods as another man talks to him. The man turns slightly, and I realize that Erol is talking to Cadmar. Cadmar looks different in this crowd with his fine silk sherwani and the sharp lines of his beard emphasizing the sharp angles of his face. But the biggest difference is in his eyes—they flash dangerously as he looks around the room. Seeing Erol's easy-going nature next to Cadmar's intensity feels wrong.

A chime rings out in the Council Room, bringing the discussions upstairs and down to a halt. The men stand in unison and face the back of the room. A beat later I realize the women are also standing, although no one can see us. I hastily join in, pulling at my saree as we wait.

Five men parade down the center aisle of the Council Room. Their features are hazy due to the distance and the veil. The men fan out in the front of the room. One of the five steps forward and ascends to the top of the dais. A monstrous marble chair awaits the man, appearing as if it was built straight out of the floor. The man assesses the mass of Ari men below him. As one, the men—and the women in the Veiled Room—place their fists over their hearts and bow, holding the submissive position.

"Rise."

The prince's voice reaches into the corners of the vast hall, sounding as if he is in the Veiled Room with us. As one, the Ari straighten. No one speaks. Then, just as Erol described, the royal vizier walks up to the stairs. He stops in front of the chair a step below the sultan's marble throne and turns. Once again, everyone in the room places their fists over their hearts and bows. Unlike our bow to the prince, the vizier bows in return to the room. His chair is on the right side of the sultan's throne—a reminder that the vizier is the right hand of the sultan. I strain, trying to see his features, but the dark purple veil makes my effort futile.

The last three men walk up two steps, stopping in front of the three chairs placed on the lowest level. As one they turn, and for the third time, we bow. These men are the Consulate—the three who are chosen by their peers to sit in on the most secret of council meetings. The coveted position that instigated Cadmar's creation of Logonkelie.

"Sit."

The entire room follows the prince's instructions in unison. The prince perches on the edge of the marble chair, and the royal vizier stands. The vizier must be tall—despite being on a lower step of the dais, his head is in line with the seated prince.

"Welcome back, councilmen. It brings joy to see your faces again, although the sadness of the loss of Sultan Gautam still lingers on in our hearts."

The vizier pauses in his speech, as though the loss of the sultan weighs heavily on him. His voice is smooth like oil, dripping easily into the ears of the Ari.

"But we must push forward to continue to do what's best for the city of Aveena."

Councilmen nod at his words. I glance at the women in the Veiled Room, but none of them move.

"We shall keep this first council meeting short in order to honor Sultan Gautam's desire for brevity." The vizier smiles, indulging a few chuckles. "And so, to business. Councilman Lobo, please present the guidelines provided by the Ordinances to the council at this time."

One of the councilmen makes his way to the dais, followed by a servant carrying a large scroll. I lean forward, eager to see the Ordinances with my own eyes even at this distance; however, nothing about the scroll stands out. Councilman Lobo faces the waiting Ari, while the servant kneels before him, holding the Ordinances above his head for Councilman Lobo to read.

"According to the Ordinances," Councilman Lobo begins, "the transition between sultans must last through three full moon cycles, to honor the late sultan. Business will proceed as usual within the city. However, it is our obligation as the Aristocracy to maintain a respectful, solemn air for all."

I hold in my scowl—the finery in the room definitely doesn't qualify as solemn. I look up at the dais, trying to gauge Prince Ajani's reactions, but his stillness reveals nothing. I don't like how the councilman speaks as if the prince isn't there, as if this isn't his father and his future that he speaks of. As I stare at the prince's statuesque form, I wonder if he feels the same.

"Prince Ajani Bahu's official coronation will take place in three moons. We will mark the beginning of his reign and the end of Sultan Gautam's at that time." Councilman Lobo pauses, gesturing to the kneeling servant to adjust the scroll. Clearing his throat, he continues, "During this time, the power of the final decision shifts to the previous sultan's royal vizier in order to ensure consistency and a smooth transition between reigns."

Grumbles break out among the councilmen. Cadmar and Erol stiffen in their seats. Cadmar appears to be clutching the arm of his chair. However, a few men nod in approval, smiling up at the vizier. Vizier Nassor's face is grave as he stands, halting Lobo's reading of the Ordinances.

"My duties as royal vizier are a burden as well as a blessing. I promise to uphold the Ordinances with the utmost respect and duty and act as Sultan Gautam would if he were still with us." The vizier pauses, making eye contact with several members of the Council before continuing. "Our goal, as always, will be to ensure that Aveena continues to be prosperous and self-sufficient. We have to ensure that the Aristocracy remains a strong, united front for our Upper and Lower City brethren. If we show weakness, the Tribes might descend. Or worse, the Lower City may grow restless."

The mumblings end abruptly, but now I'm the one clutching my armrest. Brethren? Grow restless? My white knuckles match the white of my saree, so I force my hands to relax. I do not want to draw attention from the other women, all of whom nod at the vizier's words.

This must be how Zahir felt earlier.

"Thank you for your support as we transition from the reign of his Imperial Majesty Sultan Gautam Bahu to the future reign of His Imperial Majesty Sultan Ajani Bahu." The vizier sits down on his chair and surveys the men of the council.

Councilman Lobo bows to the dais and returns to his seat. I watch as the servant scampers out of the room, filled with the urge to persuade the servant to let me see the copy of the Ordinances.

The Consulate conducts the rest of the meeting swiftly. Councilmen present information to the five men on the dais, and the Consulate determines whether the information dictates immediate action or should await further review. The speed through which the Consulate maneuvers through the requests shocks me; my assumption that the first meeting would be lengthy was wrong. Every request is designated to be discussed at a later time.

Prince Ajani does not speak again until the end.

"To thank you for your support of my father and for your future support of my reign, I invite all councilmen and their families to a feast. I look forward to speaking with each of you."

Prince Ajani's voice is an emotionless monotone. I wonder which member of the Consulate wrote his speech.

The rule of Aveena shall be entrusted to the men who retain clearer minds than their women counterparts. Women do not contain the sensibilities necessary to navigate the political landscape without succumbing to their emotions.
-excerpt from *A Brief Political History of Aveena-*

22

The councilmen file out behind the prince, talking in low whispers to one another. Unlike the voices of the prince and vizier, these whispers do not carry up to the Veiled Room. I remain in my perch watching the men leave, my mind whirring.

The royal vizier will be acting as sultan for the next three months.

My stomach knots, leaving me queasy. Of all my work as the Nightshade, not one job tangled with the royal vizier— the Ari are too afraid to cross him. Well, all of the Ari except Cadmar. I exhale slowly and resist rubbing my face in frustration. Sala would kill me if I smeared my perfectly applied makeup.

Zahir and Erol walk down the aisle, their heads bent together. If Zahir was having a hard time earlier, I bet it's nothing compared to what he's feeling now. Right before they pass underneath the balcony, Zahir looks up and stares at the violet fabric. A girl my age giggles, but her mother silences her with a look. Zahir's eyes scan the veil until they settle on my corner. He stares for a second longer, then disappears from sight. A smile tugs on my lips—I guess he knew where I would be.

The last straggler leaves the Council Room, leaving the women free to gossip. The beaked-nosed crone from earlier stretches out her wrinkled limbs as if she had settled down for a nap and not to observe the Council of the Sultan. Her eyes flash in my direction as I stand. I readjust my pallu in an attempt to hide my uncertainty of what to do next.

"Good afternoon."

One of the middle-aged women approaches me. A few streaks of silver thread their way through her straight black hair. She wears a light green kurti over jade lehenga. Around her neck swings a delicate gold chain with a small flower pendant.

I know that necklace.

I stare at the necklace, forgetting to respond to her greeting. She clears her throat to get my attention and says, "I'm Lady Asfour."

I snap out of it and bow, fist over heart, saying, "Namaste, Lady Asfour. It is a pleasure to make your acquaintance."

"And you." She seems placated by my response and continues, "You are Councilman Shaikh's niece."

I nod, waiting for her to continue. In the world of women, age takes precedence over beauty, and Lady Asfour has both.

"Erolji and my husband are close acquaintances. I believe you and your cousin will be dining with us tonight at the prince's feast."

"Thank the dunes," the crone mutters from across the room. Apparently, she had not forgotten her earlier distaste of my 'relatives.'

"Ah, Lady Shah. What a pleasure to see you today," Lady Asfour says with an innocent smile on her face. "I'm glad to hear that your rash cleared up. You need to make sure to keep your chakras aligned so that it doesn't come back."

Several women cover their giggles with their hands. Lady Shah glares at Lady Asfour. Her daughter sneers at me. I raise an eyebrow and stare back, unfazed.

"Lady Asfour, you know—" Lady Shah begins, red in the face. I'm not sure whether it's because of anger or embarrassment.

"Please don't work yourself up on my account, Lady Shah. I don't want the other ladies to blame me for the return of that heinous rash. If you'll excuse us."

Lady Asfour glides to the door, not giving Lady Shah a chance to respond. After a second, I follow, ignoring Lady Shah's narrowed eyes.

"Thank you, Lady Asfour."

Her smile is genuine as she says, "No need to thank me, dear. That old bat needs to be put in her place at least once a day or else she runs amok on the rest of us."

I snort but try to turn it into a dignified giggle when Lady Asfour glances at me. A palace servant steps out to guide us to the prince's feast, but Lady Asfour waves her off with a lazy hand. Instead, she leads the way herself. Sala and another handmaid fall into step behind us.

Everything about Lady Asfour screams dignity and refinement, the perfect Ari woman. And yet there is an underlying rebelliousness about her. I look at her necklace again, and my insides cringe. It's harder to come to terms with the job I tried to complete now that I'm confronted with the living, breathing, and dignity-saving person whom I tried to frame.

"It's a lotus, dear."

"What is?" I ask, confused.

"My necklace."

"Oh," I say stupidly.

"Do you know what is special about the lotus?"

"No, Lady Asfour."

The marbled hallways look the same even though I know I'm in a different part of the palace. The pristine uniformity continues to alienate me, making me hyper aware that I'm an outsider.

"Please, call me Farah, dear. All these formalities get a bit tiresome, don't you think?"

"I'm Lailani."

"Yes, I know, dear," she says, patting my hand. "Your uncle told me."

"Oh."

I sound like a bumbling idiot, and I'm overwhelmed with the urge to slip into the darkness and out of sight. Oblivious to my embarrassment, Farah smiles and continues talking.

"Anyway, the lotus is an extraordinary flower because it grows out of mud and dirty water. The flower pushes through the muck and blooms above the surface in the morning, revealing its beauty. By evening the petals fall away and the flower fades."

"It dies?"

"Not exactly, dear. It hides away during the night. Then the next morning, the flower reappears and blooms again. No mud on its petals, the same beauty as the day before."

"Do we have lotus flowers in Aveena?"

"Not many. They appear in the shallow parts of the canal, usually outside of the palace and Upper City. We've industrialized the canal too much for the lotus to be able to grow in the Upper City. No mud."

"So, it actually *needs* the mud?" The disbelief rings clear in my voice, making Farah chuckle.

"Not everything of value comes from something pretty."

I don't have a response to that, and Farah doesn't expect one. I thought Cadmar was different from my expectation of the Ari, and then I met Erol. Now, I'm confronted by an Ari lady who doesn't fit my idea of the Aristocracy. Do any of these people act like I expect them to?

The two of us round another marble corner into the widest hallway yet—several Ari houses could fit side by side, and the ceiling is just as tall. Beautiful turquoise mosaics crisscross the ceiling, the intersections inlaid with golden diamonds. Ari mill about, talking to each other in hushed tones.

"There you are," Zahir says. He's agitated and grabs my arm more roughly than I think he means to.

"Hello, cousin," I say calmly. I pry his hand from my forearm and interlock our arms instead, in a typical familial fashion that I've seen the other Ari use as they walk through the Upper City. His arm is tense within my own, heat radiates off of Zahir in waves.

"What took you so long, Lailani?" he says.

"Your cousin is like an overprotective brother, isn't he?" Lady Asfour says, reminding us of her presence. I laugh, which makes Zahir glare at me.

"Farah, this is Zaharian. Zaharian, this is Lady Asfour."

Zahir nods in acknowledgement of Lady Asfour as she bows to him—even though Lady Asfour is older than Zahir, she is expected to show him the proper signs of respect due to a male of the Aristocracy.

Zahir opens his mouth again, but Erol and another man walk up at that moment, stopping Zahir from asking what took us so long for the third time. Internally, I shake my head at him—he's supposed to be an Ari male, not a worried old maid.

Erol smiles and says to me, "Lailani, this is Tei Asfour. Tei, this is my niece, Lailani."

I try to extricate my arm from Zahir's, but he doesn't relinquish his grip. The result is that my bow to Tei Asfour pulls Zahir forward as well. I'm blushing, but luckily Tei Asfour will think that my flushed face is from the awkwardness of the bow—not from my embarrassment of being the unknown thief in his house.

Tei Asfour is the darkest Ari man I've ever seen. He looks as if he toils away in the sun, not in the cushy palace. Normally, Ari strive to have the lightest skin possible, often resorting to lightening remedies applied to the skin. Anything to not look like the "heathens" in the Lower City.

He smiles at me then takes his wife's arm in his own. Farah leans into her husband and whispers something in his ear. He replies in an equally low voice. Both look at each other with such love that I have to look away. Even if I had succeeded with my last job as the Nightshade, how

173

could anyone have believed that Lady Asfour would betray her husband?

"When do we go inside, Uncle?" I ask Erol.

Before he can respond, Sala appears by my side. Bowing, she says, "Lady Acharya, please allow me to adjust your pallu."

Zahir's arm tightens against mine, as if he wants to anchor me to him, but I free my arm and gesture lazily, saying, "If you must. Please excuse me."

I follow Sala through a door in the corner of the hall. Inside, colorfully dressed Ari women primp in front of floor length mirrors, the earthly rich scent of patchouli wafts through the room from the burning incense. A few sit on cushions in the corner sipping tea. Sala steers me to the farthest corner from the door and plucks at my white saree, making sure that my petticoat sits just right on my wide hips and that my pallu drapes perfectly. A quick glance around the room confirms my suspicions—Sala dressed me in all white to stand out against the vibrant colors the rest of the Ari were sure to wear.

"Instructions from Cadmar," Sala whispers.

"Fix my hair," I order.

Sala hovers by my ear and says, "Charm as many Ari as you can. Flirt if you must."

I frown at Sala, not sure I'm hearing this right, but I can't question her without the other women noticing. Sala's eyes twinkle with excitement. I raise an eyebrow, prompting her to explain.

"You've made the other Ari women jealous. Your name is already buzzing around. Use that to our advantage. Make their men talk about you, too."

The blood drains from my face, and I look down at the gold bracelets encircling my wrists to hide my sudden pallor. Flirt with their men? I haven't tried to catch a man's attention since living in the Upper City. Bile rises in my throat, but I swallow it down.

I need to push through for Tanu. For the future possibility of escape.

"That's enough," I say in the same bored tone once I'm sure my voice won't tremble and give me away. "Take me back to my uncle."

As we leave, several women glare at me. Or maybe it's just my imagination.

**A woman's value lies in her ability to
secure a prosperous match. She should
strive to reach her full potential through
proper pursuit of eligible matches, while
still maintaining her mysterious allure.**
-excerpt from *The Guide for Aveenan Gentlewomen*
given to Laila on her tenth birthday from her
father-

23

The minute we exit the women's room, Zahir hooks his arm in mine and leads me to the door. Erol waits for us there, a large vase filled with gold coins in his hands. Seeing my confusion about the vase, Erol smiles.

"Every family is expected to pay respects to the prince then head to their seats for the feast," Erol says. "Should be fun."

Zahir grumbles at my side, but we both nod and follow Erol. I gasp at the beauty of the room. The white marble fills the entire space from floor to vaulted ceiling. The marble on the floor is broken up by pale pink tiles that pattern the floor. As we pass one, I'm startled that I recognize the design—a lotus flower.

"It's rose quartz from the mines north of the Tigris Sea," Erol says. "Sultan Gautam insisted on reconstructing this room in honor of the sultana."

"Reconstructing?" I ask.

"Yes, he rebuilt it for his wife," Erol says. The look in his eyes warns me not to comment on the amount of money spent on such a frivolous endeavor.

"How romantic," I say without conviction.

We walk down the center aisle of the room towards the dais in the back where the prince and the royal vizier greet the Ari. An archway is erected behind the two men—rose-colored curtains are tied to the archway in order to reveal the latticework of the arch. At the crux of each diamond, a crystal candle holder twinkles merrily. From a distance, the prince looks as if he is surrounded by glittering jewels. Flowers overwhelm the rest of the space in bouquets and garlands, the marigolds and jasmine competing with the candles and fabric draped over the dais.

As we approach, the piles of gifts come into sight—cases of gold and jewelry, delicate fabrics, and other expenses to demonstrate the Ari's loyalty to the prince. My eyes gravitate to the young man who will be our sultan. The prince sits stiff as a board in his seat, and I wonder how long he'll be stuck in that same spot. The royal vizier stands by his side reciting the names of the family members that are in front of us. While Prince Ajani looks uncomfortable, the vizier looks completely at ease.

The royal vizier introduces the next family in his even, oily voice: "The Shah family. Councilman Jagan Shah, his wife Etana Shah, their son Pradeep Shah, and their daughter Esha Shah."

A stumpy man and his hook-nosed wife step forward. I recognize Lady Shah and her daughter, Esha. Both parents push Esha forward before they all bow. Their son fidgets from behind his parents, and I wonder if they were purposefully trying to hide Pradeep. Odd, since he seems to be around the same age as the prince.

"Rise."

I whip my head towards the prince, surprised. His voice sounds familiar, but... no, there's no way that it could be.

As I shake my head, Zahir whispers, "You okay?"

I bob my head in a nonanswer as Lady Shah speaks to the prince.

"My daughter is the most skilled girl here, Prince Ajani," the older woman says. Her daughter preens, attempting to catch the prince's eye.

"Indeed, Lady Shah."

Lady Shah apparently takes his automatic response as permission to continue. "Yes, yes, Ajaniji. She is most skilled. She sings like the most beautiful songbird—"

I can't help the snort that escapes me, but I quickly turn it into a cough when Zahir nudges me.

"She is known for making the best jalebi in Aveena, *and*," Lady Shah lowers her voice into a stage whisper. We can all hear her anyway. "Esha has been instructed in other talents as well. Talents when it comes to pleasing a husband and keeping him happy."

My eyes widen as Esha twists, sticking out her hip sensuously. If this is what Cadmar meant by flirting with the men, there is no fucking way *that* would be happening.

The prince looks over the heads of the Shah family—I'd be avoiding eye contact too if it was me. Councilman Shah shuffles his feet, looking embarrassed at his wife's boldness, and sets the gold filigree box down on the dais.

"Thank you, Lady Shah. Please enjoy the feast," Vizier Nassor states with finality.

Lady Shah and her daughter turn away reluctantly from Prince Ajani as Councilman Shah herds them to their table. The prince's face remains impassive as he watches them leave. Lady Shah glares at me before following her husband across the room.

"What did you do to that one, Lailani?" Zahir asks quietly in my ear.

"Would you believe me if I said nothing?"

"No."

I laugh and the sound echoes, drawing the looks of the Ari who are close by. I blush and look down. I can't stand being ogled like one of the peacocks in the front of the palace. Zahir stops walking and drops my arm. It's the first time I can get a good look at the prince. When I look up and into Prince Ajani's eyes, his widen in shock and recognition. I stumble slightly, and Zahir catches my elbow. My mind spins as the royal vizier introduces us: "Councilman Erol Shaikh, his son Zaharian Shaikh, and his niece Lady Lailani Acharya."

All three of us bow in unison, hands over our hearts.

"Rise."

The prince's voice sounds more melodic than it did in the bazaar the other day. Erol places our offering at the foot of the dais. When I look up, the prince is still staring at me, his impassive mask vanished. This close, I notice how his tawny-brown skin contrasts the jet black swoop of hair that falls over his forehead. Although he's seated, the prince's long limbs give away his height. The young man from the bazaar. He *lied* to the Suraksha for me.

When I risk eye contact again, he seems to want to say something.

"I, uh, welcome to the palace," Prince Ajani manages to get out.

"Thank you, Prince Ajani," Zahir says from my side. His voice brings the prince back to reality.

"I trust your journey was comfortable?" he asks, still looking at me.

"Indeed, it was, your Highness," Zahir responds. "The heat of the sun was unable to break our spirits because we left early in the morning. And we avoided fighting with the other Aristocracy trying to get through your front door."

Zahir's babbling as usual. The prince pulls his eyes away from me and looks at Zahir for the first time. Zahir smirks and bows again with a flourish.

"Just wanted to make sure that you saw me pay my respects, Prince Ajani. I wouldn't want to start off on the wrong foot with the soon-to-be-sultan because he was too distracted by my beautiful cousin to notice my bow."

I want to elbow Zahir, but he's too far away for me to do it without the prince and vizier noticing. Surprise flashes across Prince Ajani's face before he schools it back to his passive expression. The royal vizier cuts in, saving the prince from having to say anything.

"Indeed, your cousin is the talk of the night."

I cannot tell if the smooth words are intended as a compliment or an insult. I lower my lashes, as a demure young Ari woman should, and remain silent. The effort kills me inside.

"My niece is worth talking about," Erol says.

"Of course," Vizier Nassor replies.

We wait. The three of us cannot leave without permission from Prince Ajani, who is looking between Erol and the vizier, unsure what to say. *He's* supposed to be our next great sultan?

The silence extends. The prince shakes himself out of his reverie and says, "Please enjoy the feast."

Many eyes are on the three of us as we weave between tables. Several people lower their voices as we pass, and some stop talking all together. By the time we reach our table, I'm grateful for Lady Asfour's familiar smile.

"Well, that's one way to get everyone's attention, my dear," she says with a laugh.

"I'm not even sure what happened," I mutter. The Ari at the next table are trying to eavesdrop.

"Catch the attention of the prince, and you catch the attention of the Aristocracy."

I force a smile, hiding the panic threatening to overwhelm me. If only they knew why I had his attention.

If he questions me, my cover might be blown before the end of the night.

**If you think the allure of the Harem Room
is in the entertainment, you're mistaken.
The weak-minded seek out the pleasures
of the Harem Room; the power players
seek out the opportunities to shift power in
their favor.**
-Advice from Jelani Cadmar to the newest
members of Logonkelie-

24

Surprisingly, I'm enjoying the feast. Between Lady Asfour and Zahir, my nerves have vanished like the wine from Zahir's glass.

"—and Tei had no idea what to do, so he just had to marry me," Lady Asfour finishes, giggling even more. Tei Asfour smiles indulgently at his wife and takes her hand. My heart melts.

"Well, no woman knows what to do with me," Zahir begins.

"I don't doubt that, Zaharian," Lady Asfour says, gesturing with her wine glass. "You have rascal written all over you."

"Really? Where?" Zahir asks, looking down at his body in shock.

"Don't worry about it, Zahir—Zaharian," I say. "Even if you saw it, you wouldn't be able to read it anyway."

Everyone, including Zahir, laughs.

"To rascals," Zahir says, raising his wine in a toast. The clink of glasses chimes from our table. I take a small sip to avoid being rude; the sweet wine goes down smoothly, inviting me to sip more. As I take another small sip, the tingling feeling of being watched raises the hairs on my neck. I lower the glass, searching for the source.

"If you want to know who is staring at you," Farah whispers in my ear, "you'll have to look at the head table."

I resist the urge to turn. Instead, I lean into Farah and ask, "Who?"

"The same young man who has been staring at you all night."

Prince Ajani.

Nerves flutter in my stomach. I lower my eyes to hide my nerves. What is he thinking?

A servant bumps my shoulder in order to set down fresh drinks, startling me.

"My apologies, Lady Acharya. I thought you would like fresh wine," Sala says. As she pours wine into my already-full glass, she whispers, "Flirt with him."

Sala saunters around the table, filling the glasses of my dining companions. Zahir snorts, and I look at him. His jaw is clenched, but he doesn't speak. When Sala fills Tei Asfour's wine glass, she winks at me from across the table then moves into line with the other servants ringing the outer wall of the room.

A second servant sets down the next course of the meal: slow-roasted lamb in a red peanut sauce. I focus on daintily slicing the lamb—my manners can't give me away—and think about Sala's instructions. Flirt with the prince? From here?

"Just look at him over your shoulder," Zahir whispers in my ear. His breath is warm on my cheek. When I look at him, his expression is closed off; he won't meet my eyes.

Zahir turns to Tei and asks, "So papaji tells me you have a passion for plants. How do you keep them from shriveling up in the sun?"

Zahir is distracting the rest of the table for me. I take a deep breath and let it out as I finish my bite of lamb. I run my tongue over my teeth, checking for food, before turning slightly. I keep my eyes lowered, using Sala's kohl liner as a shield against the room until the last second. Then I lift my eyes and meet the prince's stare. His eyes widen as our eyes lock together. I dip my shoulder, allowing my pallu to slip down my shoulder. His eyes follow the fabric and flick back up to my eyes, drinking in my face. I smile shyly at our future sultan and turn away from his pressing stare.

"Well played, Lailani," Farah whispers to me.

"I haven't the slightest idea what you mean, Farah," I say.

Farah laughs, and I join in to cover the racing of my own heart. Maybe if I entice the prince, he won't investigate my identity too closely.

Two hours later, I push honeyed fruit around my plate, trying to hide the fact that I have no room for the overly sweet dessert. The talk at our table slows as our bellies grow full. Servants wander around the room, refilling drinks and offering mukhwas. When a servant offers the mix of seeds to me, I decline, unable to fathom another bite of anything.

"Is there always this much food?" I ask Farah.

She smiles and leans back into her cushion to discreetly allow her belly some room to stretch. "This many courses? Not all the time. Food this rich? Always. The kitchens have outdone themselves tonight, having all of the prince's favorites in one feast."

I groan but resist imitating Farah's pose. A chime sounds across the room, the reverberations echoing in the arched ceiling. The royal vizier stands and says, "The prince invites you to join him in the Harem Room for entertainment."

The prince descends from the high table surrounded by the sea of Ari. Once his sherwani disappears, whispers break out in the hall. Erol and Zahir flank me on either side, so I weave my arms with both of theirs. I love having Erol and Zahir as human shields from the prying Ari eyes. As we leave the feast, heads turn in our direction, and the whispering grows louder. I draw Zahir closer to my side.

"You've made an impression on them," Zahir says to me. A blush rises to my cheeks. Zahir glances at me and then averts his eyes, as if he cannot stand the sight of my blush.

"That probably has something to do with it," Erol says, a mischievous twinkle in his dark eyes. "Or the fact that the prince is fascinated with my niece."

I don't know how to respond to that, so I say nothing.

In the main hallway, the Asfours catch up with us. "My wife does not like the Harem Room," Tei Asfour says without preamble. "We shall retire for the evening."

Disappointment shoots through me, I was counting on Farah's presence to help bolster my nerves. Farah reaches out and touches my arm, understanding in her eyes. "You'll be fine, Lailani. I'm sure that a certain young man will ensure that you are quite comfortable in the Harem Room."

She winks and allows her husband to lead her from the hall.

"You've made a powerful ally, Lailani," Erol says, a hint of pride in his voice.

"I didn't really get the chance to talk to Tei Asfour, so I'm not sure how—"

"I wasn't speaking about Tei." He grins. "Tei might be the one sitting in the Council of the Sultan, but his wife is the one who makes the decisions."

"I knew I liked her," I say, grinning.

The men congregate in front of an archway with a shimmering red curtain blocking the view of the inner room. The design seems to be drawing appreciative nods from several of the men, but from our spot in the back of the queue, I can't see it. A few of the older women without eligible daughters say goodbye to their husbands and do not enter the room.

"What is the Harem Room?" Zahir asks, also noting the number of women who do not follow to the dark depths of the room.

"It's...well, you'll just have to see."

"Why are women leaving early? If this is where the entertainment is going to be..."

My voice trails off as the carvings around the archway become clear. Women are etched into the surface: each figure has ample curves and a tiny waist that twists provocatively, welcoming the men into the Harem Room.

"Oh."

Zahir stares at a carved woman who appears to be thrusting her breasts towards the observer. I cannot smack him like I would back in the Hathorda, so I pinch his arm. Zahir yelps, but at least he's not drooling.

We enter the Harem Room.

Fabric billows from the ceiling, creating little alcoves within the room. Nets of rope hold delicate blown glass balls suspended above each alcove. The spheres cradle blue candles, shedding a halo of blue-tinged light on the lounging cushions underneath. The councilmen have spread out in the room in small clusters. Very few women intermingle with the men, observing in silent subservience.

Erol leads us to an empty alcove, and we sit on the cushions. I move delicately to keep my saree from rumpling, curling my knees underneath myself and leaning on the cushion next to me. I might dislike Esha Shah and her ghastly mother, but I can use a few tricks from the big-nosed wench.

Servants bring out after-dinner drinks and tall, ornate hookahs. The low lights and the sweet smoke of the hookahs fill the room. A servant sets up a violet and silver hookah in front of Erol, lights a coal, and places it on top. The servant bows his way out of the alcove.

Erol takes a long drag on the mouthpiece of the hookah and blows out the smoke above him. He closes his eyes, enjoying whatever it is that men enjoy about hookah, and passes the hose to Zahir. The beat of a drum sounds in the room, and several of the councilmen whoop in response.

"What is that?" I ask Erol, but the drum drowns out my voice. The rhythm speeds up, increasing in volume and speed, reflecting the men's shouts. At the peak of the tension, a cymbal crashes and the room falls into silence. Two women appear through the curtain and pose, arms outstretched over their heads, heads back.

The infamous Harem.

The women begin their synchronized dance. They drop their heads back again, exposing their necks and swishing their long locks in the process. The drum pounds through the room, while the women lift one hip at a time, ensuring all eyes are on the simple movement before they shimmy their hips. The two Harem girls move further into the room, shimmying their hips and popping their chests the entire way. The calculated moves receive shouts of appreciation from the councilmen. The drum picks up the pace, pounding in my head as I watch the women flaunt themselves like goods for sale in the bazaar.

Dancing is popular with the women of Aveena—before I fled to the Lower City, I would dance until my heart was fit to burst from the joy of the movement. But only for the joy of dancing, not for the benefit of men.

But this was nothing like the dancing in the city.

These women were objects to be admired and coveted.

Another crash of the cymbal announces three more dancers. What little was left to the imagination when it came to their sheer pants and jeweled bra tops was answered by their swirling movements. Still in sync, the five women begin to interact with the councilmen, sashaying and swaying for specific men throughout the room. The men respond without a thought of their wives sitting next to them, reaching and grabbing whatever they could get a hold of.

My happiness with my flirty lounging position evaporates as I watch the councilmen become animals. I untuck my legs and readjust my pallu to give some semblance of coverage despite the sheer material. I mentally curse Sala for not giving me something more modest. As Zahir passes the hookah hose to Erol, I grab the pipe and inhale deeply. Sweet smoke attacks my lungs, and a cough rips through me, making my eyes water. Not the distraction I was looking for.

The music comes to an end with a final crash of cymbals. The five Harem women spread out around the room and slink into alcoves with the councilmen.

"I, uh, I need to get a drink." Zahir hurries out of our alcove.

I scoff and shake my head. Erol pats my arm. "He'll learn. They're only interested in whichever councilman is in favor. Hopefully they don't break his heart."

"He isn't thinking with his heart, just his—"

"May I join you?"

Erol and I try to stand up at the same time, almost knocking over the hookah in the process. Prince Ajani places a hand on the wobbling hookah to steady it and smiles timidly at Erol and me.

"Please sit," he says. "If you two bow then everyone will flock over here."

"Your Highness, please join us," Erol says.

Prince Ajani sits in Zahir's vacated seat. He remains upright even though the cushion tries in vain to swallow him. The overall effect is that Prince Ajani looks like he's sitting on a desert cactus instead of a cushion. The prince's nearness brings back my fluttering nerves.

"Thank you for the delicious feast, Ajaniji. I haven't had honeyed fruit that wonderful since I was a boy," Erol says.

"It was my pleasure," the prince replies.

A beat. I look down at my lap and watch the prince out of the corner of my eye.

Erol nods. "And those roast birds—what were they called again?"

Another pause.

"Quail." Although he's responding to Erol, the prince seems distracted, glancing around the room and back to Erol as if he cannot keep his attention focused in one place. Erol wears what I've come to recognize as his Ari smile—pasted on at the edges, not too overbearing, not too joyful.

"Yes, those were fantastic as well."

"The cooks outdid themselves. I am grateful for their hard work."

"If you two will excuse me for a minute," Erol says, "my old man needs kicked in."

I want to plead with Erol not to leave me, but he strolls away. Ajani glances at me, scans the room, then looks at me again. I can't tell if he's nervous or if he doesn't want to be caught staring at me like he was in the main room.

"Lady Lailani. Or is it Laila?"

"I—"

"I have to say that was quite the disguise in the bazaar. You blended in much better than I did."

He pauses, waiting expectantly for an explanation.

"It's Lailani, Your Highness, and I—" I duck my head shyly, unable to meet his earnest brown eyes. "Well, I'm embarrassed to say that I have some practice blending in at the bazaar."

"Oh?"

I lick my lips, and his gaze follows the movement. "Don't you ever need a break from all the pressure? The expectations?"

"You have no idea," he mutters darkly.

I glance at the Harem Room, but no one has realized that Prince Ajani is here. The music pulses throughout, the drum beating in time with my racing heart.

"But I do understand." I pause, then ask, "Why were you there, Your Highness?"

The silence stretches for so long that for a moment, I don't think he'll answer.

"I needed…" his voice trails off. "I'm not sure what I was hoping for in the bazaar, but all I knew was that it wasn't being here."

I freeze, surprised by his candor. He shakes his head then says with a lopsided grin, "I won't tell if you won't."

"Deal," I say, relief flooding through me at his easy acceptance of my feeble lies.

"So Lady Acharya—"

"Please, it's just Lailani." The prince's eyes widen—shit, the Ari are always formal when it comes to male female interactions. Hoping to smooth over my mistake, I add, "You seem surprised, Your Highness."

"It's just that most young women prefer that I use their title."

The words slip out before I can stop them.

"And are you very familiar with many of the young women here?" The prince's neck immediately reddens at the implication of my question. "Oh, Prince Ajani, I apolo—"

"No need to apologize, Lady Achar—I mean Lailani."

My name sticks in his mouth like honey to fruit. We sit in silence again. My hands twist in my lap, while the prince snatches the hookah hose and twirls it.

Cadmar will be pissed that I messed up the chance to capture the prince's attention. Sala will be disappointed. And then they'll kick me out of Logonkelie. And then what would become of Tanu? My stomach sinks. I have to fix it.

"You're probably wondering why I prefer to use my first name, Your Highness," I begin. I smooth my hands out on my skirt, stilling them. The prince stops playing with the hookah, waiting. "You see, this is my first time in the palace, and all of the formalities make me feel out of place."

"Really?"

"Well, yes, Your Highness. My mother always said that to know a person's first name is to know a person. I guess I'm just feeling like a stranger among strangers. That must seem silly to you—"

"No, it doesn't."

I look Prince Ajani full in the face. This close, I notice that his skin is more bronze than brown. The dark swoop of his hair, which seemed to hide his face in the Council Room, highlights his face more than anything. He also has a small dark chin beard; I can tell it's out of preference and not out of an inability to grow a full beard as the men gossip about.

"The formalities make me feel like a stranger too."

"They do?" I ask, incredulous.

He looks out at the room again, as if he is unable to look me in the eyes, as he says, "Especially since my father died. I went from being Ajani to His Highness Prince Ajani."

Is that bitterness in his voice? Carefully, I touch his hand. The contact is brief but warmth shoots through my fingers from the connection.

"I—I'm sorry for your loss, Your Highness," I say. "I know what it's like to lose someone you love."

The prince hesitates then says, "You're the first person to offer me condolences, Lailani."

192

I'm shocked. How did none of the puffed up Ari not tell the prince they're sorry for his loss? Some of my shock must have shown because the prince chuckles darkly.

"No need to look surprised. Everyone is more concerned with earning favor with the future sultan than wishing a son well wishes after losing his father. Everyone except for you, that is."

I blush and look down, unable to meet his eyes. The vulnerability that I see there makes me feel like a snake pouncing on an injured mouse.

"Sorry to be blunt, but has someone you've known died, Lailani?"

"A person doesn't have to die in order to be lost to us."

The truth escapes my lips before I can hold it in. The truth and the emotion behind it—I've tried to forget my life in the Upper City, but something about this hurting prince brings it out of me. We stare at the councilmen and Harem women, but for the first time, the silence isn't an uncomfortable one.

"I want you to call me Ajani from now on."

"Your Highness, I can't—"

"No objections. If I am to call you Lailani, then you should refer to me as Ajani. It's only fair."

"I didn't know you were so concerned with fairness."

Ajani stares for a second then bursts out laughing. I grin and secretly sigh in relief that he wasn't offended by my impertinence. After his laughter resides, he adds, "We should probably refrain from being so informal around others though."

"Can't have dear Lady Shah getting her saree in a bunch," I mutter, which brings another bout of laughter out of Ajani. I like the laughing version of Ajani—I can almost forget that he's the prince and our future sultan.

**Strength is more often found in silence
than in words.**
-Aveenan Proverb-

**Those who hold true power, speak louder
than the rest, ensuring that their voice is
the only one heard.**
-excerpt from *A Brief Political History of
Aveena*-

25

"Good evening," a cool voice says.

Both Ajani and I look up and shift further apart—I hadn't realized how we'd leaned towards each other—but the royal vizier waves lazily. "Please, don't become uncomfortable on my account."

"Vizier Nassor," Ajani says, "what a pleasant surprise. Please have a seat."

Vizier Nassor settles down on my other side. As he reaches for the abandoned hookah hose, his arm brushes against mine, sending a warning shiver through my body. Accidental or purposeful? I assess the vizier through my lashes as he inhales deeply.

The royal vizier is an impressive man. Every aspect of his appearance strategically reminds you of that fact: gaudy jewelry on each finger, making himself glitter in the dim light; expensive clothes sewn together with gold filigree; his height compacted with the feeling that he is always looking down at you. He keeps his salt and pepper hair in a top knot, adding height to his already tall stature. When he leans back on his cushion, I notice that even more rings garnish his toes. Not even the prince wears as much jewelry as the vizier.

The only jewelry that doesn't glitter in the candlelight is the black stone bracelet he wears next to the gold. The midnight stones seem to absorb the light instead of reflect it.

Although many women in the Veiled Room openly ogled the prince, I noticed that only a few were bold enough to eye the vizier. His position makes him a desirable match, but his reputation warns off potential contenders.

"Nassorji, this is Lady Lailani Acharya. Lailaniji, this is the royal vizier, Nassor Al-Sid."

I nod my head from my seated position, noting that his eyes watch every movement that I make. When he takes his eyes off me, I breathe easier. I keep my eyes lowered and do not join in their conversation.

"Ajaniji, I have been looking for you for several minutes. Some of the councilmen want to discuss an upcoming proposal to improve infrastructure. They seek your support."

The relaxed young prince disappears and is replaced by the solemn young man that stood on the dais earlier in the day.

"Indeed. What is their proposal?"

"I will let them explain it to you, Your Highness. They are sitting over there by the woman in the orange attire."

Vizier Nassor gestures across the room. The Harem woman in question notices that everyone in our alcove is now looking in her direction and pushes her breasts out further—as if they needed the extra umph. The councilman sitting nearest the woman is practically drooling over himself.

I scoff but quickly turn it into a cough so that neither of the men sitting next to me notice.

Ajani looks reluctant to leave my side. "Will you be okay on your own, Lady Acharya?"

Before I can answer, Vizier Nassor answers for me. "I'll take care of the lovely Lady Acharya, Ajaniji. I haven't had the pleasure to speak to her myself yet, though I've heard plenty about her attributes from the rest of the Aristocracy."

Although the words themselves aren't threatening, the hairs on my arms stand up, warning me against the vizier. I don't know if it's the rumors about the vizier or what he actually says that puts me on edge, but I know I don't want to be left alone with him. However, there is no way that I can gracefully find a way out of the situation. Ajani, placated by the vizier's answer, smiles shyly at me and then leaves the alcove. The vizier inhales the hookah and blows out the smoke in small ringlets, staring at me. I watch Ajani walk away and try to remain relaxed with the vizier's closeness and staring.

"You've certainly caught the attention of many, Lady Acharya."

I say nothing, as expected.

"It's understandable, of course. New young women usually draw attention in the palace, especially young women with such—" he pauses as he eyes the length of my body before saying "virtues."

I remain silent. The vizier sucks in more smoke and breathes it out of his nose. He lowers his eyes from my face to my chest, unashamedly staring at the cleavage that Sala ensured was visible in my attire. My indifference slips, and I try to hide myself from his gaze. The vizier laughs and looks at my face, taking in the new blush in my cheeks.

Damn blush.

"I apologize for being so bold," the vizier says, scooting closer to me in the alcove.

I struggle with myself, wanting to outright refuse his apology but knowing that Ari courtesy dictated otherwise. Vizier Nassor watches me closely, his amusement growing in the silence.

"There is nothing to forgive, Nassorji," I finally reply.

"Good girl. See? That wasn't so hard."

My body is on high alert, alarm bells ringing in my head to flee. Instead, I freeze as Vizier Nassor moves his leg to touch mine under the table, assessing my reaction.

"I find myself as taken with your beauty as the other councilmen. You are a sight to behold, Lady Acharya."

I stare at a burn mark on the cushion near me, refusing the intimacy of looking the vizier in the eyes. Where in the dunes did Zahir and Erol go?

"Look at me, Lady Acharya."

How would I respond to that? Then something snaps inside of me. *I will not let this man cower me. I am stronger than that.*

I meet his cold, green eyes, and jolt at their color—a djinn color—but I can't get distracted. Instead, I glare at the vizier, trying to relay that I do not appreciate his nearness. I am not some Ari to be toyed with.

"Ah, and that's what drew my attention. Your extraordinary eyes."

"Your attention?" I ask savagely. Forget politeness. It's not like the vizier has any.

"Ah, she speaks," he says, patronizing me like I'm incapable of having a conversation. "Yes, my attention, Lady Acharya. I am a most desirable match for a young woman such as yourself. Surely, you're aware of this?"

I open and close my mouth, forming answers and then swallowing them away. Is the vizier *flirting* with me?

He lowers his voice, making it more oily and smooth, as he says, "But you are Erol's niece. I hope you haven't been listening to the rumors. Gossip is not becoming of a woman such as yourself."

The vizier inhales the hookah, closing his eyes as if in ecstasy, then carefully blows rings into my face. I think he's expecting me to applaud him for blowing smoke in my face, but I just stare at him and pray that Erol or Zahir returns soon. Or even the prince. At this point one of the councilmen wouldn't be a bad option either...

"You are lucky, Lailani," he said. His lack of formality raises my hackles.

"How so?"

"You have it easier than any of us. You may coast through life, allowing men to take care of the world for you. I, on the other hand, will have to work twice as hard to maintain a semblance of civility in our society for all of us. I will continue to strain myself so that you, and other women, do not have to."

Anger bubbles beneath my skin. I put my hands in my lap, forcing them to remain relaxed and unclenched, and look down at the burn mark again. Let him think I'm demure and shy as he expects.

"You have no idea how deplorable those in the Lower City truly are, Lailani. I have a few acquaintances in the

Lower City who I have the displeasure of necessitating meetings with. Their women practically beg for me to bed them. They hope that I will give them a better life. As if *I* would take a Lower City whore into my bed. Preposterous. Especially when surrounded by well-bred beauties such as yourself in the palace."

I lower my head, my fury blazing. Is this supposed to be flirting? If I could, I would strangle the vizier. I know men and women in the Lower City who are worth more than this man and his pompous ideals.

The vizier moves closer to me—his hot breath ruffles the fabric of my pallu and his perfume overwhelms my nose, choking me with the scent of sickly-sweet oranges. Although we are not hidden in the alcove, he reaches out and lifts my chin, forcing me to meet his eyes. An icy blast streams from his touch, spreading like an icy fire down my limbs. I try to shift away but my body won't obey me. Panic rises and I glance into his smirking face.

Was he causing this? But how?

"You are quite the beauty, aren't you?" he says, turning my head this way and that, like he was surveying a prized mare at the bazaar. My head swivels under his guidance, but when I struggle to pull back, it won't move.

I allow him—what choice do I have?—and let my eyes say what my lips cannot.

"But I have angered you, my beautiful Lailani. Your stunning blue eyes give you away." He leans even closer and whispers in my ear, "What did I say to anger you, Lailani? Did my crude description of the Lower City scum offend your delicate feminine dispositions?"

Remain silent, breathe normally.

A smile appears on his long face—or rather a sneer. "Or were you jealous of the attention I received from the Lower City whores? I promise you, beautiful Lailani, if you ever wanted to come to my bed, I would treat you with the utmost respect."

Vizier Nassor runs the back of his hand on my cheek, leaving an icy chill in his wake. When his hand drops, I flinch away from his touch and lower my eyes. I hope he mistakes it for shyness. And not that I'm plotting how to kill him and make it look like an accident.

"Cousin, father wants a word with you. Vizier Nassor, will you please excuse us?"

Zahir appears at the vizier's elbow, his face the perfect Ari mask. Vizier Nassor winks at me. Slowly, he rubs my shoulder, his hand sliding under my pallu and back, the sharp iciness biting briefly into my shoulder then receding.

"Until next time, Lady Acharya."

The vizier smirks, his green eyes narrowed in delight, before he saunters across the room. I cringe as his hand snakes around one dancer's hip, pulling her along with him. I shiver, unable to shake the oily memory of the vizier's proximity.

Of my helplessness.

Zahir waits until Vizier Nassor is settled before he grabs my elbow and pulls me from the alcove. His grip on my arm is tight, and I focus on the slight pain, allowing it to distract me from what just happened. Zahir pulls me into one of the side rooms, away from prying Ari eyes. My hands tremble. I clench them as tight as I can, both arms stiffly by my side.

"Laila," Zahir speaks softly. "What happened?"

I can't look at Zahir. I can't acknowledge the concern. Instead, I look at the ceiling, blinking back hot tears. I don't know if I'm more shaken or angry, but either way I want to cry, to find some sort of release from the conversation with the royal vizier.

And the memories he stirred, burning, rancid in the back of my throat.

Zahir mutters words to me, trying to comfort me, but I don't hear him. My mind is in a different time, a different place, a different conversation. Words swirl around me—useless, privileged, submissive—each blurring into the next in a never-ending list of things that I'm supposed to be. And here I am, trying to blink back my tears instead of wiping them away for fear of messing up Sala's make up.

I have to remain composed.

I have to lock away my feelings.

I have to play my part.

If the vizier has shown me one thing tonight, it's that Cadmar and I are united on one aspect: Vizier Nassor must go.

**The Suraksha maintain the peace,
protecting the weak and upholding the
laws with integrity.**
-from The Ordinances of Aveena-

26

The dark figure paces, while I watch its progress. One end of the room, turn on its heel, and to the other side. Back and forth. A ticking metronome. Or maybe the predatory prowl of a tiger.

The figure—a man if I were to guess—seems unaware of my presence as he paces. I stretch, extending my limbs like a sleepy cat, and snuggle into the cushion. Might as well be comfortable. The darkness in the far corner of the room obscures his face.

My stretch causes the figure to pause.

He snaps his fingers.

The cushion vanishes from beneath me. I turn to see where my cushion went but am pulled short by a sharp pain. My wrists and ankles are bound with rope, forcing me to kneel.

I struggle against the bonds.

The ropes cut into my skin as I struggle. Blood drips off my wrists and stains my white saree.

I scream, but a gag materializes, stopping my scream from forming. Eyes are on me.

I look up. The figure watches me fight. Only his cold green eyes are visible, narrowed into slits in the darkness. A chill runs across my shoulders and down my arms.

I have to get out of here.

I thrash against the bonds. I search for a knife, but my lack of clothing immediately distracts me—garish yellow pants are slung low over my hips, and the bedazzled top barely hides my breasts let alone a knife.

Shit. Shit. Shit.

The more I struggle the tighter the ropes become.

The figure moves towards me—not the agitated pace from earlier, but rather a stately walk across the room. Panic fills my body.

The man nudges the rope around my ankle, and I scream in pain. He leans forward, grabs hold of my face and forces me to look into his slitted eyes. Iciness spreads from his hand. He's so close that his twisted, oiled beard nearly touches my face.

"Hello, Laila," the royal vizier says.

***

Hands are on my shoulders. Or ropes tying me down. I fight the bonds holding me and try to jump up from the bed to search for a weapon. Fabric snags around my legs, and I topple onto the floor in a tangle of sweaty white saree and sheets.

His touch, the dream, it felt real. The scent of oranges permeates my senses, disorienting me further. It was a dream. Only a dream.

But his djinn-eyes…

No, my father was wrong. Magic doesn't exist in Aveena. Djinn-eyes are an old superstition like Sala said. I had to have imagined the icy feeling from his touch. It was impossible.

I rub my wrist, the ghost ache of the ropes in the dream irritating my skin. My body aches, the bone-tired ache of exhaustion.

I never fall back asleep.

I can't bring myself to face the others. Zahir, Erol, Sala, even Cadmar… I know I can't give them the answers they deserve. Shame and fear coil beneath my skin—like the vizier's oiliness had left an invisible residue. No amount of washing could wipe away the slime of his words or the feel of his touch.

I change into the first kurti I find and then walk to the window. The delicate morning light barely infiltrates the curtains. I shove the fabric aside and stand on the window ledge. I run my fingers over the bars, realizing that the gaps between them are large—large enough for me to slip through. Like everything else in the palace, the bars are for show.

Gingerly, I lower myself as far as I can go and then drop to the ground in a crouch, escaping the only way I know how.

A cool breeze whips through my hair as I walk through the palace grounds. Trees line the walkways around glistening pools with fat shining fish just beneath the surface. Soon the trees block out the early morning sunlight, bowing over the narrowing walkway like servants before the sultan. Underbrush appears between the trees, and the meticulous order seen everywhere else in the palace shrinks. I allow my feet to carry me as I gape at the natural splendor. This must be the sultan's gardens.

I love it.

I find a secluded bench a short distance off the path. It's hidden away from prying eyes and deceiving hearts. I breathe slowly and leisurely. With my eyes closed it feels as if it's just me and the birds. After the nagging of the Council of the Sultan, the soft, unobtrusive chirps of the birds soothe my soul. Even the odd squawking of a bird somewhere behind me does not disturb my peace.

Who knew that Aveena held a place like this?

The sweet scent of mangoes hits my nose, and I glance behind me. Stumpy little mango trees grow in abundance behind my bench, their branches hanging low with fruit. The sight reminds me of the mango trees of my childhood: always reaching for the best ones near the top, begging Nana to let us eat another, juice dripping down my face.

I sigh and turn back to the path in front of me. A crowned gray lizard patters his way down the garden path. Every few paces, he stops, lowers himself to the ground, then lies in wait, before rolling back up onto his feet and moving on. He seems so focused on his path, knowing exactly where he's going, unlike me.

I close my eyes again and inhale the mango-sweet breeze, willing the rest of the world away.

Tanu would love this.

The sweet scent of mangoes transforms into the scent of overripe oranges. A cold hand caresses my face, reaching for my—

My peaceful bubble bursts with heartache. I open my eyes, but the colors look duller, less vibrant. Tanu could never come here. Not into this pit of snakes. Being a woman in Aveena is hard; being a woman in the palace is torture. I would not let that happen to her...

The scuff of soft footsteps on the worn path warn me of another's approach. I sit straighter in case it's one of the Ari coming out for an early morning stroll through the gardens, listening closely.

The footsteps stop. I feign nonchalance despite my pounding heart, waiting.

"What are you thinking about?"

Sala.

She sits casually on a rock a few paces away looking at me with knowing eyes. A sigh of relief slips out, but I don't let my guard down. What is she doing here anyway?

"Nothing really," I say, trying to cover my surprise. "How long have you been there?"

"I followed you out the window."

I splutter. "You—what?"

"Followed you out the window, yes."

I can't tell if she's amused or annoyed.

"Why?"

She bobbles her head side to side and doesn't speak.

"Well, that's not an answer," I huff, which only makes Sala laugh.

"Your point?"

I sigh and look out at the trees ahead of me before turning back to Sala. No point in pretending she's not here. Not like I could ignore her if I wanted to; Sala is the kind of woman who makes herself known.

"Come and sit with me."

"You sure you can handle that?" she asks with mock concern.

I shake my head and pat the bench. Sala makes her way through the foliage, careful to avoid stepping on the undergrowth. No wonder I didn't notice her trailing me—not even the birds are disturbed by Sala's movements. She must have made some noise to clue me in.

"You never answered my question," I say, shaking my head. "Why did you follow me?"

"And you never answered my question."

"What question?"

"What were you thinking about?"

I hesitate. Sala will see through any lie. I decide on the truth—or at least part of it anyway. "This place is so beautiful, and yet I would not bring anyone here to see it."

Sala nods and turns her eyes to the small birds in front of us. We sit in silence, but it's comfortable. Sala's unusual lack of response relaxes my shoulders and some of my tension evaporates. After a moment I ask, "Why did you follow me?"

"You looked like you needed a friend," she says, pulling her legs onto the bench and crossing them. One of the birds flutters its wings but doesn't fly away.

"A friend?"

She speaks slowly as if frightened I might run off. "Yes, binti, a friend."

"Binti?" I ask, dazed.

"It means 'sister' in the old language."

I look at Sala, studying her profile. This quieter version of Sala takes me off guard. Sala turns and cocks her head to the side, her eyes flicking over my disheveled appearance: the purple bruising under my eyes, the knots in the stupidly long hair she gave me, and the rumpled kurti I threw on.

"Tell me what happened last night."

Not a question.

I look away quickly, revealing my discomfort. Sala kneels directly in front of me so I'm forced to look at her. Just like with Zahir, I can't meet Sala's eyes. But unlike Zahir, Sala won't take no for an answer. She sticks her face inches from mine and stares into my eyes. I flinch away from her closeness.

"Laila," she says softly, almost pityingly. "Tell me what happened."

"It was a dream," I lie.

Sala stands up.

"We both know that isn't true," Sala says. There is no anger in her voice. She walks a few paces away, giving me the space that I desperately wanted a few seconds ago, then comes back and sinks onto the bench, closing her eyes briefly, then sighing. "Let me tell you a story."

"We really should—" I begin but Sala raises a hand to stop me. The sunlight filters through the branches overhead, casting shadows on her face and masking her expression. I wait for her to speak, watching her out of the corner of my eye, tension knotting my shoulders in the silence before she begins.

"I grew up in the eastern district of the Lower City. My parents were lucky enough to afford a storefront. They made ceramic pots and bowls. I didn't have any brothers or sisters, but I was never lonely either. My parents made sure that I knew I was loved and kept me involved in all they did. My first memory of Krish had to be when I was six or seven. My parents hired this scrawny boy to sweep the shop and to clean up at the end of the day. And just like that Krish was in my life."

Sala stops talking for a moment. My gut clenches, dreading the rest. "They didn't need to hire anyone, but my parents always said that we should help out those who had less than us. At the time I didn't understand because it seemed like we didn't have anything ourselves. Krish and I became inseparable, and when we got older—well, you know how things go."

I did. The passion and butterflies. The hesitancy in the first kiss. The lack of hesitancy in every kiss after. I shake my head to clear the memories, but Sala doesn't notice as she stares out at the trees.

"Krish was my everything. We spent every waking moment together. My parents already loved him like a son-in-law. They planned on passing down the shop to the two of us so that we would be able to be happy. But our bliss made us blind."

A grimace crossed Sala's face, the pain of her memory resurfacing. I can't look away.

"The Suraksha came to Krish's house one morning. They said that his father had failed to pay the new tax for three months in a row. Now they were taking their own tax. They tried to drag Krish's father into the bazaar, but Krish fought them off. He was always brave like that. His father was old and frail, he argued. They could hurt him.

The Suraksha dragged Krish to the stocks in the bazaar instead. They beat him for his insubordination, for stepping out of his place. They went too far. Afterwards, they told Krish's father that maybe by getting rid of his son he would be able to afford the new tax."

Sala stops, her hands clenched in her lap. My heart thrums in my chest, breaking for Sala and Krish. The future they dreamed of but could never have.

"After Krish's death, I was devastated. But I also wanted revenge. And not on those who killed Krish, but revenge on those who gave the orders. I kept hearing about Jelani Cadmar and his petitions to stop the use of examples. I left the Lower City behind and found Cadmar."

Sala's eyes meet mine, and I'm taken aback by the ferocity behind them. She holds my gaze, refusing to release me from her grip.

"You have to choose, Laila." My heart jumps into my throat. "I need to know if I can trust you to have my back or not."

Her voice is serene, confident. I close my eyes tightly. She trusts me even though she doesn't know me. Guilt seeps in. How much she misses Krish, the anger at the Suraksha. I squirm, wondering if she regrets telling me.

Are you really worried that she regrets telling you? Or are you more worried that you don't deserve that show of trust? A small voice asks.

I swallow, my throat dry, then stare at the dirt beneath my sandals.

And then the words spill out of me: Prince Ajani, the royal vizier, the women in the Veiled Room. Sala does not interrupt me as I pour out all of my emotions, unable to stop. I refrain from telling her about meeting the prince in the bazaar and the iciness of the vizier's touch. The former was the prince's secret to keep, and the latter, well, I wasn't going to bother her with figments of my imagination.

As I tell her about the vizier, I begin to heal. It's like sucking the poison out of a snake bite. I still feel slimy, confused, and shaken, but somehow, it's less so than when I woke up this morning.

When I finish, Sala takes my hand in hers but does not say anything. And silently I thank her for it.

Councilman Ba,
Please share the notes you've procured
from the fields regarding our production
numbers at our next council meeting.
Although I've tried to relay our concerns
to Sultan Gautam, he remains stubbornly
obtuse to the problems at hand. Perhaps
your notes will effectively persuade the
council to act where my words have failed.
-Vizier Nassor Al-Sid-

27

"We should head back, binti."

I nod. The sun, which has started to warm the palace gardens, is the only indication of time passing. I squint through the trees, but the thick canopy prevents me from seeing how high the sun has risen.

"You don't mind going back through the main door, do you, my lady?" Sala sweeps me a grand bow and gestures towards the palace. "I just don't know how happy your uncle will be with this humble servant if we crawl through the window."

"Humble servant, my ass," I mutter, rolling my eyes.

Sala rises from her bow and allows me to take the lead, remaining a step behind me. As we pass the stream that feeds into the canal, Sala whispers to me, "Was that an eyeroll, my lady? I can still kick your ass behind closed doors, you know."

I cringe and pick up the pace, while Sala chuckles.

I didn't realize how far I'd walked this morning. The vastness of the palace could easily house the entire southern Lower City. Luckily, we avoid any palace inhabitants, utilizing the foliage to hide our presence. Inside the palace, our footsteps pad softly on the marble floors. None of the Ari are awake yet, leaving the hallways deserted. I sigh in relief as we round the corner to Erol's suite without passing a single soul—I have enough attention on me without additional palace gossip.

At Erol's door, Sala turns to me and grips my shoulders, waiting until I meet her fierce eyes before she speaks.

"You are strong enough, binti."

My eyes fill with tears, but I stare at the ceiling until I feel the wateriness disappear. Without further explanation, Sala saunters into the room.

I take a deep breath and follow her inside.

"Where in the dunes have you been?"

Zahir rushes over and snaps the door closed. Before I can answer, Zahir crushes me in a big hug. Despite my surprise, I close my eyes and rest my cheek on his chest. The flutter of his heartbeat is loud in my ear, and when I inhale, he smells spicy, a mixture of cardamom and man.

"Zahir, I—"

"Don't scare me like that again."

Zahir lets go and holds me at arms' length to study my face. The warmth I felt in his arms disappears. I can't analyze Zahir's worry—or my reaction—because Sala snatches my arm back and hooks it with her own. As she leads me across the room, she whispers in my ear, "Don't forget your aliases."

Sala pulls me down onto one of the larger cushions with her, and I struggle to adjust myself so that I'm not falling into her. Erol, his eyes tired and his hair a mess around his head, sits across from us. I suppress a giggle at Erol's disgruntled appearance; clearly, he does not take well to early mornings. Someone knocks on the door, and Zahir opens it for Cadmar and Nimra. Today she's wearing the plain kurti of a maid, a hint of salt and pepper hair peeking out from the edge of her veil.

Cadmar continues speaking to her as they enter the room. "I don't trust his intentions, Nimra."

"You read too much into things, Cadmarji," she says. Her voice is soft and scratchy, barely above a whisper.

"Who don't you trust?" Zahir asks, reaching for the tray of fruit and snagging a slice of starfruit.

Cadmar sits erect on his seat, as if he is incapable of allowing himself to relax into its folds. "Nassor, of course. We need to keep an eye on him," he says more to himself than to any of us. Then he glares at me, the force of it causing me to lean back in my cushion. "You cannot go out on your own."

"I—"

"I went with her," Sala says. Everyone's attention turns to Sala, but she focuses on meeting Cadmar's eyes in a silent challenge. Cadmar breaks eye contact and looks back at me.

"Well, you still should have alerted someone where you were going. The palace is no place for you to go wandering around."

How did he find out? I can't tell if Cadmar is concerned for me or for Logonkelie. I don't ask. Instead, I arrange my kurti on my lap and wait until Cadmar's gaze moves elsewhere.

"We need to discuss last night. Erol, reports from the council?"

Erol rubs his face then sits straighter in his chair. "Most are shocked by the news that the royal vizier is acting sultan. That boy might be sitting in the sultan's throne, but Al-Sid has final say on everything. By the expressions of those close to Nassor, it was not a shock for all."

"Agreed," Cadmar says. His clenched fist is the only indication of Cadmar's anger.

"Was there a transition period when Sultan Gautam came to power?" I ask.

Cadmar and Erol exchange looks. "I'm not sure," Cadmar says slowly. "I was only a boy when Gautam became sultan."

The image of Cadmar as a child pops unbidden into my mind—serious eyes, short cut hair, grim smile, chubby toddler legs. I resist smiling and look at Erol.

"I wasn't in Aveena during the transition. Military training." Erol pauses. "To be frank, I'm not sure if any of the council would remember the transition to Gautam. He did have a long reign. However, many are not bothered by the vizier's declaration. The Aristocracy know what to expect from Nassor, even if they do not like it. They do not know what to expect from Prince Ajani, which makes them nervous."

"He seems like a spineless boy," Zahir interjects. "He never spoke for himself during the council meeting."

I look down, picking at a loose thread, my throat tight.

Disgust laces Zahir's voice as he continues, "He's got to man up if he has a chance of winning over the council. Even I can see that."

"He's not that much younger than you, boy," Erol says. "You've got to keep your temper in check if you are to survive here."

"But he's not wrong," Sala says, leaning forward. "Even the servants who've known Ajani since he was a boy are unsure about him as sultan right now."

"Report, Sala," Cadmar says.

"A please is always appreciated, Cadmarji," Sala says, batting her eyelashes at Cadmar.

"Fine, please report and stop wasting time, Sala," he barks. Cadmar's anger seems to be simmering much closer to the surface this morning, but Sala is undeterred.

Sala sits up and crosses her legs. The movement causes me to fall into her as the cushion shifts. "In the servants' rooms, many gossip about how Ajani is still mourning his father."

"His father just died," I say, unable to keep my silence any longer.

"But he's got a city to run," Sala says, not unkindly, but I still bristle at the implication. "He's known what being sultan asks of him since he was a boy. He knows he has to be strong, despite what he'd prefer to do."

Sala is right, but then I think of the young man I spoke with. The lost look in his dark brown eyes, the premature frown lines in his forehead. And the barely concealed pain. I can't help but wish that he had time to heal, to be human, before he had to be His Highness, the Sultan.

"The servants are scared of the royal vizier," Nim says, her quiet voice cutting through my thoughts.

"Scared?" Cadmar asks.

"They know his heart. They know his greed," Nim's simple statement fills the room with tension. Talking about the vizier raises the hairs on the nape of my neck. I don't want to talk about his heart or his greed; I know what they truly are.

"Lailani did well last night," Erol says, breaking the silence. I blush at Erol's compliment. "She's made a powerful ally in Lady Asfour."

Cadmar smirks, and I know that the irony does not escape him.

"And she's caught the attention of a certain prince," Sala says, nudging me with her shoulder. I feel the blush spread across my cheeks and neck. Cadmar's eyes narrow.

"He couldn't take his eyes off of her last night," Erol adds. "Which also means that most of the Aristocracy could not take their eyes off Lailani either."

Cadmar stands abruptly, tension radiating off of him as he paces away, pulling at his beard. When he turns back to us, he glares at me, the anger palpable from across the room. I freeze, holding his gaze.

Cadmar points an accusing finger at me. "You *will not* fuck up this opportunity for me—for Logonkelie."

"What?" I ask, reeling back from the vehemence in his tone. The rest of the room is shocked into silence.

"You. Will. Not. Fuck. This. Up." As he spits out each word, he stalks closer. In my periphery, Zahir shifts to stand, but Erol stops him.

I tilt my chin up in a challenge. "I have done nothing wrong."

"Drawing the attention of the prince? Really?" Cadmar scoffs.

"You told me to flirt, to charm them," I say calmly.

"The Aristocracy, yes, not the future sultan!"

Sala starts. "Cadmarji, this could work to our advantage—"

"You know better," Cadmar snaps at Sala. She opens her mouth to argue on my behalf, but I place a hand on her arm to stop her. It won't help. Cadmar gestures wildly towards the rest of the palace. "You need to stay under the radar. I thought you of all people would understand self-preservation."

"I am doing as you asked," I repeat in the same calm tone, masking my true feelings.

"A day in and we're already in the dunes…" Cadmar mutters to himself. He runs his hand over his face then his expression hardens. "I know you're used to being the center of attention as the Nightshade, but this is bigger than you, than all of us."

I open and close my mouth, astounded that he thinks I would want to be in the limelight. That I tried to draw the prince's attention. *He* came to me in the Harem Room, sought me out.

"Cadmarji, we can use this," Sala says. "If she has the prince's ear—"

"We don't need anyone looking too much into her background, especially the vizier. Too many inquisitive eyes and her alias crumbles, taking Logonkelie with it. What were you thinking, talking to the vizier one-on-one, too?"

He speaks to Sala over my head, like I'm not even there. Guilt swirls in the pit of my stomach, but I swallow it back. I did what I thought he had asked. If anyone is to blame, it's Cadmar for his lack of direction before shoving us into the palace. He should have specified. And I definitely didn't want to have that conversation with the vizier.

"From now on, for the love of Wind Mother, lie low." I nod, not trusting myself to speak. Some of the anger deflates out of Cadmar, and he adds, "Focus on building connections with the lesser Ari, those that the power players aren't paying as much attention to."

"Why?" Zahir asks. I shoot him a grateful look behind Cadmar's back.

"We need to use our influence to persuade the council to open continuous trade with the Tribes."

"The Tribes?" Zahir asks. My mind spins with the abrupt change in direction.

Cadmar nods. "Aveena has grown past her limits. Soon we will no longer be able to sustain ourselves. We need to get ahead of it."

"And building connections with the lesser Ari will do that?" Zahir doesn't hide the skepticism in his voice.

"Yes," Cadmar says simply. Zahir opens his mouth to argue again, but Cadmar turns his attention away from him, clearly moving on from the questioning. "In addition, we need to work on discrediting the royal vizier. Nimra, ensure that the servants continue to fear the royal vizier. We might not be able to do anything about how the Aristocracy view Nassor at this point, but if we can control public perception, it's a start."

Nim nods and stands to leave. "Mistress expects us to report soon. I must leave."

"Make sure I know any changes that you hear of, Nimra. Through the usual means, if possible. If we gather too often that could draw attention."

"Yes, Cadmarji."

Nim bows and leaves the room.

"Zaharian, Erol, I expect you to continue to make contacts throughout the Aristocracy. Erol, I know you are well-established, but Zaharian, you need to meet and mingle with the younger men throughout the Ari. They are the wild cards in the Council of the Sultan and might be swayed one way or another despite their fathers' opinions."

"When you say mingle, you mean—"

"Get to know them. Drink with them. Tell your stories. Talk about women with them. Common male pastimes."

"Okay." Zahir draws out the word into a question.

"Is that a problem, Zaharian?" Cadmar asks. When Zahir opens his mouth, Cadmar pushes on, "If so, I'm sure I can come up with a reasonable enough excuse to get you out of the palace. Perhaps you'd prefer to return to the fields?"

Zahir snaps his mouth shut and shakes his head once. His jaw is clenched tight, but Cadmar doesn't care as he turns away.

"Sala."

"Yes, Cadmarji."

"Help Lailani navigate the women of the Veiled Room and her assignment to stay under the radar. Run interference with the other women if necessary."

"So, babysitting?" Sala asks, disappointed.

"We need to establish her place, and you're the only one I trust to do so and keep Lailani in check."

"Keep me in check?" I ask.

Cadmar turns to me, narrowing his eyes. "Yes, keep you in check. You need to remain focused, which means no more morning wanderings. With or without Sala. And no more flirting with men high above your status. Your reputation must be spotless among the Aristocracy."

I keep my face a mask to hide my annoyance and embarrassment. Cadmar is ordering Sala to be my handler, to let me out of my cage only when he sees it to be permissible. I can feel the leash tightening around my neck as he speaks.

"Your job at this point, Lailani, is to make connections with the women and lesser Ari and remain a beautiful flower in the court."

I hate myself for accepting Cadmar's orders. I didn't leave the Upper City to become a puppet once again. I didn't become the Nightshade so that I was only valued for my beauty and marriageability.

And yet here I am.

I inhale slowly, trying to shake some of the frustration. I need to do this for Tanu. I have to get her to Bhavin no matter the cost. No matter how far I want to run away from the palace and Logonkelie. I need to buy time.

"That will be all," Cadmar says to the group. "Be safe."

I jump up, intent on escaping to my room before Cadmar can give me any more demeaning tasks, but Sala puts a hand out.

"Not so fast. Training you two," she says, pointing to Zahir and me. I groan as Zahir protests, but I'm too exhausted to argue.

My muscles ache as Sala pushes us through more and more complex yoga sequences, but at least the movement distracts me from my dour thoughts.

When caring for your garden, you must protect your plants against the natural elements of Aveena that could damage them. Frequently water and, if necessary, shade them from the sun's rays. Plant life flourishes only with absolute care and the blessings of Wind Mother—labor and magic at its best.
-excerpt from *The Handbook of Aveenan Plants* loaned to Sultana Chhavi from Farah Asfour-

28

The Sultana

The flowers in the garden flourish in a brilliance of colors. Chhavi wanders through the blooms, the sun beating down on her dark, unbound hair, unbothered by protocol. She stoops over a low-hanging vine, pruning the dead leaves from the plant, soothed by the fragrance of the lavender flowers. After days of being isolated in their Upper City residence, Chhavi finally understood Farah's fascination with plant life. The work provided the distraction she needed.

"Sultana Chhaviji," Amara says tentatively behind her, "perhaps you should rest in the shade for a moment."

Chhavi glances at the noon sun, before acquiescing to her maidservant's request. Amara and the other servants set out fruit and water for the sultana. She thanks them before sitting.

A part of her longs to invite them to join in her meal, but she knows her request will make them uncomfortable. Just as her solitary place setting makes her uncomfortable, reminding her of why she is here.

Would her loneliness ever ease? It seemed to grow with each passing day, not disappear.

And with her growing loneliness, the sultana was also experiencing growing doubt. How could her husband, who was in perfect health, pass so suddenly? How could her husband suffer from heart attacks when his father and his father before that died of natural causes?

It was too smooth. And too convenient. But for whom?

The sultana sets down her uneaten fruit, staring at the plant life around her.

"Would you prefer something else to eat, Chhaviji?" Amara asks.

"No, Amara, the fruit is fine." The sultana pauses for a second before continuing, "But I do think that I would like to go out today. Could you ready my guard?"

"Ready your guard?"

"Yes, Amara dear."

The maidservant doesn't run off to fulfill her request like she normally does. Instead, she shifts nervously from foot to foot. Chhavi cocks her head to the side inquiringly. "What is it, Amara?"

Amara takes a deep breath, steady herself, then says, "We have been instructed to keep you inside."

The sultana furrows her brow and asks, "By whom?"

"The vizier."

Amara picks at her kurti as if she expected the sultana to reprimand her for her answers. Smoothing out her features into a neutral expression, Chhavi responds casually, "Well, could you by chance do me a favor?"

"Anything, Chhaviji," Amara says, eager to appease her mistress.

"I think I would like to read out here. Would you mind returning to the palace and retrieving some books from the old palace library for me?"

"Of course, Chhaviji. What books did you have in mind?"

The sultana smiles as she relays her request. After Amara scampers off, Chhavi's face falls.

The vizier has trapped her in a beautiful prison.

Chhavi pushes fruit around her plate with her fork, her hunger forgotten. She understands why she has been gifted this mourning period. She understands that relocating to their Upper City residence is the best location for her to mourn. What she doesn't understand is why the vizier commanded her servants behind her back. Why does it matter to the vizier or those in the palace if she visits the bazaar from time to time? She can honor the tradition of the mourning period while occasionally walking through Aveena. Her ravi wouldn't expect anything different.

Sighing, Chhavi leans back, staring out at the flowers waving in the wind.

"Is the food not to your liking, Chhaviji?" another servant asks, her head bowed respectfully.

Chhavi startles, the new servant taking her by surprise. What is her name again?

She smiles and says, "It's wonderful. Unfortunately, it's me that's unsettled. Could you bring some ginger tea to my room? I need reprieve from the sun."

"Of course, Chhaviji," the servant says, bowing. She grabs the plate and hurries off. Before she disappears into the house, the servant turns and watches Chhavi. When their eyes meet, the servant ducks her head quickly.

Chhavi stares after the servant, her brows furrowed. Something about the whole interaction leaves her unsettled. The rest of the servants who joined her in the Upper City residence Chhavi knew by name, they are the same servants who she trusts in the palace.

All except this new one.

The sultana stands abruptly and strides inside, feeling exposed and in need of the solitude of her rooms. She expects the gossip and spy games in the palace, she was naive to think that it wouldn't follow her here.

Inside her room, Amari is straightening the cushions on the burgundy chaise lounge by the window.

"Amari, dear," Chhavi says.

"Yes, Chhaviji?"

"Before you retrieve the books from the palace, I'd like to write a few letters for you to deliver as well."

"Of course, Chhaviji. I'll leave when you're done."

"Thank you," the sultana says with a tired smile. "That will be all for now."

Amari leaves, and Chhavi's shoulders slump. Sadness threatens to overwhelm her, but she shoves it deep down. First, she needs to write letters.

Trust is earned, not given.
-Aveenan Proverb-

29

The aches in my body are nothing compared to the raging headache pulsing behind my eyes. I've finally escaped Sala's torture and retreated to my room on the pretense of needing to rest before another evening amongst the Ari.

I ignore Sala's knowing glance as I flee the main room of the suite.

In a few hours the council would convene, but for now, I hid in the dark. The long, billowing curtains barely block the sunlight from the windows as I soak a cloth in the basin and then lay back on the bed, pressing the damp material onto my eyes. I let the cool cloth ease the throbbing headache with a sigh.

Inhaling deeply, I sink further into the soft mattress, the one positive of this foray into the palace. Two years of sleeping in the attic of the bakery hadn't erased my longing for a comfortable bed. I will never willingly go back to my parents in the Upper City, but that doesn't mean that I don't miss some of the luxuries their life afforded.

Maybe after I take Tanu to Bhavin and she is healed, I can find a way to give her the same luxury of a comfortable bed.

Someone knocks softly on my door, and I stifle my groan.

Dragging myself up, I stumble to the door, my cloth in my hand, and open it. Zahir leans against the doorframe with his arms crossed over his chest.

"We need to talk," he says.

I glance behind him, noting that the main room is deserted. I sigh. "Now?"

"Yes," he says. His tone is firm although he speaks barely above a whisper. Apparently, he doesn't want to draw attention to our conversation. "Are you going to invite me in?"

I roll my eyes, but step back, muttering, "Do I have a choice?"

My tone is whiny even to my own ears, but I fail to muster the energy to care.

Zahir scans the room, taking in the crumpled saree on the ground and the closed curtains without a word. I toss the cloth into the basin—my aching head would have to wait—and cross my arms, waiting for him to begin.

Zahir swivels around, and asks, "Do you want to sit?"

"What do you want, Zahir?"

"Okay no," Zahir says. He rakes a hand through his curls, then states, "Cadmar doesn't trust you."

My shoulders tense, but I manage a neutral tone as I say, "That's not a question."

"Didn't say I was going to ask one," Zahir shoots back. We stare at each other, but I refuse to engage more in this conversation than I have to. The sting of Cadmar's accusations from the morning still burns in my chest. Zahir raises a brow and steps closer. I hold my ground.

"What I want to know is," Zahir says slowly, deliberately, "why?"

"Why what?" I have to tilt my head back to maintain eye contact with him as Zahir crowds my space. He's mistaken if he thinks he can intimidate me into talking.

"Why doesn't he trust you?" he asks, matching my neutral tone.

I bob my head in a nonanswer. "To be fair, Cadmar doesn't seem to trust anyone."

"Stop avoiding the question."

"Stop asking stupid questions."

We stare at each other. Zahir's jaw clenches and unclenches. I hold my breath, stubbornly staring him down.

Zahir breaks first, sighing, then slumps down on the edge of the bed. He pats the mattress next to him, saying, "Will you please just sit?"

I hesitate but then decide to acquiesce this one point. The mattress dips slightly, but I perch on the edge, ready to leave if he tries to dig into my background. I have to protect Tanu at all costs—no family ties are allowed in Logonkelie.

Zahir turns towards me, and his knee brushes my own.

"I trust you," Zahir says.

"What?" I ask, disbelief etched into my tone.

Zahir holds my gaze so that I can see the truth in his words as he repeats, "I trust you."

"We just met."

"I trust your abilities. I trust you to have my back. I trust that you won't knowingly do anything to put us at risk." I don't know how to respond, shocked that I could earn Zahir's unwavering trust in only a few days. "So, if I can see that you won't put us at risk, why doesn't Cadmar?"

I press my lips together. "I'm not in Cadmar's head. How could I—"

"But you know," Zahir says with such surety that my weak deflection falls flat on the floor. "He's an Ari, and one with power. We are nothing compared to him, but someone we've found our way here with. I'm not sure if I understand his approach—"

"Then why are you here?" I ask, desperately gripping onto the change of subject.

Zahir tenses briefly then shrugs. "Anything is better than working in the fields. Even being surrounded by asshole Ari."

Silence stretches between us.

"Something was… off this morning. Cadmar's accusations didn't make sense. It's been bothering me ever since. Why would he think that you'd purposely jeopardize everything? Why would he accuse you of being the center of attention? So, then I asked myself, if you had joined Logonkelie, you would have gone through the same tests as me, right? You would've spent weeks proving yourself to him before we ever set foot in the palace."

I cringe, the truth of Zahir's observations making me shift uncomfortably. Cadmar was a fool for thinking that the other Logonkelie wouldn't detect any of this.

"Unless you didn't. Unless you didn't earn Cadmar's trust one painstaking task at a time. But then, why are you here?"

This was the problem with lies, one tug and the whole thing unravels. I had never been good at the game of words, much to my father's chagrin. How could I ensnare an Ari to raise our family's name if I couldn't battle with words like the rest of them?

Zahir waits, watching me squirm under his gaze. There's nothing accusing there, just a desire to understand.

"Do you really trust me?" I ask.

"Yes," he answers without hesitation. "We're in this together."

Trust was such a fragile thing. Before I was the Nightshade, I had willingly given my trust to the wrong person, and he had shattered it. I had never been able to piece it back together, and I don't think it will ever be whole again.

But I could give one piece of trust to Zahir, right? One truth, one little bit of trust, and see what he does with it.

"I—" I have to clear my throat, the dryness making my voice raspy. "I–Cadmar doesn't trust me, and I don't trust him."

"Why?" he asks, calm and curious, not judgmental.

"He caught me in his office, as the Nightshade. He gave me a choice: work for Logonkelie or imprisonment." I gulp at the dryness in my throat. Zahir doesn't say anything. The moment stretches between us until it's my turn to shrug. "And so, I'm here."

"When did this happen?"

I grimace. "The night before we came to the Hathorda."

Zahir rubs his beard, thinking. "If he wanted your skills, he should have earned your trust, your respect. Not blackmailed you."

I falter, shocked. I stutter, then close my mouth.

"His mistrust of you isn't going to fix that either," Zahir mutters, more to himself than to me. Zahir turns his attention back to me. "Thank you."

"For what?"

"For trusting me." I nod, unable to speak. A small piece of trust mends itself inside my chest, melting back into place. "Even if you can't trust Cadmar, you can still trust me. And Sala and Erol."

"I know," I say.

He places his hand over mine as he says earnestly, "We've got your back."

"I know."

"Cadmar needs to learn to trust you sooner rather than later. It's obvious to the rest of us that you have no interest in drawing unwanted attention to yourself."

"Thank you." My voice wobbles slightly, but I swallow the pinpricks forming behind my eyes.

Zahir nods, then stands. He walks over to the basin and removes the cloth from it. The only sound in the room is the trickle of water as he twists the excess out. Then he walks back, offering it back to me.

"See you," Zahir says before slipping out of the room, closing the door behind him with a quiet click.

I lay back on the mattress and place the cloth over my eyes again.

That was not what I expected. The throbbing behind my eyes fades as I take slow, measured breaths, letting the tension from earlier seep into the mattress.

Zahir has my back in the palace. Sala too. And maybe even Erol, if I let him.

For once, I'm not facing the unknown completely alone.

It feels... nice.

A woman is best to be seen and not heard. Her beauty is her greatest asset; her voice her greatest flaw. She should aspire to perfect her greatest asset.
-excerpt from *The Guide for Aveenan Gentlewomen* given to Laila on her tenth birthday from her father-

30

There are more women in the Veiled Room this afternoon than there were the day before. Each has at least two extra handmaids with them to showcase their status, which means that the Veiled Room feels crowded and stuffy. Despite the increase in women, a quick glance reveals that none of the lesser Ari are present today. Frustration and relief battle silently within me—frustration that I cannot complete Cadmar's assignment and relief that I don't have to try.

A wisp of a worry floats through my head, but I push it away. There's no one here who would recognize me from the Upper City. It would be nearly impossible with how I've changed to recognize the girl I was in the woman I am right now.

Worry aside, I sit in my corner, taking in the faces around me. Cadmar wants me to make nice with these pompous peacocks?

The women have foregone their sarees for kurtis, but the tunics are adorned with jewels and gold. Although the outfits are supposed to be casual, each woman in the room strives to distinguish herself from the others through lavish jewelry and impracticality.

When Sala had pulled out my own kurti for the afternoon, I scoffed at her choice. "Are kurtis even supposed to be corseted?"

"This isn't the Lower City, binti."

Sala squeezed me into a cream colored kurti with vines of vibrant red roses curving around every inch. Sala tugged the strings of the corset for ten minutes, ensuring that all space was wiggled out of the top.

I sigh and adjust in my seat, trying to find a position that's easy to breathe in. My breasts feel like they're pushed up to my chin. The sweet, earthy scent of saffron wafts through the Veiled Room from the incense burning on silver plates. It's too strong, making my nose itch.

With a flick of my wrist, I summon Sala to me.

"Fan me," I say. Sala bobs her head and produces an ornate red fan. I ignore her as she moves behind me. *Focus, Laila.*

A palace servant, eyes lowered out of respect, offers me a tray of tender coconut and sliced starfruit. I take a small piece of coconut, noticing the marigolds garnishing the silver tray, adding elegance to the already-gleaming silver.

With Sala in place, we both begin to scan the women in the room, eavesdropping when possible. Before leaving Erol's suite, Sala and I decided that if I could not mingle with the lesser Ari, that I would call her to me and she would focus on the left side of the room, while I scanned the right. That way Sala could keep an eye on the servants and read the lips of their masters.

"...and you would not believe what that has done to her figure. She needs to be careful, or else her husband might..."

I resist rolling my eyes at Lady Pateel as she gossips. I shift slightly to listen to the next pair of women.

"...the prices of it. Her kurtis are truly a steal."

"I will have to send for her. Dhruvji was just saying how important it is to make a good impression."

"Sounds like an excuse to go shopping!"

The two women laugh softly and clink their glasses together. No new information there—everyone is striving to impress the prince.

Four women, including Lady Asfour, catch my eye. If I had seen them in the Lower City, I would have pegged them for something illegal—heads leaning in together, eyes flitting around to the surroundings, voices whispering but trying to sound casual. Here in the palace, the signs are all there, but the culprits throw me off. I try to listen, but the swish of Sala's fan in my ear hinders me.

"That will be enough," I say, waving Sala away. She meets my eyes through the slit in her veil as she bows, questioning my early dismissal. I ignore her and stare down at the flowers on my kurti, tracing their shapes with my fingers, as I concentrate hard to hear Lady Asfour's conversation.

"...happened so fast."

"Do you know when we'll meet again, Farahji?"

"There's no way to tell."

"So, you haven't heard from her?"

"No one has."

"The vizier sent her off too quickly for anything to be done. We'll just have to wait."

A peel of laughter breaks my concentration and halts the conversation. Irritated by the disruption, I find the source of the laughter. Several of the younger women titter away on the opposite side of the room, with Esha Shah in the center of the group. Although the men have not filed into the Council Room yet, some of the sillier young women keep glancing at the veil and giggling. Esha's kurti is reminiscent of the white and gold saree I wore the night before, down to the golden drops hanging from her ears and the shimmering design across her small breasts. *No, silly girl, the prince didn't like me because of the color of my saree*, I think. But then I remember the way the prince's eyes skimmed down the length of my body. Well, that's not the *only* reason.

"Oh, Esha," one particularly giggly girl whispers, "you look divine in that kurti."

"This old thing?" Esha replies, smoothing her hands over the fabric.

"Too bad the prince can't see you through the veil," another girl says a little loudly. "The council would come to a full halt and have to reconvene tomorrow."

The girls burst into laughter again. Lady Shah shushes them halfheartedly—her smug expression ruins the effort.

The slide of the bolt to the Council Room clangs into place, silencing the women more effectively than Lady Shah. Men's voices float up to the Veiled Room above. The interruption gives me a moment to process Lady Asfour's conversation. *Her?* The only *her* that I can think of is the sultana. That would make sense based on the comment about being sent off—I wondered why the sultana wasn't supporting her son during the transition. And she's the only woman who would deal with the vizier willingly.

I trace the flowers again, thinking.

But the sultana doesn't *do* anything. The sultana was just... there. A breeding horse for continuing the line of sultans, a pretty face perhaps, a figure for the woman to say that we're represented. Did Cadmar mention any meetings that the sultana took part in? And even if she was in meetings, these four Ari women wouldn't have joined…

"Oh, who's the one with the curls?"

I look up as the speaker—one of Esha's cohorts, dressed in mauve—is shushed immediately by the woman next to her. Zahir glances at the Veiled Room and winks, causing the girl in mauve to giggle uncontrollably despite the silencing looks from the older women. I cross my arms and stare pointedly out of the veil to avoid glaring at the giggling nitwit. She looks like a grape in that kurti anyway.

Once the men are in place, the chime rings, and everyone rises. The Consulate marches to the front of the room. Ajani walks to the top of the dais and instructs us to rise from our bows, and my second Council of the Sultan meeting begins.

"Welcome, esteemed councilmen," the prince says from the dais. His voice is familiar after last night's conversation. "Today we need to discuss the produce grown by our Lower City brethren. Vizier Nassor?"

The prince sits on his throne and allows Vizier Nassor to conduct the rest of the meeting. The vizier recaps the current production numbers from the farms in the outskirts of the Lower City. His lists of numbers are extensive, covering not only the production but also the cost of the equipment, the numbers of workers, and the longevity of the rate of production based off of the recent census. By the time he opens the floor for discussion, my head spins with numbers.

Men stand and declare their support or grievances with the current production rate and give suggestions. I try to memorize the conversation and speakers, but my head is already swimming with the vizier's numbers. Most of the women stare off around the room; the elder Lady Shah slumps in her chair, her chin resting on her chest. Several handmaids are signaled to come and fan their mistresses—the more the men speak, the hotter the air becomes in the Veiled Room.

Ray Lobo stands, his bald spot a beacon in the dark hair around him, and his booming voice jolts many of the women—and some of the men—out of stupors.

"Vizier Nassor, those Lower City dogs are purposefully hiding some of their production from the rest of Aveena. We give them tools and land to work, and yet we are cheated out of the produce promised to us. Just last week, one of my workers said that he did not have the order of mangos promised and that he would have them next week. But then I saw children eating mangos as I left the bazaar. This cannot be permitted."

His voice fills with indignation, and he clutches his chest, either in passion or pain, I cannot tell from this distance. His face becomes red from his rant. Several of the men around him mutter and nod to one another in agreement.

"And what do you propose, Councilman Lobo?" the vizier asks, his voice smooth as silk.

Emboldened by the nods of his peers, Lobo continues, "Vizier Nassor, I propose that we increase the number of Suraksha who patrol the production of food. Clearly, the Lower City cannot be trusted. These dogs would rather fatten their families instead of supporting the success of Aveena."

"And what is wrong with giving the families who farm the produce that they've toiled to grow?" Cadmar's voice echoes through the chamber. The whispers die instantly.

"And what do you suggest, Councilman Cadmar?" Vizier Nassor asks.

"I suggest that we increase the percentages of produce retained by the families who grow the food. If their bellies are full, then they will be happy. If they are happy, then they are apt to work harder."

Councilman Lobo's laugh cuts through the air like a knife—there is no humor in his red face as he scoffs at Cadmar.

"Did I say something in jest, Councilman Lobo?" Cadmar asks. Although he appears calm and unconcerned, after studying Cadmar's moods the past few days, I see the strain in his shoulders, revealing his fury.

Once Councilman Lobo catches his breath, he says, "Why should we give them a meter when they're already taking more? Our allowances are generous in this matter already. It is greed that breeds in these Lower City dogs, not hunger."

"And yet it was children that you saw supposedly eating the mangos? Are you suggesting that the Lower City children are so satisfied with their full bellies that it is greed that drives them?"

The gaunt faces of the children I have seen in the Lower City swim in my memory. The haunted look in their eyes wasn't from greed but from desperation. I knew a kindred, suffering spirit when I saw one. Oftentimes, I would snag some of the fruit from the Upper City on my excursions as the Nightshade in order to fill their tiny bellies. I wanted to pay forward the help that many of their parents had given me when I first came to the Lower City.

The vizier's voice draws me from my memories to the present conversation.

"But as I have said in the past, Councilman Cadmar, we must be wary of being too generous with those who do not earn it. The numbers do not lie in this matter. If we become more lenient with the farming families, then will we not have to become more lenient with the other citizens in the Lower City? And what about the merchants in the Upper City? What is their due?"

"Excuse me for saying so, Vizier Nassor," Cadmar says, his tone the opposite of apologetic. "But you speak out of ignorance of what transpires in the Lower City."

The silence following this pronouncement is deafening. Vizier Nassor strokes his beard as he contemplates his opponent in front of him.

"And you'll excuse me for saying so, Councilman Cadmar, but *you* speak out of turn."

The tension is palpable. None of the women sleep now. My racing heart demands more air, but I struggle to breathe in the damned corset. Cadmar and Nassor glare at one another from across the room, holding each other's gazes. Cadmar is the first to break the silence and the glaring contest.

"Forgive if I offend, Nassorji. It was not my intention."

Cadmar bows, fist over heart, and waits for the vizier's command to rise. The vizier glares at Cadmar's exposed neck while stroking his pointed beard. After a beat, he says, "Rise, Councilman Cadmar. I trust this will not happen again."

The prince looks from one man to the other. Unsure of what to do, he rises to his feet and says, "I believe we should table this discussion for a later meeting."

And with that, Prince Ajani descends the stairs. He's halfway out of the Council Room before the rest of the Consulate thinks to follow.

Nimra,
Keep an eye on our newest members.
Report your observations on their
interactions regularly to me. We must
protect our goals.
-C

31

Prince Ajani does not host a feast for the Ari. I can't help wondering if the mounting tension in the council is at fault for the lack of festivities.

We fall into a routine in the meantime—training in the morning then primping to sit in the Veiled Room. Every minute of the day is torturously tedious, from the ridiculous outfits to sitting like a social pariah in the Veiled Room. Each day I scan the room for potential allies amongst the women, and each day I'm disappointed by the same crowd of women run by the Shah's.

The only reprieve from the tedium is the time spent with Sala and Zahir in the morning. Although Sala kicks our asses throughout training, between Zahir and Sala's antics I manage to enjoy myself.

My anxiety simmers in my veins, threatening to overwhelm me. Despite my intentions to follow Cadmar's orders, I'm blocked at every turn. And then there's the worries swirling in my head about what will happen when I do meet some of the lesser Ari. Connecting with them, winning them over, feels impossible.

Deep down, I know that the Jade goddess will have to bestow luck upon me to get through this unscathed and unrecognized.

However, without the feasts, I haven't struggled to avoid the prince. Or the vizier.

It's temporary.

I push into downward dog, my legs no longer protesting. Sala's instructions seem less like orders and more like guidance. I tune her out, following my body's rhythm rather than her commands. The morning is the one part of the day where I'm in control. The meditation is second nature.

"And release. Savasana."

Melting onto the smooth floor, I focus on my breathing. My heart slows, and tension seeps out of my body.

Sala's voice pulls me out of my meditation, and I follow her lead to close our practice. Sala nods at me before she joins Erol for breakfast.

Zahir is splayed across the floor in his shavasanah. I sigh. Typical.

"Come on, Zahir. Breakfast."

I shake his shoulder, and Zahir jolts awake, grabbing my wrist tightly. His fingers dig into me, sending pain down my arm. Terror flits across his eyes as they meet mine, but I can tell he's somewhere else. Shaking off the shock, I say quietly, "Zahir, it's me."

I maintain eye contact, and slowly, so that he can see what I'm doing, I gently remove his fingers from my wrist. The panic recedes from Zahir's eyes as I continue to hold his gaze, and I lean away. Zahir blinks rapidly, glancing down at his hands and then back up at me.

"Laila, I—"

"Don't worry about it."

"But—"

I put a hand out to stop Zahir from speaking and say, "Don't worry about it."

I move to my usual seat, pulling a plate toward me. Zahir does the same. He tries to catch my eye, but I concentrate on my plate of food. No one else notices what happened as they discuss Ray Lobo.

The food is tasteless as my mind whirs, replaying Zahir's reaction over and over. The panic in his eyes. The painful grip on my wrist. And then the realization that it was me... Who did he think I was?

Sala and Erol talk about the council, but I ignore them.

We are all completing our assigned jobs for Cadmar without fail—and yet I feel like we could be doing more. I feel like a bird with its wings clipped, being paraded around the bazaar for show, instead of given the opportunity to fly. Not that I'm sure how to fly here, in the palace.

"Lailani!" Sala says, waving a hand in front of my eyes.

I jerk. "Hm what? Sorry."

Sala scoffs and tears another idli in half, before saying, "I was saying that there is another council meeting today."

"Oh goody," I say, unable to feign interest for yet another meeting. No wonder Aveena was surrounded by desert from all the hot air the Ari wasted in these meetings.

"Perfect opportunity to ingratiate yourself with the other Aristocracy," Erol reminds me.

I resist rolling my eyes at the older man. Erol has grown on me but he has to know that this has been a fruitless endeavor for me. From what Zahir has said, he hasn't had much luck either.

"Lovely," Zahir says. "Can't wait."

Our eyes briefly meet, before we both turn to our breakfast, pushing the idli and sambar around our plates.

Erol's chair scrapes across the floor as he pushes away from the table. "I'm going to lay down for a few. Knock if you need me."

I wait until Erol's door closes before turning to Sala with pleading eyes. She raises a brow. "What?"

"Can we please *do* something?" I ask. "I'm going crazy locked up in this suite doing nothing."

"You aren't—"

"Sala, be realistic," I say.

Zahir jumps in. "We've made no more impact with the Ari than the prince has with the council."

She opens her mouth to argue, but I hold up a hand. "Can we please just—just—"

"Just what?" she asks.

I sigh. "Just get out of here. See if we can listen to any conversations. Find out anything useful." Sala scoffs but I add, "Can we please try?"

"Cadmar won't like it," she says slowly. "We need to keep your reputation clear…"

"If I come, then she will be sufficiently chaperoned," Zahir says quickly. "He can't argue against that. And if we find anything useful then he'll have to get over his annoyance anyway."

"But Logonkelie—"

"We're doing it for Logonkelie," I say. Sala frowns, and I add, "I'll even let you put me in that orange saree that makes me look like part of the Harem."

"C'mon Sala. You know you want to get out of this suite," Zahir says.

She hesitates, mulling over our words, then smirks. Zahir and I grin at one another as Sala points a finger in our faces. "If either of you screw this up, I'll make you wish—"

"Save the threats, Sala," Zahir says, raising his hands in surrender. "We want out of this room too badly to screw it up."

Sala takes another bite of idli then stands, gesturing towards my room. "If we're going out, let's do it right at least."

Grinning, Zahir and I high five before I follow Sala.

⸏⸎⸏⸎⸎❦⸎⸏⸎⸏

An hour later and sufficiently primped to venture into the palace, Zahir and I link arms and let Sala follow behind us as we roam the palace. The servants must work all night to maintain the shine of the marbled hallways. As we pass the Veiled Room and turn down hallways I haven't yet seen, the white marble shifts to include the faintest pink stone with veins of gold running through. The arched windows reveal the palace gardens, the light peeking through and catching the gold veins in the marble.

The further we walk into the palace, the clearer it becomes that we're the only ones wandering through the halls.

The palace is deserted.

After several hallways in silence, Zahir leans over and whispers, "She only let us out to make a point, didn't she?"

"Clearly," I whisper back with a grimace. The excitement I felt at leaving the rooms has diminished with each step. "At least we're out of the suite."

Zahir chuckles. "If I had to sit around for another afternoon—"

I shush Zahir quickly and pull him to a stop. He tilts his head to the side in a question, but then he hears them too—voices around the corner.

"...Nassorji? I've known most of them my whole life."

"Ah, but now you are to be sultan. You must learn to read them as your father did." I tense at the oily voice of the vizier. If we wanted to get information, we couldn't have stumbled on a better pair—the prince and the vizier.

Zahir drags me towards an open window, and the two of us pretend to observe the garden as we strain our ears to hear the conversation.

"My father did that?" the prince asks.

"It is a skill any sultan must hone. You must be able to read between the words that a person says to you to get to the heart of what they mean."

Zahir tenses and whispers, "If only he knew to listen to the heart of what Nassor meant."

I elbow Zahir to shut him up. Even if I agree.

"They all offered their support."

"And?" the vizier prompts.

"They followed the protocols of respect given to a sultan. That's good, right?"

I cringe at the question in the prince's voice, the lack of confidence it portrays. Zahir rolls his eyes but keeps his commentary to himself.

"Yes and no," the vizier says. Footsteps echo nearby, their voices getting fainter, and I miss the next words that the vizier says. I tug on Zahir's arm, and we tiptoe towards the end of the hallway.

"What do you mean?" the prince asks.

"You need to stop hiding after the council meetings."

"But I—"

I gesture to Zahir to remain where he is and then peer around the corner. The prince and the vizier are several meters away, their backs to me.

The vizier waves a hand, and even from my distance, the glitter of his rings catches the eye. "Your Aristocracy are used to lavish banquets and parties."

"We hosted the welcome feast," the prince says, halting and crossing his arms as he looks up at the vizier.

"That was two weeks ago. You should be hosting them nightly. Or at least every other night."

"But isn't the business in the council more important?"

"Yes and no." The vizier pauses and puts a hand on the prince's shoulder. I duck behind the corner again, hiding from view. "Business happens just as often in the social events as it does in the council. More so if you ask me. We need a celebration."

The prince scoffs. His muttered, "What is there to celebrate?" is barely heard from our vantage point.

"The purpose of the celebration isn't the important part," the vizier says. "The opportunities it provides is. You want them to see you as sultan? You need to act like it."

Their footsteps drown out the prince's response as the two of them disappear around the corner. We wait a few minutes in tense silence to make sure they're truly gone before returning the way that we came. None of us risk discussing what we overheard as we head back to the suite.

"Well, that was—" Zahir begins, but Sala cuts him off.

"I need to find Cadmar. Stay here."

Before we can respond, Sala has slipped out of the suite through the servant's door.

Zahir flops onto one of the cushions, while I go sit on the windowsill, looking out through the barred windows.

"Did we actually learn anything?" I ask, running my fingers over the bars as I think out loud. "We all know that Nassor is pulling the strings."

"Yes and no," Zahir says, mimicking the vizier. I scowl at him and he laughs before sobering up. "We have a heads up about another tortuous party."

"Joy," I mutter. "Wonder what farfetched reason they'll come up with for this one."

"Two days without an argument in the council?" Zahir asks.

I snort. "Lady Shah's rash has cleared up again?"

Zahir chuckles. He sweeps his hands across the ceiling like he's reading a sign above him. "A night honoring the esteemed vizier."

"Ugh, no," I say. "I will be skipping that one, thank you."

"We could all wear every piece of jewelry we own so that we emulate his fashion sense."

"No!"

"And the men could shave their beards into little points and oil them."

"Zaharian!"

Zahir strokes on his beard like he's thinking, and I burst out laughing at his imitation of the vizier. He mimics the vizier's oily tone as he says, "My dear councilmen, I do think this is a great idea, nay the best idea I've ever come up with. Perhaps we should deem this day Nassor Al-Sid day for future reference and–"

"Zahir!" I shout through my laughter. My stomach hurts from laughing so hard, and tears stream down my face. Zahir grins and bows dramatically.

"I'll be here all–well I don't know how long I'll be here, but I aim to entertain as long as I'm allowed to be here."

"Gandmasti," I tease, sticking my tongue out at Zahir.

He places a hand over his heart, a scandalized look on his face. "Lady Acharya! How crass of you to use such language in the presence of a gentleman!"

"Gentleman, my ass," I say with a grin. I slide off the windowsill, adding, "I think I'll lay down until Sala wakes me up for my daily beauty torture. See you."

"I'll be here," Zahir says, stretching out on the cushion, "contemplating other ways to celebrate Nassor Al-Sid Day if you need me."

Giggling to myself, I close the door and meander to the bed. My face hurts from grinning, the muscles out of practice from smiling so much. I don't think I've laughed that hard since I lived in the Upper City.

**His Royal Highness,
Prince Ajani Bahu IV,
cordially invites you to an Unveiling
Celebration to follow the next council
meeting.**

32

The Veiled Room is crowded with twice as many women as usual. I guess the invitation to the unveiling sparked enough interest that the other women deigned to come. I maneuver through the women to my usual seat, sweeping my skirt out before settling into it. The whispers buzz around the Veiled Room but I tune them out, staring out at the heads of the councilmen instead.

They're not much better judging from the way the men lean in to one another, heads together. Everyone is speculating.

"Is this seat taken?" a soft voice asks.

I turn away from the curtain to a middle-aged woman who I haven't seen in the Veiled Room before. I smile and gesture towards the seat. "All yours."

The woman settles, and two palace servants stroll over to offer us refreshments. We sip the fresh sugar cane juice, momentarily savoring the sweet flavor, before I set my glass down, turning towards the other woman.

"I'm Lailani Acharya," I whisper. "I don't think we've met before."

The woman smiles and bobs her head. "Lakshmi Naidu."

"Have you—"

The chimes echo through the room, and Lady Naidu smiles apologetically to me as we both stand. I watch the Consulate procession come down the aisle, frustrated with their timing. If only they had waited another minute, I might have been able to talk to Lady Naidu and finally make headway on Cadmar's task.

"You may be seated," the prince says from the dais.

The shuffling of hundreds settling into their seats echoes throughout the Council Room before silence descends again. Anticipation is thick in the air. To my surprise, Prince Ajani remains standing instead of handing off the proceedings to the vizier.

"Today we are forgoing our normal business to honor the noble Suraksha from the city and their tireless work. Please show your appreciation to Captain Mahato and his team."

A smattering of applause reverberates through the room as ten Suraksha file in. I can't help but note that they had the Suraksha enter from the servants' door on the side of the Council Room instead of through the main doors in the back.

"Captain Mahato and his team have worked tirelessly to enact justice in the city and through their diligence and actions, we have finally been given reprieve from the menace who calls himself the Nightshade. Today we honor them and their hard work to protect us all."

I join the applause a beat late, anxiety crawling beneath my skin with each word. A cold sweat breaks out on my back, and the juice sits heavy in my stomach. The prince continues and it takes every effort to refocus on what he's saying.

"It's been two weeks without an attack from the Nightshade thanks to Captain Mahato and the city Suraksha who have gone above and beyond in the call of duty to protect our people from the Nightshade. Their protective measures, the examples they've made, and the enforcement of the wall have scared the Nightshade away."

A few murmurs erupt amongst the councilmen, but they're quickly silenced through glares from their neighbors. The prince continues in a measured voice, each sentence clearly carefully memorized for this purpose. He's stiff as he delivers his lines, probably like the vizier intended.

"The Nightshade has disappeared and for that we are grateful. Please step forward." The Suraksha line up at the base of the steps. The vizier and prince step down. A servant holds a tray up for the vizier who grabs the first medal, passing it to Prince Ajani. "As a token of our appreciation, we honor you today."

The prince repeats his words as he places the medal around each Suraksha's neck. My vision blurs as I stare unseeingly through the veil. I want to flee the room, but that would draw unwanted attention.

"Please join me in thanking our honorable Suraksha."

The Suraksha turn to face the Ari as we applaud again, this time more noticeably enthusiastic than the initial applause. From this distance the faces of the Suraksha are blurry, so I'm unable to see if I recognize any of the guards.

"Tonight, we celebrate the unveiling of the Nightshade and our esteemed guests with a veiled masquerade. We will see you all soon," the prince says.

The Suraksha file out—through the servants' door again—and then the prince exits followed by the vizier and the

Consulate. Whispers break out immediately after the final chimes ring out.

I shoot up and hurry towards the door on unsteady legs, Lady Naidu forgotten completely in my haste to escape. As I maneuver through the other women, the name "Nightshade" surrounds me on all sides. I want to cover my ears.

Sala falls in step behind me, and we rush back towards the suite to get ready for tonight. For the party. Honoring the stopping of the Nightshade. Me.

I was a fool to think that no one would notice that the Nightshade had been inactive these past two weeks. Why hadn't Velo gotten someone else to do the jobs? Keep up the ruse of the Nightshade? He cut me off but he owned the alias. He could've gotten one of his other thieves to do it.

It didn't make any sense.

I bypass the main room in Erol's suite for the safety of my room. Sala follows me in and then closes the door.

"Get it together, binti," she says softly, no heat in her tone. "You have a masquerade to attend."

I nod, my anxious thoughts swirling in my head as I passively sit for Sala's ministrations.

***

"They're serious about this," I mutter to Zahir as he escorts me towards the ballroom. The Dara family chats excitedly in front of us, but other than that, the hallway is empty. "The Nightshade? Really?"

Zahir snorts but turns it into a cough when Dhruv Dara glances over his shoulder, his disapproving look still evident through the metal mask around his eyes.

"Seems so," he whispers back. Zahir is wearing a maroon sherwani with charcoal grey diamonds accenting throughout. The leather bands of his mask emphasize his golden eyes, his curls flopping overtop of the mask.

I want to argue at the ridiculousness of it all—the blatant lie—but there hadn't been time.

"Chin up," Zahir mutters, and the two of us round the corner to where the rest of the Ari are milling about outside of the ballroom. As I tilt my face up, the dangling crystals from my mask brush across my cheeks.

The energy from the Ari sparks and glitters like the interpretations of 'veiled' around the room. Most of the women wear sheer veils over their faces, their eyes peeking out from the slit, while the men wear variations of masks over their eyes and noses, similar to Zahir's. Sala once again outdid herself with the uniqueness of my outfit–the crystal beading emphasizes my eyes but then strands dangle over my face. She heavily lined my eyes in kohl, the sparkly black glittering like the crystals of my mask. The cerulean blue of my eyes pop more than usual, their difference from the brown eyes in the room incapable of hiding.

If it weren't for the orange saree that Sala gleefully forced me in, I might have enjoyed the masquerade. Instead, my breasts were pushed up high from the blouse, which was why I had refused to wear it before now. A deal was a deal though.

I should've known better.

The doors to the ballroom are open, so Zahir and I step through to find Erol and the Asfours. The room is smaller than the first time we visited with a massive opaque curtain hanging across the room, cutting off the majority of the room from view. Instead of dinner tables, a few tall tables line the wall for Ari to mingle by. I keep my eyes trained forward, ignoring the whispers of some of the Ari as we pass.

"Lailaniji," Farah says as we approach. She kisses both of my cheeks in greeting, her eyes alight behind her sheer, pistachio-colored veil. "Stunning as always."

"Thank you, Farahji. And you as well."

"Have you met Lady Pateel?"

I bow in greeting to Lady Pateel, who returns the gesture. Tei Asfour claps Zahir on the back in greeting, folding him into the conversation with Erol and Councilman Pateel.

"Pleasure to meet you," I say. "Your veil is gorgeous."

Lady Pateel smiles, pleased, as she touches the pale blue and gold veil covering her face; the gold detailing matches the maang tikka dangling on her forehead.

"Thank you, Lailaniji," she says. "Your servants are more creative than mine, I fear. Those crystals emphasize your beautiful eyes. Such a unique color."

"Isn't this so much fun?" Farah asks, her eyes alight with excitement as she scans the room. "A veiled party! I don't remember ever having an event quite like this one before."

I smile, Farah's enthusiasm is contagious despite my nerves. "This isn't typical?"

"No, dear, definitely not," she says with a laugh.

Before she can continue, a gong rings out in the room and a hush descends over the crowd. A heartbeat passes then the opaque curtain rises, revealing the transformed ballroom, and I gasp.

Hundreds of candles sit in gold sconces along the walls; the servants must have been hanging them up for days. Crystal strands drape from ceiling to floor, the delicate strings glittering in the candlelight, reminiscent of my crystal mask. Ropes of flowers drape across the walls, high above the candles, the clusters of tiny white blooms glowing above our heads. The scent of jasmine wafts towards us as a cluster of musicians strum their instruments, the sweet, flowing melody enticing the Ari to enter the enchanting ballroom. Erol and the Asfours stroll towards a table, and Zahir tugs me along as I stare at the mesmerizing space.

A drummer taps rhythmically on his tabla drums, the soft beats an undercurrent beneath the melodic chords of the strings. Two Ari begin to dance in the center of the room, their movements smooth if not stiffly formal as their hands barely clasp one another in the dance.

"You're staring, Lailani," Zahir murmurs, laughter hidden in his tone.

"I can't help it," I say, smiling broadly. "Have you ever seen anything like it? I wonder what those flowers are. They smell familiar…"

"Those are raat ki rani," Lady Asfour says as we join their table. She points to the nearest blooms above our head. "They chose well."

"Why?" I ask. The crystals of my mask tickle my face as I stare above our heads at the small blooms.

"Another name is the lady of the night," Farah says with a shrug. "Closest they could get to actual nightshade without bringing those poisonous devils into the palace."

My stomach sinks and the nausea I've been fighting all afternoon returns with a vengeance. If only they knew the irony of using a plant called *lady* of the night. A servant approaches, offering us each a sparkling glass. I take a quick sip, hoping the bubbles will settle my stomach, but the subtle alcohol burns as it goes down.

"It's strange," Lady Pateel says, sipping her drink daintily. "I understand honoring the guards for their work, but they didn't catch the Nightshade did they?"

Farah shakes her head, watching the dancers. "Not that they mentioned."

"Just because the Nightshade hasn't struck again, doesn't mean he won't." Lady Pateel shivers. "I get all knotted up just thinking about it."

I wish I could melt into the floor and away. My mouth is dry as the two women continue to speculate, oblivious to my discomfort.

"I would assume that if they caught the Nightshade, he would be paraded around for all to see. The ultimate example to scare away others," Farah adds.

Lady Pateel nods. "Nothing less than he deserves."

The doors open again, and the Suraksha enter the ballroom, their beige uniforms dull spots in the crowd of colorful Aristocracy. My hand trembles as Captain Mahato and another Suraksha wander towards our corner, deep in conversation with two councilmen. My stomach plummets when the second Suraksha approaches—the white patches on his shaved hair familiar from the southern gate.

"Well," Lady Pateel huffs, glaring at the Suraksha, "I understand that we're honoring them and all, but really, this is too much."

Farah's grimace is barely visible beneath her veil in the candlelight. "They are tonight's honorees."

"I can honor them from a distance," Lady Pateel says with a sniff. "I think I'll see if Vihaan will dance with me."

"Go get him, Sanjaya," Farah says, nudging her along with a grin. "You're such a romantic."

Lady Pateel winks then waltzes over to her husband, whispering in his ear. After a brief moment, the two excuse themselves and join the other dancing couples. Farah and I watch Lady Pateel and her husband twirl together, sipping on our drinks in contented silence. The musicians draw out the last note, and the Ari applaud enthusiastically. As the next song begins, my nerves settle slightly. Maybe I can hide in the corner with Farah for the whole night. Then I'd be able to—

"Farah, dear," Tei says, extending a hand towards his wife, "would you honor me with a dance?"

Lady Asfour smiles broadly and accepts his outstretched hand. "Of course, Tei."

As Councilman Asfour leads Farah out to the dancing, she turns and winks at me over her husband's shoulder, mouthing 'you're next.' I shake my head, causing the crystals to clink together, then turn to join Zahir and Erol but they're both gone.

I scan the crowd for them and finally spot Zahir talking to a group of younger Ari. He gestures animatedly, clearly in the middle of a story as the men around him laugh. Even further away, Erol is deep in discussion with Councilman Laghari and Consulate Bakshi.

I'm on my own in a sea of Ari celebrating the demise of the Nightshade.

Unaware that the Nightshade walks amongst them under a different veil.

Vines
Always around
Encircling
Never ending.

The tree
Once strong
Standing
Never faltering.

Vines and the tree
One and the same?
Uniting?
Never more.

Just vines
Demanding more
Strangling
Ending.
-from an unnamed poet-

33

A servant sweeps my empty glass away, replacing it with a new one. Warmth tingles in my stomach, the nerves from earlier evaporating with each sip. The tabla drum beats in time with my breaths, and I sway to the music, savoring the sensation of crystals sliding across my cheeks.

The ballroom is truly breathtaking.

I manage to hide on the outskirts, a wallflower with the raat ki rani high above. Anytime a cluster of Ari settles at a nearby table, I flit away to another dark corner. Anytime the Suraksha are near, I slip into the crowd. Anytime I spot the prince, I disappear to the other side of the ballroom.

Cadmar will be pissed in the morning that I've squandered this opportunity, but what does he expect with the theme of the night being me?

I'm lucky that I only recognize one of the Suraksha present for the celebration.

Someone bumps into me from behind, and I stumble forward before I catch my balance.

"Oh dunes, I'm so so sorry," a feminine voice says. "I'm not used to this saree and—"

I turn and smile, recognizing Lakshmi Naidu from the Veiled Room earlier in the day. Maybe I won't fail Cadmar's task tonight.

"It's quite alright, Lady Naidu," I say, plastering on my best Ari mask as I give a tinkling laugh. "These crystals are keeping me off balance as well."

The worry pinching Lakshmi's eyes relaxes, and she returns my warm smile. "It's quite a unique design. Absolutely stunning."

"Thank you, Lakshmiji," I say, bowing my head. "Are you enjoying the celebration?"

Lakshmi fumbles with her veil, and her simple silver wedding band catches the light. Simple silver drops hang from her ears, and she's artfully draped her pallu over her neck, hiding the lack of necklace. Not that it would stop any of the Ari women from noticing.

"Of course," she recites with perfect practiced enthusiasm. "It's an honor to be invited."

The group of Ari women giggle a few tables away, and Lakshmi glances over her shoulder nervously at them. Lady Shah catches her looking and glares our way.

I sigh, drawing Lakshmi's attention back to me. "She never stops, does she?"

"I don't know what you mean," she says.

"Lady Shah, the old crow," I say dramatically. "I think her face might be stuck in that scowl. It's all I ever see."

Lady Naidu freezes, then a laugh bursts from her. She covers her mouth, quieting her laughter. I wink at her.

"She does tend to—"

"Lakshmi!" An older man barks as he saunters up. Sweat glistens on his upper lip and across his bald head. He looks to be twenty years Lakshmi's senior. He grabs her hip and pulls her towards him possessively. Lakshmi winces briefly before plastering on a soft smile.

"Nilam, dear, I was—"

"I told you to remain where I left you," Nilam says, gripping his fingers tighter into her hip. Lakshmi whimpers but hides it quickly.

"I am—"

"No, you're not," he says. "A good wife should follow her husband's commands. Do you see the other Ari women straying from their husbands?"

Lakshmi opens her mouth then closes it, lowering her eyes submissively to her husband. Before Nilam can continue his rant, I cough slightly then take a sip of my drink, drawing his attention away from Lakshmi.

"And who are you?" Nilam Naidu barks at me.

"Pleasure to meet you, Councilman Naidu," I say, bowing respectfully. "I'm Lady Acharya."

"Acharya… Acharya…" Councilman Naidu mumbles to himself then he claps his hands together. "You're Shaikh's niece?"

"Yes, Nilamji," I say, cringing as spittle hits my cheek.

Nilam nods to himself, thinking, then shouts, "Lakshmi!"

"Yes, Nilam dear?" she asks, hiding her flinch as he yells near her ear.

"Get me another drink," he orders, gesturing with his full glass towards the other side of the room. Lakshmi stumbles in her saree, and Lady Shah, noticing, cackles and nudges her cronies as Lakshmi regains her balance. Ducking her head, Lady Naidu disappears in the crowd without a backwards glance, leaving me with her husband.

Councilman Naidu leers as he steps closer, eyeing the ample cleavage being displayed by the damn orange blouse. I would kill Sala for this when we were back in the suite.

"Lady Acharya," Councilman Naidu says, leaning in, "you have the most beautiful… eyes."

I step carefully back, putting the tall table between myself and the councilman.

"Thank you, Councilman Naidu," I say through gritted teeth. "You're too kind."

"I am, aren't I?" he says, smiling smugly. "I'd love to get the chance to—"

A presence steps behind me, causing Councilman Naidu to falter and look up. I momentarily relax, assuming either Zahir or Erol came to my rescue, until the familiar sickly-sweet scent of oranges fills my nose.

"Councilman Naidu," the oily voice says.

"Vizier Nassor." Nilam fumbles a half bow before standing taller, puffing his chest out slightly.

"Mind if I join you?" Nassor asks, leaning onto the table. His elbow brushes against mine, and I tuck my arm behind my back.

"Not at all, not at all," Nilam replies, smiling broadly. "I was just telling Lady Acharya that she has the most extraordinary eyes."

"Indeed," the vizier says silkily. The hairs on the back of my neck rise as the vizier stares at me, eyes roving up and down my body.

Councilman Naidu prattles on, oblivious to the vizier's attention as he says, "By the dunes, I've only ever seen one set of eyes quite that shade. Uncommon for sure. You'd think I'd remember…"

His voice trails off, and I fidget, wishing I could vanish into another alcove. Nassor smirks and takes a step closer towards me, his fingers toying with the obsidian bracelet on his wrist. Distracted, Councilman Naidu is oblivious.

Nilam snaps his fingers and points towards me, causing Nassor to pause. "The North bazaar! That gold merchant… dunes what was his name?"

My chest constricts. He can't be talking about…

"Parth! That's it," Councilman Naidu says excitedly. The color drains from my cheeks. "I swear Parth Johri had a daughter with those same eyes."

"Oh really?" Nassor asks, now paying attention to Nilam's ramblings.

"It's been ages since I've seen that girl," Nilam adds, stroking his beard thoughtfully. "Figured he'd already married her off. Made her someone else's problem. How Parth would rant about how useless she was, always underfoot."

I jerk like I've been slapped, but neither man notices. My father lamented my marriageability, but I didn't realize that he'd complained to his customers about me too.

"It's why I've never married," Nassor says. "Wouldn't want to be burdened unnecessarily."

While Nilam drinks deeply from his glass, Nassor rubs a hand down my arm on the word 'unnecessarily.' I lurch away, but the vizier wraps his fingers around my elbow tightly, icy cold prickling from his touch. My eyes flit around the ballroom, desperately searching for another member of Logonkelie to rescue me. The sea of Ari spans in front of me, the backs of several councilmen block us from view of the rest of the room.

"You have no idea, Nassorji. You'd think that having a woman at your beck and call would have its perks but alas," Nilam sighs dramatically and waves his glass. "Not sure if the perks outweigh the problems. Have you tried the palm wine? It's delicious."

Nilam waves over a servant in his eagerness to bond with the higher-ranking man. Nassor reluctantly lets go of my arm to take a glass, and the instant I'm released, I step away, halfheartedly bowing and scurry from the corner before either man can protest.

Fuck, fuck, fuck.

Not only was I trapped for the second time by Nassor, but Councilman Naidu recognized me from my father's shop. I *knew* mingling with the lower Ari would backfire. I had a suspicion it wouldn't go well and of course—*of course*—I was recognized.

"Well, that was an interesting conversation," Zahir says, falling into step with me.

I jump, my heart leaping into my throat. How much did Zahir hear?

"You scared me!" I hiss.

Zahir places a hand on my lower back, guiding me away from the exit and towards a shadowed corner. The crystals of my mask brush against my shoulder as I glance behind us longingly looking at the exit.

"Evening, Zaharian," the younger Dara, Kumar, says, waving to Zahir as we pass. "Care to join us?"

The other young men eagerly nod at Zahir. A few appraise me when they think Zahir isn't looking. Zahir's hand tightens on my back, but he maintains his carefree smile.

"Haven't had enough of me yet?" he says.

"On the contrary, we need you to liven up this masquerade," he replies, gesturing to the elegant dancing behind him.

Zahir claps a hand on Kumar's shoulder. "In a moment, boys, in a moment. My uncle wanted me to relay a message to Lailani, then I'll be all yours."

The group grumbles, and as we walk away, I hear one of the others say, "I'd love to relay a message to her."

Zahir tenses but doesn't say anything until we're secluded. One of the huge curtains hangs nearby, partially blocking us from view. The delicate raat ki rani buds wrap around the fabric, the delicate jasmine smell perfuming the corner. Zahir crosses his arms and waits for me to say something. I mimic his position stubbornly. I don't know how much he heard, and I won't be giving away more than I need to.

If only Zahir wasn't so much taller than me. I have to crane my neck to hold his gaze, putting me at a disadvantage.

Finally, he blows out a breath, rubbing his beard thoughtfully.

"You're from the Upper City."

Shit. He'd heard that? He can't know. No one from Logonkelie can search into my history. Knowing that I was the Nightshade is enough.

I shrug. "Councilman Naidu was speculating. He didn't have any—"

"Did you know your mouth twitches?" Zahir says. He taps a finger on the left corner of my mouth. "Right here. Every time you're about to lie, this corner dips down briefly."

I close my mouth, clenching my jaw to keep from moving. Zahir watches my reactions, his eyes roving my face as he speaks.

"I noticed it when you talk to Cadmar. It happens the most with him." I flinch slightly but try to stop it before he notices. Zahir scans the room over my head before meeting my eyes again. "Don't worry. He has to figure that one out for himself. He won't get any help from me there."

"What do you want, Zahir?" I whisper.

"The truth," he says.

"I—I can't give you that."

Zahir holds my gaze, searching. After a moment, he sighs, stepping back.

"I'll cover for you," he says. "Go."

I don't look back as I rush away. I'm done with this masquerade.

Sala peels away from the wall of servants and follows me around the periphery of the dance floor. Several women spin on the arms of their partners to the music, their skirts twirling around them in the candlelight. I can feel Sala's confusion behind me, but I can't risk talking to her here.

I hurry around a group of younger men roaring with laughter. One of them stumbles back and his heel catches on the edge of my saree. Tugging the fabric free, I turn and bump straight into something solid. My slippered feet slide out from under me, but before I fall, a pair of big hands steady me. I look up into the prince's face, the corners of his eyes crinkled as he grins down at me.

"We need to stop running into each other this way," he says.

"Your Highness," I say, scrambling into a bow. "I apologize. I didn't mean—"

"It's alright, Lady Acharya," he says, touching my arm to indicate I should rise. I hadn't seen him touch any of the other young women throughout the night. Tingles spread up my arm. "Are you leaving?"

Was that disappointment in his voice? I stutter, then clear my voice. "Unfortunately, Your Highness. It's quite late, and I'm feeling a little under the weather."

One of the Consulate steps forward. "Ajaniji, if the young lady is sick, you really should—"

"It's fine, Manish," Ajani snaps.

"But sir—"

"I do need to get some rest, Your Highness," I say. I reach out to comfort him, but drop my hand quickly, realizing my mistake. I can't touch the prince. I bow, trying to hide my reach, then say, "Good evening, Your Highness."

Ajani sighs, returning my bow with a nod. "Lady Acharya."

I wait for Ajani to pass before I weave through the crowd towards the exit. More of the Ari turn to whisper as I pass by, their eyes burning into my back as the gossip. By the end of the masquerade all of the Ari will know of my run in with the prince.

So much for staying under the radar.

**When you court a young woman, be
confident in your intentions with her. Do
not court anyone if your heart is unsure.**
-Advice from Sultan Gautam to Prince Ajani
on his thirteenth birthday-

34

I absentmindedly pick at the silver swirls at the edge of my saree. Lady Laghari's brow furrows as she notices, and I force my hands to lay flat amid the indigo fabric as we wait for the men to file out. Despite the late night at the masquerade, the council met as usual. I had expected Cadmar to burst into Erol's suite this morning to chastise me for my performance the previous evening, but he's been... quiet.

The silence is worse than the anger.

The other women stir, and Lady Laghari covers her yawn with a delicate hand. Not many women appear to care about the meeting—probably because they know that they have no influence over the proceedings. Or maybe it's because the discussions don't affect them directly as the vizier rambles about the production numbers again.

The door opens and the whispering dies. I look up to see a lone male servant enter. His unorthodox presence in the Veiled Room catches the attention of every woman. He crosses the room and, to my surprise, approaches me. He hands me a small scroll, bows, and leaves without saying a word. I try to wipe the shock from my face. The only person I can think of who would send me a note is Cadmar. But why would he risk drawing unwanted attention?

"Well, who's it from, girl?" Lady Shah grumbles. I answer her with a bobble of my head and sweep from the room. Let her try and figure out what that means.

Sala follows behind me silently as I walk down the impersonal marble hallway and around the first corner. The servant who had delivered the note trails behind us, far enough away to be respectfully out of earshot.

"Who's it from?" Sala whispers by my shoulder.

"No idea," I say equally as low.

A white and gold ribbon is elegantly knotted around the small scroll, reminding me of my saree from the first night in the palace. I unroll it and skim the contents quickly.

It's not from Cadmar.

> *Dear Lady Acharya,*
> *I'd love to bump into you again, on purpose this time, if it pleases you. If you would allow me to escort you on a tour of the palace today, I would be greatly honored by your company. Kaartik will show you the way, if you oblige.*
> *Sincerely,*
> *Ajani*

"He's very informal, isn't he?" Sala murmurs, reading Prince Ajani's note over my shoulder.

"That's informal?" I ask. "Seems pretty Ari to me."

"But he signed his first name only."

"Well—I—it's from our, um, conversation."

I want to rip the paper away from Sala's scrutiny. She hasn't spoken to him. She doesn't understand how uptight the prince is, first names aside. A few women come around the corner with their servants, sending curious glances our way. I keep my face impassive, giving a formal nod as they pass, and wait until we're alone again before speaking.

"Go on," she whispers, her veil hiding the movement. I glance at the note and then at the servant waiting nearby. "Don't make the boy wait."

"What about Cadmar?" I whisper back.

Sala slips the scroll from my grasp, ignoring my desperate "Sala" as she saunters over to the other servant.

"Please, lead the way, Kaartik," she says, handing him the note.

Kaartik bows, then leads the way.

Sala mutters to me once Kaartik's back is to us, "I'll handle Cadmar. You handle the prince."

Sala falls in line behind him, with me trying to glide gracefully like an Ari while my mind churns with nerves. We are the only souls in the hallway, and the emptiness of the palace puts me on edge. My leather sandals sound like drums pounding against the ground as Kaartik leads me to my date with the prince.

My date with the prince.

My breath hitches in my throat, and the steady drumbeat of my steps falters. I don't know how I am going to do this. I wasn't lying to Sala when I told her I didn't know how to flirt with him—I've spent my prime flirting years working as the Nightshade. Men were the last thing on my mind. Unless I was stealing from them. Ahmed was the last one who...

A fine sweat breaks out across my forehead.

No, I can't think about him. Not with so much at stake.

We round the corner, and there is Prince Ajani, flanked by two Suraksha. Without the royal vizier looming over his shoulder, Ajani appears taller, more confident. Sala and I sweep into deep bows. My indigo dupatta slinks to the side.

"Please rise. Good afternoon, Lady Acharya. Thank you for accompanying me on a tour of the palace."

"The pleasure is all mine, Your Highness."

We stand several meters apart, exchanging formalities as if we have never spoken before. His face is smoothed into his Ari mask, the same mask I've seen him wear around the rest of the council. Awkwardness looms between us, and I shoot him a pleading look. I can feel Sala's presence behind me as she adjusts my dupatta.

"Shall we?" the prince asks, extending his arm to me.

I nod, not trusting my voice, and take a step toward him. My foot snags, and I stumble forward. Into the prince's arms. His very warm, manly arms. A blush sears across my face as I stand up.

"Are you okay?" Ajani asks. I look up to assure him and meet his brown eyes centimeters from my own. I can feel the heat in my cheeks deepen as I stand too close to the prince.

"I, yes," I stammer. I lower my eyes from his and try to get myself together. "Thank you, Your Highness."

I place my hand on top of Ajani's outstretched arm like I'd originally intended, one of the gestures that Sala and Cadmar had made me practice in the Hathorda.

"We're going this way, Lady Acharya," he says and gently steers me past his two guards and Sala. I risk meeting Sala's eyes. She winks at me as the prince leads me to the left, the opposite side from the guests' quarters. My cheeks continue to burn as understanding dawns on me—Sala tripped me.

Ignorant of my embarrassment, Prince Ajani turns left and leads me down a new hallway as he discusses the palace. "This is the new palace, which is where most of the council resides, when they are here. There is not any reason to visit the old palace, it is where the first sultans resided and is not very impressive. But down here…"

The prince's voice trails off as the hallway opens up to a larger room. I can't help but gasp. The ceiling soars high above our heads at least three stories up, capped by a domed ceiling. My eyes follow the lines of the structure, the crisscrossed dark wooden beams that appear to swirl and converge at the centermost point.

"How is the wood swirled like that?" I whisper.

Prince Ajani smiles and says, "They aren't actually swirled. The ceiling plays tricks on your eyes in this room."

I nod as if this makes complete sense and allow the prince to lead me further into the room. Vast marble columns line either side of the room, like soldiers lined up to support the weight of the ceiling, and in the center of the room, the marble floor is etched with a design. I can't make out the shape, so I stand on a bench to get a better vantage point.

The prince gasps and quickly grabs my waist to steady me, saying, "Lady Acharya, be careful!"

In the splendor of the room, I'd forgotten myself. No Ari would jump onto a bench to get a better view. "Would you be so kind?" I ask, offering him my hand. Prince Ajani helps me step safely off the bench, before swiftly releasing my hand. The warmth of his hands on my hips lingers, and I turn towards the design on the floor to hide the heat that has risen in my cheeks. "Thank you, Your Highness. It's a mandala?"

"Yes," Prince Ajani clears his throat and tries again. "Yes, it took five carvers and several years to complete the detailing."

"It's beautiful," I say.

Prince Ajani offers his arm, and I accept it, allowing him to lead me out of the vast room. As he speaks, I glance back for one more glimpse of the magnificent domed ceiling. "On this side of the palace we have several pieces of art that I thought you might like to see, Lady Acharya. My father is—was—a patron of several celebrated artists in Aveena. He always desired to surround himself with their work."

"If the sultan was a patron of the arts, why are the pieces only on this side of the palace?" I ask, thinking about the barren walls that line the hallways I've seen thus far.

Ajani chuckles and says, "My father liked to hold the things he loved close to his heart."

"Oh?"

"You'll have noticed the simplicity of the palace I assume?"

"Well, yes, Your Highness." If you could call the elaborate marble, domed ceilings, and etched mandalas simple.

Prince Ajani gives a half shrug, saying, "That was my father's style."

"Oh."

I struggle to add something clever, to make him laugh like I did in the Harem Room, but my mind is blank. Our steps echo in the hallway, mocking me for my inability to flirt with the prince. Maybe Cadmar was right not to trust me with the prince.

**To feel affection and to give affection
is to feel the sun from both sides.**
-Aveenan Proverb-

35

Sultan Gautam's art gallery consists of a series of small rooms with archways instead of doors. The most extraordinary parts of these tiny rooms, tiny for palace standards, are the vaulted ceilings, each mimicking the domed ceiling in the grand marble room.

"Are all of the rooms like this?" I ask.

The prince smiles and says, "Yes, something about the importance of open ceilings and viewing art."

I bob my head in a non-answer and trail behind the prince further into the room. Sala and the two Suraksha remain in the hallway, discreetly watching us through the open door. Prince Ajani settles us on the bench in the middle of the room. The distance between us feels unnatural, as if we are waiting for another person to join us. I shift from side to side. Together we stare at the wall opposite us.

"Well, what do you think, Lady Acharya?"

Is this a trick question?

On the wall is a large square canvas. The stark white of the marble contrasts with the ruby red of the canvas, ensuring that the viewer's focus is on the canvas. The problem is that the artist had only painted the canvas red.

Solidly red.

"Uh, the red really does, um, stand out against the marble," I say.

"Hm, good insight, Lady Acharya. Might I draw your attention to the wall on our right?"

The prince speaks with his courtier's voice. As we shift in our seats to look at the right wall, I glance at the prince in the hopes of understanding if he is serious or jesting, but his face is set in his Ari mask, revealing nothing. The canvas on the right wall is the same except that the paint is solidly navy blue. We stare at it in silence. Sala must be struggling to not laugh out loud at us—two overly serious Ari staring at a solid painting.

Tentatively, I break the silence. "This one seems more—"

"Gloomy."

"Yes, definitely gloomy, Your Highness."

"The artist seems to be showcasing his pain in this piece."

Um, what?

I swivel on the bench so I'm facing the prince and not the painting. His face is still in the indifferent Ari mask. As my eyes search his face, the prince's full lips quirk up in the corner. I playfully push him on the shoulder.

"You're playing me, Prince Ajani!"

The prince laughs and waves away the guards who had stepped into the room when I had shoved the prince. My cheeks turn red, and I cross my arms in front of my chest, trying to preserve some dignity.

"You were trying so hard to be serious, Lady Acharya," Prince Ajani says. "I had to see if the woman I've spoken to was still there."

"So, you tricked me?" I sputter.

"I didn't think it would be that easy," he says, shrugging. A piece of his night-black hair falls into his eyes, and before I can think about it, I reach out a hand and push the hair to the side. The prince freezes, and I pull back my hand quickly.

"Do you want to leave the gallery?" he asks.

"Please."

The prince helps me up from the bench and links our arms together. The motion pulls me closer to him, and I lower my eyes to avoid meeting Sala's gaze.

We walk further into the labyrinth of hallways and, thankfully, away from the bizarre art gallery. As we walk, the formal prince mask starts to melt away, and the Ajani I had spoken to the first night emerges. "...honestly had forgotten what my father's art gallery was like. I had thought it would have been a good place to take you, but clearly, my father had strange taste."

"And do you court all the young women this way?" I ask.

He glances at me and grins. "Oh, am I courting you now?"

"Well, I thought..." My voice trails off. Once again, I'm unsure how to answer the prince. He's keeping me off kilter. I don't like it. The unnatural Ari manners that Cadmar tried to instill in me keep trying and failing to cage my natural Laila responses.

Prince Ajani leans closer to me so that our heads are nearly touching and whispers, "Lailani, I want to spend more time with you. Though that is only if you want to, as well."

Our eyes meet, causing me to blush again. I look down.

"Of course, Ajani."

The butterflies in my stomach fight with the pit of guilt that I feel luring Ajani in. I change the subject before my guilt can give me away.

"So that was Sultan Gautam's favorite place in the palace—"

"For whatever reason."

I smile. "—so which part of the palace is your favorite?"

"Come with me," he says. Ajani's eyes light up with excitement, and I can't help grinning in response. He grabs my hand and pulls me faster through the hallways. His hand dwarfs my own, I feel like a child being led through the bazaar.

The remnants of the Ari mask evaporate from Ajani's face. It's the first time I've seen him appear his age, he's only twenty-three, after all. We bump into two Ari as we run like kids. The two councilmen shoot us disapproving stares until they realize who ran into them and hastily bow. Sala and the Suraksha, caught off guard, struggle to catch up to us.

Ajani stops his mad dash in front of a set of interwoven metal doors. A breeze enters through the gaps in the design. Wooden beams form a low-hanging ceiling and vines twirl haphazardly around the wood. A flash of blue catches my attention as a jewel-colored bird moves in my peripheral.

"This," Ajani says, grinning, "is the royal aviary."

Ajani pushes the gate open, and we step into the little antechamber.

"You have to close the gate to the rest of the palace first before entering or else the birds can escape."

"Has that happened before?" I ask.

Ajani laughs and closes the intricate iron gate in our chaperones' faces.

"Not since I was younger. Parakeets are small, but they can make a huge mess. My father was fuming. It took the servants days to recapture all the birds."

We walk through the inner gate, and Ajani secures the door behind us. Like the palace gardens, the plant life radiates with a vibrant green that isn't seen anywhere else in Aveena. Vines ensnare many of the trees, oftentimes creeping from the highest branches to the metal enclosure above. Bright magenta flowers bloom from the vines closest to the entryway, the honey-sweet smell wafting to me in the humid air.

"Come."

Ajani grabs my hand and laces his fingers into mine, making my heart leap. Our interwoven fingers feel intimate in the humid enclosure as Ajani leads me further into the aviary. A rustle of wings draws my attention to the right as a massive, red-breasted parrot takes flight. I gasp and nearly trip as I gape at the parrot. Ajani grips my hand tighter, steadying me.

"It's only a bit further."

"What is?" I ask.

I can hear the smile in his voice. "You'll see."

The chatter of the smaller birds gets louder, but we still cannot see them yet, just the flash of color here and there through the thick green leaves. The path veers off to the right, but Ajani stops and squeezes my hand.

"You'll have to be careful where you step. The ground is uneven."

I nod and let the prince guide me off the path. Ajani holds branches out of the way and offers his hand at the smallest dip in the ground. His gallantry is sweet, even if it is unnecessary. Finally, we come across a small clearing in a corner of the aviary. The soft grass looks springy to the touch. Trees encircle the clearing, allowing for a smidgen of privacy. On the far side of the clearing, long birdhouses harbor hundreds of chattering birds. The small, yellow-capped birds fly in and out of the birdhouse, bringing food to family members inside. Although the birds are uniformly yellow on top, their bodies vary in color—from emerald-green to the bright blue of the bird in the entryway to vivid orange. I'm so transfixed by the hum of activity surrounding the birdhouse that Ajani has to tug on my hand to bring me further into the clearing.

"They're beautiful," I say.

"Better than the paintings, that's for sure," Ajani says, teasing me.

I glance up at the prince and smile shyly. I have to look back at the birds to escape the intensity of his gaze.

"Here, let's sit."

Ajani leads me to the one bench. The bench is plain except for the vine design that graces the top of the bench and skirts down its sides. I let go of Ajani's hand in order to sweep my skirt the correct way to be able to sit. I finish arranging myself and look at the squawking birds. A green bird and a red one fight over territory in front of us, tittering back and forth on the railing of the birdhouse. *Not unlike the Ari women I've met so far*, I muse with a smile.

"A rupee for your thoughts?" Ajani asks.

I flash him a small smile. "Would you like the truth or a pretty answer?"

"The truth, always," he says.

I grin and gesture back at the birds. "I was thinking how some of the women in the Veiled Room squawk over territory like these two birds."

Ajani's resounding laugh causes several of the birds to take flight.

"Well, you asked for the truth," I mutter sheepishly. I try to cross my arms in front of my chest, but Ajani takes my hand again and weaves his fingers through mine.

"And what was the pretty answer?" Ajani asks, his dark brown eyes twinkling in anticipation.

"That the birds are beautiful and perfect adornments to such a magnificent palace. Or at least something like that to butter you up."

"Butter me up?"

I smile and flutter my eyelashes at Ajani like Esha Shah would. "Well, a girl's got to stay in His Highness's good graces somehow."

Ajani chuckles and slides closer to me on the bench. Our knees are a feather apart, but he doesn't close the distance. The hand that Ajani is holding bends at an awkward angle, but I dare not move. Adrenaline rushes through my veins with his nearness.

"Lady Acharya, you have no need to 'butter me up' as you say." I smile and meet his eyes. Both of us have forgotten the birds. "I always want your honest answer, Lailani. I crave it."

My smile feels brittle as I continue to meet his vulnerable eyes.

My name is Laila, I think. *And I'm not as honest as you believe.*

**The dunes, the stars, the creatures of the
sea and air, man and woman—we are all
children of Wind Mother and Sky Father.**
-from the Sacred Scrolls of Wind Mother
translated from Aramak, the Olden Tongue-

36

"Lady Acharya!"

Farah's voice halts me in my flight from the Veiled Room. Another demonstration of the vizier's power and pointless use of my time in the birdcage upstairs.

"Lady Asfour."

I bow briefly to the older woman and smile. Linking her arm with mine, Farah tows me alongside her in the opposite direction. Raising an eyebrow, I add sarcastically, "Um, good to see you, too, Lady Asfour. Of course, I'll go with you wherever you are taking me."

The older woman's laughter chimes through the hall as she leads me to the eastern wing of the palace. "Really, Lailani, how *do* you keep that prince with that tongue of yours?"

"He's not interested in me," I mutter.

Farah's laughter echoes in the marble hallway. One of the elder councilmen glares at her as she passes, but Farah ignores him. She leans closer so that our heads are nearly touching and whispers, "Oh my dear, even the blind can see he's interested."

"Where are we going, Lady Asfour?" I keep my chin up, ignoring the heat rising to my cheeks.

As we turn down another hallway, a breeze swirls around our feet, catching the skirt of my saree and playing with it. Farah clicks her tongue at me. "Just because you're embarrassed doesn't mean you need to get snippy with me, dear. Didn't Lady Shah invite you?"

"Lady Shah wouldn't invite me anywhere," I reply, resisting rolling my eyes.

Farah pats my hand, saying, "You really should work on that, dear."

"Me?" I'm struggling to keep my voice from rising. "It's Lady Shah who's had a problem with me since—"

"Since you unleashed that tongue on her, too."

I stop and tug my arm from Farah's. "That's not fair at all, Farah. She had it coming to her—"

"Of *course* she had it coming to her, dear," she says calmly. Farah looks me up and down, her eyes critical. "You don't know how to interact with women do you?"

"What?" I shout, indignant. It's not my fault that Lady Shah hated me from the moment she saw me. Everything since then she's deserved.

Farah sighs and looks at me pityingly. "You can't go barging in and expect women to respond to you. Dealing with women takes the art of subtlety and finesse, both of which you need to work on. You have spent too much time with that cousin and uncle of yours, I'm afraid."

I can't handle her assessment. She has no idea of what I'm dealing with, the pressure I'm under.

Duh, Laila. She can't know any of that. Shut up and listen to what she's telling you, my inner voice chides me.

After a moment of indecision, I ask her, "Okay, so how should I deal with her?"

Farah links her arm with mine again and pulls me along the hallway. I drag my feet, not wanting to deal with any of this. The urge to turn around and walk back to Erol's suite is overpowering.

"To start, you should come and prepare candles with me for Andheraka."

"Andheraka?"

My mind is reeling. It can't be that time of year already. Can it?

"Yes dear, the shortest night of the year?" Farah smirks at my confusion. "You had no idea that the festival was in four days, did you?"

"I—I lost track of time."

"The palace does that to you," she says knowingly.

We round the corner and meet several other women heading in the same direction. Servants carry tiffins of wicks, tiny crystal glasses, and pails of white wax through the door. The giggles and chatter of women carry through the entryway, more joyful and energetic than anything I've experienced thus far in the Veiled Room.

"Come on, Lady Acharya, time to make candles for Andheraka."

Before I stop myself, I ask, "The women in the palace still make the candles?"

Farah looks long and hard at me. I try not to squirm under her gaze. Why can't I keep my big mouth shut? My tongue indeed...

"Of course, Lailani. Didn't your family do this in the Upper City?" she asks. I bob my head in a nonanswer, already furious with myself for opening my big mouth. "Why does it surprise you that we would do it up here then?"

Think quick, Laila.

"I, well, everyone just seems so—refined here," I say with a shrug, hoping she thinks I'm still in awe of the palace. "It's hard to imagine."

She pauses, giving me another look, before saying, "Participating in traditions reminds us that we're human."

We enter the suite, cutting off more discussion. How does Farah do that? Just drop knowledge like it's not significant at all. My awe of Lady Asfour continues to grow the more I talk with her.

Inside the suite, the cushions have been pushed to the perimeter of the three walls. By the vast windows, servants huddle over hot wax, pouring the burning liquid into the small crystal glasses and setting the wicks. The window shades are flung open to allow the heat of the melting wax escape as the servants work. Ari women sit on the cushions around the room, applying decorations to the finished candles. I scoff—of course the Ari wouldn't make the candles themselves—but luckily the sound is drowned out by the cacophony of women's voices.

Farah leads me to two empty cushions against the far wall. As we pass through the center of the chaos, women shoot us furtive glances over their candle-work. I chance a glance at Lady Shah, poised in the centermost cushion surrounded by her posse. Her eyes narrow as they watch me, adding to her already-sour disposition, but for once, she does not sling any insults my way.

"Let me guess," I whisper to Farah as we settle into the cushions, "Lady Shah wanted me to be left out?"

"And do we always give Lady Shah what she wants?" Farah asks playfully. As two servants bring a small bowl of glue and paint brushes, she adds, "Subtlety and finesse."

Years have passed since I was able to celebrate Andheraka. Before I escaped to the Lower City, my mother and I would spend many afternoons leading up to the festival, making and repurposing the candles. I would handle the hot wax while she did the decorating. My mother could always make the delicate paper and a few jewels we had into miniature works of art. One year, when we ran out of paper early, mother found petals and leaves, which she dried in the sun and adhered to the candleholders. She was renowned on our street for making the best candles, and we would display them prominently in our window in the days leading up to Andheraka for passersby to admire.

I did not inherit her gift.

"I give up, Farah," I announce. Twenty minutes later, and all I have to show for it are two crinkly wads of paper stuck haphazardly onto one side of the candle and several giggles from the woman next to me as I growl in frustration.

"It's—" Farah says and then begins to laugh. "Well, it's horrible, dear, but at least you're trying."

I sigh and stare around the room. The scent of sandalwood is heavy in the air from the candles, mingling with undertones of glue from our supplies. Esha Shah is showing off her perfectly bejeweled creations to her friends. Although Esha is always fishing for compliments, this time around she's earned them.

"Here." The young woman sitting next to me hands me a handful of jewels. She smiles shyly before continuing her delicate paper flower construction.

"Thank you——?"

"Lady Tahan."

I bow my head in acknowledgement. "Lady Acharya."

"I know."

"Thank you, Lady Tahan."

At least all I have to do with the jewels is glue them on. I apply the pieces around the two paper wads that I've already created. Part of the reason that I'm struggling with the candle is because I'm not giving it my full attention—although I'm participating, I know that Cadmar would want me to work on learning information that he could use. Unfortunately, my brain seems incapable of doing both. I give up on listening to the conversation between Lady Ba and her neighbor and ask Farah, "So, is Andheraka the same as in the Upper City?"

"What do you mean, dear?" Farah asks. Her tongue is in between her teeth as she delicately sets the paper flower she's been constructing onto the edge of the candle. "Ah, there!"

"That's beautiful, Farah," I say.

"It will never be as beautiful as the real thing, but it will pass," she says. She sets her finished masterpiece to the side and waves to a servant to bring her another candle. "Now what was it you were asking me again?"

"Andheraka. Are the celebrations the same as in the rest of the city?" I ask again.

"Of course! Like I said, Lailani, traditions are important. The ceremony will take place outside in the palace gardens. I believe Councilman Lobo's granddaughter has been chosen to begin the dancing this year."

Lady Pateel snorts. I tilt my head questioningly, inviting her to explain.

"Well, Lady Acharya, it's always amazed me that Councilman Lobo was able to have children, seeing as, well, you know." She gives me a sly grin.

"Seeing as what?" I ask. Both Farah and Lady Pateel giggle.

"There have always been rumors you see," Farah begins. "About, um, Ray Lobo's...preferences."

"Oh. *Oh.*"

One of my jewels falls off. I sigh and push the candle away. I don't have time to fight with candles and decorations anyway.

"Here," Farah says, thrusting a candle into my hand. "Hold this for me, dear."

Lady Asfour applies delicate paper flowers to the candles as I hold them for her. After a few moments of concentration, I remind her of my original question. "So, Councilman Lobo's granddaughter will start the dancing?"

"Oh, yes," Farah says.

"And the dancing will carry into the night like it does all over Aveena," Lady Pateel adds. "It's really quite lovely."

"You're such a romantic, Sanjaya," Lady Tahan says, nudging Lady Pateel.

"Well, it's true!"

"'Lovely' isn't how I would describe it," Lady Tahan rolls her eyes at me, sharing a private joke. I smile tentatively in return.

"How would you describe it then?" Lady Pateel asks.

"Stiff."

We laugh at the disappointed look on Lady Pateel's face. I relax further, enjoying the conversation with the women around me and grateful for the simple job Farah was having me do.

"I heard that the dancing in the city can get quite raucous," Lady Pateel says, sniffing. "I would much prefer stiff and beautiful than that craze."

"Oh, I don't know, Sanjaya," Lady Tahan says with a grin, "I think I could use some raucous dancing if you know what I mean."

I laugh with the others, ignoring the look Lady Shah sends us from across the room.

"What about you, Lady Acharya?"

"Hm?"

"Which would you prefer?"

"I'm used to the raucous dancing in the city," I say without thinking. The three women around me pause and stare. "I—I mean that I've never celebrated Andheraka in the palace, so it's going to feel strange compared to—compared to what I'm used to."

Farah swoops to my rescue. "Of course, dear. But you shouldn't worry too much about it. You'll catch on fine."

"Especially if that young prince of yours is leading you around," Lady Tahan says slyly.

I blush and look down, unable to hide the small smile playing on my lips. The women around me laugh again, but, for once, I feel like part of the laughter and not the subject of it.

Several minutes pass in comfortable silence. For the first time, the women in the room feel like real women to me, not just Ari. The excitement brings about a carefree aura amongst them, softening their normally stiff and competitive natures. Even Lady Shah seems less prickly as she glues emerald jewels in swirls around her candles.

"You know what's odd?" Lady Pateel says as she waits for a servant to bring her a new candle. I'm only half listening as the warm breeze soothes me further, making me sleepy and content. "The Nightshade's silence. Vihaan and I were discussing it just last night."

"I thought after the celebration, he would strike again, just to prove he's still out there," Lady Tahan adds.

"That's what Vihaan and I were thinking," Lady Pateel says, nodding.

Fear prickles down my spine, draining the color from my face and banishing my sleepiness. Farah gestures for me to rotate the candle I hold for her. I struggle to keep my hands from trembling as she adds, "You really do worry too much about that sneakthief, Sanjaya. That's the real power he holds over us—fear."

"I don't know," Lady Pateel says slowly. "You remember what happened to the Chandras."

The three women around me fell silent. I racked my brains for the name, but like most of my jobs as the Nightshade, I had hidden the memory from myself. Taking a deep breath, I ask, "What happened?"

Farah sighs. "I forget that you weren't here, Lailani. You were too young to care about the news at any point."

I bob my head, waiting. The chatter of the other women fills our silence, until Lady Tahan speaks. "It was quite horrible, really. Councilman Chandra was on the rise, but the scandal—"

"No one has heard from them since," Lady Pateel whispers.

"Everyone knew it was the work of the Nightshade, it had his telltale signs, but a ruined reputation cannot be repaired."

Lady Tahan's voice drops off, and she refocuses on her candle, as if afraid to speak further about the Nightshade.

"Farah?" I ask.

Farah sets the flower down and fixes me with her direct stare. "Councilman Chandra was on the rise as Lady Tahan mentioned, and whenever you rise, there are those who wish you to fall. Councilman Chandra was framed for communication with the Tribes. Papers were found in his home, correspondence between himself and the head of one of the Tribes, revealing that the Tribes would support Chandra as sultan if he were to overthrow Sultan Gautam."

The rest of the color must have drained from my face, because Farah pats my hand reassuringly, adding, "You have nothing to worry about, dear. It was all false, and the Tribes have never threatened Aveena."

The women fall silent again, their eyes on their candles. As I hold the candle out for Lady Asfour, memories surface, the close encounter with the two city guardsmen, the ease of slipping through the unlocked front door like I owned the house myself, the pride that seared through me as Velo handed me the bag of money, the joy of being able to support Tanu and Dada...

"What happened to the Chandras, after?" I ask, determined to hear the full story.

"Banishment from the palace and hefty fines," Lady Pateel says with a shudder.

"At least it was only that," Farah reminds her.

Guilt sinks into my stomach, removing the remnants of pride that had surfaced with my memories.

"Lady Asfour, your flowers are wondrous!" Lady Dara exclaims nearby. Her voice brings us back to the present.

"Thank you, dear," Farah says, smiling. "Your jewel design is, um, quite unique, Lady Dara."

Lady Dara winks at me and says, "I'm hoping that Dhruv takes the hint."

I laugh with the other women to cover up the coldness that has rooted in my chest, guilt for my actions as the Nightshade.

A person of two minds is a liar;
a person of three minds is a hypocrite.
-Aveenan Proverb-

37

After saying my goodbyes to Farah, Lady Pateel, and Lady Tahan, I follow Sala through the weaving hallways back to Erol's suite. Despite the knot of guilt about the Nightshade, the glow of success settles in my chest, outshining the guilt, making me feel that for once, something has gone smoothly with the women in the palace. Lady Shah left me alone, preferring to ignore my presence altogether, with the exception of several disapproving glares shot my way. And after being surrounded by the air of excitement for the festival, I can't help feeling excited for the sense of normalcy that Andheraka will bring to my palace life.

The sense of normalcy is fleeting.

Cadmar awaits us inside of Erol's suite. I haven't had direct contact with him since the second day in the palace, which has suited me just fine. Unlike Cadmar, the other members of Logonkelie trust me.

"We've been waiting," Cadmar says without preamble.

"Lady Asfour had Lailani join in with the other ladies in preparation for Andheraka. It was a good opportunity for Lailani," Sala says simply. She grabs a handful of grapes from a nearby platter then settles on a cushion near Cadmar.

"Where's Erol?" I ask.

"Mingling with some of the older councilmen," Zahir answers. He's stretched out across two cushions, his arm slung across his eyes.

I nudge Zahir with a toe. "Why aren't you with him?"

"I was getting a headache from their talking, so I left," he says dramatically.

"Imagine that," I reply sarcastically. I sink onto the cushion next to him, not bothering to keep my saree unrumpled–I know Sala will shove me into a new silk contraption for the feast tonight. "Someone talking too much for you, Zaharian."

Zahir scowls, but Cadmar stops our banter by saying, "I have a special assignment for you two."

I freeze, unsure if I can handle another Ari kiss-ass session or more instructions to flirt. So far all of Cadmar's instructions have been outside of my scope of expertise. I prefer to be hidden in the shadows and invisible, and my experience in the palace so far has been anything but that.

"What is it this time?" Zahir asks, failing to hide the dread in his voice. I cover my smile, knowing that Zahir feels the same way as I do about our assignments.

"We have an opportunity with Andheraka, and I want you to take advantage of it. Use the festival as a distraction to weaken at least one of the vizier's supporters. Cast doubt on their credibility."

"How?" I ask.

Cadmar waves a hand dismissively at the two of us. "You should decide amongst yourselves."

Zahir rubs his eyes. As if that will rid us of the stress of the palace. "Anyone in particular?"

"Sala continually reminds me that you both are capable. You have full reign to play it how you will so long as we are discrediting the vizier's supporters." A spark of excitement ignites in me. The opportunity to plan like I used to, work like I used to. Banishing the knot of guilt in my stomach, I sit up straighter, trying to reign it in and keep up a professional facade. This will be different from the Chandra's anyway—I have control of the target. Cadmar continues, interrupting my thoughts. "Make sure to stay away from the vizier himself."

Zahir scoffs. "Gladly."

"Is it just Zahir-Zaharian and I completing this?" I ask.

"I will assign Nimra to you as well."

Sala stirs from her cushion. "Cadmarji, I think I should—"

"No, Sala."

"But I—"

"It is time for them to fly on their own." The finality in Cadmar's tone leaves no room for argument. The tension radiates briefly between them before Sala breaks first, gazing out the window instead.

Zahir and I exchange looks, but don't comment.

"When can you spare Nim?" I ask.

"I'll send her after the feast this evening."

I nod and stand. "Well, if that is all, Cadmar—"

"Actually, I wanted to have a word with you, Lailani."

Surprise and trepidation run through me, but I school my features into the Ari neutrality that I've perfected. Cadmar gestures to Zahir and Sala, not bothering to look at their faces as he dismisses them. Zahir looks at me sympathetically as he and Sala disappear into the suite.

As the door snicks shut, I cross my arms and say, "If this is about the prince, I promise I've been trying to avoid him. It's just—"

"This is not about the prince, although if you were to try a little harder to avoid him..." Cadmar's voice trails off as I snort.

"And how would you have me avoid a direct invitation?"

"I–well–I didn't come to talk about the prince." Clearing his throat, Cadmar continues, "Let's discuss this assignment."

I barely tamp down on my sarcasm as I say, "Isn't that what we were discussing with Zahir and Sala?"

"Do you remember what I said to you the first time we talked?"

Flashes of that last failed job as the Nightshade swim in my memory. A knot reforms in the pit of my stomach as I think about the one rule of Cadmar's that I've never followed.

"If you are referring to your...expectations, I've adhered to your—"

"No, that's not what I'm referring to."

My face crumples in confusion as I struggle to remember the rest of the deal, the conversation that altered my existence so thoroughly. Cadmar grips my arm, the hard angles of his face softened as he says, "I want for you to have a purpose, to care about the work that you are completing. I want you to approach this assignment with that sense of purpose, with the desire to see change."

I falter, stepping slightly away from Cadmar. This is not the brash, cold Cadmar I am used to.

"Why do you care?" I ask.

The Ari mask snaps back into place, making me question whether Cadmar had ever softened at all. "I want more for you than to just survive. It's what I want for everyone who works with me."

"And why should I care what you want?" My tone is rife with bitterness. "Last time I checked, I'm the only one you work with that is blackmailed into being here."

Cadmar stares at me, slowly taking in my defensive stance and my words. "Does it matter how you joined us now that you see the problems with the vizier yourself?"

"How can I trust you, when you don't trust me?" I shoot back.

"But you trust Zahir and Sala," Cadmar says, a statement not a question.

"They let me choose to trust them."

And without giving Cadmar the opportunity to respond, I sweep into my room and shut the door.

<hr/>

Although I know that I need my rest, I'm awake before dawn on the morning of Andheraka. I slip into the main room of our suite and silently cast open a window. Sitting on the ledge, I stare out to the palace grounds. Night still wraps herself around the palace, and when I lean forward, I can see the stars from this window, unlike the view from my room.

Excitement has been coursing through my body since we created our plan, combining with the excitement for the festival itself.

Dark anticipation fills me. Finally, the chance to bring out the Nightshade, to don my alter ego. Finally, the opportunity to put my skills to full use.

I miss the night. The darkness and shadows shielding me. The thrill of success, of being invisible.

The desire to become the Nightshade again overshadows the guilt I feel knowing the ramifications of my actions. Of the fate of the Chandras.

It *is* different this time.

I slide my hands around the bars of the window. The metal is slick with the morning dew and still tinged with the warmth from yesterday's sun. I rest my forehead against one of the solid bars. The urge to slip out through the window and into the night overwhelms me. I long for the freedom.

I squeeze my eyes shut, closing myself off from the temptation.

Tonight, I think.

Soft steps tiptoe across the room. I keep my eyes shut, allowing my ears to track the steps across the room. Ten steps away. Four steps. At two steps, the shuffling stops. With my eyes closed, I can feel his eyes watching, unwilling to disturb me.

"Good morning, Zahir," I whisper.

I can almost hear the smile in his voice as he says, "Good morning, Laila."

Zahir sits on the windowsill next to me. His knee nearly touches my own, and the energy that I feel around Zahir tugs at me, wanting me to close the gap, sending tingles. I savor the feeling, my head resting against the metal, Zahir's now-familiar presence warming me.

I turn my head and look at him. The faint moonlight reflects on his eyes, making them appear like lodestones in the darkness. Zahir smiles, still watching me closely, and nods to the bars I'm leaning against.

"Wouldn't be planning on sneaking out, would you?" he whispers.

"Not after the last time." I pull my knees to my chest and lean against the frame, turning away from the night and towards Zahir. "Plus, I have an engagement tonight that requires my full concentration."

"Do you now?" Zahir asks, pulling at his beard. Then in his best Ari voice, "I hope you don't plan to get into any trouble, sweet lady."

I stick my tongue out at Zahir. "Oh, of course not, ji."

For the first time since the Hathorda roof, Zahir and I sit in silence, watching the rays of the sun pierce the morning sky.

After several minutes, Zahir gestures to the shimmering black cloth waiting in the center of the room. Together we lift the soft material and drape the fabric over the windows, dimming the initial rays of the sun. Sunlight catches on the glitter woven into the fabric.

"Might as well do the rest of the suite," Zahir says, handing me a stack of smaller cloths in the same shimmery black fabric. I cover the unlit lamps on one side of the room, while Zahir drapes his fabric over the smaller window near his door. Once I drape the fabric over the window and sources of light in my room, I go back out to the main room and sink into one of the cushions.

"Let the fasting begin," Zahir says with a bow as he walks into the room.

"I can already hear your stomach growling. How have you survived Andheraka all of these years?" I tease.

Zahir lays on the floor, hands behind his head, and stares at the ceiling, like he's actually contemplating my question. I nudge him with my foot, and he sends me a lopsided grin.

"You should've seen the feast I had at midnight last night. Even Anik Ba would be able to survive a day of fasting with the amount of food I guzzled down."

"Where did you get the food?" I ask.

"I asked nicely," Zahir says with a wink.

I snort and exaggerate rolling my eyes for Zahir's benefit. "Uh huh. Horseshit."

"What?"

"You? Ask nicely?" I scoff again and lean into the cushion. Laughing with Zahir helps ease the tension coursing through my body in anticipation of tonight.

"Hey now. One of us has to know how to do it."

I glare at Zahir. "I'm not going to respond to that."

"You just did."

"Dunes, you're obnoxious."

Zahir winks at me again. "It's what makes me so irresistible."

"If irresistible is code for wanting to slap you across the throat to get you to shut up, then yes."

"Only if you kiss it to make it better afterwards."

"Pig," I say. I try to sound like I'm disgusted but my grin gives me a way. Zahir smiles and starts to speak but then something over my shoulder shuts him up. I turn on my cushion to see a bedraggled and sleepy Erol in the doorway.

"Could you two wait until the sun is up to bicker like the council? *Some* of us want to sleep before tonight."

"Go get your beauty sleep, Erol," Zahir says innocently. "Everyone knows you're in desperate need of it."

Erol glares, but then a yawn takes over, ruining the image. I laugh and stand up.

"We should try to rest, you know," I say to Zahir. "We've got a long night ahead of us."

"That we do."

Instructions followed.
All is well with two friends.
N.

38

The hours drag by until the beginning of the festival despite it being the shortest day of the year. I alternate between pacing in my room, observed by my tailless lizard who has returned, and pacing in the main room, observed by a bemused Erol. We don't even have the norm of meals to distract us from our task later, fasting is required in anticipation of Andheraka.

At midday, Nim interrupts my pacing to go over the details of our plan once more.

By the afternoon, I convince Sala to lead me through one of her yoga sequences to channel my pent-up energy. I force my body into increasingly more complicated poses, using the slow burn in my muscles to burn away my excess nerves. By the time Sala dresses me for the evening, my mind has sunk into focused precision. Sala has braided my hair into a beautiful, complicated arrangement on top of my head. She managed to make sure that my hair won't budge during any of the night's activities.

My cropped choli is filled with iridescent sparkles, glittering over my chest and shoulders. I run my fingers over the exquisite golden material, selected for its practicality as much as its beauty, before fastening my skirt high on my hips, hiding the black dhoti I wear underneath.

"That should work," Sala says from over my shoulder.

"You're sure that you cannot see the dhoti underneath?" I ask, twisting in the mirror to check each angle.

"The skirt is long enough if that's what you're asking. You ready?" Her voice is low, only a slight tremble revealing the trepidation she feels for us. We considered using Sala in our plans, but Cadmar's instructions were clear.

I grab her hand and give it a reassuring squeeze. "Sala, this is what I'm good at."

"That doesn't mean that the circumstances haven't changed," she says.

"I'm ready. I promise." I turn back to the mirror, checking my skirt one more time. "You are such a mother hen."

Sala smiles, but it doesn't clear the worry from her eyes. "Only to those who need it."

I open my mouth to argue, but Zahir's arrival stops me.

"You ready to go, Laila?" he asks from the doorway.

"Of course," I reply. I take his offered arm, letting him escort me to the beginning of the festival. "You really should use my Ari name," I say softly.

Zahir bobbles his head in a non-answer, causing his curls to bounce happily around.

"I want you to remember who you are."

Ever the overprotective older brother, as Farah says. "I know who I am, *Zaharian*. C'mon we've got festivities to attend to."

Sala follows us out to the palace gardens. Like the windows in Erol's suite, every window we pass is covered with shimmering black fabric, blocking our view of the dying sun. Faint light resiliently illuminates our path through the curtains; soon, the palace will be swathed in absolute darkness. I try to retain my focus on the task ahead, but Zahir won't stop muttering about the plan in my ear as we make the short walk to the ceremony.

"Remember to wait until the end of the retelling but right before the hour of silence," he says.

"I know, Zaharian."

"If we try to leave once the hour has started, they won't let us."

"I know, Zaharian."

"The timing must be perfect."

"It will be, Zaharian."

"And we must be back in time for the beginning of the dancing."

"Zahir!" I whisper fiercely as I pull him to the side of the hallway. His eyes open wide as another pair of Ari pass us on the way to the gardens, shooting us curious looks. I wait until they are out of earshot before I continue. "I know the plan. You need to stop."

"But—"

I slap my hand over his mouth to cut off his response. His golden eyes widen but it works. "No buts! We both know what we are doing. If you keep talking, you'll ruin my focus that I've honed all day."

Tentatively, I remove my hand from his mouth. He rubs his beard, then asks, "Your focus?"

I sigh and look to the ceiling for patience, count to three, and then meet his eyes. "Yes, Zahir, my focus. Before a job, I always spend hours focusing on my task. If you keep badgering me, you'll ruin it."

"Oh, I, uh, sorry, Laila."

I link my arm with Zahir's again and continue walking towards the gardens.

"You have to trust me, Zahir, like I'm trusting you," I say in an undertone. "I appreciate your concern for me, but you've got a lot to learn when it comes to how I work."

Zahir is saved the necessity of answering me as we approach the doors to the garden. Two servants open the doors, revealing the crowd milling about in the gardens.

The steady beat of a drum cuts through the thrum of the crowd. A hush descends over the Ari scrambling to take their seats surrounding the circular stage in the middle of the garden. Zahir and I snag two seats on the outermost circle. My heart beats in time with the increasing fervor of the drum.

A crescendo and then silence.

A shadow walks to the center of the stage, a woman dressed in the same shimmering black used to cover the windows in the palace. The only skin visible under the swaths of fabric are her hands and the glint of her eyes.

Slowly, she extends her arms and walks in a circle, looking at the Ari sitting on each of the four sides before speaking. Her voice is deep for a woman's voice and charged with emotion as she tells the story of Wind Mother and Sky Father:

"Sky Father and Wind Mother were fighting. Sky Father's indifference towards their people angered Wind Mother. She believed that his distance made him uncaring and unsympathetic to their needs. Wind Mother accused Sky Father of being incapable of understanding their people because he was never among them. Sky Father knew that he understood their children because he could see everything that they do. From his distance he was able to see their triumphs and their failures; he alone could see the big picture whereas Wind Mother was too close to their people to know what was good for them."

Masked actors join the narrator on the stage, however, instead of watching them, I close my eyes, focusing on the woman's words, the emotion that she pours into every syllable.

"Their argument was so disruptive to the world that they had created together that the earth trembled. Animals fled the dry earth and hid in the dark depths of the ocean. Mountains slid into the sea. Without the mountains to protect her, the desert clung to the dry earth, pushing herself against the ocean and resisting falling into her depths. The stars disappeared, terrified by the argument between their parents.

The children that Sky Father and Wind Mother were arguing about hid as well. They could not hunt or gather or build or bind. The humans huddled together out of fear for the battle raging between their parents."

The narrator's voice drops away, leaving the crescendo of the drum in her wake. Taking a deep breath, I open my palms to the sky, opening myself to Wind Mother.

In a whisper that carried over the crowd of still Ari, the narrator continues:

"One by one, the people lit candles to coax the stars out of hiding, to show their distant cousins that there was nothing to fear. The people hoped that by showing their parents the light in the darkness, that Sky Father and Wind

Mother would remember their love for one another and for their children.

After several hours of waiting, one small child began to move slowly throughout the candles, singing and dancing as she went. She imitated the fluid nature of Wind Mother as she twirled around the candles; she imitated the sturdy, ever-present nature of Sky Father as she stomped in time to her song. Drums joined in, drowning out her voice, but filling the hearts of everyone present. Soon all of Sky Father and Wind Mother's children, big and small alike, were dancing through the sand and stomping to the drums. Each held a candle in his or her hand as they moved through the lights that they had lit in the stars' absence."

Zahir's gentle tug on my wrist pulls me out of my reverie. Under the cover of the third and final crescendo of the drums, Zahir and I slip behind a tree and back towards the doors to the palace. As we walk, the narrator's voice follows us, whether a blessing or a curse, I'm unsure.

"The earth slowed its trembling, transfixed by the hypnotic dance of the people. Animals stopped diving into the depths of the ocean, and the desert was saved from joining the mountains in the ocean depths…"

"Lean on me, so it's believable," Zahir mutters, tugging me closer so he can wrap an arm around me.

I slump into Zahir's arms, letting him drag-carry me the final steps to the door. The narrator's final words weave through the air, indicating the last few moments before the hour of silence: "One by one, the stars peeked through the darkness, curious about the moving and twinkling lights below them. The song carried across the sands and to the sky, finally halting Sky Father and Wind Mother in their argument.

From above, the two looked down on their people, touched by their bravery and unity in the moment of darkness..."

"Now or never," I say under my breath as we approach the guardsman.

"What are you—"

"Good evening, noble Suraksha," Zahir says, cutting off the man's question. "We will need to return to our room shortly. My cousin is feeling faint. She must be attended to if she will make it through the night."

The guard looks at me. I try to look woozy as the two men talk.

"Everyone must attend the hour of silence."

Zahir waves a hand, nearly dropping me in the process. "Well, as you can see, my dear fellow, my cousin cannot stand on her own, let alone perch quietly for an hour like the delicate flower she is. You really ought to let us back in so that her fainting doesn't make a scene."

"But—"

"But really. Can't you hear the narrator finishing up her lovely retelling? If we keep discussing the situation like this, we will be here until the morning feast, and we can't have that. My father will not be happy if my dear, sweet cousin hasn't arrived in time to dance with the other Aristocracy due to your admirable attendance in your duties."

"But—"

I moan slightly, trying to appear on the verge of passing out. I flicker my eyelashes, rolling my eyes up before refocusing on the guard in front of me. His gaze focuses on me for a moment. I can see the internal struggle he's fighting, deciding whether to disobey orders or to cause a scene. The whole time Zahir keeps talking in a fierce whisper, not giving the man time to think.

"...always been a bit delicate, you know. And with the fasting today, it's really no surprise that she's feeling this way. I mean look at the amount of skirt she has. That would weigh you down too if you were feeling faint already. Oh no, look at her eyes. Can't you see that she needs to lay down right now? C'mon good man, you really need to let us in before she can't walk anymore. My father—"

"Alright, alright," the guard says.

He grabs the door and pushes it open for us, and we hobble in. Zahir gives him a cheery wave and says, "Thank you, good sir. You really have no idea how much you've—"

The guard pulls the door closed, rubbing his head when he thinks we cannot see him anymore.

"Well, that was rude of him to close the door in my face," Zahir says indignantly.

I pinch his arm and flash him a grin. Zahir grins back and then we hobble down the hallway and around the corner. The shadows loom in front of us, inviting us in. As we pass one of the shimmering black curtains, I snatch it from the wall and ball it up, holding it to my chest.

"Now, where is…" Zahir's voice trails off as he stares into the darkness.

"She'll be here," I say.

"Oh shit, there you are." Zahir jumps as Nim emerges from the shadows. "How did you—"

"Never mind that," I say. "Nim, do you have everything?"

Nim holds out two small scrolls and my lockpicks. I nod and lead the two through the nearest servant's door, so that we're out of sight. The servant's hallway is deserted, as we knew it would be but I send Zahir to check nearby just in case. I set down the black fabric I stole and untie the back of my skirt.

"I could do that for you if you would like," Zahir says from my shoulder. "I am an expert in—oof."

I elbow Zahir in the stomach then step out of the skirt and hand it to Nim.

"Not the time," I mutter.

Nim holds my yellow skirt while I wrap the black fabric around my glittery choli. We had decided that it would be too inconspicuous if I were to wear a black choli to the festival—sun colors were obligatory attire. Zahir has already removed the outer layer of bright clothes and stands ready in his sneak suit. As I tie the black fabric around me, securing the loose ends, I'm aware of our hour slipping away. At least ten minutes were wasted, and my inner voice is urging me to get going, but I know that we cannot be sloppy.

"Alright, Zahir, can you check the black fabric?"

I spin slowly, giving Zahir the opportunity to make sure that the fabric covers the entirety of my gold choli.

"You can see little hints of the gold, but it looks like part of the glitter in the black fabric."

"That was the point," I say with a smile.

I slip the crumpled scrolls Nim brought and my lockpicks into the secret pocket in my dhoti.

"We will meet you in the gardens before the dancing begins."

Nim's face remains expressionless as she nods, but Zahir looks paler under his curls.

"Let's go, Zahir," I whisper. The two of us slip down the servant's hallway and out of sight.

When executing a task that requires discretion, ensure that you are well and truly alone. No matter the professionalism of the disguise or expertise of the plan, unplanned guests will ruin your task every time.

--excerpt from *Tricksters Among Us: Spies, Thieves, and Liars* Banned by the Council of the Sultan in the year 214-

39

The darkness presses in from all sides. I embrace the thick night as I slink through the corridor, blending in with the shadows.

FORTY.

Forty minutes to slip through the empty palace and back. Left. Right. Another right.

The path that Nim had shown me the day before is etched in my mind. Zahir follows close behind, watching our backs as we move through the hallway.

A shuffle of feet around the next corner gives me a half-second of warning. I slip next to the nearest window, pulling Zahir with me. We allow the black fabric to fall over our heads. Praying that the rest of my body is covered well enough, I crouch against the wall barely aware of Zahir's warmth next to mine as I close my eyes and focus on my breathing, running my fingers along my anklet. In and out.

The tension in my shoulders fades. In and out. A shiver, a familiar caress. In and out.

The cooling sensation shifts to where Zahir leans against me.

My ears pick up the shuffle of feet again. I listen to the quiet noise pass us by, feeling like a child playing hide and seek. I don't dare look in case my gaze alerts the person that someone is hiding.

The footsteps grow fainter and fainter, finally disappearing. I remain crouched for another minute before tapping Zahir's shoulder, indicating that we should continue to Ray Lobo's suite.

Two more turns, and we arrive.

Without hesitation, I pull my lockpicks from the band on my wrist and get to work on Ray Lobo's lock while Zahir watches my back. I feel the tingling in my fingers as I tumble the lock in record time and slip inside the suite, closing the door behind us. Inside, I grin, grateful for the additional practice on Erol's suite doors that I had conducted yesterday.

I take a step, but Zahir grabs my shoulder, holding up a finger. Nodding, I crouch, touching the smooth stones of my anklet, grounding myself while I breathe and wait, while Zahir moves throughout the suite, checking the other rooms.

THIRTY.

Finally, Zahir returns and signals the all-clear.

Ray Lobo's personal door isn't even locked as we enter the garish room. Even in the darkness, the obscene orange the councilman uses to decorate his bedroom hurts my eyes. Behind me I hear Zahir's scoff, but I ignore it as I maneuver around the cushions in the corner, carefully avoiding the curling rug underneath his massive bed.

Most of the men choose to wear gold jewelry to show off their status, but Lobo is one of the few councilmen whose choice in necklace rivals the gaudiness of some of the women. When I walk up to the dresser, his favorite necklace is displayed prominently on a bust: the large gold beads, the solid square of gold pendant, and to finish the look, red tassels dangling from each bead and dripping from every corner of the pendant.

"He would want to stare at it from his bed," Zahir whispers, his breath tickling my neck.

Rolling my eyes in response, I tuck the tattered scroll Nim had prepared behind one of the other necklaces. The edge is just visible when I stand. Perfect.

I'm to the window and through the bars in a matter of moments. I lower myself to the ground in the back gardens and begin to wind my way through the less popular area, Zahir close behind. The dark shapes of the mango trees rustle in the darkness as we move past the vegetation. Andheraka is on the other side of the palace gardens, near the pretty flower arrangements and trim trees. I revel in the wildness of this side of the gardens. Even the stars cannot see me as I make my way through the night.

The Festival of Darkness for the Nightshade. How appropriate.

TWENTY.

Zahir grabs my arm, pulling me out of my reverie, and points to a tiny black ribbon tied to one of the bars of a nearby window, marking our second target for the night. Nim had worked last night, ensuring our ease into this second room.

My fingertips barely graze the bars on the window. Before I can look for something to stand on, Zahir grabs me by the waist and lifts me. My muscles strain with the effort as I pull myself through the bars and then onto the window ledge. Before I can catch my breath, Zahir is beside me, his body centimeters from my own. That unnamable energy sparks between us, mixing with the adrenaline and causing heat to rise to my cheeks. Zahir's golden eyes bore into my own, diving into my soul. As he leans closer, I close my eyes, my breath catching in my throat, unsure of what I want to happen.

Zahir's arm skims my own as he reaches down and unties the small black ribbon. A second wave of embarrassment courses through me as I take the ribbon from him and tie it to my drawstring bag. Without looking at Zahir, I enter the room.

Councilman Laghari's room is bland in comparison to the bright orange of Lobo's. We pass through quickly, and into the main room to move onto the real target: Laghari's son. Zahir had suggested that he would be the most believable candidate for the scandal we were creating.

I cross the main room in four quick strides, determined to distance myself from Zahir if possible. As I try to enter the younger Laghari's room, a hand snatches my arm, digging into my flesh. A yip escapes my mouth, and I turn, ready to admonish Zahir for revealing our cover, and come face to face with an infuriated servant.

"What are you—"

The servant grunts and his nails tear into my arm as Zahir's body slams into him. The momentum sends me crashing into the wall. Stars cross my vision as pain slams

into the back of my skull. Through my haze I watch Zahir
and the servant wrestle next to me.

"Guard—"

Zahir jams his elbow into the servant's stomach, winding
him. Before Zahir can incapacitate him, the servant punches
him across the face, sending Zahir staggering. As the servant
tries to run, I kick out my legs, tangling the man and bringing
him crashing to the floor next to me. Before the servant calls
for help again, Zahir leaps on top of the prone man and
slams his head on the ground, knocking him unconscious.

The returning silence is punctuated by our combined
gasps for breath as Zahir and I struggle to regain control.
I stare down at the servant, infuriated with myself for not
checking the room before charging in.

A rookie mistake.

"We should check the rest of the rooms," Zahir whispers.

I nod and force myself to stand, the pain in the back
of my head dulling to a throb. We make quick work of the
rest of the rooms, relief rushing through me at the sight
of each empty room.

"We need to finish this," I say. Although the fight was
over in seconds, I've lost track of my internal clock, making
me antsy to get out of the councilman's suite.

"You take care of Laghari's son, I'll deal with the servant."

I nod and slip into the room, breathing in the darkness
and letting my mind sink into my focus once again. I move
through the room in the pitch black until I reach the dresser.

Zahir's shuffling in the next room distracts me for a second,
but I keep my fingertips light on the top of the desk, feeling
for the edges, trying to map out the desk through touch.
The scrape of the wood tickles, my pinky nudges several

papers. I move to another part of the desk, not wanting to disturb the loose pages.

I finally find what I'm searching for: a small wooden box that many Ari use to store their correspondence. I slip the other scroll out of my bag and slide it behind the box, as if someone had shoved it back there in haste.

I shuffle carefully back to the door.

"Zahir?" I whisper into the dark room.

Silence greets me. A shiver of fear threatens me, but I push it away. I cross the room and into Councilman Laghari's bedroom. A shadow hovers by the window, waiting for me.

Zahir.

"Bout time," he says, flashing me a grin.

"The servant?"

"Taken care of."

I chew my lip, hesitating. "What about when he wakes? Won't he go running to his master?"

"Taken care of," he says, the moonlight illuminating the savage grin on his face. I tilt my head, a silent indication to explain. Zahir winks and pulls a small vial from his pocket. "Diluted fenugreek oil mixed with ashwa leaves. He'll be in the dunes with that headache but no memory of how he got it."

"Where'd you get that?" I ask. I could've used an oil like that a few times.

Zahir gives a half shrug, saying, "Cadmar, of course."

Of course. And he had the nerve to ask me to trust him. Clearly, I wasn't supplied the same as the rest of Logonkelie. But the annoyance is fleeting as the rush of adrenaline courses through me, charging the air around us.

"Let's go," I whisper. Exhilaration fills me. *This* is what I've been missing these past weeks. The night, the silence, the thrill. Instead of dropping down to the ground, I pull myself on top of the bars around the councilman's window and up onto the low roof.

"Laila," Zahir warns, the whisper not hiding the concern in his voice.

"Follow me," I whisper, not giving Zahir a chance to respond.

I know we should go back and get back into the Ari fray, but I can't bring myself back to that reality quite yet. I glance around, looking for the lurking palace guardsmen as Zahir pulls himself up, but there's not a soul in sight. Grinning, I race towards the next roof, quickly assessing my handholds before hauling myself up to the top. I'm now in line with the treetops of the short mango trees, their sweet smell tantalizing as I pass. Across another rooftop and up another wall.

"Laila—" Zahir tries again, but I ignore him, allowing the thrill to push me higher and higher through the maze of rooftops.

The only parts of the palace that are taller than us now are the minarets at each corner. I race across the roof, hidden by the shadow of the massive tower, nearly skipping in my exhilaration.

Freedom is infectious.

If I hurry, I know that I will make it for my favorite part of the festival.

The hairs on my arms rise in anticipation as the drum reverberates slowly in the night air. Each beat sends a pulse through the silence, marking the end of the hour of silence and the beginning of something greater.

"Laila, we should head back," Zahir says, panting from the exertion.

I hold up a hand, silencing him, as the drums pick up speed. My body quivers in excitement, knowing what is coming next. We remain crouched at the base of one of the minarets. Waiting.

I stare at the garden where all of the Ari are gathered, holding my breath.

Tiny lights start to appear, pinpricks in the darkness. Gradually, the pinpricks spread, becoming more numerous, fanning out in every direction.

Three large torches are lit and whisked off into the darkness. I watch in fascination from my perch as the torches speed through the front of the palace, disappearing under the wall, and then blaze again in the night as the torchbearers gallop down the road from the palace.

The Ari candles are lit, so I turn towards the torch making its way to the southern part of the Upper City. I know we're cutting it close, but I'm desperate to see the light reach the Lower City.

I need to feel connected to Tanu.

A drum in the Upper City joins the pounding of the palace drum as candles are lit in the Upper City. From our vantage point, the little flickers of light look like the stars that they are meant to represent. The light spreads. More torches are lit. The candlelight grows in waves, spreading like the sun's rays from the palace through the streets of the Upper City.

Almost there.

I can't crouch hidden any longer. I stand, gripping the rough sandstone wall in front of me, and lean over. As if by standing, I could hurry the light into the Lower City. Distantly I register Zahir's gasp and the hand gripping the back of my choli, anchoring me to the roof.

And then the light's there. It has to be. With Tanu.

I spread my arms wide, closing my eyes to the glowing pinpricks of man-made stars in front of me. I can see her excitement as Dada leans over to light her candle, the pure joy of a child sparkling in her eyes. The wind circles me, gently tugging at my black clothes, filling me with the same inexplicable joy.

"Thank you, Wind Mother," I whisper.

**Dance is the language with which every
child of Wind Mother can understand. The
movements are words of the soul.**
-from the Sacred Scrolls of Wind Mother
translated from Aramak, the Olden Tongue-

40

"Where have you been?" Nim asks as she tosses my
yellow skirt to me.

"We got held up."

Zahir grimaces but doesn't correct my statement. Nim's
eyes glance at Zahir, but she doesn't question us further.

"Let Cadmar know about the servant, will you, Nim?"
Zahir says as he jumps up and down, trying to pull his pants
over his sweat-streaked black sneak suit.

"Of course."

The ties of my skirt keep slipping out of my hands as I
scramble to get back into my festival finery. Nim clucks her
tongue, sounding like Sala, and fixes my skirt for me. As I
pass her the ties, Nim grabs one of my hands, examining the
small scrapes on my fingers, the only evidence of our roof-
climbing. I shrug and pull my hand out of her grip, unwilling
to offer further explanation, and adjust the black fabric
covering my gold choli into a dupatta tied across my body.

Once we're dressed, Nim slips out of the servants' hallway
to distract the guardsman by the garden door. Zahir shoves

a candle into my hand as we follow discreetly behind. The drums have picked up their pace, indicating that the dancing will begin soon.

"We shouldn't have done that," Zahir mutters in my ear, his breath warm on my cheek as we join the crowd of Ari.

"You didn't have to come."

"That's horseshit and you—"

"Stop worrying," I whisper back. I kiss Zahir on the cheek, then light my candle.

"If Cadmar—"

"It's done, so hush," I say, cutting off Zahir. If he isn't careful, he'll cast suspicion on us with his worrying. Zahir grumbles something that sounds suspiciously like "women" but has the sense not to draw more attention to us as servants walk through the crowd, handing out pieces of shimmery black fabric. It is tradition to tie the black fabric into a dupatta over colorful clothes in order to remind us of the darkness in all of us.

Since my dupatta is already in place, I use my newly lit candle to glance down at my skirt. The pattern is off-center in the front, so I tug on the material, correcting it before anyone else notices.

The voice of the narrator breaks through the drums, silencing them.

"And so, in order to make us one with our ancestors, we reenact that fateful night."

A small girl pauses at the edge of the stage, holding her candle high above her head. She stands frozen, all eyes upon her, before beginning to sing. Her small voice is surprisingly strong as she sings wordlessly through a scale, her voice sliding up and down through notes in a slow, haunting call through the night air. My hair stands on end, and I watch transfixed as she begins to dance across the stage.

The girl, Ray Lobo's granddaughter, picks up the pace. The drums join in with her, followed by several flutes and a sitar. A few younger Ari join in with the girl.

The same exhilaration that I felt on the roof fills me again. I grin, overcome with my success and the joy of the night.

"C'mon, cousin," I say, trying to tug Zahir's hand towards the front of the crowd.

"Uh, hard no," he whispers back.

I raise an eyebrow at Zahir, but he doesn't budge. I shrug and disappear through the crowd before Zahir can elaborate. By the time I reach the front, a few more people have joined the dance. I pause on the edge, savoring the soft grass on my bare feet, then excitement overwhelms me, and I leap into the dancing. I can't help the wicked grin on my face as I dance without reserve, my candle held high above my head as the thrum of the drum matches the rhythm of my heart.

I am free. I am in control.

My heart sings the two thoughts over and over again as my personal mantra through the dancing, finally feeling like something has gone right.

The music lulls, and I sway in the crowd, one in many. The rest of the Ari have joined the dancing in the past hour. Candlelight flickers all around me as we move. I drift slowly in my corner of the crowd, not seeing the faces around me, almost able to imagine that I'm not in the palace at all, but in the Lower City, where I long to be.

I twirl slowly—my eyes closed in bliss—and straight into someone's arms. I open my eyes to find the prince smiling down at me. I step out of his arms quickly. He grins and offers a hand.

"Shall we dance, Lailani?" he asks.

I nod and take his hand, swallowing my nerves. We circle each other, neither breaking eye contact, our candles twinkle as twin lights in the crowd.

The drums speed up, and soon Ajani and I are laughing and dancing with the crowd. Our feet stomp out their own beat. Our hands occasionally let go as we dance, but they always find each other again. Whirling around in the darkness makes me feel as if for once the Ari aren't watching my every move. Even Ajani seems lighter, freer, like me. His eyes crinkle from the laughter, and his hair flies around him.

I lose track of the night. I don't know if I dance with the prince for hours or minutes, but soon the drums die off, leaving the faint trill of the flutes. I stop in my tracks and stare at the sky. The stars are disappearing, and the top rays of the sun are peeking out from the edge of the world. The Ari spread out as the last notes of the flute die away, indicating the beginning of the second hour of silence. Quiet weaves through the crowd as everyone finds a place to watch the sun rise.

Ajani grabs my hand and starts to weave through the crowd. I tug my hand out of his grasp. He looks at me, and I widen my eyes, silently asking him where we are going. He grins and shrugs, bobbing his head side to side. *You'll see.*

I sigh but follow him anyway.

The prince beelines for the palace wall. At the edge of the garden, he glances around, making sure we weren't followed by other Ari. Then he slides behind one of the flowery bushes lining the wall. I slip around the bush and then stop in my tracks. Ajani approaches a small door in the wall. I thought the only entry point in the palace wall was the front entrance…

Ajani grins at the surprise on my face and opens the door. We disappear into the wall, up a flight of steps, and to the top of the palace wall. A startled Suraksha moves towards us when we appear, but Ajani waves him off. The guard nods and walks the other direction.

If I thought my rooftop position was perfect for seeing all of Aveena, it was nothing compared to seeing Aveena from the palace wall. Buildings stretch out before me. People mill about in the streets, tiny in the distance. I feel safe, away from the judgment of the Ari and from the eyes on my every move.

Safe from the reality that surrounds my existence in the palace.

The night fades. Purples and pinks paint the skyline, the deep orange at the base blending with the dunes. I stare at the beautiful sunrise and sigh.

Ajani moves closer and tentatively wraps his arms around me. I tense at his warmth at my back, but then relax into his hold, leaning against the prince. His arms tighten slightly as I rest my head on his chest.

We watch the sun rise over Aveena, entwined together. Safe from the eyes of the Ari.

"It's incredible," I murmur, more to myself than to Ajani. His chest rumbles against me as he mutters his agreement.

After another heartbeat, he sighs and steps away from me, and I miss the warmth of him. I turn and meet his eyes. Ajani's hair looks windswept from our dancing, and a sheepish smile tugs at the corner of his mouth. He runs a hand through his hair and says softly, "I should probably get down to break the fast with everyone. They'll be expecting me."

Disappointment shoots through me, but I push it down, ignoring the feeling for another day. I smile instead and lace my fingers through his. He glances down at our hands, and I can tell he's pleased.

"Of course, oh Prince of Aveena," I say, teasing.

Ajani laughs, shedding the last remnants of the serious prince for a moment. I lean in, drawn towards this version of him: just Ajani. Not the prince. Not our future sultan. Simply, Ajani.

He tugs my hand, giving the Suraksha a nod before pulling me through the secret passage. "The vizier will be disappointed in me."

"Why?" I ask, my joy soured by the mention of the vizier.

We approach the door, and he opens it, peeking out into the grounds to check that no one will see us exit the door, before saying, "I didn't dance with all the young women, as he asked."

I grin, my heart racing at the knowledge.

Very few Ari remain in the garden, and we're easily able to skirt around the edges to avoid them. As we near the entrance to the palace, Ajani tugs me behind one of the trees. When I round the trunk, we're face to face, and I can't help but savor the miniscule distance between us. His eyes darken as he glances at my lips, and my breath catches. Ajani leans forward—

"Where did he disappear to?" a woman asks from on the other side of the tree. Ajani and I freeze, both of our eyes darting to the pathway.

"No idea," another woman replies, disgruntled. "Maybe we should try the feast?"

Their footsteps carry away from us and down the path, their voices fading. Ajani exhales the breath that he was holding and rests his forehead on my own, his shoulders shaking with silent laughter.

"I should go," he whispers when he finally regains control of himself. I reach up and run my fingers through his dark hair, pushing it back to the side. "The vizier will be waiting for me."

"I understand," I whisper back. I take a small step back, needing a little distance, but our fingers remain entwined. "Thank you for the night, Ajani."

He lifts my fingers and kisses them lightly, holding my gaze as he does so. Warmth tingles through me. "No. Thank you, Lailani."

He flashes me another smile before stepping out from behind the tree. I lean against the trunk as I listen to his steps fade away down the path, giving him a head start so that the Ari are unaware of our private moment.

Emotions flood me as the night flashes through my mind. The freedom of climbing the roof. The exhilaration of the success of our mission. The dangerous proximity to Ajani, forbidden, yet so tempting.

The confidence of being the Nightshade rushing back to me from where it's been hiding since I'd been trapped into that deal with Cadmar.

I have single-handedly created, and ruined, the reputations of the Aristocracy during my tenure as the Nightshade. I have the power, and I shouldn't be afraid of the palace. Of Cadmar. Of the vizier. They are pawns in my game, and I need to prove it to them.

I glance at the sky. The sun hasn't even crested the wall. I have at least an hour before the morning feast's crowd will begin to dissipate. There's plenty of time to work.

I slip around the tree and down the path towards the palace. No one sees me as I enter. I glance around the deserted marble hallway before sliding back into the servants' corridor, holding my breath. It's equally as deserted, and I breathe a sigh of relief before untying the colorful skirt for the second time in less than twelve hours. The black choli and the lehenga will have to do—I can't risk going back to Erol's suite and running into other members of Logonkelie.

I hide my discarded skirt in an alcove, then braid my hair back, weaving it around my head like Sala does. The lockpicks slide into the braid easily. I untie the black dupatta and drape it over my head and face like the palace servants. As long as no one gets too close, my disguise should work.

I walk purposefully down the corridor, following my memory of Sala's map in my eye toward my destination.

The royal vizier's suite.

Knowledge is power.
He who holds the knowledge, holds the
power.
—excerpt from *A Brief Political History of*
Aveena—

41

I am the Nightshade. I am the Nightshade. *I am the Nightshade.* I repeat the mantra, chanting to block out everything else. A cart with linens stacked on it sits beside a cracked door. I grab a stack of the linens and balance them on one arm, leaving the other free just in case. No matter how lightly I step, my footsteps echo. I'm giving myself twenty minutes. Twenty minutes to get in and out of the vizier's suite without being detected.

I am the Nightshade. I am the Nightshade.

I am the Night...

His hot breath on my face. The sickly-sweet smell overwhelming my nose. His words dripping into my ear.

I hate him.

"No, no, no," I mutter, shaking my head to erase the memory of the vizier's chilly gaze. I have to stay focused. I bend down, reaching for my anklet. I run my fingertips across the smooth stone. Breathe in. Breathe Out. One. My tightly woven hair itches, distracting me. I roll my head side to side. The soft crackle in my ears. Breathe in. Breathe out.

Two. The itchy pull of my fake locks on my scalp subsides. My stance shifts subtly, a lightness filling my bones. The room blurs, but I don't blink. Breathe in. Breathe out.

A shiver shoots from the top of my head down my spine, and the hallway springs into hyperfocus.

I'm not Lailani. I'm the Nightshade.

I stand and stride forward. Most of the servants are at the feast, but I pass a straggler in the dimly lit hallway. Their eyes slide over me, ignoring my presence.

Breathe in. Breathe out.

Left. Right. Right again. Left.

TWENTY.

There it is: the servants' entrance to the vizier's chambers.

Just looking at the door brings back memories of Vizier Nassor's oily touch. My breath hitches in my throat, and my focus slips. I hesitate, clutching the linens to my chest.

"Speed it along, Nene. His Royal Pain-in-the-Ass doesn't like to be kept waiting."

I jump, spinning around, but the teenage girl is already down the hall, her stack of clean linens expertly balanced on her head as she walks.

Don't slip up like that again, I chide myself. *You might not be so lucky next time.*

I grasp the door handle, using it as my focal point, and ease the servant's door open. By the time the door is open, I'm back in my Nightshade zone.

SIXTEEN.

The vizier's suite is the mirror image of Erol's. The room is empty, as I knew it would be, but I still breathe a sigh of relief. I pause to memorize the small details: the corner of the rug is curled up; two pillows are scattered in the walkway; two exits from the main room; three windows, most likely barred.

I glide silently to the vizier's study, becoming one with the shadows cast by the dim light filtering through the black drapes on the windows.

The door is locked, of course. I pull my lockpicks from my hair and set to work on the lock. It's one that I'm unfamiliar with—definitely not the usual Ari design. I grit my teeth to keep from grinding them as my picks slip, not finding the proper positions to tumble the damn lock. Frustrated, I tug the veil away from my face. The air feels icy against the sheen of sweat across my face.

FOURTEEN.

The lock tumbles, the click shouting into the silence. I freeze, straining my ears for any sound. The soft padding of a servant's slipper is barely perceptible down the hall. I push open the door, hasten inside, and shut it before the servant arrives.

Tinkling water distracts me. I scan my surroundings, the servant already forgotten. The office is laid out just like Erol's: desk with a chair against the right wall, a small bookshelf on my left. The only oddity in Vizier Nassor's office is the ornate fountain in the left corner of the room. I make my way to it, careful to not touch anything. The stones of the tabletop fountain are purest black. The water cascades over the black rocks, reflecting the light in the room. Gold glints from the edges of the fountain basin, a stark contrast to the black of the basin's depths. Recognition tingles in the back of my mind, but I can't place my finger on it.

TWELVE.

I gulp and involuntarily take a step back from the fountain. The hairs on my arms prickle the longer I look at the rivulets of water. I tear my eyes away and shake my head. I'm being silly—it's just a fountain. With familiar stones.

There's one other difference between the vizier's office and Erol's. No window. The light in the room comes from an oil lamp hanging dead center in the room. The flame flickers in a non-existent breeze.

Why is it lit?

I should leave. Now.

The trickle of the fountain laughs at me as I flounder. My instincts tell me to run. I force my heartbeat to calm down. I squeeze my eyes shut. I have to do this. I am the Nightshade.

I open my eyes and prowl towards the desk. A deep, dark part of me smiles. I want to do this.

I want to know the vizier's secrets.

Stacks of papers clutter the vizier's desk. I memorize the title of the top document of each stack in order to reconstruct the vizier's organized chaos. The sound of the fountain trickles into my mind, invading my efforts.

TEN.

I'm ready.

I slide the silk gloves over my hands, ignoring their slight trembling, and begin to sift through the pages. Incoherent numbers flash at me from each page. The titles are all abbreviated.

Shit, I'm in the dunes with this pile, I can't make sense of this. The numbers float out of my head as soon as I read them.

I put the stack down, grinding my teeth. I *will* have better luck with the second stack.

It's clear after a minute of skimming the pages that I'm getting nowhere fast. I throw the stack down hard, causing several of the documents to fly off of the desk. *Shit.* Now, I'm being careless. If only the damn fountain would stop tinkling.

My time is almost up, and I've gotten nothing.

EIGHT.

I rub my face in frustration and think. Nightshade Laila would've been in and out already. Not helpful. Lailani would have a servant do the work for her. Also not helpful. Nim would just memorize everything and let Cadmar figure it out. Not an option. Sala would come up with more curses than I know to describe the situation. A waste of time. And Zahir would ask the fountain what to do.

I smile briefly at the thought of Zahir. Still not helpful though.

So, what am *I* going to do?

Screw Logonkelie's process. Time is ticking, and I need *something* to report back to Cadmar. I pull open the desk drawers at random. My edginess causes the contents to roll, but I'm past the point of caring: if the royal vizier doesn't know people spy in this dunes-damned place then he will now.

I glance nervously over my shoulder but keep going. The bottom drawer sticks when I tug on it. Hmmm. Another lock? From my angle the drawer looks just like the others.

"Where are you, little lock?" I mutter.

My gloved fingers skim the sides of the desk—still nothing. I kneel on the floor for a better angle and slide my hands across the undercarriage of the drawer.

Ah ha.

My left hand locates a metal piece at odds with the rest of the wooden desk. Hastily, I pull my picks out and shove them into the lock, but the gloves muffle my touch. I rip them off and run my bare hands on the bottom of the drawer until I rediscover the lock. I close my eyes, allowing my other senses to expand, and focus on the feeling of the picks and the metal of the lock. I place the pins, straining to hear the telltale click of the tumbler, and am rewarded.

SIX.

Instead of sliding forward like a normal drawer, the bottom drops open like a flap revealing a stack of letters tied with twine. I pick up the letters and carefully untie the twine. On the top letter, I find a sharp, choppy scrawl of handwriting, like the author was angered by the very pages he was writing on.

The vizier's handwriting.

I flip through the letters, aware of time slipping away, skimming. A handful are written in the vizier's hand, but the rest vary. A thrill of excitement replaces my trepidation as I skim. Cadmar wants more information about what the vizier is planning. We need this.

A sentence catches my attention, so I begin reading:

Ji,

Your attention to detail and concern is noted. Although the evidence you've provided is convincing, you promised your discretion in this matter

As a sign of good faith, I am overjoyed to present on your behalf. I will ensure that I reflect your discretion with my fellows, presenting the information as my own.

I trust that after I have shown my faith, the evidence will vanish? If so, we shall move forward with equal footing and equal faith in this partnership.

-J.S.

J.S.? My brain scrambles, trying to decipher who the author of the letter could be. One of the Ari for sure, but which one? And this evidence he mentions... if it needs discretion then it must be sensitive information. I wonder what the vizier has over J.S. to earn his "good faith".

Initials jump out at me: R.L.; R.A.; S.L.; A.B.; D.D.;V.P. The list is extensive as I continue to skim.

I flip through another few letters until my heart beats erratically when I see Zahir's name written in the vizier's hand. The top half of the letter is torn, revealing a scrap of the message.

the young Shaikh. His hot-headedness has not gone unnoticed. He will earn his due when the new order is established. Zaharian's insubordination will be addressed.

-N.A

Insubordination to be addressed? The violent beating of my heart fills my ears as worry for Zahir washes over me. I thought that he had kept a safe distance from the royal vizier; what had he done to get on the vizier's bad side?

Memories of the first night in the Harem Room flood back to me: the hatred in Zahir's eyes as he pulled me away from the vizier, the tight grip he had on my hand as I numbly followed him out of the room.

Of *course* the vizier had noticed that Zahir had shielded me from his onslaught. Is that what instigated this letter? FOUR.

I shake my head and frantically resume reading the vizier's letters. I need to get out of here, but not until I have something worthwhile to take back to the Logonkelie.

Ji,

It has been drafted carefully as you instructed. The walla was most accommodating with your specifications. He promised the paperwork shall be ready in time as well as his future services if needed.

Please confirm that the work pleases you.

Your loyal servant,

-R.L.

The letter pre-dates the others, but only by a week or two. I think back to the first council meeting. What paperwork? The only paperwork that was brought to the Council of the Sultan was the copy of the Ordinances.

The same paperwork that dictated that the vizier should preside as ruling sultan.

My racing heart stops mid-beat.

It's all circumstantial. I need concrete proof that we can *use.*

Ji,

We have secured the sultana as you requested with her loyal servants none the wiser. She will return after it is too late.

As always, I await your instructions.

-M.

The *sultana* is involved?

Will return after it is too late.

Too late for what? Everything about the vizier's letters elicits more questions than answers. I thought the sultana's absence was odd, but no one else seemed concerned. Hardly anyone mentioned it. Many of the women in the Veiled Room actually appeared pleased with the absence of the sultana. Lady Shah and her daughter were certainly trying to establish their own little circle of Ari women with the lack of competition.

How did the vizier "deal" with Sultana Chhavi?

A scrap of paper falls out of the shuffle of letters onto the ground. I pick it up, about to put it back into the stack until Ajani's name snags my attention. The vizier's handwriting is cramped, more jagged and angry than his other letters.

I squeeze my eyes closed and open them again, hoping I misread the name. I didn't.

I bend closer to read the tiny inscription next to his name: *to be dealt with.*

I'm so absorbed by the horror of these four words that I don't notice that the trickle of the fountain has vanished.

**As sultan, you are responsible for all of
Aveena, from the Aristocracy to those in
the Lower City, from men and women to
children See that you care for and protect
all equally, and you will be a beloved
sultan.**
-Advice from Sultan Gautam to Prince Ajani
on his twentieth birthday-

42

"This *is* a surprise."

A long-fingered hand grips my chin and jerks my face up. I flinch and try to pull away. The few self-defense moves that Sala beat into my body spring to mind, but his grip tightens on my chin, iciness proliferating from the contact, immobilizing me.

"Look at me, sneak," the vizier says coldly.

I keep my eyes downcast, knowing their blue will give me away.

"Look. At. Me."

His nails dig into my chin, and freezing pain shoots from the contact. I struggle to endure, but the pain grows too great and I acquiesce. Blue meets green. The vizier's face alights with interest.

"Well, well, Lady Lailani. Or is that even your name?"

The vizier releases my chin, and I try to stand up, but he places firm hands on my shoulders, forcing me to remain kneeling on the floor. He taps my shoulders once and I freeze, a cold sweat breaking out across my body and panic tightening my throat. When it's clear that I cannot rise, the vizier pulls my veil off and sits on the chair. I can barely breathe, can't think. I'd love to slap the smirk off his face, but that's impossible.

The green of his eyes is brighter, more vibrant, than I've ever seen them.

"I rather like you on your knees, Lailani. It's a position I could get used to."

I want to throw up on his ornate sandals. Nassor rests on ankle on his knee, getting comfortable.

"No response, Lailani? How unlike you." He presses a finger to my lips, his eyes brightening once again. "You may speak."

"You know *nothing* about me," I spit out.

Nassor clicks his tongue disapprovingly. "Ah, there you are. I like a little fight in my women, after all. But we've been over this already, have we not?"

Vizier Nassor pauses to look me over slowly. My face burns, and fear sears through me. I can't see a way out without either getting thrown into Niraash or revealing Cadmar's plans. Nassor strokes his beard thoughtfully.

"First, I would appreciate if you would return my correspondence to me," he says, tapping my shoulders once again. The iciness dissipates, and I slump back, able to move of my own accord again.

"H-how?" I stutter, staring at him in shock. Magic wasn't real. It didn't exist, but then… Nassor's eyes brighten again as he stares down at me.

"Djinn-eyes."

My words are a whisper. The vizier smiles as he notes my fear.

"My correspondence?"

I hand over the letters, my fingers trembling. The vizier's smile widens.

"Lailani, Lailani, what am I going to do with you?" he says. I struggle to breathe normally. "I'm really quite disappointed you're a sneak, you know. You fit so well into my plans as my wife."

My eyes widen, causing the vizier to leer.

"You were a perfect candidate: an alliance with the opposing side, beautiful. Your untapped…potential. Even your little fling with the boy prince helps." He tilts his head to the side, contemplating me. Sighing, he weighs the letters in his hands. "Now, what use shall I put you to, Lailani?"

Nerves clench my stomach, but I keep my face in an impassive mask, ignoring the bead of sweat trickling down my back. The vizier observes me closely, gauging my reaction.

"You're surprised that I'm not asking you who you work for."

It's not a question.

"You are at my mercy and will do what I say, or else I will destroy you. Whoever you worked for in the past is inconsequential." His light tone makes it sound as if we were discussing that night's meal and not blackmail and a death threat. "Luckily enough, I need another spy, and you are so aptly placed in Shaikh's chambers. You will report back to me every three days."

"How am I supposed to report to you?"

Vizier Nassor's backhand throws me to the ground. The sharp sting of the slap disorients me for a minute. When

I look up at him, he leans back in his chair, examining the back of his hand, a faint smile twisting his face.

"You will speak when spoken to, and you will address me by my formal title at all times."

I nod but don't speak—my eyes water from the slap, but I refuse to cry in front of this monster.

Nassor continues as if nothing had happened. "In addition, you will keep the ear of the prince and keep him distracted for me."

Distracted from what? But the stinging in my cheek stops me from asking. I need to get out of here. The vizier reaches down and strokes my face where he slapped it. I flinch, but he grabs my hair tightly, holding me in place. My heart hammers in my ears, nearly drowning out his next words.

"Where did you disappear to, little sneak?" the vizier asks cooly.

"I–I didn't–"

The vizier's hand tightens in my hair, and I can't help the cry of pain that escapes me. Nassor tsks, looking down his nose at me in disdain.

"I'll ask once more," he says slowly, his green eyes narrowing, "and you will not lie to me. Where were you during the hour of silence?"

The panic makes me dizzy with the adrenaline coursing through my body, urging me to flee. I've fought so hard not to be in this position again. Bile rises in my throat, but I swallow it down, trying to think through the haze. Two words finally rise up: get out.

"I broke into Lobo's rooms," I force out. Nassor tilts his head and studies me. The sickly orange smell of his perfume clogs my nose.

"And what did you do?"

"I–" I swallow roughly, forcing myself to speak, "I left a scroll."

There is no warning. The hand in my hair tightens painfully as the vizier strikes me again with his free hand. I cry out from the force, unable to move because of the hand gripping me in place.

"Tell the truth or else I'll find another way to get it out of you. Maybe through that curly-haired bastard of a cousin of yours? I'd have rid myself of him already if his disappearance wouldn't cause a stir."

My stomach drops. I grit my teeth against the pain, and finally say, "A scroll to frame him for working with the Tribes. Lobo and Laghari's son both."

Nassor throws me away from him, and I land hard on my elbow. He stands swiftly, stepping over my prone body like refuse in the street, and opens the office door. "Kaan!"

The sliver of light from the door falls across my face, but I don't move. There's nowhere to run. A soft male voice murmurs from the hallway, but I can't discern what he says.

"Lobo and Laghari's rooms. Remove scrolls that insinuate correspondence with the Tribes. Go."

Nassor shuts the door swiftly then moves over to the seat. I can feel his eyes on my face, staring at where he had hit me.

"I am disappointed that our marriage is no longer a possibility, Lailani. Your skin is beautiful when reddened by a firm hand. I would have enjoyed that immensely." He sighs and waves a hand towards the door. "Three days, Lailani."

I recognize the dismissal and bolt out the door. As I leave, I hear the renewed trickle of the fountain, laughing at my retreat.

Remove all emotion from your decisions.
Success stems from emotionless precision
and ruthless cunning.
-excerpt from *The Thief's Guide* Banned by the
Council of the Sultan in the year 151-

43

I sprint through the servants' hallway, shoving surprised servants aside as I flee. I don't stop until I hurl myself into Erol's suites. The echo of the slamming door fills the empty room. I squeeze my eyes shut.

What in the dunes just happened?

Vizier Nassor's cold, calculating face smirks at me, mocks me. My eyes fly open.

I can't escape him.

I slam the back of my head against the door, trying to force the vizier's face from my mind. My feet slide out from under me, and I sink to the floor. Hugging my knees to my chest, I stare unseeingly at the ornate gold rug. A dull ache thrums from the back of my skull, where I smacked it against the door. At least the pain of it drives the sting out of my slapped cheek.

I have lost control.

Magic. He has *magic*.

I should turn myself into Cadmar. Tell him which rule of his I've been breaking since he forced me into this deal.

341

Then at least I'd know the outcome. I could gather my bearings easily in prison.

Stop it, Laila, the voice in the back of my mind snaps at me. *Find your control.*

Since when did my consciousness start sounding like Sala?

I sigh and sit up straighter. Cadmar and Sala will be back from the feast soon. I need a plan.

The need to cry fills my chest, presses against the backs of my eyelids, but I force the feeling away. I walk into my room. The click of the lock fills me with peace of mind. For at least a few minutes, I am alone.

The rays of the morning sun illuminate the orchid that Ajani had sent to my room after our date, casting red light on the magenta flower. I grab a quill and paper from the writing desk in the corner and sit on the ground next to my flower.

"Alright, orchid, now what?"

Silence meets me, but after the nagging trickling of the vizier's fountain, the silence is a blessing. A fervor takes over me, and I scrawl haphazardly over the paper. Ink splashes each time I dip the quill, but I don't pause to clean it up.

The morning sun rose past my window by the time I finish. My tailless lizard soaks up the warmth as I look at the notes scribbled over three pages of scratchy paper. The first page is a list of things that could get me caught, things that keep me trapped and out of control. My stomach sinks at the length of the list—even the edges of the page are filled with the threats I face, real and imagined. The royal vizier and all of the ways he threatens me makes up much of this first list; however, Cadmar's deal, Sala's friendship, and Ajani's interest also make the list. Zahir's name is followed by a question mark. I can't figure him out, but right now I have more pressing issues. I cross him off the list.

I shuffle the pages and glance at the second page. The list makes me laugh out loud. It's supposed to be all the things that I have control over. I tear up the page, letting the pieces fall to the floor.

The only thing I have control over is myself. And that's dependent on who's threatening me that day.

I look at the last page. The notes are sloppy, but as I reread them, I'm impressed with the amount of information that I remember from the vizier's letters. I think I've written down most of the initials to decipher later.

I stare at the page.

I cannot present this information to Cadmar without giving myself away to the vizier but I can't destroy the list either. My gut tells me that whatever the vizier is up to will not be good for Ajani or Cadmar's plans or Aveena.

Or myself for that matter.

The doorknob to my room rattles, and I jump, nearly spilling the open ink bottle onto the floor.

"Lailani!" Sala's voice rings from outside my door. "You there?"

"Coming," I say.

I fold the page with the vizier's list and slip it into the secret pocket that Preeti sewed into all of my kurtis. It's the only place that I can be sure that no one will find the list. I rip up the other pages and sweep the fragments of paper into my palm.

"Lailani, we're waiting!"

My clay chamber pot sits discreetly in one corner. As the door rattles again, I drop the pieces of paper into it, hiding the evidence of my fear.

I open the door, and Sala winks at me, dragging me into the main room. Erol and Cadmar are already there, waiting on me. Cadmar paces between the cushions, while Erol sits placidly in his usual spot.

"About time. I was about to pick your lock if you took too much longer."

"I just needed a minute to clean up."

I shrug and allow Sala to pull me down onto a cushion. She raises an eyebrow, staring hard at me. "You okay?"

"Of course."

The lie sticks in my throat.

Sala puts out a hand to stop Cadmar's incessant pacing. If it were any other member of Logonkelie, our leader wouldn't tolerate the nonverbal order. Luckily, Sala can ground Cadmar when needed. Zahir is half-slumped in a cushion, barely keeping his eyes open after our long night. Erol's door is already closed, the lucky bastard is probably already sleeping off Andheraka.

Cadmar marches over to the windows and tugs the black fabric free, haphazardly throwing it to the floor. The morning light bursts through, and Zahir hastily throws his arm to cover his eyes.

"Well?" Cadmar asks, glancing between Zahir and me.

Zahir grumbles something unintelligible, and Cadmar nearly growls in frustration.

"Mr. Juma if you don't—"

"Everything is fine, Cadmarji!" Zahir says, sitting up and glaring at Cadmar. The bags under his eyes are prominent from across the room. "We got in and out without anyone noticing."

"And the councilmen?" Cadmar crosses his arms, waiting for Zahir to respond.

"We framed them for getting cozy with the Tribes," Zahir says with a shrug. "Can I go to bed now? My head is pounding, and I—"

"Maybe you should have slowed down on the wine," Sala says, smirking. "If you can't handle it…"

She lets her voice trail off, laughing, and nudges me. I give a half-hearted smile but can't shake the guilt bubbling up in my chest. Zahir opens his mouth to argue, but Cadmar cuts him off. "Bed, now."

But even his normally serious mask cracks with a small smile. Zahir drags himself off the cushion and stumbles to his room, muttering about nosey people minding their own business. As his door snicks shut, Cadmar turns back to me, appraising. I bury my sweaty palms in the folds of my skirt to hide their tremble.

"About last night…" Cadmar begins.

He can't know about the vizier… can he? My heartbeat pulses in my throat, and I swallow heavily, attempting to clear the dryness. I need more time.

"You did well."

My stomach feels like it sinks through the floor. "I—uh—it was a team effort," I say lamely.

Cadmar walks over to a tray laden with fruit and peruses the options. "I meant about the prince. He couldn't keep away from you." Cadmar settles on a slice of dragon fruit and turns.

"But you didn't want me around him," I say. Please Cadmar, keep your word, I silently plea. It's my only hope at protecting Ajani from myself.

"You're going to disobey me anyway," Cadmar says with a rueful smile. "You can't stay away from him, even if it's good for you."

"I try to," I mutter, my voice nearly a whisper.

Cadmar runs a hand over his face, and for the first time, I notice the bags heavy under his eyes. Those aren't just from Andhereka–they're too deep-set.

"We'll try it your way, Sala," Cadmar says. "Lailani, I expect you to pursue this avenue. Having the prince's ear could be vital to our objectives."

"Pursue?" I ask.

"He means flirt, binti," Sala says, "which means you'll have to brush off those rusty skills."

"My skills aren't—I mean—" I stutter, unsure how I want to respond to this turn of events. Sala laughs her full-bellied laugh.

"Binti, you look like we asked you to kill someone." Sala nudges me with her shoulder then grins at Cadmar. He looks like he's regretting his decision already. "It's the right move, Cadmarji. You'll see."

"Keep the prince's attention, Lailani."

I can't swallow, my mouth parched as if I had traveled through the dunes for days. I nod, and Cadmar claps me on the shoulder, saying, "Get some rest."

I fake a yawn, trying to pretend I'm tired. My heart hammers in my chest, fighting against the guilt smothering it. As I close the door, I can hear Sala saying to Cadmar, "See, I told you to trust them."

Cadmar's response is muffled as I lean against the door, squeezing my eyes shut.

What have I done?

Both Cadmar and the vizier want me to pounce on the prince like a tigress and her prey. Their desire to use our budding relationship makes me nauseous. If only I had stayed away, resisted his charm, his kind eyes, the vulnerability of our stolen moments, I might have been able to protect Ajani.

I hit my head, muttering, "Stupid, stupid, stupid" as the guilt writhes through my veins, sinking into my skin, weighing me down.

I've done despicable things in the name of the Nightshade, things that I've only recently realized the span of my impact. I've stolen, lied, and framed others. I've justified my choices for the past years in the name of saving Tanu. I would do it all again because it was the only choice I had, the only hope of healing Tanu.

But this? This I cannot do. Ajani is too kind, too good for Aveena. As much as I crave another stolen moment in his presence, I need to keep my distance, protect him the only way I can. I can't save him from the snakes in the council or Cadmar's plans or whatever the vizier has planned. I can't even save myself from their machinations.

But I can save him from me.

**There is duality found in nature that is
unlike any other part of Sky Father's
creations. Life and death are equally
served from the same branches. The
prudent gardener respects and honors this
duality.**
-excerpt from *The Handbook of Aveenan Plants*
loaned to Sultana Chhavi from Farah Asfour-

44
The Sultana

Books lay scattered around the sultana as she pours over the page of her newest conquest: *Friend or Foe: Poisonous Plants to Avoid.* The oil lamp flickers as Chhavi rubs her eyes, exhaustion threatening to make her retire early for the night.

The door swings open as Chhavi starts to read again, the entrant saying, "No, no, Mahnoor dear. There is no need for all of that."

The sultana glances away from her book to see Farah Asfour waltzing into the room, staring at the chaos of books spread around on every surface. Farah bows, grinning, as she says, "Well, sultana, you surely seem well-rested."

Chhavi stands and embraces her friend. Her eyes water, but she holds back the unshed tears. Farah returns her hug fiercely, before pulling away and examining her face. "You look—"

"Worn, I know," Chhavi finishes for her.

"I was going to say beautiful as always."

Chhavi snorts but gestures to the empty seat. "How did you manage to come here, Farahji? I haven't had a single visitor."

Farah grimaces and says, "It was made clear to us that no one should disturb you during your time of mourning." Farah scoffs and adds, "Men. They think that they have the answer to everything."

"I'm sure they think they do," Chhavi replies with a small smile.

Amara and Mahnoor enter the room and set down chai and biscuits for the two women before bowing her way out of the room. Chhavi reaches for her cup, allowing the warmth to seep into her cold fingers before taking a sip.

"Tell me what's been happening. How is Ajani?"

Farah sips slowly from her cup before answering. "Ajani is... fine."

"Fine?"

Farah sets her cup down and leans towards the sultana, placing a hand on her arm. "He is mourning his father as we knew he would be. He is trying to deal with the council, but they are—unwelcoming at best. The vizier has taken over running the council—"

Chhavi splutters. "The vizier has what?!"

"Taken over running the council. Per the Ordinances. He's helping everyone 'transition' between sultans as he says." Farah can't hide the bitterness in her voice on the last part.

"How does that work?" Chhavi asks, trying to control her temper.

"Ajani opens the council meeting and closes it. The vizier runs the rest."

Chhavi's jaw drops but she closes it quickly, the reaction not becoming of an aristocratic woman. Her chai clinks loudly on the saucer as she sets her cup down harder than she intended. "Then how can Ajani prove to the council his capabilities as sultan?"

"Therein lies the problem." Farah's face is grave now. "As I said, he's fine, Chhaviji, but I worry for him. You know how those men are."

Chhavi nods, frowning. "The more you shout and puff your chest, the more they respect you."

"Exactly," Farah says, sipping her chai. "I'm unsure if Ajaniji is puffing his chest enough to compete with the rest."

Chhavi grabs a biscuit and swirls it in her chai, contemplating these last words. The entire reason she agreed to leave was to help Ajani show his prowess as sultan and yet...

"He's met a girl," Farah adds, smiling. Chhavi's head snaps up in surprise.

"Do I know her?"

"No, she came with the new arrivals at the beginning of the season." Chhavi stares at Farah, waiting for her to elaborate. Farah grins and adds, "Don't look so morose, Chhaviji. He's a grown man after all."

"Is this why you said he was fine?" Her biscuit tastes dry and bitter, and she shoves the plate closer to Farah, no longer hungry.

Farah laughs. "Yes, Chhaviji. And don't worry. You would like her. She's got—a fire about her. She keeps him on his toes."

The sultana mulls this over, sipping from her chai, not tasting the warm spices. Her son, her *only* son, has met a girl. And she has no idea who this woman is.

350

"Are you sure——" the sultana begins but her friend waves a hand, cutting her off.

"Chhaviji, even if you were there, there is nothing you would be able to do. He is a young man now and soon-to-be sultan."

Chhavi's brow furrows as she asks, "Soon-to-be?"

"That goes along with the Ordinances as well," Farah adds. "Three months of mourning, the vizier as the transition between rulers, and then the crowning of the new sultan."

Chhavi nods as if this makes sense, but unease tickles the back of her mind.

"What of the other women? How are they faring in my absence?"

Farah shrugs and bobs her head. Chhavi narrows her eyes at her closest confidant, unwilling to accept her non-answer.

"They are... as to be expected."

"And what's that supposed to mean?" Chhavi asks, her frustration mounting. This seclusion was supposed to help with the transition, and instead, everything is falling apart.

"Some are lost, unsure how to proceed with all of the changes happening so fast. A few are simply waiting for your return and instruction."

"And the rest?"

Farah sighs, tugging at the chain of her lotus necklace, before replying. "They are striving to fill your place amongst the women."

"Lady Shah——"

"Is one of the main ones, yes. But Chhaviji, she is not alone."

The sultana sits back in her chair, contemplating this new information. When she had followed the vizier's advice, she didn't pause to think about how her absence would impact the women she ruled; she didn't question whether they would continue on without her. But now she wondered—would the women wish to continue when she returned, or would all her work be for naught?

Farah reaches out a hand, clasping the sultana's in her own. "Do not fret, Chhaviji."

"How can I not? Everything we've worked towards—"

"We will find again," Farah says soothingly. "Our progress is not lost."

"But Lady Shah—"

"Lady Shah is nothing but a bossy old hag. Do not worry about her. Besides—" a mischievous twinkle fills Farah's eyes "—a few of the new ones are helping to keep her in check."

The sultana opens her mouth to protest, but Farah squeezes her hand reassuringly. "Chhaviji, we are doing our best with the circumstances. As for Lady Shah, well, an empty vessel—"

"—makes much noise," Chhavi finishes with her friend. "You're right. I just worry."

Farah gestures to the books scattered around the room. "Speaking of worry, what in Wind's name are you doing?"

Chhavi stares around at the scraps of parchment, rubbing the back of her neck. "I—I'm not sure," she starts hesitantly, trying to find the words to describe the knot in her gut.

"Are you considering the life of a scribe?" Farah jokes.

Chhavi gives her a small smile in return. "Something feels… off. I can't describe it, Farahji, but that's it. My husband's death was too sudden, too smooth…"

Chhavi's voice trails off as she notices the pitying look on Farah's face.

"Chhaviji, are you sure you're not—"

"Trying to catch the wind?"

"Well, yes."

"No, I'm not sure. But I feel as if I need to try. The thought won't leave me alone."

Farah hesitates, then says quietly, "It won't bring him back, Chhavi."

"I know," the sultana replies, her shoulders shrinking in on herself. She takes a deep, steadying breath, fighting off the grief that threatens to overwhelm her. Farah watches, sorrow clear in her eyes.

"He had a heart problem, Chhaviji."

"And that's what's bothering me," the sultana whispers, staring down at the chaos of books around her. "His father had a strong heart, and his grandfather before that. As far as I know, no one in Gautam's family suffered from a weak heart."

"Are you sure?"

"Yes."

Farah sits up straighter in her chair. "Then what do you need me to do?"

"Farahji, I—"

"Just tell me, Chhavi. How can I help my Wind sister?"

Chhavi embraces her friend, holding her tight. Tears glisten on both women's cheeks when they draw apart.

Chhavi spent the better part of the night devising a plan with Farah before the other woman had to slip back to the palace. As she watched her friend disappearing into the darkness, Chhavi sent a prayer up to Wind Mother to look over them both.

Ji,
I have done as you asked. Although I did
not look at the note you had me deliver,
as instructed, the recipient's paleness
after reading your message rivaled the
desert sands. I'm confident that your
persuasiveness has prevailed again.
-R.L.

45

My imagination is taking over.

As I watch the Council of the Sultan file in, everything seems foreboding. Brows furrowed in concentration. Fists clenched. Sharp whispers that escalate before the speaker is shushed. Furtive glances before putting heads together to talk.

But I have to be imagining it. Nothing has changed in the two days since the vizier caught me. Everything should be normal.

Right?

The silence in the Veiled Room weighs on my shoulders. A few whispers. A shoulder nudge here. Concern etched into the older women's faces. Under the guise of summoning a servant, I scan the faces of the women around me, struggling to determine what has changed. Then it hits me: none of the younger women came today.

"Lady Acharya?"

The servant breaks protocol to get my attention; I hadn't noticed the woman's approach. Even she looks nervous, her eyes darting around the room.

"Refreshments, please."

"And some citrus water."

Farah Asfour sinks into the seat next to me as the servant rushes off. I want to ask her if everyone is as tense as I'm imagining, but the chime announcing the Consulate rings, cutting off my opportunity to speak.

The routine formalities of the council are second nature to me now. Ajani walks to his marble throne—I place my fist over my heart and bow with the rest. Vizier Nassor ascends—I bow despite my desire to remain standing. The Consulate moves up the dais, and after one final bow, everyone sits.

I can't look at Vizier Nassor, even through the veil. My stomach churns at the sound of his oily voice amplified throughout the room, and I fight the urge to cover my ears.

I want to leave. Right now.

I squeeze my legs together to hide their trembling and slow my breathing. Instead of looking at the vizier, I focus on the prince. As usual, Ajani says nothing as the vizier begins the meeting. His posture is rigid but gives no hint to his current mood.

"...so you will understand the need to move it up on the agenda today," the vizier finishes saying then sits back down. I shake my head, trying to focus on what is happening. What's the point of coming if I'm not listening?

"Your obsession with numbers, although admirable, Nassorji, is too focused. More goes into running Aveena than just the numbers," Consulate Kabir Bakshi says, gesturing to emphasize his point.

"And yet, if we do not look at the numbers, we will set future generations up for failure," Nassor says calmly. A shiver races down my spine. "We are at fault for their destruction if we do not pay attention to the signs."

Consulate Reyanash stands, a placating smile on his face as he eyes Consulate Bakshi. Not for the first time, I wonder why the council voted in Reyanash to the Consulate, giving the Al-Sid family a stronger foothold in the Council of the Sultan. A look passes between Reyanash and Nassor before the former begins to speak.

"My cousin knows that more goes into running the city than just numbers, Kabirji," Reyanash says in a mollifying tone. "However, he simply desires us to use the calculations as a basis for further action. That is all."

Manish Reddy, the third member of the Consulate, slams his hands onto his chair, the sound echoing in the vast chamber. Ajani jerks at the noise.

"It all comes down to the same thing!" Manish keeps his voice barely below a shout. "Nassor, we respect you and your service, but this goes too far this time. Kabir and I have already expressed our concerns with your ideas, and yet you insist on rolling right over us. We are not flies to be swatted down by family Al-Sid!"

Manish's shoulders are heaving by the time he finishes. The tension radiates throughout the council, and even from my height, I can see how Ajani watches wide-eyed, unsure what to do.

Say something, I think, silently urging Ajani on.

"Are you done, Consulate Reddy?" the vizier asks in a deadly calm voice.

"Not quite—"

Nassor cuts him off. "I didn't expect an answer. Let me rephrase: you are done, Consulate Reddy."

"You do not have the ability—"

"You'll find that I do, Manish, seeing as I have the power of final say."

Manish leans back in his chair, seething, his anger palpable.

Cadmar jumps up and begins to speak, interrupting the power struggle on the dais.

"My fellow councilmen, we have a duty to the whole of Aveena—" A few groans punctuate the silence. "—We have been charged to protect those in our care. We must honor that charge and seek to protect the interests of all the people of Aveena."

"And how do you propose we do that, Councilman Cadmar?" a man on the far side of the room asks. I don't recognize him; I'm sure he hasn't spoken in the council before. Farah touches my arm and mouths, "Dhruv Dara."

I stare at Farah as my already-churning stomach drops to the floor. *Dhruv Dara.* One of the letters had the initials D.D. I turn back to the proceedings, hiding my shock from Farah.

"...it is vital to our survival. We are a city-state, afterall, Councilman Dara. We have to rely on everyone within our walls for survival," Cadmar says.

Another man stands and says, "Forgive any perceived rudeness, Councilman Cadmar, but I do not think you mentioned a concrete plan in that statement. Without any definite steps, we cannot proceed down this route. Uncertainty can also be detrimental to our survival."

I look at Farah who mouths, "Vihaan Pateel."

Another name from the letters? I can't be sure without checking the parchment hidden in my pocket.

Ray Lobo stands. My left knee jiggles of its own accord. I don't try to hide it as I lean in to focus on the conversation. Ray Lobo exudes more confidence as he faces Cadmar than I have seen before. I shiver despite the heat.

"Excuse me, Cadmarji, but do you not own a house in the Upper City?"

Cadmar's eyes narrow and he says, "Yes."

"You have an *unusual* pastime, do you not?"

A few men snicker at Lobo's sarcastic tone. Cadmar stills, waiting until the men regain control before answering.

"If you're referring to my library, then yes."

"And do you purchase books for this library?" Lobo smirks at Councilman Dara, not bothering to look at Cadmar as he questions him.

"It is unclear what my library has to do with our current discussion of food in Aveena, Councilman Lobo," Cadmar says. His cool persona disintegrates with the fire in his glare.

"Well, it would seem to me, Councilman Cadmar, that you enjoy the privileges of being Aristocracy. Although you pretend as if you are above us, you are complicit in the same faults that you have identified in your fellow Councilmen." He opens his arms, inviting nods of agreement, a sneer reminiscent of the vizier's plastered on his face. "I find it distasteful that you would go so far to tell *us* how to keep house when you have not attended your own."

Murmurs follow this pronouncement. Cadmar's gaze sweeps the Council Room, assessing the faces of his fellow Ari. Erol touches his arm, and Cadmar sits down.

He will not win today.

For the first time since the meeting began, I force myself to look at Vizier Nassor. Although most of his face remains neutral, the side of his mouth is turned up in triumph.

Ray Lobo speaks again. I wonder if the vile old man has ever felt this important in his whole life. That must be how the vizier won him over—by appealing to Lobo's pride.

Lobo's chest is pushed out like a peacock showing off its magnificent tail.

"My fellow councilmen, we *do* have an obligation to those in the Lower City." Lobo's use of Cadmar's words does not go unnoticed. "Our obligation to our Lower City brethren is to ensure that they are living a morally just life in accordance with the Ordinances. We must remain strong and united. We must show those who break the Ordinances how wrong they are. And we must have pity on those less fortunate than ourselves."

Lobo pauses for effect, making eye contact with those around him. The drastic improvement in his speech-making leads me to believe that someone—perhaps a certain vizier—has been coaching Lobo on what to say.

"The increase in thievery and crime in Aveena is *our* responsibility." Lobo pounds his chest with his fist in a show of passion. "We must educate the Lower City scum, instruct them, and reveal to them how wrong their ideologies are. That is not to say that the people are bad people—I would never insinuate that an entire group of people is bad at heart—I am saying that their way of thinking is wrong. We must eradicate their undesirable habits in order to purge Aveena."

Ray Lobo pauses to meet the eyes of those around him. The air hangs heavy, expectant, for what will follow.

I want to vomit.

"Councilmen, help me take back our city."

The picture that Councilman Lobo paints of the Lower City raises my hackles. Their *thinking* is wrong? We are *helping* them by becoming stricter? But as I look through the veil, the nods of many of the councilmen are visible from my high perch. I grip the arms of my chair in an effort to keep my hands steady; my white knuckles contrast against the rosy red cushion of my chair, its jarring opulence.

I am alone.

The dust from the street coats my lungs. I struggle, coughing, through the crowds. My hands tremble as I pull my bundle to my chest, sheltering the last piece of my mangled heart from the foreign streets of the Lower City.

I need food.

Cold sweat drips down the back of my neck into my disheveled kurti. I think it used to be blue to match my eyes, but I can't remember.

I stumble into the next alleyway. The rough wall catches on my clothes as my legs wobble and give out beneath me. I pull my bundle closer, ignoring the stone jutting into my back, and shield myself from the onslaught of dust and sand kicked up by a cart passing by.

I could give up. Just sit here until I wither away and become part of the sand.

I can't cry. My chest is empty, devoid of emotion, as if the events of the past months sucked me dry.

Someone taps my shoulder. I don't look up. *Let me be*, I think. The second tap is harder, more insistent. I lift my head wearily. My eyes blur out of focus, and it takes me a minute to recognize the mango held in front of my face. My eyes follow the arm up to the face of an older woman. Her wrinkles are permanently engraved into her skin. The white wisps of her hair escape the braid she's tied them into. Her kurti is unrecognizable in color like mine, although cleaner.

"C'mon. Eat it, girl."

Her words smear together in a whispered rush. I stare at her, uncomprehending. She grunts and pushes the mango closer to my face.

"Eat."

I struggle to adjust the bundle in my arms so that I can eat the mango. The old woman sighs and sits down next to me on the street. Her knees crack as she lowers herself to my level, but she doesn't complain.

"Let me. You eat."

I pull the bundle closer, mistrustful. The Lower City is known for its crime. What if she runs off with all I have left?

"Dunes, stop bein' so stubborn, girl. I couldn't run if Wind herself carried me."

I gingerly pass my precious bundle to the woman in exchange for the mango. At home, mother would cut mangoes into quarters, giving us each a spoon to delicately scoop the sweet flesh out of the skin.

My teeth rip into the skin of the mango. A guttural groan of relief escapes my mouth as the juices hit my tongue and dribble down my face.

Pure ambrosia.

The woman, ignoring my monstrous eating, sings softly to herself. Probably to cover up the inhuman noises I make as I squish through the remainder of the mango. Soon, all that is left is the large seed in my hand. My teeth graze the seed as I search for any last bit of mango on its surface. A fly lands on my hand, attracted by the sticky juice dripping down my arm.

Ray Lobo's droning voice brings me back to the present. No longer starving. No longer dirty. But more alone than I ever felt in the Lower City. Lobo is vilifying my people, painting them as murderers and thieves.

He couldn't be further from the truth.

All produce shall be equally shared for the good of all.
-from The Ordinances of Aveena-

46

I'm in a haze as I navigate back to the suite to prepare for the feast tonight. The last thing I want to do is primp and subject myself to the tension amongst the Ari, but there's no escaping it.

As Sala is about to open the door to the suite, a loud crash sounds on the other side. Sala and I exchange a panicked look and hurry into the suite.

A vase lays smashed in the entryway. As we enter, Cadmar sweeps his arms across the desk, sending everything crashing to the floor. Papers flutter through the air as the glass ink bottle shatters against the wall. Nothing escapes his wrath.

After the destruction is absolute, Cadmar slumps onto a paper-strewn chair and presses the heels of his hands in his eyes. Hard. His frustration fills the room like the horseshit that Ray Lobo spewed in the Council Room filled the minds of his fellow Ari. Sala and I remain frozen by the door, unsure what to do.

"Never thought I'd see that," Zahir mutters behind me.

I jump and turn, finally noticing Zahir and Erol right behind us. Erol's jaw is clenched tight as he surveys the damage.

"I'm done now," Cadmar says, not bothering to look at any of us. "You can come away from the door now."

I pick my way through the shards of broken glass and smeared ink. Erol and Sala rush over to Cadmar, but I keep my distance, watching him warily from the other side of the room.

"It's not the end," Erol says, patting Cadmar on the shoulder. He glances at the mess on the other chair and chooses to remain standing instead. "We've always known we would have to play the long game. Let's regroup and—"

"No," Cadmar snaps.

The edge in his voice makes me recoil on myself even though it's not directed at me. Roaring starts in my ears as Cadmar rants and raves, furiously pacing back and forth. I can't get a full breath in, my skin crawling as...

"Laila, come back to me," Zahir murmurs. He runs his hands soothingly on my upper arms. "Take a deep breath in now. That's good. Let it out, Laila. Again."

Sala says something, and Cadmar's voice rises again, but Zahir puts his hands on my face. "Focus on me right now."

My heartbeat slows, and soon the roaring recedes. I take a full, trembling breath, letting it out slowly.

"There you go," Zahir says. "You good?"

I nod, not trusting my voice, and step back. Zahir shifts to face Cadmar, putting his body partially in front of mine, and crosses his arms.

"And the way that he shut down Manish! He's one of the Consulate and should have the chance to speak. But Nassor can't handle anyone disagreeing with him!"

"Why didn't you bring up the Tribes?" Zahir asks. Cadmar falters in his steps and turns towards us like he'd forgotten we were there.

"Excuse me?" Cadmar asks. I shift from one foot to another, uncomfortable with the underlying danger in his tone.

"Why didn't you bring up the Tribes?" Zahir repeats. He gestures towards the door. "Councilman Dara asked you for a specific plan. You could have told them."

Cadmar gapes then snaps his mouth closed and waves his arms wildly. "They can't hear when the vizier has sunk his poison so deeply in their ears. It's not the time."

"Then what are we doing here? I thought our goal was to help Aveena survive," Zahir says coldly. Although he doesn't raise his voice, I can feel the tension vibrating off of him as he questions Cadmar. "We've been kissing ass with the Ari for weeks, and what do we have to show for it? The least you could do is—"

"Do not tell me what I should and should not do, Mr. Juma," Cadmar roars.

Zahir doesn't flinch, but I cringe away, hating myself for hiding further behind Zahir's back as he faces the councilman. Behind Cadmar, Sala and Erol exchange a panicked look.

"Cadmar," Sala says tentatively, touching his elbow to get his attention, but he jerks his arm away and turns angrily on Sala.

"You!" Cadmar says, pointing a finger in Sala's face. "You were supposed to be watching them, making sure they were performing their roles. What have you been doing all this time?"

The silence is deafening as we all stare in shock at Cadmar as he seethes in Sala's face. She looks like Cadmar slapped her, the color draining from her face. She stands taller, pushing her shoulders back, her back rigid.

"Jelani—"

"For once, address me with the respect I deserve, Ms. Khatri! I am from one of the oldest families of the Aristocracy. I have earned the deference due to me," Cadmar yells, his face ruddy with fury.

After a beat, Sala crosses her fist over her heart and bows. No one moves as Sala holds her bow, prostrate before our leader. Cadmar's chest heaves, his nose flared, as he glares at the back of Sala's neck.

Cadmar deflates, then touches Sala's shoulder gently. She doesn't move.

"Sala," Cadmar says softly. Sala remains bowed. Cadmar runs a hand over his face then says, "Rise."

I stare over Zahir's shoulder, tears threatening to spill down my cheeks as I look at Sala's passive face. Sala, the one who pushes me to share and laugh and trust them. When I see her statue-like face, all I can think is of her undying loyalty to this Ari who destroyed our room. How her heartbreak had been transformed into purpose by Cadmar.

But buried beneath good intentions, Cadmar was just like the rest of them. Power hungry. Volatile. Uncaring of the hearts they cared for.

Cadmar buries his face in his hands. His muffled "I'm sorry" is barely audible.

"I forgive you," Sala says, her shoulders sagging in relief. She guides Cadmar back to his chair, forcing him to sit down. "We've weathered bad council meetings before. What's really bothering you, Jelani?"

"The vizier grows in power. Men who we had won over to our side have changed their allegiance. I want to know how the vizier has managed to get ahead of us. There is something that we're missing."

He says the last sentence under his breath, more to himself than to her. I swallow back the guilt rising inside me. This isn't my fault. I haven't even reported back to the vizier yet. And even if I had, I'm doing it to protect them.

I glance at the back of Zahir's curly head.

Well, to protect one of them at least.

"We need to figure out what advantage Vizier Nassor has over us. I want to know how he is winning over these men. I want to know who works for him."

My stomach plummets at his words.

I work for him.

"We'll figure it out, Cadmarji," Sala says reassuringly. "We always do."

The end result of a good deed is a slap.
-Aveenan Proverb-

47

The vizier's added jewels glimmer darkly in the lowlights of the Harem Room. I've scampered around the Harem Room three times, avoiding the inevitable meeting with my new blackmailer. Leaning into the blue fabric behind me, I stare across the room, trying to locate the tall figure of the vizier again. Spindly fingers grip my arm tightly, jerking me around to face the vizier. Nassor smirks at me. He knows my feeble attempts to avoid him failed.

"Grace me with your presence, Lady Lailani. I have need of your council."

The viper can't keep the smugness out of his voice as he pulls me to a shadowed corner in the back of the dimly lit room. Instead of sitting on the cushions, Vizier Nassor pulls me to the side of the abundant drapery, obscuring the council's view of us. I force my face to relax into the smooth, emotionless mask that the Ari wear. The vizier leans closer, shadows emphasizing the harsh lines of his face, and whispers, "Very good, my dear. You've been practicing."

I long to pull my arm away but resist. The bastard wants to get under my skin, to make me blister with frustration. The vizier's sickly-sweet perfume of over-ripe oranges fills my nostrils, choking me with its pungent smell.

"What do you have for me, my beautiful little spy?"

"Don't call me that."

"But it's what you are, dear. And seeing as I own you, you will tolerate whatever name I see fit." My skin crawls. Just because Aveena doesn't have slaves, that doesn't mean there aren't other ways of making a slave of a person. The vizier continues, "Or should I check in with a certain gold merchant in the Upper City? I hear that he has a daughter who looks just like you."

No, no, no. He didn't remember. He can't have.

The vizier's smile widens. "Councilman Naidu proved to be more useful than I ever considered. Not many with djinn-eyes such as yours."

"It's not—I'm from—"

"Shh," the vizier says, pressing a finger against my lips. "No, no, no. I don't want to hear that. Tell me what you have for me."

"My uncle is frustrated by what happened in the council today," I say. I need to give this viper some information without telling him everything.

"Go on."

"My uncle thinks you have something to do with it, but he doesn't know how."

A smirk.

"Just your uncle? Or others?"

I freeze.

"Just my uncle," I whisper.

"You lie. I know he works with Jelani Cadmar and Tei Asfour." I struggle to maintain my indifferent mask. My palms begin to sweat, but I twist my hands into my saree, refusing to let the vizier see me falter. The malice in the vizier's voice is laced with joy as he says, "Try again."

He wants to punish me. He's *enjoying* this. Panic starts to filter through my body with the realization.

"They wish to find a way to stop this attack on the Lower City. They believe it will do more harm than good."

The vizier's fingers dig into my arm, threatening to break the skin. His smug mask does not slip. "You're being coy with me, little spy. Need I remind you that I am in the one in power here?"

Vizier Nassor steps closer to me, towering over my head like a minaret over the palace. The rotten orange smell swamps my nose, and I resist coughing. I try to lean away from his imposing form, but he grabs my shoulder. Iciness floods through my body, painfully cold, as the vizier traps me between himself and the wall with his magic. Vizier Nassor could overpower me in this moment, and no one would know. Fear spikes of its own volition, sending adrenaline coursing through my body. Run. Flee. Get away.

Nassor steps away, stroking his beard, his smirk growing. The chill disappears, but I'm left quivering. My attempt at an emotionless Ari mask failed.

"How do my opponents plan to stop me?"

My hands tremble. I push my palms against the wall behind me.

"I do not know—"

"Lies."

"Truly, I don't—"

Vizier Nassor slams his fist into the wall, and my head jerks to the side as his fist catches some of the loose strands of my hair. The rise in the belly dancers' music hides the noise of his fist against the wall and my gasp of pain.

"Let's try this again, my beautiful little spy. How. Do. They. Plan. To. Stop. Me?"

I can't breathe. I can't keep the mask up.

"They plan to talk to some of the men who are in the middle. And they plan to bring people from the Lower City to speak to the council. To plead their case and show that the Lower City folk aren't villains."

Vizier Nassor's cold eyes bore into mine. I'm staring death in the face. Then his face breaks into a venomous smile. It's worse than the coldness. Vizier Nassor runs his hand down my cheek like that first night in the Harem Room.

"Good girl."

His hand continues down my cheek and caresses my neck like a noose. Suddenly, the vizier is pressing his weight into me, his long fingers cutting off my air and my scream. He lowers his head down to my ear and says, "Next time, *Lady* Lailani, you answer when I tell you to do so. Now be a good girl and distract the prince for me. I have business to attend to."

The vizier kisses my cheek possessively and walks away.

My limbs won't respond, the fear flooding through my body immobilizing me like the vizier's magic. I squeeze my eyes shut as memories surface.

Rough hands.

Pain.

Pleading.

A crash of a cymbal startles me out of the spiraling, repressed memories.

I'm in the palace, not the Upper City.

I stumble out from the corner, wandering the Harem Room, hopelessly searching for comfort. The sights blur: the dancers become writhing shapes, the patrons ornate blots. A chill fills my chest, solidifying the mental trap gripping me, and exhaustion floods through me as the adrenaline seeps away. I'm lost in a sea of unfamiliar faces and reeling emotions.

Someone tugs on my elbow, and I wrench my arm out of their grasp. It's the vizier coming back. I spin and—

"Oh, Your Highness."

I hastily cross my fist over my heart and bow. The few Ari women who braved the Harem Room hone in on the two of us.

"Lady Lailani, there is no need for such formality."

I rise from my bow and look up into the prince's face. The haze of smoke paired with the dim lights make it difficult to read his expression. We stand in awkward silence before I register that I need to respond. I search for the right words—formal enough to appease anyone listening but casual enough that the prince won't think anything's amiss.

"I—"

"Would—"

We speak at the same time and both stop, waiting for the other to continue. Ajani grins, officially breaking the awkwardness. My smile is forced, cracking at the edges with the strain of pretending I am okay. The guilt rises as the vizier's parting order to distract Ajani rings in my ears, but I swallow it down.

"Would you like to sit, Your Highness?" I ask. I tilt my head to the side. Ajani follows the gesture, noticing for the first time the small gaggle of women observing our exchange.

"Ah, yes, of course, Lady Lailani," he replies.

He offers his arm—the epitome of Ari manners—and leads me away from the snooping aunties. We settle far away from the dancers. A servant sets down an array of delicacies on a gold-trimmed plate. Before the servant leaves, Ajani gestures to the curtains. The man nods and readjusts the fabrics to hang in front of our alcove. Through the sheer material I can just make out the women putting their heads together. Ajani is warm next to me, and a flash of him holding me on the wall flitters across my mind. He is the comfort I need after the vizier. I relax, shoving the vizier's trap into the back of my mind to deal with later. Ajani sighs and leans his head back onto the pillows, completely oblivious to the gossip.

"Long day, Your Highness?"

Ajani doesn't open his eyes as he says, "Don't call me that."

"You'll have to get used to it at some point, you know."

He groans, which makes me smile. His reluctance reminds me of one of my friends from the Upper City—he didn't like to be reminded of his responsibilities either.

"I can tell you're laughing at me, Lailani."

"I would do no such thing," I say in my best mock-scandalized voice. "You wound me deeply that you think I would be capable of such chicanery."

"Chicanery?"

"My father uses that word all the time," I say without thinking.

"Your father?" Ajani asks.

I scramble to stick to the story Sala drilled into my head before entering the palace. "Yes, my father. Before he died, of course. He would tell Uncle Erol that my cousin and I were full of chicanery. As kids."

"You said 'uses' though."

"I forget sometimes—" I glance down, not finishing my sentence. Ajani's hand covers mine.

"I do, too."

Ajani leans closer and his spicy scent surrounds me. The smell transforms, becoming the rancid orange odor of the royal vizier. My heart races. The hand over mine traps me, makes me vulnerable.

I wrench my hand out from under Ajani's and pull it to my chest. My body perches on the edge of the cushion, ready for flight. The prince is stunned. Or maybe hurt? It's hard to read the emotions flickering in his dark eyes.

I lower my hand slowly. I'm incapable of meeting Ajani's eyes; instead, I look over his shoulder. This second wave of adrenaline seeps from my body, leaving me drained.

Drained and unsure how to fix this.

"I'm sorry."

Wait, what?

My eyebrows furrow in confusion as my eyes snap to his face. The prince watches the belly dancers on the other side of the room, while his hand runs through his hair. He's looking but not really seeing.

Sorry for what?

"Lailani, I owe you an apology. I've been distant lately. You probably feel like I've led you on."

Ajani finally meets my eyes. Tentatively—as if afraid of rejection again—he reaches for my hand and holds it between both of his.

"It's not fair to you. I courted you so openly, and during Andhereka…" His voice trails off. I can tell the memory affects him as much as it affects me. Heat rises to his cheeks, and he clears his throat, continuing, "…and then didn't speak to you. I understand your hesitance to be close to me right now. I know how women talk. I'd hate to stain your reputation with my distracted courtship. Please accept my apology."

Ajani bows over my hand and places his forehead against it. Before anyone notices, I lift Ajani's head from my hand.

"There is nothing to forgive, Your Highness."

"Please, let me make it up to you. Tomorrow."

His eagerness is endearing, pushing the last remnants of the vizier away. I nod, and his answering grin sends warmth through my heart. We stare into each other's eyes, and his face changes. The energy around us ignites.

I look away and say, "Well, Your Highness, I think I should find my cousin and get him to escort me back. It's late, and I have a very exciting day planned for tomorrow."

"Funny enough, so do I, Lady Lailani."

Ajani stands and helps me to rise from the squishy pillows. A servant opens the hanging fabric, removing the barrier between us and the rest of the Aristocracy. The dancers are mingling with various councilmen. As we pass by the alcove where the Ari women perch, several glare at me. I smile and pretend not to notice. Ajani leads me to the group of young Ari men laughing near the entryway of the Harem Room. A servant cleans up the slew of empty glasses from the table behind the Ari. The men—really boys—lean heavily against the wall, sway in place, or throw back more drinks so they can hand the empty glasses to the servant.

"—so then I told her that she could rub my magic lamp anytime."

The young Ari around Zahir burst out laughing. One slaps Zahir on the back and says, "Zaharian, I don't know how you get away with this shit."

"It's the curly beard. Women don't know how to handle the curls," Zahir says with a wink. As we approach the men, I notice that several have used beard wax in an attempt to curl the ends of their meager mustaches. The beard, indeed.

"I think the wax has gone to your head, cousin," I say.

At my comment, several of the young men turn, losing their balance in the process. A few eye me up and down openly before noticing who I am with. Those who weren't already bent over from losing their balance bow to the prince. Pathetic drunks. Zahir—the steadiest of the group—looks to the prince before bowing. His eyes never leave Ajani's face, as if he doesn't want to expose his neck to the future sultan. Luckily, Ajani doesn't notice Zahir's rudeness; his attention is on the two who ogled me so openly.

"Sorry to break up the party, gentlemen, but Lady Lailani wishes to return to her rooms," Ajani says formally.

Zahir steps forward and says, "Very well, Your Highness. Cousin, shall I escort you back?"

I nod and link my arm with Zahir's. I look back at Ajani and smile. "Until tomorrow, Your Highness."

"Tomorrow."

**There are no friends amongst spies and
thieves. Contacts, yes. Associates, yes.
Friends, no. Everyone is expendable.**
-Advice from Velo to Laila in her
first year of being the Nightshade-

48

The stress of the highs and lows from the Harem Room
leaves my body feeling as if it's been beaten like a rug.
My steps drag, and Zahir keeps glancing at me when he
thinks I'm not looking.

"Stop doing that."

"Doing what?" Zahir asks innocently.

"Checking in on me. I can feel your eyes on me every
other step."

"You're walking slow."

"I'm tired."

"Even for tired, you're walking slow."

I stop walking and glare at him. "Are you going to keep
analyzing my every step? It's annoying."

Zahir crosses his arms, jaw clenched. "Are you going to
pout like a child if I do? Because that's annoying."

We glare at each other for a second. Zahir's mouth twitches,
and I can't keep my face straight anymore. We both laugh. I
link my arm through Zahir's, the tension broken.

"Want to walk near the canal?" Zahir asks.

My body aches, but I say yes anyway.

Outside, the breeze whips through the length of my pallu, tugging it around. I shiver and move closer to Zahir, using his warmth to combat the cool breeze. He stiffens— *what's his problem?*—but leads us to the edge of the canal, slowing his pace so that my worn body can keep up with his longer legs. The moon illuminates the world around us, glistening off of the water below and casting a silvery light throughout the garden.

"It's beautiful."

"Better than the Hathorda rooftop?" Zahir asks.

Zahir speaks so quietly that I almost don't hear it. His question takes me off guard. I look at Zahir, but he's pointedly watching the water below. "Well, it's different here for sure," I say.

"Different?"

"Obviously. But better? I'm not sure about that."

Zahir stops walking and finally meets my eyes. His eyes catch the moonlight, making them seem overbright. Unlike the prince, where his eyes reveal his emotions, Zahir's eyes mask what he's thinking. My arm is still entwined with Zahir's, and suddenly, I feel too close. We are only a breath away from each other; Zahir's warmth is scorching, and his eyes…

I step back, trying to find some normalcy. Ever since we've entered the palace, things have been… different. I can't put my finger on it. Zahir resumes walking, and despite the chill of the breeze, I keep a small distance between us, resisting the urge to move into Zahir's warmth again.

"I'm worried for you, Laila," Zahir says softly, under the cover of the canal.

"Huh?" I ask, forcing myself to focus on Zahir's words and not being next to him. The rush of the canal hides our voices from prying ears.

"I'm worried for you, Laila."

I pause, collecting myself before I respond. He can't know about the vizier. If that viper knew that I'd been found out, I wouldn't be the only one who might disappear. I could not risk Zahir getting hurt because of my failure...

"Why?"

"I don't trust the prince."

"The prince?" I ask stupidly.

"Yes, the Ari that you spend more and more time with." Zahir's arm tenses under my own, like he's reigning himself in. "You're letting him court you again, aren't you?"

"Yes."

Maybe if I speak quietly enough, the canal could carry my voice away from here, away from this conversation.

"He doesn't have honorable intentions with you, Laila. He's going to use you and then leave you. You don't hear what everyone is saying about the two of you. You've broken protocol once already." Zahir's voice rises. He takes a deep breath, getting himself under control before continuing in a furious whisper, "And luckily for you, I think I was the only one who noticed that you two disappeared during Andhereka. If you keep going off alone with him, well, he is a man..."

Zahir's voice trails off, his implication hanging in the air between us.

I stare at my friend, the person who I thought I was going through this palace hell with together. Loneliness hits me, tears threatening to fall as his words worm their way under my skin.

I shove Zahir away. I can barely control my voice, wanting to shout at him but afraid of being overheard. "Why did you bring me out here? To berate me? To warn me? I'm not some child! You're the last person I need this from, Zahir."

"Or maybe I'm the first person you need this from," Zahir replies. He looks to the sky, running his fingers through his hair in exasperation. Zahir's anger matches my own, but he has a tighter rein on it. He speaks softly, passionately, as he says, "Look, Laila, I don't trust him. And you clearly do."

"I—"

"Don't lie to me. I see it in your face when you look at him."

"Cadmar wants me to get close to the prince, Zahir. You know that."

"But is that all you're doing?"

"Of course it is."

Zahir stops. I cross my arms and refuse to look at him. Out of all the people who I thought I had to worry about tonight, Zahir was the last one on my list. Why can't he have my back? I can take the shit from Cadmar and the vizier. I can deal with the prince. But Zahir is supposed to have my back. I trusted him.

"You don't get to say this to me."

It's Zahir's turn to glare. "And if not me, then who?"

"I have to deal with everyone else's horseshit. I have to prove myself to everyone else. Since when did I have to prove myself to you, Zahir?"

Tears slide down my face. Without giving Zahir another glance, I rush back to Erol's suite by myself.

Zahir doesn't stop me.

**Courtship is a choreographed dance.
Be coy, not too forthcoming with your
affections. Tease him with the chase.**
-Advice from Lady Shah to her daughter-

49

Ajani planned ahead this time.

His eyes are alight with mischief as he leads me to the aviary. I try to match his excitement, but the puffiness under my eyes is barely concealed by makeup, threatening to expose my utter exhaustion. Sala and the two guards trail behind us at a distance. Ajani's hand is warm in mine; he doesn't bother with protocol. I smile, allowing him to pull me along. Allowing him to pull me closer.

"What are you smiling about, Lailani?" Ajani asks.

"You."

His grin is pure man. The look sends a thrill through the butterflies already dancing in my belly. Ajani leans closer as we walk through the marbled hallways and whispers in my ear, "I'm glad that you're thinking about me."

A blush creeps into my cheeks, and I have to lower my eyes from the intensity of his stare. It's been a long time since I've let a man lead me around like this. The blush in my cheeks darkens at that thought. Ajani laughs, appearing like the man that he is and not the somber Ari statue he's pretending to be.

The double iron gate greets us at the aviary entrance. Ajani opens the first gate and bows jokingly, indicating that I should enter first. He swings the gate behind him, shutting out our chaperones with a stern look.

"There are some benefits to being the next sultan," Ajani whispers as he opens the next gate. I smile shyly, his good mood infecting me. I can almost pretend that it's just the two of us hidden away from the world: that the rest of the Ari aren't gossiping about us; that he isn't the most powerful person in Aveena; that I'm not a liar; that the vizier isn't blackmailing me…

Ajani reaches from my hand, bringing my thoughts back to the present. He laces his fingers through mine. The motion is more intimate now that we're alone.

Get out of your head, Laila, I tell myself. I breathe and focus on relaxing my shoulders.

"So, Prince of Mysteries, what is so special about our rendezvous today?" I ask.

"Hm, Prince of Mysteries? Maybe I should add that to my list of titles."

I playfully smack him on the arm and say, "Careful. Your ego is showing."

The prince stiffens when I smack him, but then the moment passes. He points out different birds hiding in the foliage above our heads. I nod and "mm-hm" at the appropriate points, but inside I'm chiding myself. I cannot forget who I am talking to. I can't talk to Ajani like I would Zahir.

Zahir.

His warnings about the prince's intentions swim through my mind. He knows why I'm here. Zahir should know that I have to play the role Cadmar assigned to me.

But are you only playing a role? my inner voice asks me. I push down her taunt and refocus on the present.

"...and that small black one with the bright blue back in the underbrush over there is a Fairy-Bluebird."

"Fairy?" I ask, interrupting Ajani's monologue.

"Well, in the old days before the city of Aveena was built, the Fairy-Bluebirds were believed to be omens by our ancestors."

"Omens of what exactly?" I eye the black and blue bird with suspicion. I don't need omens to complicate things further.

"When our people were nomadic, the Fairy-Bluebirds were supposedly omens to our ancestors sent to give hints on whether to continue your journey or not."

"Do you believe it?"

"Believe that a bird could tell me what to do?"

"When you put it that way…"

Ajani laughs and leads me off the path towards the creek. "Lailani, no bird can tell you what to do. Only the Ordinances can do that."

I slow down and tug on his hand. Ajani looks at me, confused. All the playfulness slips off his face.

"Isn't it weird that you just said a *paper* can tell us what to do?"

He lets go of my hand, unsure of how to respond.

"Lailani, that is just—" he hesitates, "—the way things are in Aveena. We need the Ordinances."

"We do?"

I tread carefully. Ajani likes me, but that might not stop him from calling me traitorous if I question the Ordinances.

"Yes, we do. Could you imagine the chaos if we did not have the Ordinances?"

"You are the prince," I say softly. "You have a voice despite the Ordinances."

Ajani runs his hand through his hair and says, "They give us a way to govern our lives."

A shrill bird call fills the silence between us. *You're right, little bird*, I think. *That's horseshit.*

"And yet no one has seen them."

"I have," Ajani says. I tilt my head, waiting for him to continue. Ajani shrugs. "The original is in my father's—I mean *my* tower."

"That makes sense, I guess," I say. I smile, trying to dispel the tension between us, and step closer to Ajani. I move the hand ruffling his hair away and reach to fix it myself. His black locks are soft under my touch as I run my fingers through, combing his hair back into its swoop.

"If you keep that up, you'll end up looking like Wind did your hair," I say, trying to regain the playfulness of earlier.

I finish fixing his hair and look into Ajani's face.

"Oh, I, um, I'm sorry, Your Highness. I didn't mean to presume…"

I'm so close to Ajani that his breath warms my cheek as I stutter like a fool. I can see flecks of green in his dark brown eyes this close. And that heat…

I step away and resume walking. A tangle of emotions wars in my head. Zahir's warning battling my perception of the soon-to-be sultan. The guilt of dishonesty with the budding hope.

"Where do you think you're going, Lady Lailani?" the prince asks. He grabs my arm in the tender spot left by the Vizier's rough fingers. I wince but the prince doesn't notice as he steers me away from our bench and towards the creek.

Our bench?

Maybe Zahir is right, and my emotions are clouding my head.

The babble of the creek greets us. Ajani sweeps his arm out in a grand flourish. His voice becomes serious but his grin ruins it as he says, "Your courtship awaits, oh beautiful lady."

A silk blanket, finer than any I've ever slept under, sprawls across the springy grass of the creekside. Sunlight shimmers off the small crystals woven into the edge of the purple silk—understated elegance by Ari standards. On top of the blanket, clear crystal dishes lay in neat rows. The crystal is so pristine that its presence does not hinder my ability to see the food inside: neat little cakes, fruit slices, nuts, and what looks like a decanter of wine on the end.

"Your Highness, I—"

"It's just the two of us, Lailani. Let me forget my title for a few minutes."

I smile in return, meeting his hazel eyes.

"Thank you, Ajani."

"I did tell you I owed you. I thought about the art gallery again, but I've had enough of that for the year."

I laugh. "Maybe enough for two years at least."

Ajani helps me to sit on the silk blanket before settling himself next to me. I stretch out my legs and lay down on the silk blanket, closing my eyes. The trickle of the creek and the twittering of birds above calms my nerves and allows me to relax. I can almost pretend that I am not an imposter sitting with the soon-to-be-sultan.

Zahir is wrong, I think. *He doesn't see this side of the prince that I see.*

"What would you like, Lailani?"

I sit up quickly—too quickly—and blood rushes to my head. A flush warms my cheeks, catching the prince's attention. I bite my lip, and Ajani's hazel eyes follow the motion.

"Sorry, what did you just ask?" I ask, flustered that I had not been paying attention.

Ajani grins, his eyes resting on my mouth a second more before he speaks.

"I asked what you would like, Lailani."

Ajani had uncovered the beautiful crystal dishes, while I lounged.

"Please let me get it, Ajani," I say, reaching for one of the crystal plates. Ajani gently slaps my hand away.

"I'll be the one serving this meal if you please, Lady Lailani. I intend to pay my debt."

I pause, thinking, then shrug my shoulders. I lay on my side and say, "You choose." Then, even softer, I add, "I trust you, Ajani."

The flustered young man in front of me contemplates the plates of food for a minute. He carefully serves two identical plates of food with an array of options from each of the dishes.

Prince Ajani challenges every notion I have of the Ari. Most men would have insisted that I serve the meal. The idea that they could serve the food to me would not have crossed their minds.

And yet here the prince serves me food.

"Why did you do that?" I blurt out as Ajani hands me my plate of food.

"Do what?" he asks.

"Serve the food."

He cocks his head to the side, causing his hair to fall into his eyes. "Did you not want me to?"

"I, well, I'm just confused. Most men won't even lift a finger to help with food, let alone serve it. And then here you are, Prince of Aveena. And you're serving me food..." I cut off my babbling as Ajani laughs. "What?"

"You're the most honest woman I've ever met, Lailani."

I snort and pop a grape into my mouth. "I hardly believe that. With all these women around you like jewels in the sand."

Ajani appraises me, watching for my reaction as he says, "You have no need to be jealous of the other women."

I nearly choke on my grape. "Jealous? I'm not—"

"Lailani, you are unlike any other woman that I've ever met."

I open and close my mouth, stunned. A tiny bird lands on the far corner of our blanket and tilts his head to the side, saving me the necessity of responding. The vivid orange of his beak pops against the subtle blue of his feathers. I offer a corner of flat bread to the bird, trying to tempt him to come closer. He blinks then flies away in a rush of wings.

"I guess your birds aren't fond of naan." I eat the bite of rejected bread and set my plate to the side. "Who built this anyway?"

"My grandfather built it for my grandmother as a wedding present."

"Does your family do anything the normal way?"

Marriage was little more than a business contract between families in Aveena. Most parents wed their children off for the right bride price or to gain a powerful ally in the new in-laws.

Ajani shrugs. "The men in my family believe in honoring the women in their lives. They believe through showing the utmost respect that they will receive respect and loyalty in return."

"They do not think that women owe their men respect and loyalty?" I ask carefully, pushing the food around my plate.

"Respect is something earned," Ajani says simply.

We sit in silence for a minute, while I think this over.

"Is that why the sultana isn't in court?" I ask.

Ajani takes a sip of wine before responding. "In a way, yes. My mother is showing her respect to my father by observing the period of mourning dictated by the Ordinances."

"How long will she be gone?"

Ajani's mouth tilts up at the corners. Now I'm the one staring at his lips. I look away to the creek, heat stirring in places I'd rather not mention.

"Are you anxious to meet my mother?"

Ajani's teasing tone pulls a smile out of me in return. I nudge his shoulder with my own.

"Now *you're* looking too much into this," I say. "I was just curious."

I lean back on my elbows and stare at the canopy of leaves above my head. A few rays of sunlight warms my face, the brutal heat weakened by the journey through the trees above. I can feel Ajani's eyes watching my every move.

"The Ordinances dictate that the sultana is to remain in mourning until the next sultan is crowned."

My head snaps up, and I look into Ajani's hazel eyes.

"So that means that she won't return until the coronation."

Ajani runs his hand through his hair. I grab his hand and weave my fingers through his to stop him from messing with his hair.

Ajani stares down at our entwined hands and says, "Can we not talk about this anymore? Vizier Nassor knows the Ordinances. Even though I do not like the situation, it cannot be helped."

My heart skips a beat at the mention of the vizier's name. What does he have to do with the sultana's absence from court? But I recognize the closing of a topic. Instead of questioning Ajani further, I squeeze his hand gently.

"Okay, what would you like to talk about, Ajani?"

"I like it when you say my name," he mutters so quietly that I almost don't hear him.

"Ajani?"

"Yes, Lailani?"

He looks nervously between at our entwined hands and my lips before finally meeting my gaze. My breathing catches in my chest as I look into his eyes.

"You can kiss me if you like."

Ajani leans in, hesitating a few inches away from me. I meet him the rest of the way. When our lips touch, a spark ignites in my stomach, causing butterflies to erupt in joyous flutters. His lips are warm against mine, his kiss tentative. I close my eyes and allow myself the moment, reveling in the tenderness of his kiss.

She is hiding something. She's disappeared again. I hate to disappoint, but when I followed, I lost her. Let me know how to proceed.
-N.

50

A flash of light catches my attention out the massive open window. I stare out at the distant dunes. The humid air leaves me feeling sticky, but still, I watch the distant desert.

Again, a flash of purple-white lightning erupts, fighting the setting sun to illuminate the sky.

I hope they're preparing.

I try to shake the dread coiling in my chest bred from my years in the Lower City. Their thatched roofs cannot withstand the unpredictable desert storms, leaving a path of destruction in their wake. If I was there, I'd be helping Dada secure his roof, ensuring that he and Tanu were safe. He's getting too frail to do the work himself.

I have to believe a neighbor stepped in to help.

I force my gaze from the lightning and focus on the surface of the palace's outer walls. There. And there. A path illuminates in my mind's eye. It can be done.

I pretended to be ill tonight, unable to join yet another feast.

Ajani's kiss has lingered on my lips since the aviary, the heat mingling with my guilt. I've replayed our date over and over again in my mind.

But something feels off.

Once I pushed the desire away, Ajani's words sank in. The sultana, the Ordinances, the royal vizier—connected and yet…

I glance furtively around to check for observers then step onto the window ledge. Wind tugs at my pantlegs, more fervent with the impending storm. Before I can reconsider, I reach for the first handhold and pull myself up, letting instinct takeover as I climb to the sultan's tower. The rough sandstone is familiar, the slight pain in my fingertips welcome. Sweat trickles down my back, causing the black kurti to stick to me, but I don't break my concentration. A large balcony looms overhead, my entrance to the tower summoning me forward.

My arms tremble as I pull myself over the edge and sink down to the floor, listening. The wind whispers through the open archways into the sultan's tower, causing the pale green curtains to billow and flutter in its wake. Otherwise, silence greets me.

Sticking to the shadows, I slither inside then let my eyes adjust to the darkness. The large shapes of chairs and cushions come into focus. A sitting room then. I tiptoe past towards the nearest door. It's slightly ajar, so I push it open a breath further and peer inside. What looks like a massive bed emerges from the shadows. I back away and move to the next door. As tempting as it is to explore Ajani's rooms, I don't have the time.

The next door leads to a narrower corridor. I take a chance and follow it. The hallway is lined with frames but in the darkness, I can't tell the subject of the art. I shake my head thinking of Ajani's father's gallery, and a ghost of a smile crosses my face.

At the end of the hallway, I'm met by another door. I try the handle, but it's locked. I pull my pins from my hair and pop the lock easily.

I breathe a sigh of relief at the stacks of shelves filled with scrolls. This has to be the right place. I gently close the door behind me then turn on the nearest oil lamp to give myself the barest light to search by.

I walk to the centermost shelf and scan its contents. Scroll after scroll perches in its rectangular home. Little plaques line the bottom of each row, labeling the documents. The crinkled ends of the scrolls protrude slightly from the shelving, causing me to bend in order to read the plaques. Crop production and council notes are among the first scrolls I see.

I walk to the other side where some of the scrolls seem older, more fragile, and skim the labels on these. Several have a strange script, not the common tongue of Aveena, and I swallow my gasp. Aramak. The language of the Tribes.

I've only seen it once before, when my father was approached by one of the Tribes to trade. He turned them away quickly, refusing to do business with them.

I shake my head and go back to scanning the labels. I'm about to give up when I finally see it. I set my lamp down carefully on the desk and gingerly pull the Ordinances from their shelf. The edges are brittle and yellowed with age, and a puff of dust whooshes out of the shelf as I free the scroll. My nose tickles, and I rub it absentmindedly as I carefully roll out the scroll.

Ajani had said that these were the original Ordinances. The very laws that Aveena was founded on.

I stare down at the scroll. Now that I'm directly confronted with the words responsible for my life, I'm unsure if I want to read them.

I inhale slowly, keeping my eyes shut. As I exhale, I open them, renewed with determination. The flop of the scroll echoes faintly through the office as I begin to read the Ordinances.

❦

The lines of the Ordinances blur before my eyes. I push back in my chair and stare at the ceiling to give my eyes a change of pace. It's not here. Whatever answer I am looking for is not in this damned scroll.

The problem is that I don't know what I was looking for to begin with.

There is no convenient message saying, "Here's what the royal vizier is up to, here's how to get out of him blackmailing you, and here's a surefire way to bring the two halves of the council together. And as a bonus we've included instructions on how to fix your friendship with Zahir!"

I need to leave, the feast will be winding down soon. I stare down at my pages of notes. There are three things I'm confident in.

One, there is nothing in the Ordinances dictating the length of time appropriate for mourning a deceased sultan and instating the new one.

Two, there is nothing in the Ordinances insisting that the sultana should show her husband proper respect by mourning in solitude for three months.

Three, there is nothing in the Ordinances that explicitly states who should be in charge until the rise of the next sultan.

I rub my hands over my eyes, squeezing them closed. My body aches from sitting hunched over the Ordinances. My brain feels fuzzy from overwork, incapable of processing one word more.

My instincts nag me to continue, but I can't think through the fuzz. I'm close to figuring it out... whatever *it* is. The three major decrees that the royal vizier made since Sultan Gautam's death were not written in the Ordinances.

What is the snake playing at?

The miserable are very talkative
-Aveenan Proverb-

51

The burnt orange of my gold-lined saree shimmers in the light of the hall. The tiny bells on the hem and down the blouse jingle each time I shift in my seat, announcing my discomfort to the table. Erol, Zahir, and I sit with new dining companions tonight—Anik Ba and his petite wife Chutki are on my right while Ray Lobo, Dhruv Dara, and his wife Nyein Dara are on the left of Zahir. I suspect the vizier's hand in the arrangements: somehow Erol, Tei Asfour, and Cadmar have been strategically assigned to opposite corners of the room.

Or maybe my imagination sees conspiracies wherever I go.

The spice of chicken tikka masala wafts up from the steaming copper serving dishes placed in the center of our table. The smell stirs childhood memories of my mother stirring her simmering masala. A different time and a different place. My ridiculous gold bracelets force me to scoop the tikka masala delicately with my naan. The chains of the bracelet loop around my wrist and around my middle finger with small golden bells dotted along the way.

"Chutki, can you not see that my plate is empty?" Anik Ba barks at his tiny wife.

"Well, I—"

"*Well, I*," Anik says, mimicking his wife's nervous tone. "Even Councilman Lobo noticed that my plate was empty before you did, and he's across the table."

Ray Lobo smirks at poor Chutki before turning back to his conversation with Dhruv.

"What dish would you prefer, Anikji?" Chutki asks, peering up at her colossal husband.

"*What dish would you prefer?*" Anik mimics again. A slight jingle indicates the fists I'm forming under the table. Erol places his hand on top of mine, discreetly reminding me where we are.

"Anik, have you tried the masala? The cooks have outdone themselves this evening," Erol asks.

"My wife failed to serve me that one, Councilman Erol, so no, I haven't."

Chutki lurches forward, almost knocking over the wine glass in her husband's thick hand in her hurry to get to the chicken tikka masala. Her dark cheeks burn copper like the serving dish by the time she's managed to portion out food on her husband's plate.

I set my naan down and lean away from the table, unable to eat more. The way Chutki flits around her boulder of a husband erases my appetite.

"Have you heard the news, Erol?" Anik says between sloppy bites of masala.

Erol sips his wine before responding. "What news?"

"Apparently there have been mumblings in the Lower City. Unrest."

"Unrest? How so?" Erol's feigned calm baffles me.

Anik scarfs down another bite of masala-covered naan, splashing a few drops on his belly, before continuing.

"You know that my cousin's son is one of the captains over the Suraksha at the eastern gate. He says that the Lower City scum have been meeting in groups. Talking. All organized like."

"Nonsense," Ray Lobo interrupts. "Those lice don't have the ability to organize."

"It's true," Anik insists. He gestures around, causing a glop of the tikka masala to fall squarely in the center of his round belly. He ignores his wife as she cleans the mess while he talks. "My cousin says that he has forbidden his family to pass through the gate into the Lower City. He doesn't trust what those Lower City lice have in mind."

"I heard that—"

"Rumors, all of it," Ray cuts off Councilman Dara. "I have it from the vizier himself that these are simply rumors to get under our skin. No foundation at all."

"The vizier himself, you say?" Erol asks. "And do you have many conversations with Vizier Nassor, Councilman Lobo?"

"That's between me 'n' him, isn't it?"

"'Him and I'," Erol corrects softly.

"Excuse me?"

Erol bobs his head and chooses to pick up a cracker instead of answering. My bells tinkle as I shift in my seat. The women at the table wait in uneasy silence. Finally, Councilman Lobo sighs through his teeth and resumes berating us with his thoughts.

"Eh, these Lower City criminals get restless every few years. Nothing a good tightening of the leash won't fix," Ray says.

My eyes widen. *A tightening of the leash?* Fury boils under my skin. Councilman Lobo revels in the attention from our table.

"These Lower City lice need to be reminded why they need us. 'What we give, we can also take away.' I'm sure the vizier will quash these 'rumors.'"

Anik nods his approval, while Councilman Dara stares at his plate. Erol's time in the palace shows through the calm facade he wears throughout Lobo's tirade.

"Surely you cannot blame them for being disgruntled at the accusations being thrown their way?" Erol asks evenly.

"Blame them? Of course I blame them! What reason do they have for being disgruntled?" Ray Lobo's ruddy face reaches a new level of redness thus far unseen. His voice rises, causing a few Ari to glance over. "These damn Lower City lice are overly sensitive to everything when they bring it on themselves. Don't like a tighter leash? Then don't pull on it. We don't need you to be a bleeding heart for them, Councilman Shaikh."

My bells scream in the silence following Lobo's rant as I stand abruptly, drawing the attention of the men at the table. Ray Lobo smirks at me. Out of the corner of my eye, I see Chutki fidgeting with a napkin. I open my mouth to speak, but Zahir's subtle shake of the head stops me. All the angry words that I had felt bubbling to the surface a moment ago die down.

Erol speaks first.

"Well, I think it is time we retire for bed. Zaharian? Lailani? If you would be so kind as to assist an old man like myself?"

Zahir and Erol rise from their chairs and maneuver towards the door. I follow behind, my fists clenched. As I pass Ray

Lobo, his withered hand clasps onto my wrist. I look down my nose at the twisted old man below me.

"Watch yourself, girl." His grip tightens. The golden bracelets cut into my wrist, but I don't flinch. "Those of us looking out for your best interest would hate to see anything happen to you. Or your curly-haired cousin."

I wrench my wrist out of his grasp and flee. I can feel Ajani's concerned eyes watching me as I leave.

My fury roars in my ears as I follow Zahir and Erol back to the suite. Erol excuses himself the minute we enter, his shoulders slumped under the strain of the evening. I slam open the door to my room and stalk in.

"Laila, you shouldn't have—" he begins but I interrupt him.

"Why did you stop me, Zahir?" I can't control the tremor in my voice. "*Someone* needs to tell them to get off their high horses and get the stick out of—"

"And that someone should be *you*?" Zahir asks from my doorway. He crosses his arms over his chest as he watches me fling the golden bracelets against the wall.

"Well, it's clearly not going to be you," I yell. The bells on my pallu jingle. I growl and tear it off as well. Zahir takes a deep breath before responding.

"No, it's not going to be. That's not my role, is it?"

"No, your role is to watch and do nothing, right? To let them, let them—"

"Let them do what? What they're going to do anyway?"

Anger flashes in Zahir's eyes as he strides towards me across the room. He grabs my arms and holds me in place, forcing me to look at him.

"We. Can't. Stop. Them."

Each word hisses out like a slap to the face. I glare at him and try to jerk out of his grasp. Zahir holds me tighter, his golden eyes staring into my own.

"Do you think I *want* to stay quiet? To pretend I'm one of them? Sniveling and ass-kissing and—"

"Obviously you'd rather sit back and judge than stand up to them. Just like you sit back and judge me when I'm doing the same thing you are." Zahir pushes away from me and stares. In my fury it's easy to ignore the hurt and disbelief etched onto his face.

"We have to be one with the Ari, Laila, or we risk death. This isn't some game. This isn't being the Nightshade and blissfully ignoring the ripples of your actions. We are surrounded, and we cannot fall into their game."

The truth of his words stings. I cross my arms protectively over my chest, glaring at him.

"I know that this isn't a game," I say defensively.

"You aren't acting like it. Get your head focused, Laila, or else we'll all be caught. Stop playing games with Cadmar. Stop playing games with the prince. Stop playing games with me. Just stop."

"That's what it is then," I say bitterly. "You're jealous, aren't you?"

Zahir runs a hand over his beard and just stares. The silence stretches out between us, crushing the last remains of our easy friendship. I don't know how to take it back, to fix it.

"I know what I'm doing, Laila," he says quietly. "Do you?"

Before I can respond, Zahir strides through the doorway and snaps it shut behind him.

I stare at the closed door after he leaves. How *dare* he…

Words fail me. I throw myself onto the bed and scream into the overstuffed pillow adorning it. I'm not sure who I'm more upset with—the Ari, Zahir, or myself.

We found a mystical combination of desert
and arable land. The melding of sands
and prosperous fields allow us to survive
without relying on our neighbors, or worse,
indebting us to the Tribes.
—excerpt from *A Brief Political History of
Aveena*—

52

"What are you wearing? You look like a priestess of chastity."

I raise my eyebrows as Esha Shah and her group of cronies approach. Esha sneers at me and I smile back. It throws her off her game when I appear unaffected by her stupidity.

"Why *thank you*, Esha. Isn't the fabric just *divine*?"

I twirl in front of her, allowing the bejeweled navy to spin out around me. I stop spinning with my back to her. The fabric wraps tightly around my legs and emphasizes my butt. Looking over my shoulder, I add, "Prince Ajani couldn't believe how it moves. Or maybe he was just fascinated by other... assets."

I wink at a stuttering Esha and sashay towards the Veiled Room.

"Her face turns splotchy when she's mad," Sala whispers.

"I know."

I grin at Sala, making her cackle. We part ways at the door to the Veiled Room, and I saunter over to my usual seat. The encounter with Esha puts an extra spring in my step, and I make sure to sweep out the skirt dramatically before settling into my chair. As Esha's group enters the Veiled Room, I feel Esha's glare, but I ignore her, scanning the heads of the men below.

Several of the councilmen choose new seats today, forcing everyone to rethink their seating. A few councilmen towards the front, including Ray Lobo, joke loudly with one another, clapping each other on the back. Zahir's curly head sits a few rows back next to Erol, his rigid posture giving away his discomfort. He notices the new arrangement as well. My heart contracts, thinking back to our argument a week ago…

The chime sounds. The procession starts.

To my surprise, Prince Ajani stands after the formalities. He runs his fingers through his hair—he's nervous. The vizier looks up at him, surprised, but he hides his shock.

"Fellow councilmen" —mutterings— "today I will begin the discussion regarding those in our care in the Lower City."

I clasp my hands in my lap and freeze in my chair.

"Our duty is to take care of *all* of Aveena, including those in the Lower City. We must—"

"We must ensure that we are taking care of the interests of all parties involved," Nassor cuts in smoothly. Ajani glances at him before trying again.

"Which is why, we should—"

"We should consider how to best care for those around us," the vizier finishes Ajani's sentence, giving the appearance of a unified front. My hackles rise as I watch the two men standing on the dais, staring each other down. After a beat, the prince slowly lowers himself into his seat with a nod. The vizier turns back to the councilmen, a smug smile twisting the side of his mouth. "Our food production…"

I sag into my chair, disappointed. Ajani was about to take control of his council. Or at least speak for once. Maybe our conversation in the aviary made him consider his position, inspired him to be more than a puppet. At least he tried…

The royal vizier drones on the dais. It's the same speech as the day before and the day before that. His oily voice curls around me like smoke from the candles and sinks into my stomach. Bile rises in my throat, his voice conjuring the feel of his body towering over mine in the Harem Room. Pressing against me. Sweat trickles down the back of my saree. I shift in my seat, struggling to adjust the tightly wound fabric now sticking to my thighs.

In a desperate attempt to escape the vizier's voice, I watch the council instead. On the left, Ray Lobo nudges Anik Ba next to him and nods. A few rows behind Ray, Dhruv Dara fiddles with his handkerchief while he mutters to Jagan Shah. One of the Consulate members—Reyanash Al-Sid—watches the vizier with rapt attention.

Zahir and Erol are on the right side of the Council Room. They were forced to find new seats when they arrived due to Vihaan Pateel and his brother. Cadmar sits toward the front on the right side of the room, arms crossed as he listens to the vizier preach.

Wait a minute.

I scan the heads of the Council Room again, taking inventory of the new seating arrangement. The sweat that had risen turns to ice.

The new seating arrangement isn't an accident.

Vizier Nassor speaks to the left side of the room, never fully addressing those sitting in the other section.

He knows.

The hidden letters. The lists of initials.

R.L…Ray Lobo.

A.B…Anik Ba.

J.S…Jagan Shah.

My gaze flits over those that the vizier is addressing, the councilmen on the left side of the room, and my stomach plummets. The letters, the men whose names were there, sit on one side of the room. Unified.

They're isolating those who do not support the vizier's policies.

Bile rises in my throat. I watch Zahir's curly head, Erol's silvery ponytail, Tei's stout frame, and Cadmar's short buzz.

They've been isolated. *Targeted*.

And they don't realize it.

The vizier's voice carries throughout the vast room, smooth and precise, not overwhelmed by emotion, but I cannot focus on the words he's dripping into the eager ears before him. As he waves a hand to emphasize his next point, the lantern light glimmers off of the rings adorning his fingers.

The council listens to him. Many nod in approval, nudging their neighbors conspiratorially.

Unlike when Ajani spoke.

Defeat surges through me, threatening to overwhelm me.

The veil blurs, dread seeping into my soul, oozing from every pore. I'm surprised women around me cannot feel it, the trepidation tempting me to succumb to its cold embrace.

Refocus, Laila.

I force myself to refocus on the vizier, to listen, thrusting my dread down into the hidden depths of my heart. To be dealt with later.

"—and with the implementation of a stricter protocol, we can ensure that Aveena runs self-sufficiently. We must run self-sufficiently for Aveena stands as a lone and proud city amongst the primitive nomadic tribes."

Nods of agreement from the council.

He knows how to unify a group behind a cause.

Vizier Nassor gestures to a servant waiting at the foot of the dais. The trembling man ascends the stairs, hands a roll of parchment to the vizier, and then bows low to take his leave.

But no one can propose a change to the laws except the sultan...

The realization staggers me, and I slump back against the chair. The royal vizier fills the role of sultan until Ajani's coronation.

He has the power to change laws.

"This decree" —Vizier Nassor unrolls the parchment with a flick of his wrist—"creates the positions of Overseer and Manager of Sales. Both positions will create a middle-man between our hard-working farmers and those who depend on their toils. Overseers will be instituted with each portion of farmland. They will keep a close eye on the Lower City and will monitor the production of the plot of land and the produce grown, reporting the numbers to the palace. The Manager of Sales will inventory every fruit, vegetable, and grain, making sure that what is grown makes it to the market. The Manager of Sales will sell the produce in the bazaar for the farmers, allowing them to focus on what it is that they do best: farming.

By signing this decree, we will do what is best for the entire city. We will pay homage to Sultan Gautam's memory by taking care of his city. We will fulfill our duty as caretakers of Aveena."

My brain scrambles to make sense of his oily words, smoothly delivered to the waiting council. Surely no one will sign this, this *monstrosity* of a decree.

But reality sinks in as I watch the Ari. The bolder councilmen puff their chests out and nod to their neighbors, buying into the vizier's words about their duty to Aveena. The conniving councilmen centered around Ray Lobo smirk as they imagine the ways they could gain from this sort of decree. And the others? Those left are either horrified, dumbfounded, or intimidated.

I stare at the prince, willing him to do something. If only my thoughts could reach him, encourage him, tell him to do the right thing.

But Ajani remains silent on his cold throne.

My eyes flit to Zahir next. *Speak, Zahir,* I plead silently with him. A tremor runs through his body then he stills. Tension? Or Fear? He sees through what the vizier proposes—I know he does. He worked in the fields, he *knows* what it's like there. He's smart enough to sift through all the fancy words and smoke and realize that the vizier is legalizing slavery. But Zahir says nothing. Just like he does in every council meeting. He has the opportunity to make a difference, to have a voice, but he does nothing.

I suppress my growl of frustration. Why the dunes am I stuck in this veiled prison?

Several minutes tick by—or maybe it's only seconds— before Cadmar stands. His short frame seems smaller across the room, isolated on the far side from the rest of the council.

"Nassorji, with all due respect we *cannot* pass such a heinous decree."

"And why not?" Someone barks from the mass of councilmen on the left side. Several nods of agreement follow, but Cadmar pushes on.

"Because we have to take care of everyone in Aveena, not just our own interests. If we do not show compassion, then who will?"

Anik Ba doesn't bother to stand as he says, "But this does take care of everyone in Aveena. Vizier Nassor explained so when he spoke. Were you not listening, Cadmar, or has your jealousy of the vizier led you to become deaf to any ideas other than your own?"

Ray Lobo cackles next to Anik, the wretched sound echoing in the vast hall. My skirt becomes wrinkled due to my clenching hands; even from my vantage point, I can see the crimson tinging Cadmar's ears.

"I do not speak from personal feelings, Councilman Ba—"

"Of course you don't," another voice interrupts, sarcasm dripping from each word.

"—I speak for those who are not represented here. Compassion will go a lot further in the long run than stricter rules. We need to come together and—"

"And protect our city!"

Nods follow the last shout. I look from Erol and Zahir to Tei Asfour, willing them to support Cadmar, bolster him, shout 'down with the vizier!,' anything.

They do nothing.

"I beg of you, Councilmen, think! Think of how you would feel at the end of the day if you didn't have autonomy over your own lands. If you had someone constantly looking over your shoulder and insisting that you've lied to them. This cannot happen!"

Cadmar's words ring through the air passionately, but they fall on deaf ears.

Ray Lobo stands. Turning, he addresses the men in the rows sitting behind him, ignoring Cadmar altogether.

"The Lower City should be grateful to us for the jobs and the land we've provided them. They owe it to us and to the city to embrace any new decrees that increase productivity!"

Men nod and murmur to each other. Cadmar stands alone, unable to captivate the attention of the audience around him.

They are too far gone.

"Councilmen—"

"Sit down, Cadmar," Ray Lobo snaps at him.

"I have just—"

"And I have had enough of your bleeding heart!"

Cadmar looks around the room into the hostile faces of the other councilmen. When he meets the eyes of the vizier, I swear the vizier winks at him from the dais. Cadmar lowers himself to his seat, defeated.

It happens quickly after that, man after man streams before our eyes to sign the new decree. Each signature feels like a cut to the flesh—death by a thousand cuts for the Lower City. The tightening of the leash.

A few tears escape, and I let them trail down my face.

Ajani looks like a statue. Or perhaps a painting of a man instead of the real flesh and blood. He is an ornamentation for the council, nothing more, saying nothing. Doing nothing.

The vizier sends out messengers to post the decree throughout Aveena. Vaguely, I realize that the papers were already prepared.

In a daze, I stand as Prince Ajani Bahu the IV, future Sultan of Aveena, proceeds out of the Council Room, followed by the man who holds the power.

Nowhere is safe from the gossip and plotting of the Aristocracy. It's part of their nature. The sooner you accept it, the easier it will be.
-Advice from Sultan Gautam to Prince Ajani
after the first rumor was started about him-

53

The Sultana

Chhavi carefully prunes back the emerald leaves of the rangoon creeper. The vine is tightly wrapped around the arch, the clusters of coral-colored flowers dangling over her head as she meticulously snips the errant branches. Her upper back aches from the angle, but she had promised the vine that it would be next. She had to keep her promises, even if they were only to the plants in her garden.

The last browning leaf falls by her feet, and Chhavi steps back, placing her hands on her hips as she surveys her work.

Perfect.

According to one of her books, the rangoon creeper would flourish after a good pruning, and Chhavi couldn't wait to see it.

Chhavi wipes her face with a cloth, then meanders over to the shaded table, where Amari placed her usual afternoon chai. This had become her ritual in the afternoons, a break from trudging through tome after tome without any clue as to what she was looking for. Chhavi allows herself this—honest work in the garden followed by her afternoon tea.

She closes her eyes, humming appreciatively, as she sips the spiced warmth, heavy on the ginger just like she preferred. Chhavi didn't know what she would have done if Amara hadn't come with her to the Upper City.

Her chai is gone all too soon, and the sultana stands, stretching her neck and shoulders before wandering back into the house. The afternoons are always quiet now that she didn't attend the council meetings regularly, Chhavi muses. Although she'll miss the simplicity of her routine, she is itching to get back to the palace.

A thump around the corner startles her out of her reverie.

The door to her chambers is ajar. Odd. Amara left for the bazaar an hour ago.

Chhavi steps on the threshold and stills. Mahnoor's long braid swings back and forth as she shuffles through a desk drawer. The servant bends to read something closer, and Chhavi realizes that it's her notes from her reading.

"What are you doing?" Chhavi barks from across the room.

Mahnoor jumps and drops the papers. As she turns, a page flutters off the desk and onto the floor. Mahnoor dips into a bow and says quickly, "Chhaviji, I am simply organizing—"

"Amara cares for my personal chambers, not you."

Mahnoor's eyes flick to the door, but the sultana crosses her arms, blocking the servant's only exit from the room.

"What are you doing, Mahnoor?" Chhavi demands.

Mahnoor stutters, saying, "Amara asked me to—"

Chhavi holds out a hand, and Mahnoor closes her mouth quickly.

"We will see about that," the sultana says icily.

Footsteps pads behind her, and Chhavi turns to see Rajesh, one of her manservants, approaching.

"Everything okay, Chhaviji?" he asks. "I heard raised voices."

"Please detain Mahnoor until further notice," the sultana commands, gesturing towards her room. "We'll have Captain Sanjit interview her when he returns from the bazaar with Amara."

"As you wish," Rajesh says.

He crosses the room and escorts Mahnoor out. Her head hangs as she walks past, but she doesn't try to plead her case with the sultana again.

Chhavi rubs her temples, the impending headache already forming. As if Farah's note that Amara smuggled to her this morning hadn't been enough, but to be betrayed by one of her own? Her silk saree sighs as she shuffles towards the sitting room. She'd had her suspicions that a spy was in her residence, even secluded here in the Upper City, but the palace games always exhausted her. If only...

"—posted everywhere."

"But what about—"

"Can't you feel it? The city knows."

"It's eerie."

"Crowds just standing. Staring at the decree."

Chhavi's heart races. This *couldn't* be the same decree that Farah wrote her about.

"That's not all," one of her guards growls. What is Captain Sanjit doing gossiping with the servants? "They're angry."

"Of course they're—"

"You don't understand," the guard. "There's talk."

"A few hotheads—" a serving maid says, brushing off his concern.

"It's not just a few," Amara says. "Everyone is talking. Men and women. Merchants and Lower City folk. The bazaar was buzzing. I left as quickly as I could."

Chhavi pushes the door open, startling her household into haphazard bows. "Tell me what's happened."

"Chhaviji, do not worry yourself—" Captain Sanjit says with a placating smile.

Chhavi stands at her full height, meeting her guard's eyes. "I asked a question, Captain."

"Yes, sultana," he says, bowing his head. He clears his throat then reports, "The vizier has posted new decrees throughout Aveena. The people are infuriated."

"Well, of course they're—" the errand boy stops when everyone turns in his direction. Captain Sanjit glares at the youngling. Before anyone continues, a male servant bursts through the door, sweat pouring down his forehead. The sultana is shocked to see the utter terror written on the man's face.

"They've set fire to the south bazaar. At least a dozen guardsmen were killed before they could react."

The words float in the air for a brief moment before everyone bursts into action.

Chhavi's captain snaps orders to secure the residence. Chhavi is ushered into her room with three of her serving maids. They are commanded to barricade the door with the furniture. Before he leaves, the captain hands each woman a blade, instructing them how to use it should their home be infiltrated. The cold metal of the handle chills Chhavi's hand, foreign and terrifying at the same time.

Chhavi and Amara tremble next to each other, blades rattling against their bangles as they listen to the rest of the household move to protect the Upper City residence.

To protect the sultana.

The Aristocracy never forget that the Lower
City outnumbers them, fifteen to one. I'd hate
to see what would happen if the Lower City
realized it too.
—excerpt from *Human Error: a Study of Human
Thinking—*

54

Electricity from the lightning storm pulses through the
palace. The threatening wind sneaks through the arched
windows in the hallways, allowing nature to creep into the
feast. The normal chatter is jarring as the eerie calm of the
storm tempts us into believing we're safe from its rage.

The end of my pallu crumples in my hand. I cannot escape
the fear of the storm that two years of living in the Lower
City ingrained in me. A giggle escapes one of the women
before it is hastily hushed. A few men, like Ray Lobo, relax
and smirk, drinking in the tension like a fine wine.

Cadmar radiates anger and defeat.

Even the food seems off—not as vibrant or delicious as
I've come to expect.

I glance at the head table. At my prince. Ajani. His shoulders
are rounded as he stares into his cup, a lost man about to
drink his sorrows away. My heart sinks for the boy I've come
to care for, but it pales in comparison to the despair I feel
after the vizier's decrees.

Next to the discouraged prince sits the only man in the room who appears oblivious to the tension and electricity: Vizier Nassor. The vizier is dressed ornately for the occasion— gaudy rings adorn every finger and the edge of his sherwani is lined with real gold.

He looks like a sultan.

Vizier Nassor meets my eyes. He raises his wine glass, toasts me, and drinks.

I push my plate away.

"Lailani, are you feeling okay?" Erol asks in my ear.

"I—"

The enormous doors to the dining hall groan open, and a sweaty servant hurries to the head table. He tumbles out of his bow in his haste to approach the prince. His hands shake as he whispers to the prince and the vizier. The rest of the Consulate lean closer, trying to hear the news.

I pick at the jewels lining my magenta pallu, watching Ajani's face. He turns white under his coppery skin, his eyes wide like the servant's. The vizier's face doesn't give away his feelings, but when he stands, his fists clench at his sides, the only sign of worry in his body.

The still hall is the quiet before the storm.

Vizier Nassor addresses the Ari. The prince's ashen face stares in shock. He looks like a frightened boy.

"My friends, terrible news has arrived from the city." The vizier pauses, and we wait, hanging on to his every word. "A riot has broken out—"

Muttering interrupts the vizier at the word 'riot.' Fear is etched into the faces in the hall. I freeze in my seat, waiting for an explanation. Panic starts to set in.

"Our valiant Suraksha are trying to contain the riot and to push the violence into the Lower City. Their goal is to minimize the damage to at least two of the three sections of the city. The riot will burn itself out there."

The Lower City? But…

"It appears that our Lower City brethren do not understand the generosity in our new decree. Once the Suraksha have subdued the individuals in charge, we will be able to… educate them further." Nassor's somber expression can't contain his sneer. My heart flutters in my chest as I hang onto his words. "Until such time, I ask that you please return to your suites to await further news. The safety of our Aristocracy is crucial to the continued survival of Aveena."

What about the safety of those in the city? What about…

I do not move from my seat. A tremor of fear shakes its way down my spine.

Ari women cry and look to their men for comfort. Several of the families rush out of the room—the Shah family in the lead.

A riot…

"Come, Lailani."

Erol's voice does nothing to penetrate the fog infiltrating my mind. Fear ensnares me. Unlike the pompous Ari around me, my fear isn't for myself but for…

Someone bends down near me and grips both of my shoulders.

"Laila, come on."

Zahir's use of my real name pulls me out of my daze. I turn my head and stare. In the depths of Zahir's eyes, I see the same fear that has trapped me—fear for those we know in the city.

"Zahir, what about—"

"I know, Laila. I know."

"We can't stay here."

"We don't have a choice."

Zahir's eyes soften. It's the first time since we argued that I see the old Zahir. He places his hand on my cheek, keeping me focused on him as he speaks, low and soft, amidst the chaotic Ari and flashes of colorful fabric around us.

"Laila, we have to go back to the room. We have to wait. There is nothing that we can do in the city that isn't already being done."

The words pain him. Zahir isn't just talking to me—he's reminding himself as well.

I nod and allow Zahir to help me to stand. The fog of fear clouds my mind, incapacitating me. Zahir laces his fingers through mine. I focus on the warmth of his hand and the back of his curly head as he weaves through the crowd of panicked Ari and servants. Back down the long, cold marble corridors, past the opulent decorations. I try to stare out of each massive window as we pass, looking for... who knows what in the distance. Fire? Shouts? A white flag?

They are pushing the riot into the Lower City.

It will burn itself out in the Lower City.

The fog dissipates from my mind as we walk through the door. Zahir leads me to my room, unaware of the change. His eyes are distant.

"Do you want me to stay with you?" he asks softly.

I look at Zahir again. His eyes are glazed with worry. The panic I've been feeling washes over. I run to the window before Zahir can react.

"Laila!" he shouts.

But I'm already gone.

I sprint through the palace gardens, the electricity in the air shooting through my veins. Above, the palace Suraksha rush toward the front gate, ignoring my mad dash below. They are more concerned about keeping people out than ensuring that everyone stays in. A crack reverberates ominously in the night as purple lightning streaks across the sky, halting the Suraksha in their tracks.

The storm has arrived.

"Where do you think you're going?" A burly guard grabs my arm, nearly yanking it out of the socket. "Get back inside with the other Aristocracy like a good girl."

I twist in the guard's grip, struggling to free myself.

"Let go," I growl. The guard's grip tightens as he begins to drag me back towards the door into the palace.

"Orders are to keep everyone inside."

Oblivious to the searing heat in my shoulder, I thrash back and forth, trying to buck the guard's grip. The burly man grunts as he pulls me along. As we near the palace, he turns his attention away from me to fumble for the door handle, and I snatch my chance, jabbing my thumb into the pressure point on the side of his neck.

The guard collapses in a heap near the door, but I'm already sprinting towards the wall. The wind roars in my ears as I crash through the delicate foliage, taking the most direct route to the secret door. The door that Ajani showed me during Andhereka. I slip through without hesitation.

And without a plan.

Lights flicker in the distance as I tear down the hill towards the Upper City. I run on instinct—a primal animal—all logic lost.

One thought drives me through the haze of fear: Tanu.

Another peal of lightning, closer than the first, shatters across the sky. The rumble of thunder fights with the roar from the wind. I stumble over something on the ground as a dust cloud swirls to life over the dunes in the distance. Losing my balance, I topple down part of the hill, clawing at the hard earth to stop my fall. I slam against a cart at the bottom, knocking the wind out of my already-burning chest. I don't stop. Somewhere in my fall, I lose one of my delicate slippers.

Keep moving.

The first houses of the Upper City blur by. As the ground levels out, I sprint faster, my bare foot slapping against the dusty ground. I'm racing Wind. Racing time. Racing from the fear that chases me out of the palace.

They are pushing the riot into the Lower City.

As I cross into the Upper City bazaar, a new rumble meets me, different from the storm building overhead, assaulting my ears.

I see the first signs of the riot. Carts overturned. Wood splintered. Fabrics slashed. The detritus of the riot wrenches at my soul.

She has to be safe.

I leap over a fruit cart, attempting to maintain my dead sprint through the wreckage. My feet tangle in my underskirt, and I crash into the rough ground. Knees scraped and bloody, I pause long enough to tear away the underskirt and discard it in the bazaar dust. I rip off the magenta pallu and fling it to the side. The floaty material descends onto an overturned cart.

In the dark, it looks like blood.

I charge forward without the unnecessary weight of the Ari opulence holding me back.

The emptiness of the bazaar gives way to disheveled streets. Here the houses show the damage of the riot as if they had joined the battle.

The fires visible from the top of the palace hill flicker closer, answered by the lightning above. The distant sounds that I had heard in the bazaar turn into an all-encompassing cacophony of shouts.

I trip over a form in the darkness. The boy groans as I glance back at him. Horror fills my chest. He isn't older than eight. Hrithik's age. A slash runs from his collar to his stomach. Blood seeps into the ground around him, forever marking the spot of his death.

The shadows around the boy's face contort, and suddenly I'm looking into Tanu's face. I gasp and stumble away from her and she reaches towards me. The pain in her eyes…

My heart screams in desperation as I leave the boy to die alone and forgotten.

It will burn itself out in the Lower City.

I can't stop.

Poison
Leaches into my city
Causing pain
Creating destruction

And all I wonder
Who are you truly?
-from an unnamed poet-

55

The roar assaults my ears.

A man reaches for me, a jagged knife in his hand. I freeze, but then another body slams into him. The sound of his head colliding against the sandstone wall is indecipherable in the chaos.

I dodge, weave, and duck, avoiding engaging in the riot.

Pieces of wood and rocks fly overhead. Smoke fills the air, the flicker of flame illuminates the outline of people as they fight and die.

Bodies. Everywhere.

Standing and fighting. Yelling and crying.

In the darkness and confusion, I can't tell who's a rioter and who's a Suraksha. They all bleed the same.

Panic constricts my heart.

A slamming pain to my skull.

Stars floating past my eyes.

A hand on my shoulder.

A near miss with a torch.

I sprint through the riot, fighting the inevitable ebb and flow of bodies. Smoke fills my lungs as a cart turns into a bonfire, sparks reaching for the night sky. Lightning strikes the roof of one of the buildings. Even the flames want to escape the madness that has overtaken Aveena.

I cough, my eyes watering.

My head aches.

I surge forward.

A weeping woman lays protectively over an unmoving man. Blood and sand mix together around him.

A teenager runs past. The golden jewelry in his arms catches the light of fires, sparkling in the crowd. Before he can react, another man stabs the teenager in the back, snatching the gold from his dying grip, and disappears into the mob.

The wall looms ahead. I scratch and claw my way forward, desperately trying to reach the gate. Bodies cram into the space, squished against the wall. The wall, a mockery of protection.

A body slams into me, pushing me against the rough sandstone of the nearest house. One hand grabs my breast while another forces my skirt higher. The man's ragged breathing fills my face.

My screams blend into the cries around me as I thrash against the building. The man's weight pins me to the wall. His hand digs into my wrist, restraining me. Helpless.

Just like I was helpless when confronted by the Vizier.

Just like I was helpless when trapped into working for Cadmar.

Just like I was helpless when I escaped with Tanu.

Tanu.

I jerk my arm down and twist it out of his grip. The man grunts, but I jam my finger into his eye. He yowls. He lurches forward, and I elbow him in the temple.

He crumples to the ground.

I run, keeping the wall at my back, then slip in between the houses. My hands shake uncontrollably as the adrenaline courses fiercely through my body. My stomach heaves, and I vomit.

A hand holds my hair away from my face. The bile rises again, and I'm unable to stop it as I throw up a second time. My body quakes.

"Get it all out, Laila."

I whip my head around, causing my body to protest the further abuse.

Sala stands next to me—one hand holding my hair, the other holding a knife.

"Sala, I—"

I'm out of lies.

"If you're done, we need to keep moving."

Sala shouts over the chaos. Her face is hidden in the shadows of the flickering fires outside of our alleyway; her voice reveals nothing. If Sala had wanted to kill me, she could've done it already.

And yet she's here. Holding my hair and watching my back.

I nod and stand.

"Into the Lower City?"

I nod again.

Sala swears and then leaps back into the fray. We keep the houses to our backs as we fight to move through the surging crowd. The tight press of bodies is almost impenetrable.

Pulses of anger thrum through the crowd, matching the power of the storm above.

Sala veers away from the south gate and follows the line of houses leading towards the eastern side of Aveena.

Battle rages. I watch as a Suraksha cuts down an elderly man with his sword. The body barely hits the dusty ground before another person leaps onto the Suraksha's back. The pair flail around, the Suraksha trying to dislodge his attacker. The man on the back hits the sultan's soldier repeatedly with a piece of wood. The flailing weakens. The assailant stabs the ragged edge of the wood into the Suraksha's side. The shrill cry of the guard reverberates in the alleyway merging with the cries of the riot.

Sala snatches my hand and pulls me forward, away from the horrific scene.

I knew the Suraksha.

Heat and smoke coat my throat. I struggle to swallow the lump that's formed. Then the image of the dying boy flashes through my mind again.

Tanu.

My animal instincts scream at me to claw, bite, and scratch through the crowd, but logic finally breaks through. I pass Sala and indicate for her to follow me.

I know how we're going to get over the wall.

⚬⚭⚬⚭⚬⚭❦❧⚭⚬⚭⚬⚭⚬

My hands are raw and bleeding. Dizzy spells force me to stop often. Sala had bandaged up a long gash on my arm that I hadn't realized was there.

Yet my need to see Tanu, to protect her, fights off the pain more effectively than any herbal remedy.

We make it over the wall using several rooftops and luck. Once I stopped fleeing like an animal, I remembered ways to cross the wall without going through the gate.

The distant roar of the riot grows fainter and fainter as we weave through the mud-walled shacks of the Lower City. Most look abandoned, but a few have terrified faces peeking out from the windows. Sala doesn't ask where we are going, and I don't tell her.

After cacophony behind us, these streets feel hushed. Thunder erupts overhead, and I jog the last few blocks. Sala follows behind.

And there's the house.

I rush to the cart outside and stand on it to peer through the window. Inside, Dada rocks back and forth, singing a song that I cannot hear. Wrapped in his arms is Tanu—precious and perfect. Even from here I can see her little eyes fighting to stay awake against Dada's calming power.

My shoulders sag in relief. She's okay.

I watch as Dada sings, closing his own eyes, a small smile despite the tension that's visible in the rest of his face. Tanu's head lolls forward and rests against Dada's chest. My heart longs to switch places with the old man.

I tear my gaze away from the pair and step off of the cart. I walk past Sala and approach the larger building across from Dada's house. My hands find the familiar holds in the side, and I climb. My body strains with each movement, but I ignore it. I wipe my eyes on my shoulder. It must be the dust and smoke from the riot making them water.

I collapse onto the roof and crawl towards the small shelter that I built years ago and curl up inside. Sala joins me, still uncharacteristically silent. She's waiting for me to speak. I can't find my voice.

The purple lightning moves away, racing over the endless dunes, away from Aveena. The sandstorm follows the vicious lightning, relieving Aveena of the storm's most destructive force. As the harsh wind dies down, the first drops of rain thunk onto the roof.

I reach underneath a sack and pull out a crossbow. I load the weapon then set it on the wide ledge, ready to protect.

Wind Mother gifts sisters of the soul to those who need them most, giving her daughters the chance to survive and thrive with one another.
-from the Sacred Scrolls of Wind Mother translated from Aramak, the Olden Tongue-

56

The minutes of silence that follow as Sala and I watch the shack are punctuated by the riot sounds carried over the wind. Adrenaline seeps from my body, leaving me wrecked in its wake. The animalistic side evaporates.

Blood and pain. Heartbreak and violence.

This isn't my Aveena.

"If you're going to throw up again, try and do it over the side."

Heat rises to my cheeks. "I wasn't going to—"

"I threw up the first time I saw a man killed in front of me."

Sala's voice is low and harsh. I glance at her, but she's staring towards the riot; her profile cuts a dark line against the gentle rain. I look away, swallowing the emotion fighting to break free. Sala grabs my hand. The warmth helps ease the pain in my heart.

"How did you know?" I whisper.

"Zahir," she says simply. My heart tightens.

Sala followed me into the riot. She watched my back. She didn't question me. She still doesn't.

I take a deep breath and draw strength from our linked hands.

"I was raised in the merchant district in North Aveena. My father owned—owns one of the largest jewelry stores in Aveena. He knows as much about fine gold and precious gems as he does about climbing up the social ladder. He married my mother for her status; she is a lesser cousin in the Ba family and the closest to a true Ari wife he could manage."

I feel Sala watching me. I push forward, needing her to understand but unable to meet her eyes.

"I knew from a young age what he expected of me. As his sole daughter it was my duty to marry for the benefit of the entire family. If I married well, then the family would be lifted up by my good fortune."

"When I was seventeen, I met Ahmed. His family were also merchants, but from the less-reputable East Aveena market. He was wonderful…at first." My eyes blur as the memories flood back. "His eyes would come alive when he looked at me. I would meet Ahmed late at night by the canal. I couldn't imagine anything more romantic—a secret affair, a handsome lover, a moonlit walk by the canal. Ahmed stole my heart and swept me off my feet. His gentle kisses sent thrills through my body, and Moon felt like she smiled down on us, hiding our secret."

I extend my left ankle, gesturing to the smooth stone anklet I wear.

"I don't understand how it works or why, but—" I swallow my nerves. Sala deserves the *whole* truth. "When I rub the stones and concentrate, a coolness settles over me. I—well, it's like no one notices me. I-I'm not sure why, and I promise I haven't done—"

Sala squeezes my hand, and I stop rambling. "It helped you meet with Ahmed undetected?"

I nod, tucking my foot out of sight again. I stare at Dada's house, gathering my strength to tell the next part.

"As the months moved on, Ahmed's hands grew bolder, his kisses rougher. I loved him so much, I–I would just playfully push him off. Remind him to ask my father for my hand." I pause, bile rising in my throat, but Sala squeezes my hand, lending her support. I owe her the truth, but my voice is barely a whisper now. "Then one night... No longer playfully, I begged him to stop, but h–he had me pinned. He told me I wanted it, that I–I had been teasing him the whole time. I couldn't move as he, as he..."

I can't make myself say the words, even three years later. A tear slides down my cheek silently, cutting a path through the soot from the riot. Sala puts her arm around my shoulder, pulling me closer, silently comforting me. Waiting until I'm ready.

I take a deep, steadying breath, and continue.

"My body knew before I did. I couldn't stand the smell of my morning cardamom tea. My breasts became tender. I couldn't walk the three flights of stairs to my room without getting winded. Our servant was the first to notice that I missed my cycle. She must've told my mother." My voice trails off, overwhelmed by the sadness threatening to take over. I suck in a shaky breath. The onslaught of memories are relentless, making me feel as if I'm sixteen, scared, and helpless again. "My father barged into my room, yelling so loud I thought people on the street could hear him. 'Whore!' he shouted, 'How could you shame our family so?' I tried to tell them, but I kept tripping over the words. I watched as my mother cried in the corner. Not happy tears. Tears of shame. She blamed me for bringing the family to such a low point, for dishonoring them."

My throat feels dry and scratchy as I push through. The distant shouts of the riot break through the deluge of memories, giving me the perspective I need to continue.

"I was in a haze—terrified of my parents' reactions. Then they were gone, and I could hear my father yelling downstairs and my mother's mumbled responses. And I–I crept towards the stairs to listen."

Fear and heartbreak and betrayal. I look at Sala for the first time since I started my story. Her face is barely visible in the shadows.

"They were going to marry me off to *him*. I was *his* problem now, they said. And I–I couldn't face that future. If Ahmed would do that to me while courting me, what would happen to me after our marriage? And before my parents walked back upstairs, I shoved clothes in a bag and climbed out of the window. Climbing was easy after all those nights I snuck out to meet Ahmed."

"I ran to the Lower City and hid. I nearly starved, nearly lost Tanu, until the people in the Lower City helped. They took care of me, feeding me even though they couldn't afford to share. And when Tanu was born, I loved her instantly, despite what Ahmed did. But I couldn't–I tried to take care of us, but I–" I gulp in another breath, trying to calm myself. "An older woman led me to Dada. His wife and child died in childbirth years ago; he's been lonely since. Dada loves Tanu like she was his own…"

Pressure builds up inside me, struggling to break the dam of emotions that I've held in for years. I've had to be strong. I've had to be the rock for myself and for Tanu.

I force myself to take one shaky breath after another. I need Sala to understand all of it, the whole truth.

"Starving in the Lower City while pregnant wasn't–wasn't good for Tanu. She's perfect, to me, absolutely perfect, but–" I look at Sala, willing her to see the truth. "I didn't notice until she started trying to walk. Her feet, they're not right. She can walk but its challenging."

When she sees me falter, Sala coaxes it out. "What else, binti?"

"She'd be fine if it was only her feet. There are plenty of others in the Lower City who manage a good life with similar injuries. But–but her eyes. Sala, she's losing her sight."

"But she's so young," Sala whispers.

"I know," I respond. "I need to get her to Bhavin. No one can find out. If they do, they'll–they'll…"

My voice cracks, and I tear my eyes away from Sala's compassionate gaze. Frustrated, I swipe at my eyes, trying to erase my tears from existence. As I lift my hand, Sala grabs it and holds it in place. She has both of my hands in hers, now. I feel her eyes on me, but I stare at the rain instead. Maybe I can throw my tears into their midst. Then I could retain my strength in front of Sala. Be more resolute like her.

But Sala doesn't let go of my hand.

"I'm sorry," I mutter.

"For what?" Her calm voice masks her thoughts.

"For being"—I shrug—"like this."

"Laila, look at me."

I don't want to see her revulsion at my weak tears, but I force my eyes to meet hers. Sala speaks each word slowly, as if afraid that I won't comprehend their meaning.

"Laila, let yourself feel your emotions. Don't apologize for having them."

A sob erupts from my throat as her words crumble the last of the dam that has held me together for three years. I collapse onto Sala's shoulder and cry.

No one knows every detail of the past three years. Not the complete story. I haven't trusted anyone with the knowledge, only giving away small pieces of truth. I'm lightheaded as I sob, the pressure in my chest lifting with each passing tear.

It's the only way for the anger, resentment, joy, and fear to escape my body at the same time.

**There are some situations from which
there is no exit or escape.**
-excerpt from *The Thief's Guide* Banned by the
Council of the Sultan in the year 151-

57

The pastels of the morning sky wash away the terrible night. The beauty of the sunrise feels impossible after the horrors. The fires and shouts of the riot had died down during the pale hours before dawn.

Aches that I had ignored during my frantic flight into the Lower City batter my body in the rising dawn.

"We need to tend to your injuries," Sala says when she notices me moving. She had insisted that I try and sleep, taking up my vigil over Dada's shack in my stead.

I wince as I sit fully up. The cut in my arm throbs with my heartbeat, but its not the only pain radiating through me.

"Binti," she whispers, "we need to go."

"I know."

With that, we slip from the rooftop, Sala carefully monitoring my descent, and into the street. I pause at Dada's window, pressing my hand against the imperfect glass, before letting Sala guide me away.

The frequent patrols of Suraksha and my battered body make our progress slow as we wind through the Lower City.

Eerie silence fills the streets causing the hairs on my arms to stand up.

Sala stops me with a hand, then whispers, "Any idea tricks for getting into the Upper City, oh Nightshade?"

My mind scrambles for a second before it hits me.

"I have a way," I whisper back.

Sala gives a curt nod, and I take the lead. As Sala watches my back, I silently maneuver through the streets, poised to flee at the first sign of Suraksha. I wished Sala had picked a different outfit last night—my tattered magenta attire is too vibrant for the Lower City, even in its ruined state.

Finally, we approach the canal. I cast a furtive look around, checking for patrols of Suraksha or nosy Lower City neighbors, before flitting over to the other side of the canal fence. When I glance back, Sala's eyes widen in surprise, but I shrug and gesture over. Sala grins and crosses the fence. Her grin falls when she glances down into the canal, and I turn to see what has caught her attention in the water. Lumps impede the smooth flow of the water. Lumps that look a lot like bodies...

I gulp but lower myself into the tunnel through the wall. The damp ledge of the canal wall is slick beneath my weakened fingers, but I cling on, waiting for Sala to follow.

"We need a plan. Where are we going?" I whisper, the trickle of water hiding the slight echo of my words in the tunnel.

"What do you mean?" Sala asks.

"We've been lucky so far with the patrols. But you know they don't care about the Lower City."

There's a long pause then Sala says, sighing, "You're right. I was so concerned with getting off that roof before daylight that I didn't think it through."

"Would we be welcome at the Hathorda?"

"Course. Why wouldn't we be?"

With that settled, we cross through the canal tunnel. On the other side, Sala keeps an eye out for Suraksha while I lead us towards one of the better buildings for climbing. It's slow moving across the rooftops with my injuries, but at least there's less of a chance of being caught by Suraksha up here.

Sala doesn't hide her bemusement as she helps me lift a wooden plank, lowering the other end onto the Hathorda roof. We tiptoe carefully across then pull the board in after us.

"Do I want to know when you figured that one out?" Sala asks.

I chuckle and share my first smile since confessing my secret to Sala. It feels good. Normal.

"Did you think Zahir and I liked the fresh air?" I quip.

Sala crosses her arms, clearly irritated that we had slipped out on her watch.

"No, I just thought you and Zahir had a thing for each other."

"What?" I shriek.

Sala laughs at my shock. I stutter, trying to explain, which only makes Sala laugh harder.

"Zahir and I are just friends! Well, at least I thought we were… *Friends*, Sala. And would you stop laughing at me?"

Sala bends over, hands on her knees, laughing uncontrollably. I shove her, and soon we're both hysterical. Sala claps her hand on my shoulder, leading me into the Hathorda.

Sala and I keep vigil in the Hathorda. We kill time by training, laughing, and talking in the Logonkelie room. I tell her everything I can about Tanu, gushing like a new mother.

In a way, I am.

Sala listens. She hugs me when the stories become painful, laughs with me when I tell her my failures, and cries with me when I can't handle the pain of loss. Sala produces a healing balm, and I rub it across the cuts and bruises that pepper my body. After two days, most of them are healed.

Aveena is shut down. The silence is heavy with mistrust and loss.

The vizier waits in the back of my thoughts, nagging me. His smug face when he tells the court about the riot flits back to me as I try to sleep at night.

He was happy about the riot... *Why?*

On the second day in the Hathorda, Sala and I venture down into the tavern. Scorch marks grace the entryway, and several of the tables lay broken in a corner. The barmaid recounts how she and the other barmaid who was working barricaded the doorway and smothered the flames as best they could. The wreckage adds to the rough-and-tumble nature of the Hathorda.

Over our simple dinner of rice and goat, I come clean with Sala about the vizier—my failed reconnaissance into his rooms, the lists of Ari names that I jotted down, my forced betrayal of Logonkelie. She hides her disappointment, but I know she's hurt that I didn't confide in her sooner.

She has to know how hard it is for me to trust. *Was* for me to trust. I have no secrets from her now.

"What drives me crazy," I say between bites, "is that I don't know what he's planning. He's the *vizier*, he's already the most powerful man in court."

Sala stares at the swaths of fabric around us, unseeing, her brows furrowed in concentration.

"The problem with powerful men," she says, "is that they always want more."

Both of us remain silent. The burgundy fabric behind Sala conjures images of blood mixed with sand, darkening the ground underneath the guilty and the innocent, death not caring which was which. I shudder and look away.

Sala shakes herself out of her reverie and takes a swig of her beer before adding, "What I am struggling to figure out is how to explain your flight to Cadmar."

"What?" I choke on my rice, making my eyes water.

Sala looks at me sternly. "You've completely blown your cover."

I ring my hands together. How had I *not* thought about this? I glance at the dilapidated entryway, tempted to disappear into the city, but Sala places her hand on mine, stilling the panic.

"I assumed that since you believed and trusted in me…"

"I do, binti, I do," Sala says. "But Cadmar is married to his rules, and you're in direct violation of his biggest one."

"I thought…"

My voice trails off. I'm not sure what I thought. I knew the risk I ran joining Logonkelie in the first place, but I chose it to buy more time.

Sala squeezes my hand, but her reassurance is negated by her solemn words. "I will help you, but I can't trust you for Cadmar. He has to do that on his own."

"That's right," a voice growls from the door.

Our heads snap up in unison as Cadmar strides into the tavern. Six armed men follow him, their blades unsheathed; none of them wear the uniform of a guardsman. Fury radiates off Cadmar as he looks between the two of us.

"Cozy, are we?"

Sala jumps to attention. "Cadmarji, let me explain—"

"That's enough."

His voice cracks like a whip across the empty tavern; the barmaid disappears into the back. Sala frantically glances between me and Cadmar.

"Cadmarji, Laila has—"

"I will deal with you later, Ms. Khatri"—Cadmar spits out— "I thought you knew better than to endanger those who trust you."

Sala bows her head, but not before I see the tears in her eyes. The panic. I stand and face his fury head on. He has to believe me…

"Cadmar, I—"

"You've been dishonest with me since the beginning," he growls. With each word, Cadmar steps closer, a predator cornering his prey. "You've been sneaking away to see that brat of yours the entire time. You've been feeding information to the vizier, undermining everything that we've done."

I want to flinch away from his words, to escape up the stairs and across the rooftops, but I stand tall and look him in the eyes.

"I've done what you've asked of me." I reach out—to grab his hand or to stop him, I'm unsure—but drop my arm uselessly by my side. "I've fought for your cause, Jelani."

"Don't you *dare* address me. You do not have that privilege."

I cross my fist over my chest and bow low to the enraged man. My words come out in a whispered plea. "I am yours to command, Cadmarji. I have been the entire time." I straighten and meet his dark eyes. "But I will not deny that I joined knowing that I could never be compliant with your rules."

I wait, holding his gaze. The silence stretches out in the room—no one dares to move, to breathe. Cadmar's eyes narrow, and I know I've lost.

"You knew the deal when you joined us. And now you've endangered us all."

I do not fight as the armed men surge forward. My injured arm protests as they jerk my hands behind my back and bind them. I do not cry out.

I lift my head and follow my captors to Niraash.

Defeat is inevitable.
-Advice from Sultan Gautam to Prince Ajani-

58

Playful rain patters across the bars on the lone window above my head, happily splashing its way into oblivion. I lean my head against the damp wall and squeeze my eyes shut. Breathe in. Breathe out. One. Breathe in. Breathe—frustration bursts out of my chest, and I scream. My chains rattle as I slam my hands against the wall and kick my feet. And still, I keep screaming.

Echoes taunt me back.

It's my fault I'm here.

Swirls of possibilities run through my head, drowning me in what if's. What if I had told Cadmar about Tanu from the beginning? What if I had told Sala everything about the vizier when we were in the palace?

But what if's are futile, like my scream.

Water splashes onto my face—I don't know if it's the happy rain here to torment me or tears.

So many things I don't know.

My chains chafe against my wrists as I collapse on the floor, succumbing to the sobs splitting my body apart. The sound echoes down the dark cavernous passage leading away from my cell.

I've cried more in the past two days than I have in the past two years.

I failed everyone.

I failed Tanu.

I failed myself.

The dangers of Niraash do not lie in the prison itself. They lie in the depths of the mind, the torturous moments of silence and solitude where one must confront their own transgressions.
—excerpt from *Human Error: a Study of Human Thinking*—

59

Time passes. The rain stops, but my window remains dark. My cell is pitch black, save for the grayish light peeking through the window.

How long have I been down here?

What's the point in knowing? I should accept my fate.

Hopelessness fills me as I think of Tanu's form curled in Dada's arms. Did Cadmar leave them alone? How will they survive without my help?

The scraping of the bars. The rough grunt of a Suraksha. The thump of my food bag.

"What—" I croak, trying to talk to the guard.

The bars slam shut, and the Suraksha's steps fade into the blackness.

I crawl in the dark towards my food bag. My chains scrape against the ground as I sweep my hands back and forth, searching. The shapeless mound silhouettes against the greyish light a few feet away. I scurry towards it. My chains snap tight, bringing me up short. My hand reaches, willing the food nearer. I try to slide the metal cuff further up my arm to give me some leeway. Nothing.

Laughter bursts from me—maniacal and desperate.

Tears fall again.

No one knows where Niraash is hidden.
How they've kept it secret all these years
is a mystery. Probably because no one who
enters ever leaves.
—excerpt from *A Brief Political History of*
Aveena—

60

The screeching of the iron bars across the ground jolts me from my stupor. I rub my sleepy eyes on my shoulder and cringe away from the lamplight. Two Suraksha stand in the doorway, staring. The light cast from the lamp hits the angles of their faces, illuminating the aggressive tilt of their mouths. Their eyes peer through the shadows.

A shiver runs down my spine. A warning.

The chains restrain me from standing, so I sit up as straight as I can, exuding defiance. I refuse to be the fearful street rat they expect.

The taller of the two speaks first, the deep rasp of his voice raising the hairs on my neck.

"We don't get many women down here."

My breath hitches in my throat, but I manage to keep my voice calm as I say, "No doubt you don't get many women in the city either."

The other guard laughs. "Heard you like to tumble guards up at the palace. How about you try one of the Suraksha?"

"Happen to see one around?" I ask, looking around the cell. I push my confusion about his words to the side; I need to keep them talking. "All I see here are a couple of dogs."

The first one growls, and I force myself to laugh. I tilt my head towards him, saying, "See? This one even growls like one."

He steps forward, his broad shoulders blocking the lamplight, but the second Suraksha puts a hand on his chest. The first guard shakes off his hand and glares at his companion, and I seize the opportunity to drive a wedge between them.

"That's right, big boy. Stand down like a good doggie. I'm sure you—"

Pain flares in my skull as the Suraksha slams my head against the stone wall. I try to blink the stars out of my vision, resisting the urge to puke over the floor. The guards argue nearby, and I sit up again, struggling to focus on their blurring forms.

"—get control."

"The bitch deserves—"

"We have our orders, Vijay. Stand down."

The one who slammed my head—Vijay—seethes in the corner as the other Suraksha approaches me. Fury simmers under the surface, at me or Vijay I cannot tell, but he reigns it in. Cold. Calculating.

I gulp and start to speak, but the guard cuts me off.

"Shut it, bitch."

He grabs one of the manacles chained to my wrist and tugs it toward him. I yelp as the iron cuts into my already raw skin, scraping it further.

"Greetings from the vizier," he says.

Panic takes over and I try to pull my chained wrist from him, all common sense vanished from thought at the mention of the vizier. I thrash, scratching at the guard, but Vijay pins me to the wall, making sure my head collides again.

"Remember, we don't mistreat our prisoners," the second Suraksha says as he pulls a pouch out of his pocket. He leers, the coldness in his eyes freezing me to my core. "That's why we won't leave a mark."

The guard pulls a grainy handful out of the pouch and grinds it into my bloody wrist. I bite my cheek to keep from giving them the satisfaction of hearing me scream as salt and rock sear into my wound. The rocks tear into my raw, sensitive skin, shredding it further under the manacle. But it is overshadowed by the incessant burning from the salt. Tears stream down my face as I groan, trying to find relief from the pain.

As the Suraksha drops my wrist and snatches the second, Vijay whispers in my ear, his spit hitting my cheek.

"But who would believe a little bitch like you, anyway?"

The Council Room is long—longer than in real life. The aisle stretches out like the canal, cutting through the crowd of faceless councilmen jeering on either side. A shiver runs through me, urging me towards the dais.

I need to see what is happening.

I surge forward and fall. Golden manacles gleam in the flickering candlelight of the Council Room; my wrists and ankles are bound. The gold chains disappear through the massive doors.

Laughter bursts from the watching Ari.

I need to see what is happening.

I stand and tentatively pull at the golden chains. They resist but give in. I take a step forward and drag the clinking chains. They follow. The chains are heavy, forcing me to concentrate on each step as I drag the glittering weight behind me.

I build a rhythm—step, pull arm, step, pull arm. Sweat beads down my face, but I ignore it. My right wrists stings, and I notice a gash forming under the gold cuff. Soon both ankles and wrists are rubbed raw.

But I need to see what is happening.

After hours—or maybe just a few minutes—the dais looms closer. Three figures stand at the top, but I can only make out their outlines—a large violet veil hangs in front of them. The unnamed desire to see past the veil thrums through me. I pick up speed—step, pull arm, step, pull arm—my breathing becomes ragged.

I'm level with the councilmen, dragging my golden chains past their seats. A hand reaches out and touches my cheek. I yelp and jerk my head out of the way, but then a hand from the other side of the aisle grabs my behind. Before I can reprimand its owner, the hand lets go.

My fierce scream does not stop the hands. They pet, stroke, slap, grab, then disappear back into the crowd. The only part of me they do not touch is the golden manacles. I lean all my weight into the chains, trying to move into a sprint past the faceless councilmen.

I need to see what is happening behind the veil.

My wrists and ankles bleed freely as I stumble to the end of the aisle. I grip the veil and tear it away. The fabric flutters down from the ceiling—as if in slow motion—revealing the men behind it.

Prince Ajani stands, his face impassive like the first time I saw him in the palace. He stares straight ahead, his eyes glassy and unfocused. A viridian smoke swirls around the prince's ankles then licks its way up his legs and torso until the green mist encompasses his entire frame.

Vizier Nassor waits in the shadows behind Ajani.

Panic fills me. I have to get to Ajani. I try to run forward, but the golden manacles start to tug me back down the aisle. Ajani stands blissfully unaware as Nassor emerges from the shadows. His eyes glow the same viridian hue of the mist.

My body slams to the ground. The chains clink as I'm dragged backwards away from the dais. I try to scream for Ajani, but my voice stops working.

The vizier extends a hand, his golden rings taunting me, and curls his hand over Ajani's shoulder. The moment he touches the prince, Ajani's face contorts. He writhes in pain, screaming so loudly it rattles my bones.

And I know he's suffering the vizier's icy cold grasp.

"Ajani!" I shout, struggling to reach him.

My manacles cut into my wrists, but I fight them. A hand grabs a wrist, but I push it away.

I have to get to the prince. I have to save him from—

"Will you calm down?"

My eyes snap open. A small figure huddles in front of me, tugging at the iron cuffs chaining my wrists to the wall. Each tug causes my eyes to water as shards of rock dig further into my damaged wrists. I blink, trying to make out the face in the darkness.

"Hrithik?" I whisper.

"Duh. Now stay still."

I sit up and offer him my wrists, wincing from the pain. Hrithik inserts a large iron key into the hole and twists. My right manacle springs open.

"But what are you—"

"What does it look like, binti? I'm getting you out."

I stare at the little boy.

"But, Hrithik—"

"Call me bhiayya. We're family now."

"Sala."

He smiles and nods. Hrithik opens the cuffs, and the bruised and raw areas sting with the flood of fresh air to my wounds. I relish the bite.

"Let's go. We don't have a lot of time."

I stand and sweep Hrithik into a hug.

"Thank you, bhaiyya."

"Ew, binti, let go," he whispers, pushing me off him.

I grin and follow the boy out of my cell. Hrithik leads me through the cavernous tunnels of Niraash without hesitation. As the tunnel rises towards the city and the exit, Hrithik veers to the left.

"Where—"

Hrithik waves his hand to shush me. I snap my mouth shut and follow him down the smaller passageway. The twists and turns of this tunnel make the walls feel like they're closing in on us.

Hrithik stops, and I bump into him. He gestures to the grate halfway up the wall. I raise an eyebrow at him, and he shrugs and indicates that I should lift him. I sigh and push Hrithik up towards the grate. To my surprise, it swings inward—it's already open.

Hrithik grips the ledge and pulls himself inside. Peeking his head out, he points to a crate a few feet away, then gestures to the ledge.

I nod.

The crate sticks to the mud around it. I wiggle it back and forth, cringing when its creak echoes down the passage. Hurriedly, I set the crate below the grate, the muffled thunk making my heart race faster. I press my back against the wall, listening for the footsteps I'm sure will come.

"Come on. Don't wait fer trouble."

"For," I say, correcting him. Did he use the Lower City slang last time I saw him?

I wipe my sweaty palms on my rags then test my weight on the crate. The old boards hold. For now.

"Quickly!"

"I know."

His nagging reminds me of Sala.

I push off the crate and leap for the grate opening. My hands grasp the ledge as the crate splinters and collapses beneath me. I scurry into the hole and after Hrithik, ignoring the new chunks of dirt that grind into my tattered skin. My wrists burn, but adrenaline keeps me going.

Hrithik's knowledge astounds me. Left, right, right again, left—his confidence never falters. The further we crawl, the more hopeful I become.

I'm escaping.

We round the last curve, and a dim light meets us. I hear pacing footsteps, but Hrithik doesn't pause. A hand reaches down to help Hrithik leave the tunnel altogether. The wizened hand helps me out of the tunnel...

"Velo?" I ask.

His toothless grin greets me.

"'Ello, girlie."

Few leave Aveena of their own free will.
They fear the unknowns of the desert.
They fear the magic of the Tribes. Better
to remain safe within Aveena's walls.
-excerpt from *A Brief Political History of
Aveena*-

61

"Didn' think you could get rid of me, did you?"
"But I—"

The dead rat nailed to my wall. My last conversation with Velo.

"I think you're wantin' to say 'thank you,'" Hrithik says with a grin.

I smile at the boy and do as I'm told. Velo waves off my thanks and gestures for us to follow him. The Suraksha had made sure that I couldn't see where we were going when they brought me to Niraash. Even now with Velo leading the way, I can't reorient myself.

As we scurry through side streets, I notice the scorch marks that mar the sides of buildings and the excessive debris littering the streets. Patrols of stern-faced Suraksha force us to hide often. There never used to be as many patrols before the riot.

Hrithik surprises me—his steps are light as he maneuvers through the side streets and blends with the shadows. I limp behind him, my injuries making it impossible for me to match his silent steps.

Finally, we pass a landmark that I recognize: Ahmed's family's business.

"Niraash is in Eastern Aveena?" I ask Velo under my breath.

"And underground, too."

Velo leads us to the Hathorda. We cross the last few rooftops with ease and drop onto the familiar space. Sala leaps forward and crushes me in a hug. I blink back tears as I hug her back.

As I hug my sister back.

"You sent them?"

"Of course."

"But what about Cadmar? Logonkelie?"

Sala holds me out in front of her so I can see her face.

"Cadmar is wrong."

My heart lifts as I hug her again.

"Not that this isn't sweet, but we best get on with it," Velo's voice says behind us. I grin and hug him too, taking Velo completely by surprise. I grab Hrithik and pull him into a hug next. Each hug gets easier, a little more weight lifted off of my chest.

"Your ma better watch out, bhaiyya. Velo here might snatch you up for his own uses."

Hrithik wiggles out of my grip then crosses his arms over his chest. Velo winks at him, and Hrithik sticks his tongue out back.

"He wouldn't dare cross my Ma," Hrithik says confidently.

"Too right."

The four of us sit on the roof. My body protests the movements, and I shiver slightly. I'm weak and clammy. In the wake of the adrenaline fleeing my body, my injured wrists and ankles scream for attention.

"Here," Sala says, offering a bowl of clear broth. "Prove you can hold this down before I give you anything else."

Hrithik and Velo munch on chaklis—spicy, crunchy swirls of snacks, favorites in the Lower City—while I sip the broth. My sips turn to gulps as I drop the spoon and drink from the bowl itself. Each gulp warms me, pushing the shivers out of my worn body. It's the best bowl of broth I've ever had.

As I eat, Sala fills me in.

"It was Nim who trailed us from the palace. She's been doing extra work for Cadmar ever since the vizier started gaining power in the council. Cadmar reacted without thinking about it. He had a whole story cooked up for your disappearance and everything. It's like he planned on having something happen with you."

"That's what happens when you blackmail someone, I guess. I never trusted him either." Bitterness taints my voice.

"But binti—"

"It is what it is," I say with a shrug. I didn't want to hear her explanations for why I should trust Cadmar. Especially after being in Niraash. Especially after the vizier's guards. "So, what did he tell the Ari about my disappearance?"

"You're the height of scandal, girlie," Velo says with a chuckle. I look to Sala, waiting for clarification.

"He's not wrong," she says. "Erol put out that you had shamed and disgraced him by tumbling some guard, so he sent you away."

The broth forms a hard lump in my throat as I swallow it. I cough, trying to dislodge the feeling. My eyes water.

"Seriously?" I ask once I gain control.

"Don't think the irony doesn't escape me," Sala says with a half-hearted smile.

"Poor Ajani," I say softly.

"He'll be alright," Sala says. "He was always going to be heartbroken over you anyway."

I nod and sip my soup. Ajani's soft brown eyes, his unguarded smile, the way he messes up his hair when unsure or frustrated. I have to— no, need to—let it go.

Let *him* go.

Sala watches me closely. I can't tell if she's checking that the broth will stay down or if she's making sure that I won't be stupid about the prince who was never mine.

"What about Tanu?"

"What about her?" Sala asked, surprised.

"Did Cadmar—?"

"Cadmar would never do anything to Tanu. She's innocent in all of this."

I nod, unsure of whether to believe her. "What about the other Ari? Do they know the Nightshade was caught?"

"Actually, no," Sala says before snatching one of the chaklis from Hrithik. Hrithik tries to take it back, but Sala keeps it out of the boy's reach.

"I wonder why Cadmar didn't tell them…" I mutter, more to myself than to the group.

Velo scoffs. "It's obvious, girlie."

"It is?"

"He doesn't want to taint his reputation." Velo shrugs and adds, "Better for me."

I grimace. I wouldn't be surprised if Velo had been training replacements to masquerade under my guise so he could keep business going. Dunes, if I were him, I would.

After a few moments of silence, she pulls the healing balm out of her hidden pocket. Opening the container, she scoops a dollop onto her hands then moves towards my ankles.

"Sala, don't. I'll get—"

"What happened?"

Horror flickers across her face as she takes in my mangled ankles. Gently but firmly, she grips my hand in hers, angling it so she can assess the extent of my wounds. Velo glances at the cuts before blocking them from Hrithik's view.

"C'mon, lad, we need water. Those need cleaning."

Hrithik nods vigorously and lets Velo lead him downstairs. While they are gone, I tell Sala about the vizier's guards. Her horror turns to deadly fury as she listens.

"That bastard," she growls. "I'll cut off his—"

"We got water," Hrithik sings from the doorway.

Gentle steam rises from the basin of water as Sala gestures them over. She then instructs them to find a small tool in her room before guiding my feet into the basin. Dirt swirls away from my wounds, the soapy water stinging my ankles. I grit my teeth, knowing that I need to get them clean or risk infection.

Hrithik and Velo return and hand Sala a tiny tool before leaving again. Sala lifts my foot out of the water and places it on her leg.

"You're going to have to stay still."

I nod as she begins digging at what's left of my skin with the pincer-like tool. Sala works meticulously, pulling piece after piece of rock from my ankles and then my wrists. After she deems them clean, Sala gently massages the cooling balm into my injuries. The sting recedes into a small burn, and I can't help but sigh in relief.

"Once you're fixed up, we need to get going again, girlie."

I jump, I didn't notice that Velo and Hrithik had returned.

"Get going?"

"We can't stay here. You gotta get out of the city."

"But I—Sala?" I turn to her, hoping that she'll have a different answer. Hoping that she can fix this.

"Cadmar won't back you, the Suraksha knew you were imprisoned, and they'll know you're gone soon."

Sala's eyes plead with me not to argue. I look down at my raw wrists. Leave Aveena? And go where? I think about Sala and Ajani. I think about Erol and Zahir. How could I leave them?

I think about Tanu. If I left, I wouldn't see her again; if I took her with me, then I would force her into a life of running from my mistakes. And what kind of life would I leave her to in Aveena? Between the vizier's enslavement of the Lower City and the violent uprisings in response, she would never be safe. She would always be seen as less than human—because of her poverty, because of her blindness, because she is a woman...

"Binti?" Sala's voice is tentative, careful.

The red skin on my wrists glares at me, reminding me of the golden manacles from my dream.

Oh shit.

I grab Sala's hands and meet her eyes, willing her to believe me. To hear me out.

"Sala, I know what the vizier is going to do."

Hrithik's small form curls up in the corner of the roof. Sala and I covered him when he'd fallen asleep in the middle of eating another chakli. Velo disappeared soon after, agreeing to meet us in a few hours.

"Nassor built up followers, showed others how good he'd be as sultan, carefully undermined the prince at every turn," I say as I prowl back and forth across the roof. I clench my fists to keep the tremors of anger under control.

Sala nods and adds, "He even hinted that the riot was the prince's fault instead of his own."

"What?"

"This was after you ended up in Niraash," Sala says, waving away my disbelief. "The rumors have been—brutal. All spread by the vizier's chosen few."

It all falls into place, according to Sala. Even the way the councilmen had changed since Sultan Gautam's reign. I explain about the Ordinances and how the vizier had created those rules to give himself time.

"That's what he plans for tomorrow!" Sala shouts, slapping her forehead.

Hrithik stirs and rolls over. I wait until I'm sure he's asleep before whispering urgently, "Tomorrow? Sala, what's happening tomorrow?" The pit in my stomach grows, panic replacing the warmth leftover from the broth.

"The vizier called a 'special' council meeting to vote on 'current matters.' This *has* to be it."

"Have they had special meetings before?"

"We've never had a riot before."

So, Sala and I planned until the morning light burst over the rooftops. I covered Hrithik's eyes with the blanket as he slept—he would need his strength for what we had to do later.

**The royal line has been deigned by Wind
Mother and Sky Father themselves.**
-from The Ordinances of Aveena-

62

The Aveenan sun beats down on my head. It's always hot after a storm, but today the sun is scorching. As Hrithik and I leave the shelter of the buildings, we're exposed to the late morning sun's fury.

"If you keep twitching like that, they'll think yer crazy," Hrithik whispers from my side.

I elbow him and say, "It's 'you' not 'yer,' bhaiyya. Don't make me tell your ma that you've been spending too much time with Velo."

Hrithik sticks his tongue out at me, and I return the gesture. The light-hearted moment is short-lived as we arrive at the top of the hill. The Suraksha waiting at the gate are heavily armed, making them more intimidating than the first time I arrived with Zahir months ago. They glare at us, squinting against the sun, assessing any threats we might pose. I shift in my seat but relax the rest of my body, making sure my face is pleasant and neutral. Although I wear a veil, the guard's eyes feel as if they can penetrate through the fabric and uncover my true identity. Next to me, Hrithik grins and waves like the kid he is. Velo loaned us the cart to help with our ruse, and Hrithik's mother loaded it with expensive fabrics and bejeweled sarees.

"Stop there," one of the Suraksha says. "Name and identification."

"My name is Hrithik, and this is my Auntie—" I bow my head and avert my eyes from the guard. "—she's helping me today cause Ma is too sick to come and one of them fancy ladies needs new pretty clothes. We brought all sorts for her to try on. Ma's the best seamstress in Aveena, and I'm the best helper. Ma says so. Do you know which fancy lady I'm talking about? She's got the—"

"Enough," the Suraksha growls, cutting off Hrithik's babble. He gestures to the other guards, who move to the cart. "Every cart goes through inspection today."

He keeps his hand on his sword and his eyes trained on us as the other Suraksha encircle the cart. They shuffle through the fabrics, causing Hrithik to cry out.

"Careful! Those are *expensive*!"

The guard who watches us steps forward menacingly.

"Watch how you talk to your betters, boy," he snaps.

I rest my hand on Hrithik's arm, but he shakes it off and points to the Suraksha throwing fabrics to the side. "And is *he* going to pay for that if it rips? My *Ma* trusted me to do the job and do it well, and I'm not going to let her down, sir. If the lady likes what we make and I talk nicely, then maybe she'll become a regular customer, and I can make Ma proud. We could meet other fancy ladies through the one, and then we'd have customers all the time! Can't you see why this is so important? So, tell them to be nice to my clothes. Please."

The guard moves his hand from his sword and rubs his temple before calling back the other Suraksha from the cart.

"Alright, go in, boy. And mind yourself around the lady. They prefer *silent* help."

A guard slaps our donkey, and the cart lurches forward. I keep my eyes downcast the entire way—they're too much of a giveaway. The whole way through the gate, Hrithik talks to the main guard.

"Oh, Ma already told me that. I plan on being completely silent and standing by the side. I might say 'that looks nice' or 'try this' but nothing more. The lady won't even know I'm there, I'll be so—"

The Suraksha walks into the post and closes the door in Hrithik's face. Hrithik grins and winks at me as a servant leads our donkey next to the other servants and merchants. Hrithik reminds me of Zahir—his ability to chatter nonstop is more distracting than a Harem girl with fireworks. My heart squeezes at the thought of Zahir—did anyone tell him what happened?

I shake my head and push Zahir out of my mind. I killed any chance our friendship might have had with my lies.

Once we're through the gate, Sala appears in her black veiled attire on the premise of helping us unload the cart. Although none of the other servants heed us any mind, my heart still thunders in my chest. We have to make it to the council meeting on time. I have to help him.

Sala's knowledge of the servants' passageways astounds me as she maneuvers nimbly through the discreet paths. Being led around the palace like a child makes me question what I'd been doing in the palace for all these weeks, I feel useless. Hrithik smiles and chatters away to Sala, causing the few servants we pass to smile indulgently at the cute babu in the hall. Sala had been right the night before—Hrithik is the perfect distraction. None of the servants we pass glance my way. Their eyes go straight to Hrithik's messy hair and bright, eager smile.

We round the corner and slip through an unmarked door. I sigh and set the fabrics down on the nearest cushion. Erol's suite feels like home after the events of the past week.

"Where are Erol and Zahir?" I ask.

"Playing nice with the other Ari as usual," Sala says, sifting through the fabrics. "They're trying to get a hint about this special council meeting."

"You didn't tell them?"

"How could I? Plus, they're safer if they have the same reactions as everyone else when you come in," Sala hands clothing off to Hrithik then turns to me. "Okay, let's get you ready."

"Ready?" I ask.

Sala gestures to the muted colors of my sensible kurti and veil. "We can't send you into the Council of the Sultan like that."

"I'm not pretending to be Lailani anymore. She's long gone."

"I *know* that, but you can't go in looking like that. We need some of Lailani and some of Laila," Sala says, hands on her hips, a slight frown creasing her face.

"This isn't part of the plan, Sala. I need to get into the council now. You said it started at one."

"I lied," she says, pushing me into my old room.

Hrithik follows the two of us, carrying the pale blue and gold bundle.

"*I* knew it was part of the plan," he says.

I sigh and resign myself to Sala's will.

Sala flits around me, primping as she goes. My eyes barely twitch as she applies kohl to my lids, but thankfully she foregoes the rest of the cosmetic torture. The blue and gold bundle isn't another saree contraption as I expected. Instead, Sala helps me into a flowing blue dhoti that cinches at the ankle and a navy short kurti so dark that at first it appears black. Gold detailing lines the sleeveless kurti and high neckline tying into the large gold criss-crossing stripes on the pants. Sala finishes by tying the matching blue and gold pallu across my body to rest on my hip.

As she works, I think about what I'm about to do. What I'll say to the Council of the Sultan. Nerves worm their way into my stomach and wiggle there. How will I get them to listen? I think back to Cadmar's speeches, the vizier's pomp, even Ray Lobo's tirades. I can't help but worry about the major flaw in this plan: I'm a woman.

"Sala," I say, grabbing her hands and forcing her to stop fixing my hair. The desperation in my voice gets her attention. "I know you don't like this part but—"

"You said you lied to me about what time the council meeting started."

"Yes?" she asks impatiently.

"When does it actually start?"

"Two thirty."

"We have to go." I stand and cross to the door in a few steps. Hrithik jumps up to follow me, eagerness written all over his face.

Sala crosses her arms. "I made sure we had enough time to—"

"I need to break into the vizier's rooms. Now."

Sala stops short and stares at me. "I don't think—"

"Look, Sala. Those Ari bastards won't listen to some girl walking into their midst, no matter how much I look like one of them. But if I have *proof*…"

I watch as Sala works through the possibilities— weighing the risks of my idea. Her incredulity at my suggestion turns into hard resignation as she realizes that it's the only way.

"You've got to be in and out of there." She pauses, chewing her lip. "And I think we need to wait for the vizier to be safely in the council meeting."

"So that he can't come running in."

She is brilliant.

Sala nods. As her fingers fly through my hair removing the last vestiges of my Ari persona, Sala and I plan to break into the vizier's rooms.

At least this time I have someone watching my back.

If my heart beats any louder, it will alert the Suraksha of my presence. My head feels light—and off-balanced— without the extensions hiding my short locks; Sala insisted that my hair needed to be fully Laila, not Lailani. My hands are clammy as I near the servant's entrance to the vizier's suite. Clammy and cold hands are never a good sign…

I push the thought away and take a deep breath. *Focus, Laila.* I slow my breathing, allowing my mind to still. When the last servant disappears, Sala waves me through the vizier's door.

His rooms are exactly the same as the last time I was here. I tiptoe to the office door and remove my picks from my short hair. I tumble the lock on the first try.

He didn't even bother to change the lock to his office, I think as I slip inside. *Asshole.*

The sound of trickling water greets me, the fountain remains in the corner of the office. I fight the urge to smash it into oblivion and head to the desk. Skipping over the rest of the papers, my fingers find the latch on the secret compartment, and I pop the lock. The door falls open.

It's empty.

Cursing under my breath, I reach into the smooth edges of the secret compartment, feeling into the corners before I admit defeat.

The vizier did change one thing about his office: the letters are no longer there.

"Shit, shit, shit, shit, shit."

The words do nothing to calm the panic rising in my stomach. They won't believe me without proof. I won't be able to save Ajani without those letters.

I close my eyes and breathe. I need to think.

I don't bother closing the secret compartment as I sift through the papers on the vizier's desk. Once I'm sure that the letters aren't sitting on top, I move to the other drawers in the desk. I throw the contents on the ground after examining them—the vizier will know I've been here either way. The smooth wood makes my fingers tingle as I run my hands over the desk, through the perimeter of each drawer, and against the back wall.

Nothing.

"Think, Laila. If you were the vizier, where would you hide it next?" I mutter to myself.

"What about in your room?"

The voice at the door makes me jump. I spin and sink into fighting position before I see Hrithik's grinning face. He waves a bundle of papers.

I run forward and grab the bundle, hastily untying the twine to flip through the pages.

"Bhaiyya, this is it!" I want to whoop from excitement but catch myself—we're still in the vizier's rooms after all. I lead Hrithik through the sitting room and out the servants' door. In the hallway, I pick Hrithik up and spin him around.

"You are the most brilliant, wonderful, sneaky boy around."

"Binti, put me down!"

I smile and oblige. Sala ruffles Hrithik's hair and leads us away from the vizier's rooms.

"Where did you find it?" Sala asks.

"I checked under his bed. Interesting little box there."

"Good work," she says. Hrithik beams.

We hurry through the hallway. I can feel my heart pounding in my throat, knowing that I'm going to have to confront *him* soon.

Sala stops outside of the servants' door leading into Erol's suite, and I run into her. Hrithik chuckles as Sala glares at me, but his chuckle turns to a groan as Sala says, "Bhaiyya, I need to you to wait in here."

"But—"

"No one can know you were involved."

"But—"

I kneel down in front of Hrithik and look into his face. His chin is set stubbornly as he plants his feet, refusing to move.

"Hrithik, does your Ma work hard in the shop?" I ask.

"Yes. You know—"

"And does she love what she does?"

"Yes, but—"

"Do you like helping her?"

"Of course."

"Then you have to stay here. If anyone found out you were helping me, then your Ma would lose the shop, and you'd both end up in Niraash. You have to pretend like you didn't do any of the amazing things that you did today." Hrithik's shoulders sag and the fight leaves him. He nods and slips through the door.

"Good job," Sala says.

I shrug and say, "It was all true. He just needed to hear it."

"Hopefully the Ari will react to you the same way."

I nod. The elation at finding the letters evaporates at the reminder of what I'm about to do.

Sala, reading my thoughts, grabs my hand and squeezes it.

The wide marble halls are empty except for our footsteps. The lack of activity in the normally bustling palace pushes my nerves further on edge. It's as if the entire palace is holding its breath.

Instead of leading me on the usual path to the Veiled Room, Sala leads me around a different corner. Massive golden doors confront us. I freeze, a shiver running down my spine, they're the golden doors from my dream.

A single Suraksha patrols in front of the door to the Council of the Sultan. He relaxes his stance as we approach. Making sure she has the guard's attention, Sala kisses me on the cheek. The Suraksha practically pants as he watches Sala saunter up to him, swinging her hips back and forth as she walks. She puts a hand on his cheek and runs it down to his neck.

He never stood a chance.

Sala braces her body against the limp guard, guiding his body to the floor.

I walk to the golden door and place my hand on the ornate handle.

**He who does not know says 'lentils'
so that his opinion will be heard as well.**
-Aveenan Proverb-

63

No one notices the grumble of the golden doors over the raised voices and heated words. I slip through the gap, aghast at the scene before me.

The men arguing before me don't look like members of the Aristocracy. All decorum has been abandoned as they shout at one another.

They are self-serving children.

"—need to round up the lot of them and have them executed!"

"Gandmasti! We cannot kill people off like that!"

"When Sultan Gautam was—"

"Sultan Gautam is dead!"

On and on the men go, yelling over one another in their passion to be heard. On the dais, Ajani's head whips back and forth, struggling to keep up with the speakers. Behind him, the vizier sits smugly, a faint smile on his face.

He is enjoying this.

"We need to get those Lower City lice under control!"

"You need to get yourself under control!"

"Councilmen!" Ajani bellows over the roar. "That's enough! You are members of the Aristocracy and members of the Council of the Sultan. You need to act like it!"

Heavy silence follows his words. Pride surges through me as a few of the councilmen nod and sit in their seats. That's right, Ajani, I silently urge him on.

But then Ray Lobo points a finger at my prince.

"And who are you, *youngling*, to tell us how we should behave? We were members of your father's council while you were still on your mother's teat."

Ajani reels back from the vehemence in Ray Lobo's tone. He stumbles over his words as he says, "I am your prince and soon to be your sultan."

"Some sultan," Ray says as he gestures to the councilmen around him. "The only thing you've had to say since sitting in your father's seat is to tell us how to behave! Where were your opinions when we were making plans for Aveena?"

"Probably thinking about another set of teats!" Anik Ba says, laughing cruelly. Several other councilmen cackle. Heat rises to my cheeks at the innuendo, but it's overshadowed by the rage simmering beneath the surface. These fucking hypocrites and their–

"Too bad that guard also had her teats on his mind, too," another voice shouts.

"That's not—" Ajani starts.

"Leave the decision-making to your elders, *boy*," Ray Lobo snaps at Ajani.

The council bursts into arguments again. I don't know what to do, how to interrupt this chaos. We hadn't planned on a complete derailing of the council when we concocted our haphazard plans.

From my vantage point, I can't miss Ajani's pleading look to vizier, the clear ask for help to reign the councilmen in.

"No," I whisper, but it's too late.

Twisting his beard, Vizier Nassor stands gracefully. The fine silk of his black kurta matches the gold adorning his body, making the vizier look like the epitome of Aristocracy. Like the epitome of a sultan.

"Councilmen, this young man has raised a valid point," Vizier Nassor says smoothly. "We are not acting like the council that we used to be under Sultan Gautam."

Prince Ajani sits on his seat, allowing the vizier to calm his council down for him.

"No, no, no," I mutter. "Come on, Ajani. Take control."

But Ajani remains seated, trusting the vizier to lead. Dread curls in my stomach.

After the vizier ensures that he has every listening ear, he continues speaking. "However, I am forced to agree with Councilman Lobo. Prince Ajani has not acted like a sultan since joining our midst."

Ajani clutches the arms of his chair. The color recedes from his face, leaving him ashen and pale under his dark skin. My mouth dries as the vizier speaks, his oily voice freezing me as effectively as his magic. I need to speak, to stop this, but I'm petrified of the snake in front of me.

"It pains me to say this, but perhaps Gautam's heir isn't fit to rule in his stead. It has happened before, and the Ordinances have the answer for us as they always do." Vizier Nassor snaps his fingers, and a servant rushes up to the dais. The man kneels and holds a scroll open for the vizier to read. "*In the instance that the sultan dies without a male heir or the heir is deemed unfit to rule, the Council of the Sultan can elect to promote the royal vizier of the deceased sultan to the position of sultan."*

Vizier Nassor looks up from the scroll at the awaiting council. His eyes glitter in anticipation as he looks at the stunned crowd. "That would be me."

"That's horseshit and you know it, Nassor."

Every head in the council turns as I walk down the aisle and into the Council of the Sultan.

"Lailani?" Ajani's whisper is inaudible due to the outbreak of shouts from the council—most like in shock because sanctity of the Council Room has been tarnished by the presence of a woman.

I ignore the councilmen around me, my eyes fixed on my prey: the vizier.

Nassor's smug expression has vanished, and a crease forms in his brow as he stares me down. I stop in front of the dais, glaring at him. The vizier shakes his head, then waves his hands, silencing the angry councilmen.

"Lady Acharya, this is no place for a woman. Especially a woman of ill repute. You must leave at once."

I cross my arms over my chest, not breaking eye contact with the vizier. "Well, then I guess it's a good thing that I'm not Lady Acharya, so you'll—"

"You will leave. At once," the vizier insists.

"What, Nassor? Afraid of a woman? Or afraid of what I might tell these men about you?"

The royal vizier's fists clench at my words, the only sign that I've affected him. Mutterings break out in the Council Room. The vaulted ceilings amplify the sounds until I feel surrounded by the whispers of the councilmen.

Ajani stands. Silence falls amongst the Aristocracy as they wait for what he will say.

"Vizier Nassor, we will listen to what Lady, uh, what this lady has to say."

Ajani's words ring with confidence, but he hides his trembling hands behind his back as he speaks.

"Your Highness, this woman is a spy," Nassor says dismissively. "I caught her weeks ago in my office, trying to steal important information."

"Of course I'm a spy. Didn't I just say that my name isn't 'Lady Acharya'? What else would I be?" I snap at the vizier. He huffs but clenches his jaw. The prince looks between the two of us, uncertain. I take a step forward, imploring him, "Ajani, please."

The whispers break out again, this time joined by the female voices tittering away in the Veiled Room at my lack of formality. I ignore the mix of emotions building inside and focus on the prince, *my* prince, hoping he'll listen.

After a long considering look, Ajani nods.

"But Your Highness—" the vizier begins, but the prince cuts him off.

"You are not sultan yet, Nassor. As I see it, I still have the right to rule this council. Sit. Down."

Vizier Nassor does nothing to hide the loathing in his eyes.

"Lady Ach—Lail—well, you have the floor," the prince says and gestures to the room at large as he sits on the marble throne.

I swallow the nerves rising in my throat as the Council of the Sultan falls into a deadly silence at Ajani's words. The men look mutinous, ready to strike me down; I can feel the daggers the women are glaring at me from the Veiled Room.

But the time to hide died when I ran through the streets of Aveena while houses burned and brother killed brother.

"Councilmen, I have not been honest with you. Vizier Nassor is right in one account: I am a spy. I lied about my identity and deceived you all—including those I lived with—in order to sneak into the palace. But the lies that I have told amount to nothing compared to the lies that your royal vizier has told."

A few men cough to hide their disbelief, but I push on.

"My name is Laila, but most of you know me as the Nightshade."

"That's horseshit." Ray Lobo stands and shakes a finger at me. "The Nightshade is a man. Only a man could pull off the disastrous work he does."

I raise an eyebrow at him. "Only a man, Lobo? What makes you so sure?"

"Well, I, uh, I happen to know someone who hired the Nightshade. He spoke to a man to explain the details of the job."

"You mean the job you paid twenty-five gold rupees for?"

"I never—"

"You never paid to have a few of Consulate Reyanash's papers go missing?"

Red flushes Ray Lobo's face as he stutters, trying to deny his involvement. I smirk and wink at Lobo. "It's okay, Councilman, your secret is safe between us."

The men do not bother to lower their voices as they turn to their neighbors. I wait, knowing that I need to give them time. Vizier Nassor's voice cracks through the room, silencing the councilmen for me.

"This is some claim you have, woman, but knowing the details of one job doesn't make you the Nightshade."

I pace back and forth in front of the dais, using my new knowledge of each name in the council to jog my memory of the jobs I've performed for them.

"Councilman Laghari hired me to hide incriminating letters in Councilman Pateel's office at home so that the Suraksha had something to find when they came knocking. Councilman Ba hired me to sneak into Councilman Dara's house to remove the family ring he had left there after screwing Councilman Dara's wife. Councilman Shah hired me to steal the necklace from Councilman Asfour's wife and hide it in Councilman Cadmar's office to frame them for an affair."

The employers of each job turn white or sink further into their seats; the victims of each job redden or crane their heads to glare. I open my arms wide, gesturing to the councilmen around me, and ask, "Is that enough proof for you, Nassor?"

I glare at the vizier, ignoring Ajani's shocked face behind him. I can't look at him. Not yet.

"But those jobs are *nothing* compared to the job you've been pulling. Isn't that right, Nassor?"

"You will address me—"

"I will address you however I damn well please."

"Your Highness, she's out of control and overly emotional. This exactly why women shouldn't—"

"Shouldn't be ostracized from the Council of the Sultan," Ajani finishes, cutting off the vizier. "Be careful, Nassor. You're starting to sound guilty."

Only those of us close to the dais hear the prince's final line to the vizier. My heart soars with pride.

"Your Highness," I say, looking up into his familiar face, "everything the vizier has told you about the Ordinances is a lie. He's been buying himself time to try and become sultan himself."

"How would you know what's in the Ordinances?" Nassor snaps at me.

"I've read them. An original copy of the Ordinances is stored in the sultan's tower. The Ordinances don't say how long the mourning for the previous sultan should be; they don't say the vizier should rule in the intermittent period between sultans; and they *definitely* don't say that the council can vote to put the vizier in as the new sultan."

"And they do not say that the sultana must remain in isolation until the next sultan takes the throne."

Every head in the Council Room turns to see a beautiful older woman walking through the golden doors.

Wind Mother gifts select few dominion over. Her powers. These special skills are neither good nor evil. She trusts the wielder to choose wisely.
-from the Sacred Scrolls of Wind Mother translated from Aramak, the Olden Tongue-

64

"Mother?"

Sultana Chhavi floats down the aisle of the Council Room; her immaculate saree glitters as she walks through the crowd of stunned men.

When Sultana Chhavi reaches me at the end of the aisle, she stops and bows with her hand over her heart. Gasps reverberate in the cavernous room. My cheeks redden, and I hastily return the gesture to the sultana.

"Sultana Chhaviji, you and this woman—" Vizier Nassor begins.

"Have never met," his mother responds coldly. "However, it seems that she and I have both seen through your horseshit."

The vizier sputters, pointing a finger at both women. "I—you know that—"

"What I know," the sultana cuts him off, "is that you've lied to this council, and you've manipulated those you've been tasked with helping, Nassor. You are a disgrace to the position you hold."

The vizier's aura of oily calm disintegrates with the arrival of the sultana. His anger is palpable to the entire council as he glares at us.

"I have protected this city from itself, Chhavi! As vizier of this council, I'm ordering you gossiping women to leave and take your lies elsewhere."

I begin to speak, but the sultana lifts a hand to stop me. Her derisive laughter is low and menacing as she ascends the stairs of the dais. Sultana Chhavi bypasses the enraged vizier to approach Ajani on the top of the dais. Ajani watches her as she approaches him, climbing each step of the dais slowly, gracefully.

Sultana Chhavi bows to her son then places a hand on his arm as she turns to the Council of the Sultan. Everyone recognizes her literal rise in power as she stands on the top of the dais with Ajani.

"Vizier Nassor imprisoned me in our Upper City residence in the name of mourning. He claimed that the Ordinances deemed it so. Like all of you, I blindly followed his directions."

Several of the men shift in their seats—the truth of her words making them uncomfortable.

"But unbeknownst to the vizier, I suspected him even then."

"Sultana Chhavi, I must—"

"You must shut up and sit down when your sultana is speaking, Nassor."

The sultana's voice cracks through the air, silencing the vizier's impertinence. I smirk as I watch the vizier lower himself into his seat.

"My beloved husband's death was too… clean. His heart attacks so evenly spaced out. I took every book on poisons from the library and used my exile to read them, following my intuition. My *woman's* intuition." The sultana glares at the vizier. "And do you know what I discovered, Nassor?"

My heart stills as I listen to the sultana. Poison? The vizier grips his seat, the whites of his knuckles blending into the white of the marble. The council waits for the sultana's words with bated breath.

"Nightshade has very particular effects, doesn't it, Nassor?" Sultana Chhavi whispers. She throws a small green branch at the vizier, and he flinches away from it. Sultana Chhavi's voice rises as she continues. "Once given, the drinker must continue to consume the poison or else suffer death. When the dose of the poison is decreased too much, nightshade causes the victim to display signs similar to a heart attack. You poisoned Gautam for a *year* before killing him."

"You have no proof," Vizier Nassor says carefully. His eyes are fixed on the sultana.

"Your guilt is my proof," the sultana says simply.

"Unfortunately, that is not enough to incriminate a member of the Consulate, sultana. Your lies will go no further today."

"Would *this* be enough to incriminate you, Nassor?" I ask, removing the bundle of letters from my hidden pocket. The vizier's face pales, and I smile. "Shall I read some of it to the council? I'm sure—"

"Enough!" Nassor screams, his voice cracking in his rage. He stalks down the dais and rushes me. His hand clamps on my throat, icy pain sears from his touch as he cuts off my breath. His eyes glow emerald as he claws for the stack of letters. Shouts of shock reverberate through the Council Room as several men move to restrain the vizier, but he waves a hand and an emerald mist appears, freezing them in place. Gasps of shock and fear echo around me, but all

I can focus on is the sickly green glow of the vizier's eyes as my vision blurs.

I will myself to fight, to claw at his hands, but the ice freezes my limbs. A ringing in my ears blocks out the frantic shouts. Bright spots appear as the vizier squeezes tighter.

At least they'll know the truth.

"Laila!" Zahir's panicked voice reaches me above the rest.

I wish I had the chance to explain to him.

Darkness creeps in, and the vizier's manic leer grows. He leans closer and whispers in my ear, "Aveena is mine."

No.

The calming cool from my anklet pushes against the vizier's ice. The vizier's eyes widen in shock. My arms are heavy, but with each pulse from my anklet, more movement comes back to my limbs.

I claw at the vizier's hand, and like Sala taught me, twist sharply, taking his arm with me.

"You bitch!" the vizier screams. His arm hangs limply by his side. The viridian mist dissipates as his obsidian bracelet slides across the marble floor.

"Never" —I rasp, glaring at the vizier— "touch me again."

The councilmen stop shouting.

I bow at the foot of the dais then ascend to Ajani. I lower my head again; to the audience behind me, I'm showing the deference due to the sultan. But I hold Ajani's eyes, reminding him of the girl he thought he knew.

"Your Highness, this is the vizier's correspondence. I removed it from his chambers before I came to the council." Ajani takes the proffered letters, flipping through the pages. "You should find evidence of the vizier's manipulation and lies within its pages."

"Lies!" Nassor shouts.

None of the councilmen approach the vizier as he looks from side to side, searching for his supporters.

Ajani stands, holding the attention of the entire room for the first time since his father's murder. He pushes his shoulders back, authority oozing from his voice as he orders, "Guards, arrest Nassor Al-Sid for the murder of Sultan Gautam."

"No! Lies!" Nassor growls as the Suraksha swarm from the golden doors into the hall. The disgraced councilman's shouts permeate the silent council as all watch Nassor Al-Sid being dragged out. "You cannot do this! I should be sultan, not you, boy! The city will perish if—"

The golden doors slam shut, cutting off the former vizier's poison from the council once and for all.

His Royal Highness,
Prince Ajani Bahu IV,
officially announces the imprisonment
of Nassor Al-Sid, former viȝier,
on the following charges:

-Poisoning and subsequent murder of
Sultan Gautam Bahu
-Treason against Prince Ajani Bahu
-Improper imprisonment of Sultana
Chhavi Bahu
-Blackmail and manipulation of numerous
members of the Council of the Sultan
-Fearmongering and endangering of the
Aveenan populace
-Deceit and dishonoring the position of
royal viȝier

Further information or evidence of
Nassor Al-Sid's crimes against Aveena
will be rewarded.

65

The days following the vizier's arrest blur into a flurry of motion and finery. Somehow between reorganizing the remaining council, discovering the depth of the vizier's maliciousness, and meeting individually with every member of his council, Ajani found time to instruct a servant to direct me to a new suite. Nerves have kept me trapped in the beautiful room, afraid to venture into the rest of the palace—or try to escape. I'm still unsure of Ajani's reaction to my identity now that the truth has been revealed.

Or at least the majority of the truth.

The council knows nothing of Logonkelie, and in the aftermath of that tumultuous council meeting, I have managed to protect Cadmar, Erol, and Zahir from the palace investigations.

I rest my back against the windowsill in my room, staring out over the gardens. Ajani must have known I would love this view. Bird calls reach my ears from the nearby aviary paired with the distant trickle of the canal. The breeze brings the sweet smell of the flowers to me as I stare out at the setting sun.

A knock on my door startles me and I perch on the windowsill, contemplating a quick escape into the gardens.

But no, I'm done running.

The knock pounds again—two knocks and a slap. Familiarity wrings my heart as I open the door to—

"Cadmar?"

He bows his head and asks, "May I come in?"

I back away, allowing Cadmar access. He settles onto a divan in the furthest corner of the room, waiting for me to join him. I hesitate, remembering the hatred in his eyes during our last encounter when he had me arrested.

"Laila, please, sit. The walls—"

"—have ears," I finish for him. I sit across from Cadmar, the 'please' throwing me off more than anything. Bags line the bottoms of Cadmar's eyes, the only sign of the stress he's endured over the past weeks. And has he always had this much white in his short beard?

"I'm sure I'm the last person you want to see right now."

I shrug. "Not the last."

Cadmar grimaces. "I wanted you to know how thankful we all are for you bringing the vizier's actions to light. The council has much to do in order to repair the damage that the vizier caused."

"How are Zahir and Erol?" I ask. "Sala? Nim?"

"Each of them are wrapping their heads around the whirlwind you stirred in their own way." Cadmar pauses then adds, "They want to see you, but we all agreed that in the immediate future we need to keep our distance."

I nod, but my heart crumbles a bit. I look to the ceiling, waiting for the burning tears to subside. Once I'm sure that I have them under control, I stare impassively at Cadmar again, waiting for the reprimand. Or for the banishment from my Logonkelie family. Or perhaps a new blackmailed agreement…

"Laila, I—I owe you an apology." My jaw drops, his words rendering me speechless. Cadmar keeps his eyes on his sherwani under the pretense of adjusting the fabric as he continues, "Sala told me the full truth—your entire experience with the vizier amongst other things. She made me realize that I was wrong to act so rashly after the riot."

"Cadmar, I—"

"No, let me finish." Cadmar meets my eyes, revealing the worry that I've never noticed there before. "Even these last few days, you've protected all of us. You've allowed my lies about your unfaithfulness to the prince to remain, in order to keep Logonkelie out of the investigation. I am in your debt. You have helped me to protect those I care about most. Thank you, Laila."

Cadmar extends his hand to shake my own, acknowledging me as an equal.

"You're welcome, Jelani." My mouth is dry as I return his grip. Before I can rethink it, I add, "Since I've protected those you care about most, will you help me protect those I care about?"

Tanu's safety hangs between us, and I can't help the anxiety that rises. Cadmar squeezes my hand, then lets go.

"Your secret is safe with me."

Relief washes through me, making me lightheaded. Cadmar dips his head and walks towards the door. Before he pulls it open, I remember.

"Wait! Jelani!"

Cadmar turns, quirking an eyebrow at me, reminding me of those first few days in the Hathorda before the palace.

"Nassor's bracelet? The one with the black stones?"

Cadmar's mouth tightens, and I know before he answers.

"Gone."

<hr>

I watch Prince Ajani from behind a tree in the aviary. He sits on our bench, his hands clasped in his lap, waiting for me. His white sherwani gleams against the vivid green backdrop of the aviary. Rings glimmer on several more fingers than he used to wear them.

Pulling my head back around the tree, I close my eyes and calm my fluttering heart. I can't tell if it's nerves or feelings or both making my heart pound this way. Although I've been avoiding Ajani, his official summons couldn't be ignored.

When Ajani hears me approach, he stands—he seems taller with the shadow of the vizier over him—and smiles shyly. I smile back but stay a few feet away. Neither of us know what to say, and Ajani begins to tug on his hair without thinking about it. The nervous gesture is so familiar that I laugh.

"So not everything has changed then?" I ask.

Ajani smooths his hair back into place with a grin.

"I guess not. Please, sit with me, Lailan—Laila."

Although he catches himself, Ajani's fumbles over saying my real name. His discomfort reminds me of the promise I'd made myself before walking into the aviary. I sit on the opposite end of the bench, maintaining my distance, and turn so I can read his face easily. His eyes take in my position on the bench, registering the space, before he lifts them to look into my face.

"Laila—"

"Your Highness—"

We both speak at the same time and then stop. I smooth my hands out on my kurti to keep myself from fidgeting with the edge.

"I thought we'd gotten past formalities a long time ago, Laila," the sultan says softly.

"I wasn't sure how you'd feel now," I say. Ajani's face tightens, so I add, "but clearly you haven't become too big-headed in a week."

"I'd like to think that I'm not big-headed at all," he teases.

"Well then you haven't looked at your hands recently. The additional gold screams 'big-headed future-sultan'."

Ajani laughs, and it warms me to see him relax again. He reaches for my hand and takes it in both of his. I close my eyes and savor the feeling.

"Laila, I don't want to lose you."

I open my eyes and stare into his beautiful, vulnerable face.

"Ajani, you don't really know me."

"I'd like to."

His earnest face squeezes my heart, making what I know I have to say even harder.

"Our relationship is full of lies, Ajani. It's not—"

"But there are so many true feelings mixed with those lies. That's the truth that I want. I want to get to know you, Laila. Not Lailani, not the spy, not the Nightshade. You."

His words hang between us, and my heart aches to give him the answer he wants.

"Ajani, I don't even know myself yet."

He sighs and runs a hand through his hair, looking out at the aviary; his other hand still holds on to mine. Neither of us let go.

When we do, it will be for good.

"What do you plan to do from here?" Ajani asks after several minutes of silence.

"I—I don't know."

The uncertainty of my future plagued me over the week, but unlike the other upheavals in my life, it didn't scare me. For once there wasn't some oppressive power keeping my back against the wall, fighting for survival. Ajani cleared my name soon after that fateful council meeting. When a few members of the council protested, he heard them out then explained firmly that my part in revealing Nassor's plans outweighed any damage that I had done as the Nightshade.

"Sorry, what?" I ask. Ajani had spoken, but my mind was somewhere else.

"I was saying that if you won't let me court you then will you at least be a part of my council?"

"Your council? As in the Council of the Sultan?"

"Well, I will be sultan, so naturally…" his teasing trails off as he registers the disbelief in my face. "Laila, you are the only person I trust."

"But—"

"No. You're the only person who will tell me the truth. You're the only person I know who has the strength to call me out when I need it."

"But I'm not Ari. I lied to you for months. I used to spy and steal from these people," I'm babbling, and I know it. "I'm a woman."

"Yes, you are," Ajani says and jokingly looks me over. I glare at him, making him laugh. "You're the only person I know who openly glares at the sultan. I need you."

"I—" I falter. "Can I think about it?"

"Of course."

Ajani pauses, then pulls a small, folded piece of parchment. He hesitates, then hands it to me. I begin to open the paper, but his hand stops me.

"Please, let me leave before you open it."

I nod, confused by his shyness. Ajani stands, and I stand with him.

"I'll expect an answer from you soon, okay?" The question at the end of the statement softens the order.

"Okay, Ajani."

Before I can rethink my action, I hug him fiercely. Ajani stiffens then hugs me back. I'm the first one to let go. I step back to add some distance between us, and then I bow with my fist over my heart, clutching the little piece of paper in my hand.

By the time I rise, the prince is walking down the path and out of the aviary.

I wished for the day
My heart flew away
And soared through the stars.

I wished for the time
For a love so sublime
The radiant sun would sigh.

I wished for you.
That wish came true.
A love that could be ours.

I wish you would stay
And beside me lay—
But my heart you'll deny.

66

My eyes blur as I read and reread the little slip of paper. The finality of the words turn into tears slipping down my cheeks. I pull my knees close to my chest, curling up on the bench, and allow myself to cry over Ajani one last time.

He knew that I would break it off with him. But he'd tried to fix it, to fix us.

Time passes—seconds, minutes, or hours. The birds chirp around the aviary. A ray of sun breaks through the trees above and shines on my tear-stained face. I close my eyes and try to think of nothing at all.

A crunch of twigs sends my head shooting up. The sultana walks down the path to me. I haven't been this close to her since the day we stormed the Council Room—separate and yet united. The normal swarm of Ari women is non-existent as she makes her way to the bench. I wipe my cheeks, eliminating remnants of my tears, and scramble up to greet her with a bow.

"Please sit down, Laila. My back aches from all the bowing today already, and my feet need a rest."

The sultana's voice is willowy and musical, it is one with the rustle of leaves in the aviary. We sit, and I observe the woman in front of me. The sultana sits straight and tall with her simple red saree draped elegantly around her. I'm jealous of her grace. Her copper skin is smooth, marred only by the laugh lines fanning out from her almond eyes—the same shade of brown as her son's. I look away from those eyes, my emotions too raw to look into them. She glances at the paper in my hands and smiles, deepening the laugh lines in her regal beauty.

"My son has always possessed a poetic heart. It is something that is a strength and a weakness as a ruler."

I look down at the paper clutched in my hand. "I had no idea."

"It's not something he shares lightly."

I nod, sending a short tendril of hair into my eyes. I shove it behind my ear—the months of long hair made me forget how cumbersome short hair could be.

"Lady Shah has had a great many things to tell me about you, Laila," the sultana says. My head snaps up, and I wait—knowing Lady Shah, whatever she's had to say to the sultana cannot be good for me. "Lady Shah seems to be under the impression that you've shamed the entire council, seduced Ajani, and used your—what did she say—oh yes, 'womanly wiles' to get Ajani to do what you want."

Redness colors my cheeks, but I stand my ground. "I did no such thing. Yes, Ajani and I have—*had*—a relationship, but it wasn't like that."

"Then what was it like?"

I can't read the sultana's emotions—she hides them better than any other Ari I've encountered. I want to think through my answer, but her waiting face leaves me little time to construct a response. Plus, I'm sure she would see through any lies I might tell her.

"It was—he courted me. Well, not really me, but Lady Lailani. He took me around, and we talked and—"

Sultana Chhavi laughs softly. "Calm down, child. I know that Lady Shah can be an obstinate old hag when she wants to be."

My shoulders slump as I breathe a sigh of relief. The sultana smiles at my reaction. I can feel the heat leaving my face.

"So, you and my son are finished?"

"Yes, I ended it."

"Why?"

"I need time. To figure out who I am now."

Sultana Chhavi nods in approval. "So wise for one so young. You've certainly stirred the pot while I've been away, Laila."

I don't know how to respond to that. I don't feel wise. My heart screams for me to fix things with Ajani and make it work somehow. And stirring the pot is an understatement.

The sultana leans back against the bench and closes her eyes, enjoying the sunlight through the trees. I wait, not wanting to be the first one to break the silence. If she only wanted to know about my relationship with her son, she would have left, wouldn't she?

"Ajani told me that he wants you as part of the Council of the Sultan."

My breath hitches in my chest. I release it slowly then say, "I asked him for time. To think on whether I should—"

I stop speaking as she opens her eyes and stares at me. Those eyes—so similar to her son's—bore into me as if she is looking into my soul.

"You must take the position, Laila."

"But I—"

She places a firm hand over mine. "No but's. You need to take the position, and you must be a part of my women's council as well."

"I thought the sultana didn't have a council."

"Oh, I don't, my dear." A mischievous smile crosses her face. "The secrecy is what makes it so fun."

I open my mouth and close it again. The groups of whispering women. The concern for when she would come back. It all makes sense now.

I've underestimated the Ari women.

"I—can I think about it?" I ask, echoing the words that I said to her son.

The sultana pats my hand then rises.

"See you soon, Laila," she says before wandering out of the aviary.

I inhale deeply, sinking into the peaceful atmosphere of the aviary, its privacy. Tilting my head back, I let the sunlight fall on my face, bright behind my eyelids.

The weight of my impending decisions sits heavily on my shoulders, dampening the peace of the aviary. As much as I believed that the council needed to change, that they needed new perspectives to guide that change, I didn't believe that the person could be me. I'm just Laila, a thief from the Lower City, not a member of the council.

But if I left, who would watch Ajani's back?

I cover my face with an elbow, groaning.

I've had enough of the palace, of the games, of the lies and manipulation. All I really want is to see a friendly face.

Really just one specific friendly face.

I jump up quickly and start walking towards the exit.

There are no obligations trapping me in the palace anymore. I'm free of Logonkelie. I'm free of the vizier. I'm free of the Nightshade.

I'm just me. Just Laila.

And there was a young girl who I wanted to spend time with.

***

"So, then Dada said I need to be nice to Rishabh cause he's our neighbor so that means we be nice," Tanu prattles. Her hand is warm in my own as we wander back through the Lower City to Dada's house. "But I don't think I need to be nice to Rishabh."

I had to bite back a grin at her pouty attitude. "And why not?"

Tanu sighs dramatically, letting go of my hands to wave hers around to emphasize her point. "Cause he's a no good gandmasti that's why!"

"Tanu!"

"What?" she asks, innocently batting her eyelashes up at me. Wispy hairs frame her tiny face, all escaped from the braid hours ago in the press of the crowd.

"You can't go around calling people that," I say.

She wrinkles her nose as she looks up at me. "I heard you say it."

"Well, I– oh," I say, rubbing my hand through my short hair feeling guilty. She probably *had* heard me say that. "Well, that's an adult word, Tanu and you're not an adult."

I smile and grab Tanu's hand to start walking again. There. Problem solved. In the short breath of silence between us, the sounds of the bazaar behind us carry. I glance at each gap between the ramshackle huts and the surrounding roofs as we pass, ensuring Tanu's safety back home.

After a few steps, Tanu says slowly, "You know how I know I'm going to be an adult?"

"Hmm?" I ask as I turn to look behind us. A few others are walking home, but none too close to us.

Tanu tugs on my hand to get my attention. I smile down at her again. "I'll know I'm an adult when I have a baby."

"Umm what?" I splutter, my eyes widening in shock.

Tanu nods her head vigorously, her eyes, so like my own, earnest as she explains to me. "Isha was talking about babies and how her daughter was having a baby soon. Isha's daughter is an adult and so having a baby makes you an adult."

"I, well, that is true," I say, still struggling to keep up with her three-year-old logic. If only Dada had gone with us to the bazaar. He would know what to say.

"How do I get a baby anyway?" Tanu asks innocently.

I inhale my own spit and start coughing uncontrollably. The tickle in my throat won't go away. We round the corner and luckily Dada is waiting outside for us.

"You okay, Laila?" Dada calls from his chair. I wouldn't call it a porch, rather he has just moved one of the chairs from the table outside so he can sit in the cool evening air.

I wave a hand and take a deep breath, finally getting the coughing to subside. "How was it, Nene?"

Tanu skips forward and gives Dada a massive hug. Her small frame appears even tinier against Dada's massive one. "Fun! There were so many people, and we got to try all these sweets. And we saw Rishabh, but I just ignored him. It was easier than being nice to him."

Dada laughs, his weathered skin crinkling near his eyes. He ruffles Tanu's hair and then nudges her towards the door. "Get washed up for bed now, little troublemaker."

Tanu sticks her tongue out playfully but then skips over to me and gives me a big hug.

"Thanks, Lala."

"Of course, Tanu," I say, grinning. I can't help the warmth in my chest from her hug, the lightening of my heart as I watch her skip off and into the house. Happy I could spend the day with her. The fear that I felt during the riot hasn't disappeared but seeing Tanu well and whole has gone a long way to assuring me of her safety.

I pass a handful of colorfully wrapped sweets to Dada as he stands. "For you," I say. "Tanu says they're your favorite."

Dada's laugh echoes through the alleyway. "That girl," he says, shaking his head. "Those are her favorite sweets for sure, so they must be everyone's."

I grin and shake my head too. "I should've known."

A dusty little boy runs up, his bare feet slapping against the dirt road. Once he reaches us, he bends over, catching his breath. In ragged pants, he asks, "Can Tanu come and play?"

I glance at Dada, unsure of who the kid is. Tanu pops her head out of the house and pleads, "Oh please oh please oh please."

Dada smiles patiently then waves her on. Tanu squeals, then races down the street with the little boy, whose mother waves to Dada as the kids reach her. I'm grateful for what Dada gives her: the chance of a normal life. Candy and friends and play. I'm incapable of giving her what she deserves.

"Care to join me?" Dada asks.

"I'd love to," I say.

Dada stands and ambles towards the house. "I'll just get you a chair."

"I can get it," I say, but Dada waves me towards his vacated seat. Stubborn, old man.

He steps tenderly, his gait slower than usual.

"Are your legs bothering you?" I ask.

"Some days," Dada says vaguely.

Before I can respond, Dada stumbles, collapsing onto the sandy ground.

"Dada!" I shout, rushing towards him. "Dada! No, no, no."

He doesn't move.

Gently I roll him to face the bloodred sky of the setting sun. Dust coats his prone form. Wind tugs at his threadbare kurta, the only sign of movement from the gentle giant.

The World of the Nightshade

Glossary

Andhereka: Also known as the festival of lights.

Aristocracy: The upper class of Aveena who are tasked with ruling the city; commoners call the Aristocracy "Ari."

Aveena: City-state nestled between the Tigris Sea and the desert; created 400 years prior when the original Aveenans separated from the Tribes, tired of the nomadic lifestyle.

Bazaar: The marketplace; there are bazaars both in the Upper City and the Lower City and the quality of the merchandise is reflective of which part of the city you are in.

Bhavin: A magic-filled oasis in the desert with healing waters; it is said that anyone who bathes in the oasis will be healed of their ailments.

Choli: Fitted blouse.

Consulate: Composed of three of the Aristocracy, voted by the other members of the Council of the Sultan. These three men, along with the royal vizier, provide closer guidance to the sultan.

Dhoti: Pants.

Djinn-eyed: A superstition, particularly in the Lower City, that those with brightly colored eyes are tainted by mischievous spirits.

Dupatta: Long scarf that is draped over the shoulders.

Hathorda: A seedy tavern frequented by Aveena's underworld.

-ji: Honorific title added to the end of a person's name.

Kurti: Tunic top; kurti is a woman's version; kurta is the men's version.

Lehenga: Long, pleated skirt traditionally worn with a choli and dupatta.

Logonkelie: The secret organization that Jelani Cadmar created to enact changes in the Council of the Sultan.

Lower City: On the furthest outreaches of Aveena, closest to the desert; mainly lower-class commoners live here.

Niraash: Aveena's hidden prison; no one knows where it is.

Ordinances: The ruling document created by the original Aristocracy when founding Aveena.

Rangtiu: The Festival of Colors.

Royal Vizier: The sultan's right-hand man; the sultan himself appoints this position.

Saree: Garment created by a length of fabric draped around the body.

Sherwani: Men's attire; knee-length coat.

Sky Father: One of the deities worshipped by Aveenans.

Suraksha: The guards throughout Aveena; can be stationed in the city, in the desert patrol, or in the palace.

Tribes: Nomadic people who live in the desert outside of Aveena.

Upper City: The area between the palace and the Lower City; mainly occupied by merchants, upper class commoners, and the personal residences of the Aristocracy when not living in the palace.

Veiled Room: Balcony room that overlooks the Council Room; women are allowed here to observe the happenings of the council.

Walla: Vendor or shopkeeper.

Wind Mother: One of the deities worshipped by Aveenans.

The World of the Nightshade

Characters in order of Appearance

Laila Vaish: Works as the Nightshade, a thief for hired; used to live in the Upper City before running away and becoming the Nightshade.

Tei Asfour: Councilman and married to Tei; one of Cadmar's allies.

Farah Asfour: Member of the Aristocracy and married to Tei; one of the sultana's allies.

Velo: power player in the Aveenan underworld; mediates the jobs between the Ari and the Nightshade.

Jelani Cadmar: Councilman with the reputation for arguing with the royal vizier and standing up for commoners.

Dada: Elderly man who lives in the Lower City and takes care of Tanu.

Tanu: Laila's young cousin who has several birth defects.

Chhavi Bahu: Sultana of Aveena and Ajani's mother.

Gautam Bahu: The late sultan; passed away from heart condition.

Ajani Bahu: Prince of Aveena and next sultan.

Amara: One of the sultana's trusted maidservants.

Nassor Al-Sid: The royal vizier for the late Sultan Gautam Bahu.

Sala Khatri: Member of Logonkelie and Cadmar's right hand woman.

Zahir Juma: New member of Logonkelie with Laila.

Nimra: Member of Logonkelie.

Nali Burjandi: Locksmith to the Aristocracy.

Hrithik: Son of Preeti; helps with deliveries.

Preeti: Designs and supplies the clothes for Logonkelie.

Erol Shaikh: Councilman and member of Logonkelie; masquerades as Zahir's father and Laila's uncle in the palace.

Zaharian Shaikh: Zahir's Ari alias in the palace.

Lailani Acharya: Laila's Ari alias in the palace.

Reyanash Al-Sid: One-third of the Consulate; Nassor Al-Sid's cousin.

Kabir Bakshi: One-third of the Consulate.

Manish Reddy: One-third of the Consulate.

The Shah family:

  Jagan Shah: Councilman

  Etana Shah: Jagan's wife; desires to increase her family's status through favorable marriages.

  Esha Shah: Daughter of Jagan and Etana.

  Pradeep Shah: Son of Jagan and Etana.

Ray Lobo: Councilman and supporter of Vizier Nassor.

Krish: Sala's former love.

The Pateel family:

  Vihaan Pateel: Councilman.

  Sanjaya Pateel: Wife of Vihaan.

The Dara family:

  Dhruv Dara: Councilman.

  Nyein Dara: Wife of Dhruv.

  Kumar Dara: Son of Dhruv and Nyein.

The Naidu family:

  Nilam: Councilman.

  Lakshmi: Wife of Nilam.

  Parth Johri: Gold merchant in North Bazaar; Laila's father.

Acknowledgements

Ever since I dreamed of publishing *The Nightshade*, I've fervently read every author acknowledgement page of every book. We're talking hundreds of acknowledgements, and each one gives me the same hope, joy, and thrill as the last.

So these pages mean a lot to me because you all mean a lot to me.

First, I'd like to thank all the wonderful professionals who helped to make *The Nightshade* a reality. To my amazing editor, Hannah Teachout. Hannah, you understood the heart of my story and your feedback was instrumental to bringing it to life. Thank you to JCaleb Designs for the absolutely amazing cover art. I'm obsessed. End of story. Jen, you helped me become part of the Books with Maps club! Goals accomplished. Thank you for taking on this project and getting as excited about maps as me.

Secondly, I want to thank my critique partners. Carrigan Richards, you've been a huge support, sharing your publishing knowledge, commiserating over plot holes and feedback, and being that person who understands that my characters talk to me, and I need to do what they say. Thank you! And Charles Daugherty, I've grown so much as a writer because of your feedback! You push me to add more detail to bring the story to life, and your feedback has made this story better than I could have imagined. And thanks for catching dais for me (not dias… what was I thinking).

Thank you as well to all the beta readers who've read one version of *The Nightshade* or another: Pamela Brown, C.B. Deem, Doreen Edwards, Claire Remley, Katie Sanders, and Dale D'Souza. A special thank you to Dale for helping me with all things desi, and to Amey Creasy for teaching me about the parts of a saree. And thank you to Allison Blanchard for all of our discussions on publishing, writing, and creative chaos. I really needed those conversations! And thank you to my creative writing students—I know I was the one teaching you, but you all taught me more than I could ever have imparted to you. The discussions, the workshops, the writer community pushed me to say confidently "I am a writer" and I'll forever be grateful. So, here's to the Avatar references during workshop, the head of lettuce for class parties, the white van (don't ask), writer's block, people watching for character development, and getting way off topic like us creatives tend to do.

Thank you to Bri and Jose Rodriguez-Rivera. You both were the first friends that I told that I was even attempting to write a book, and your enthusiastic support gave me the confidence to keep trying. Bri, you've been my biggest cheerleader and source of encouragement, especially when I was struggling through the imposter syndrome in the beginning. You kept me going. Jose, you're the only person who has read every single version of this book other than me, from the shitty first draft all the way to now. I'm so proud to hand you the final version, beautiful cover and all, and say thank you. You saw the vision and helped to bring it to life. This book would not be the same without you!

Thank you to Steve for your emotional support. If you know, you know.

And to my family, your support has meant the world to me. Writing a book is a terrifying, personal adventure, and each and every one of you have cheered me on and uplifted me when I needed it. Thank you to my in-laws for all your encouragement, and a special thank you to Efrain for buying me that book on indie publishing years ago. I finally read it, and it was what I needed to make *The Nightshade* happen. To my sisters, Liana and Siena, and my found sister, Sarah, thank you for listening to all my writing problems, uplifting me, and helping me to believe in myself. You each are the Sala to my Laila, the unwavering support of a binti.

Mom and dad, words cannot express how grateful I am for your support of my writing and this book. Thank you.

To my own kiddos, Zeke and Evie, I love you. You can do anything you put your mind to.

And to my wonderful, amazing hubs. You encouraged me when writing was just a pipe dream, and *The Nightshade* was just a seed of an idea. You supported me as I discovered who I was as a writer (still doing that by the way). You helped me through the rejections, especially the painful ones, and pushed me to keep going. You watched the kids so I could disappear into my writing cave for hours then reappear completely scatterbrained but so happy with having a writing life. You researched small business things for me (because that's my least favorite part of this whole process so you took it on for me). You always help put life in perspective. I am so grateful for you. Thank you does not begin to cover how much I appreciate your support. I love you.

And thank you to all the readers who've taken the chance to pick up this book and read it. It is a dream to have it in your hands.

About the Author

Shay Rodricks started her storytelling journey in musical theater and obsessively reading fantastical worlds from her favorite authors. She fell in love with writing as a way to tell the stories she wants to read and explore the worlds she wants to explore.

She studied History, English, and Theater at Mercer University, although her parents believed she majored in extracurriculars from all her involvement on campus. Currently, Shay is a board member for Broadleaf Writers Association based in Atlanta, Georgia, where she aims to help bring writers together.

Her titles other than author include: coffee queen, tattoo addict, trashy tv lover, wishful dragon rider, world traveler (when she can afford it), and dancer. Shay currently lives in Atlanta, Georgia, with her wonderful hubs, their (mostly) angelic kiddos, an old man dog, and a ball python named Steve.

Follow Shay on:
Instagram and TikTok @authorshayrodricks
www.authorshayrodricks.com

www.ingramcontent.com/pod-product-compliance
Lightning Source LLC
Chambersburg PA
CBHW010650100726
47901CB00012B/2495